I0784600

J. Allan Dunn

Rimrock Trail

OK Publishing 2021

J. Allan Dunn

Rimrock Trail

A Tale of the Arizona Ranch and the Three Musketeers of the Range

Published by

MUSAICUM

Books

- Advanced Digital Solutions & High-Quality book Formatting -

musaicumbooks@okpublishing.info

2021 OK Publishing

ISBN 978-80-272-7585-4

Contents

CHAPTER I
GRIT

"Mormon" Peters carefully shifted his weighty bulk in the chair that he dared not tilt, gazing dreamily at the saw-toothed mountains shimmering in the distance, sniffing luxuriously the scent of sage.

"They oughter spell Arizona with three 'C's,'" he said.

"Why?" asked Sandy Bourke, wiping the superfluous oil from the revolver he was meticulously cleaning.

"'Count of Climate, Cactus, Cattle — an' Coyotes."

"Makin' four, 'stead of three," said the managing partner of the Three Star Ranch.

Came a grunt from "Soda-Water" Sam as he put down his harmonica on which he had been playing *The Cowboy's Lament*, with variations.

"Huh! You got no more eddication than a horn-toad, an' less common sense. You don't spell Arizony with a 'C.' You can't. 'Cordin' to yore argymint you should spell Africa with a 'Z' 'cause they raise zebras there, 'stead of mustangs. Might make it two 'R's,' 'count of rim-rock an' — an' revolvers."

Mormon snorted.

"That's a hell of a name for a man born in Maricopa County to call a gun. *Revolver!* You 'mind me of the Boston perfesser who come to Arizona tryin' to prove the Cliff Dwellers was one of the Lost Tribes of Israel. He blows in with an introduction to the Double U, where I was workin'. Colonel Pawlin's wife has a cold snack ready, it bein' middlin' warm. The perfesser makes a pretty speech, after he'd eaten two men's share of victuals tryin', I reckon, to put some flesh on to his bones. An' he calls the lunch a *col-lay-shun!* Later, he asks the waitress down to the Rodeo Eatin' House, while he's waitin' for his train, for a serve-yet. A *serve-yet!* That's what he calls a napkin. You must have been eddicated in Boston, Sam, though it's the first time I ever suspected you of book learnin'."

It was Sunday afternoon on the Three Star rancheria. The riders, all the hands — with the exception of Pedro, the Mexican cocinero, indifferent to most things, including his cooking; and Joe, his half-breed helper, — had departed, clad in their best shirts, vests, trousers, Stetsons and bandannas of silk, some seeking a poker game on a neighboring rancho, some bent on courting. Pedro and Joe lay, faces down, under the shade of the trees about the tenaya, the stone cistern into which water was pumped by the windmills that worked in the fitful breezes.

The three partners, saddle-chums for years, ever seeking mutual employ, known through Texas and Arizona as the "Three Musketeers of the Range," sat on the porch of the ranch-house, discussing business and lighter matters. One year before they had pooled their savings and Sandy Bourke, youngest of the three and the most aggressive, coolest and swiftest of action, had gloriously bucked the faro tiger and won enough to buy the Three Star Ranch and certain rights of free range. The purchase had not included the brand of the late owner. Originally the holding had been called the Two-Bar-P. As certain cattlemen were not wanting who had a knack of appropriating calves and changing the brands of steers, Sandy had been glad enough, in his capacity of business manager, to change the name of the ranch and brand. Two-Bar-P was too easily altered to H-B, U-P, U-B, O-P, or B; a score of combinations hard to prove as forgeries.

There had been lengthy argument concerning the new name. Three Star, so Soda-Water Sam — whose nickname was satirical — opined, smacked of the saloon rather than the ranch, but it was finally decided on and the branding-irons duly made.

Sandy Bourke had dark brown hair, inclined to be curly, a tendency he offset by frequent clipping of his thatch. The sobriquet of "Sandy" referred to his grit. He was broad-shouldered, tall and lean, weighing a hundred and seventy pounds of well-strung frame. His eyes were gray and the lids sun-puckered; his deeply tanned skin showed the freckles on face and hands as faint inlays; his long limber legs were slightly bowed.

Not so the curve of Soda-Water Sam's legs. You could pass a small keg between the latter's knees without interference. Otherwise, Sam, whose last name was Manning, was mainly distinguished by his enormous drooping mustache, suggesting the horns of a Texas steer, inverted.

As for Mormon, disillusioned hero of three matrimonial adventures, woman-soft where Sandy was woman-shy, he was high-stomached, too stout for saddle-ease to himself or mount, sun-rouged where his partners were burned brown. His pate was bald save for a tonsure-fringe of grizzle-red.

All three were first-rate cattlemen, their enterprise bade fair for success, hampered only by the lack of capital, occasioned by Sandy's preference for modern methods as evidenced by thoroughbred bulls, high-grading of his steers, the steadily growing patches of alfalfa and the spreading network of irrigation ditches.

Business exhausted, ending with an often expressed desire for a woman cook who could also perform a few household chores, tagged with a last attempt to persuade Mormon to marry some comfortable person who would act in that capacity, they had reverted to the good-humored chaff that always marked their talks together.

Mormon, with stubby fingers wonderfully deft, was plaiting horsehair about a stick of hardwood to form the handle of a quirt, Sandy overhauling his two Colts and Sam furnishing orchestra on his harmonica. Now he put it to his lips, unable to find a sufficiently crushing retort to Mormon's diatribe against words of more than one syllable, breathing out the burden of "My Bonnie lies over the Ocean."

Mormon, in a husky, yet musical bass, supplied the cowboy's version of the words.

"Last night, as I lay in the per-rair-ree.

And gazed at the stars in the sky,

I wondered if ever a cowboy,
Could drift to that sweet by-an'-by.

"Roll on, roll on,

Roll on, li'l' dogies, roll — —"

He broke off suddenly, staring at the fringe of the waving mesquite.

"Look at that ornery coyote!" he said. "Got his nerve with him, the mangy calf-eater, comin' up to the ranch thataway."

Sam put down his harmonica.

"My Winchester's jest inside the door," he said. "But he'd scoot if I moved. Slip in a shell, Sandy, mebbe you kin git him in a minute."

"Yo're sheddin' yore skin, Sam. Got horn over yore eyes. Mormon, you need glasses fo' yore old age. That ain't a coyote, it's a dawg," pronounced Sandy.

The creature left the cover of the mesquite and came slowly but determinedly toward the ranch-house, past the corral and cook shack; its daring proclaiming it anything but a cowardly, foot-hill coyote. Its coat was whitish gray. Its brush was down, almost trailing, its muzzle drooped, it went lamely on all four legs and occasionally limped on three.

"Collie!" proclaimed Sandy. "Pore devil's plumb tuckered out."

"Sheepdawg!" affirmed Sam, disgust in his voice. "Hell of a gall to come round a cattle ranch."

The gray-white dog came on, dry tongue lolling, observant of the men, glancing toward the tenaya where it smelled the slumbering Pedro and Joe. It halted twenty feet from the porch, one paw up, as Sandy bent forward and called to it.

"Come on, you dawg. Come in, ol' feller. Mormon, take that hair out of that pan of water an' set it where he can see it."

Mormon shifted the pan in which he had been soaking the horsehair for easier plaiting and the dog sniffed at it, watching Sandy closely with eyes that were dim from thirst and weariness. Sandy patted his knee encouragingly, and the tired animal seemed suddenly to make up its mind. Ignoring the water, it came straight to Sandy, uttered a harsh whine, catching at the leather tassel on the cowman's worn leather chaparejos, tugging feebly. As Sandy stooped to pat its head, powdered with the alkali dust that covered its coat, the collie released its hold and collapsed on one side, panting, utterly exhausted, with glazing eyes that held appeal.

Sandy reached for the pan, squatting down, and chucked some water from the palm of his hand into the open jaws, upon the swollen tongue. The dog licked his hand, whined again, tried to stand up, failed, succeeded with the aid of friendly fingers in its ruff and eagerly lapped a few mouthfuls.

Again it seized the tassel and pulled, looking up into Sandy's face imploringly.

"Somethin' wrong," said the manager of the Three Star. "Tryin' to tell us about it. All right, ol' feller, you drink some more wateh. Let me look at that paw." He gently took the foot that clawed at his chaps and examined it. The pad was worn to the quick, bleeding. "Come out of the Bad Lands," he said, looking toward the range. "Through Pyramid Pass, likely."

"Some derned sheepman gone crazy an' shot his-self," grumbled Sam. "Somethin' bound to spile a quiet afternoon."

"Not many sheep over that way," said Mormon. "No range."

Sandy rolled the dog on his side and found the other pads in the same condition. Running his fingers beneath the ruff, scratching gently in sign of friendship, he discovered a leather collar with a brass tag, rudely engraved, the lettering worn but legible.

GRIT.   Prop. P. Casey.

"They sure named you right, son," he said. "We'll 'tend to P. Casey, soon's we've 'tended to you. You need fixin' if you're goin' to take us to him. You'll have to hoof it till we cut fair trail. Sam, fetch me some adhesive, will you? An' then saddle up; Pronto fo' me, a hawss fo' yoreself an' rope a spare mount."

"What for? The spare?"

"Don't know for sure. May have to bring him back."

"A sheepman to Three Star! I'd as soon have a sick rattler around. Mormon, yo're elected to nurse him."

Sam went into the house for the medical tape, then to the corral. Sandy bathed the raw pads softly, cut patches of the tape with his knife, put them on the abrasions, held them there for the warmth of his palm to set them. Grit licked at his hands whenever they were in reach, his brightening eyes full of understanding, shifting to watch Sam striding to the corral.

"One thing about a sheepman is allus good," said Mormon. "His dawg. Reckon you aim on me tendin' the ranch, Sandy?"

"Come if you want to."

"Two's plenty, I reckon. I do more ridin' through the week than I care for nowadays. I'll stick to the chair."

"Prod up Pedro to git some hot water ready. Keep a kittle b'ilin'. No tellin' what time we'll git back," said Sandy. "I'll take along some grub an' the medicine kit. Have to spare some of that whisky Sam's got stowed away."

"Goin' to waste booze at fifteen bucks a quart on a sheepman?" grumbled Mormon.

"Not if you an' Sam don't want I should," replied Sandy, with a smile. He knew his partners. "Now then, Grit," he went on to the dog in a confidential tone, "you-all have got to git grub an' wateh inside yore ribs. Savvy? I'm goin' to rustle some hash fo' you. You stay as you are, son."

He pressed the dog on its side once more, in the shade, and went into the house. Mormon followed him. Grit watched them disappear, gave a little whine of impatience, accepted the situation philosophically as he listened to sounds from the corral that told him of horses being caught, and drooped his head on the dirt, lying relaxed, eyes closed, gaining strength against the return trip.

Sam rode to the porch on his roan, Sandy's pinto and a gray mare leading, and "tied them to the ground" with trailing reins as Sandy came out bearing a pan of food, a package and a leather case. Mormon showed at the door.

"Where'd you hide yore bottle, Sam?" he asked.

"Where you can't find it, you holler-legged galoot. Why?"

"Fill up a flask to take along, Sam," said Sandy. "Here, Grit, climb outside of this chuck."

He coaxed the collie to eat the food from his hand while Sam brought the whisky.

"Load my guns, Mormon," he requested.

Mormon did it without comment. The two blued Colts were as much a part of Sandy's working outfit as his belt, or the bridle of his horse. Sam buckled on his own cartridge belt, holster and pistol, fixed his spurs, tied the package of food to his saddle, filled two canteens and did the same with them. Sandy-offered the pan of water to Grit who drank in businesslike fashion, assured of the success of his mission. He stood up squarely on his legs, eased by the plastering. They were only tired now.

He shook himself vigorously, sending out the dust with which he was powdered in all directions, making Mormon sneeze. He stretched his muzzle toward the mountains, threw it up and barked for the first time. As Sandy and Sam mounted, the latter leading the gray mare, Grit ran ahead of them and came back to make certain they were following. Then he headed for the spot in the mesquite whence he had emerged, marking the opening of a narrow trail. The horses broke into a lope, the two men, the three mounts, and the dog, off on their errand of mercy.

Mormon watched them well into the mesquite before he put back the hair in the water the dog had left and went on with his plaiting: As he handled the pliant horsehairs he talked aloud, range fashion.

"On'y sheepman I ever knowed worth trubblin' about was a woman. Used ter knit while she watched the woollies. Knit me a sweater — plumb useless waste of time an' yarn. If I'd taken it I'd have had to take her along with it. Wimmen is sure persistent. Seems like I must look like a dogie to most of 'em. They're allus wantin' to marry me an' mother me. I sure hope this one don't turn out to be a she-herder. 'P' might stand fer Polly."

CHAPTER II
CASEY

The two men followed the dog across the flats, through mesquite, through scattered sage and greasewood, mounting gradually through chaparral to barren slopes set with strange twisted shapes of cactus. When it became apparent that Sandy's hazard had hit the mark, as they entered the defile that made entrance for Pyramid Pass, the only path across the Cumbre Range to the Bad Lands beyond, Sandy reined in, coaxed up Grit, resentful, almost suspicious of any halt, lifting the collie to the saddle in front of him. Grit protested and the pinto plunged, but Sandy's persistence, the soothe of his steady voice, persuaded the dog at last to accommodate itself as best it could, helped by Sandy's one arm, sometimes with two as Sandy, riding with knees welded to Pronto's withers, dropping reins over the saddle horn, left the rest to the horse.

"I figger we got some distance yet," he said to Sam. "Dawg was goin' steady as a woodchuck ten mile' from water. Reckon my guess was right, — he wore his pads out crossin' the lava beds, though what in time any hombre who ain't plumb loco is trapesin' round there for, beats me. There is some grazin' on top of the Cumbre mesa, enough for a small herd, but the other side is jest plain hell with the lights out, one big slice of desert thirty mile' wide."

"Minin' camp over that way, ain't there?"

"Was. There's a lava bed strip of six-seven miles at the end of the pass, then comes a bu'sted mesa, all box cañon an' rim-rock, shot with caves, nothin' greener than cactus an' not much of that. There's a twenty per cent. grade wagon road, or there was, for it warn't engineered none too careful, that run over to the mines. I was over there once, nigh on to ten years ago. They called the camp Hopeful then. Next year they changed the name to Dynamite. Jest natcherully blew up, did that camp. Nothin' left but a lot of tumbledown shacks an' a couple hundred shafts an' tunnels leadin' to nothin'. Reckon this P. Casey is a prospector, Sam. One of them half crazy old-timers, nosin' round tryin' to pick up lost leads. One of the 'riginal crowd that called the dump Hopeful, like enough. Desert Rat. Them fellers is born with hope an' it's the last thing to leave 'em."

"Hope's a good hawss," said Sam. "But it sure needs Luck fo' a runnin' mate."

"You said it." Sandy relapsed into silence.

At the far end of the pass the dog struggled to get down. They looked out upon a stretch of desolation. Sandy had called it six or seven miles. It might have been two or twenty. The deceit of rarefied air was intensified by the dazzle of the merciless sun beating down on powdered alkali, on snaky flows of weathered lava, on mock lakes that sparkled and dissolved in mirage. The broken mesa, across which ran the road to the deserted mining camp, mysteriously changed form before their eyes; unsubstantial masses in pastel lights and shades of saffron, mauve and rose. Over all was the hard vault of the sky-like polished turquoise.

"I'll let him give us a lead," said Sandy, "soon as we hit the lava. We can foller his trail that fur. Sit tight, son." Grit whined but subsided under the restraining hands.

"How about a drink 'fore we tackle that?" asked Sam, nodding at the shimmering view.

"Better hold off for a while." Sandy took the lead, bending from the saddle, reading the trail that Grit's paws had left in the alkali and sand. Cactus reared its spiny stems or sprawled over the ground more like strange water-growths that had survived the emptying of an inland sea than vegetation of the land. Once the dog's tracks led aside to a scummy puddle, saucered by alkali, dotted with the spoor of desert animals that drank the bitter water in extremity. Then it ran straight to a wide reef of lava. Sandy set down the collie. Grit ran fast across the pitted surface, ahead of the horses, waiting for them to cross the lava. They had hard work to get him to come to hand again, but he gave in at last to the knowledge that they would not go on otherwise.

"Sand's too hot fo' yore pads, dawg," said Sandy, "Raise the mischief with that tape. Shack erlong, Pronto. Give you a slice of Pedro's dried-apple pie when we git back, to make up for workin' you Sunday." The pinto tossed a pink muzzle and his master reached to pat the dusty, sweat-streaked neck. Alkali rose about them in clouds. Grit's trail, though blurred in the soft soil, was plain enough. The two riders went silently on at a steady walking gait. Talk in the saddle with men who make range-riding a business comes only in spurts.

"Never see a prospector with a dawg afore," said Sam at last. "An' that a sheep dawg."

"Dawg 'ud be apt to tucker out in desert travel," agreed Sandy. "Mean one more mouth fo' water."

He, like Sam, speculated on the kind of man P. Casey — if it was Casey they were after — might be. If not a sheepman or a prospector, a third probability made him an outlaw, a man with a price on his head, hiding in the wilds from punishment. It sufficed to them that he was a man whom a dog loved enough to bear a call to help his master.

Slowly, the mesa ahead took on more definite shape. The shadows resolved themselves into ravines and cañons. They entered a gorge filled with boulders and rounded rocks, over which the sure-footed ponies made clattering, slippery progress. Here and there the gaunt skeleton of a tree, white as if lime-washed, showed that once cottonwoods had flourished before the devouring desert had claimed the territory. The cactus was all prickly pear, the gray-green flesh of the flat leaves starred with brilliant blossom. Along one side of the cañon, mounting zigzag, showed the remains of a road, broken down by landslip and the furious rush of cloud-burst waters.

Making this, finding it free of wagon sign or horse tracks, Sandy picked up Grit's trail once again. The collie wriggled, shot up its muzzle, whined, licked Sandy's face.

"Nigh there," suggested Sam. Sandy nodded and let the dog get down. Grit raced off, nose high, streaking around a curve. When they reached it he was out of sight. The road had been built up in places on the outer edge with stones, dry-piled. They had fallen away, the grade following, so that sometimes all that was left for passage was a ledge along which the horses sidled carefully in single file, stirrups brushing the inside bank. The zigzags ended, the cañon narrowed, deepened. Sandy looked down to the dry bed of it four hundred feet below. The road rose at a steep pitch, cliff to the right, precipice to the left, stretching on and up to the summit of the pass.

Suddenly Pronto shied violently, tried to bolt up the cliff, scrambling goatwise for twenty feet to stand shivering and snorting. Sandy's balance was automatic, the muscles of his knees clamped for grip, he gave the pinto its head, trusting to it to establish footing. He saw Sam's roan dancing in the trail, the led mare plunging, dust rising all about them. Left-handed, a Colt flashed out of Sandy's holster, barked twice, the echoes tossing between the cañon walls. In the road a rattlesnake writhed, headless, its body, thicker than a man's wrist, checkered in dirty gray and chocolate diamonds.

"Git down there, you hysteric son of a gun," he said to the horse. "It's all over." The pinto hesitated, shifted unwilling hoofs, squatted on its haunches and, tail sweeping the dirt, tobog-ganed down to the road, jumping catwise the moment it was reached, away from the squirming terror. Sandy forced him back, leaned far down, tucked the barrel of the gun under the snake's body and hurled it looping into the gorge. Sam got his roan and the mare under control as the dust subsided.

"More'n a dozen buttons," said Sandy. "Listen!"

Grit, unseen, ahead, was barking in staccato volleys. There was another sound, a faint shout, unmistakably; human. The men looked at each other with eyebrows raised.

"That ain't no man's voice," said Sam. "That's a gal." He looked quizzically at Sandy, knowing his chum's inhibition.

Sandy was woman-shy. Men met his level glance, fairly, with swift certainty that here stood a man, four-square; or shiftily, according to their ease of conscience, knowing his breed. Sandy was a two-gun man but he was not a killer. There were no notches on the handles of his Colts. In earlier days he had shot with deadly aim and purpose, but never save in self-defense and upon the side of law and right and order. Among men his poise was secure but, in a woman's presence, Sandy Bourke's tongue was tied save in emergency, his wits tangled. Whatever he privately felt of the attraction of the opposite sex, the proximity of a girl produced an embarrassment he hated but could not help. He had seen admiration, desire for closer acquaintance, in many a fair face but such invitation affected him as the sight of a circling loop affects a horse in a remuda.

He gave Sam no chance for banter. Action was forward and it always straightened out the short-circuitings of Sandy's mental reflexes toward womankind. He touched Pronto's flanks with the dulled rowels he wore, and the pinto broke into a lope. A big boulder was perched upon the nigh side of the road. Grit came out from behind it, barked, whirled and seemingly dived into the cañon. Coming up with the mare, Sam found Sandy dismounted, waiting for him.

What had happened was plain to both of them. The rotten, hastily made road collapsed under the lurch of a wagon jolting over outcrop uncovered by the rains. Scored dirt where frantic hoofs had pawed in vain, tire marks that ended in side scrapes and vanished.

Sam got off the roan, the tired horses standing still, snuffing the marks of trouble. Far down the slope Grit gave tongue. The cliff shouldered out and they could see nothing from the broken road. How any one could have hurtled over the precipice and be still able to call for help without the aid of some miracle was an enigma. They listened for another shout but, save for the barking of the dog, there was silence in the grim gorge. In the sky, two buzzards wheeled.

Sandy poured a scant measure of water from his canteen into the punched-in crown of his Stetson, after he had knocked out the dust. Sam did the same, giving each horse a mouth-rinse and a swallow of tepid water so they would stand more contentedly. Each took a swift swig from the containers. Sandy untied the package of food and the leather medicine kit, Sam slapped his hip to be sure of his whisky flask. Aided by their high heels, digging them in the unstable dirt, they worked down the cliff, rounding the shoulder.

A wide ledge of outcrop jutted out from the cañon wall jagged into battlements. Piled there was a wagon, on its side, the canvas tilt sagged in, its hoops broken. A white horse, emaciated, little more than buzzard meat when alive, lay with its legs stiff in the air, neck flattened and head limp. A broken pole, with splintered ends, crossed the body of its mate, a bay, gaunt-hipped, high of ribs. It lay still, but its flanks heaved, catching a flash of sun on its dull hide.

Between the wheels of the wagon knelt a girl in a gown of faded blue, head hidden behind a sunbonnet. She leaned forward in the shadow of the wagon. Sandy caught a glimpse of a huddled body beyond her. Grit sat on his haunches, head toward the road, thrown back at each bark. Sandy reached the ledge first. The girl did not turn her head, though his descent was noisy. He touched her gently on the shoulder, telling himself that she was "just a kid."

She looked up, her face lined where tears had laned down through the mask of dust. Now she was past crying. Her eyes met Sandy's pitifully, holding neither surprise nor hope.

"He's dead." She seemed to be stating a fact long accepted.

"He's dead. An' he made me jump. You come too late, mister."

The man lay stretched out, head and shoulders hidden, his gaunt body dressed in jeans, once blue, long since washed and sun-faded to the green of turquoise matrix. The boots were rusty, patched. The wagon-bed, toppling sidewise, had crashed down on his chest. Rock partly supported the weight of it. Sandy picked up a gnarled hand, scarred, calloused and shrunken, the hand of an old prospector.

"Yore dad?" he asked, kneeling by the girl.

"Yes." She stood up, slight and straight, with limbs and body just curving into womanhood. "The hawsses was tuckered out," she said, "or Dad c'ud have made it. They didn't have no strength left, 'thout food or water. The damned road jest slid out from under. Dad made me jump. I figgered he was goin' to, but his bad leg must have caught in the brake. We slid over like water slides over a rock. He didn't have a hell-chance." As she spoke them the oaths were merely emphasis. She talked as had her father.

Sandy nodded.

"Got an ax with the outfit?" he asked. Then turning to Sam as the girl went round to the back of the fallen wagon and fumbled about through the rear opening of the canvas tilt: "Man's alive, Sam. Caught a flirt of the pulse. Have to pry up the wagon. Git that bu'sted end of the tongue."

The girl handed an ax to Sandy mutely, watching them as Sandy pried loose the part of the tongue still bolted to the wagon, getting it clear of the horses.

"Think you can drag out yore dad by the laigs when we lift the body of the wagon?" he asked her. "May not be able to hold it more'n a few seconds. May slip on us, the levers is pritty short."

She stooped, taking hold of a wrinkled boot in each hand, back of the heel. A tear splashed down on one of them and she shook the salt water from her eyes impatiently as if she had faced tragedy before and knew it must be looked at calmly.

The two men adjusted the boulders they had set for fulcrums and shoved down on the stout pieces of ash, their muscles bunching, the veins standing out corded on their arms. Grit ran from one to the other with eager little whines, sensing what was being attempted, eager to help. The wagon-bed creaked, lifted a little.

"Now," grunted Sandy, "snake him out."

The girl tugged, stepping backward, her pliant strength equal to the dead drag of the body. Sandy, straining down, saw a white beard appear, stained with blood, an aged seamed face, hollow at cheek and temple, sparse of hair, the flesh putty-colored despite its tan. Grit leaped in and licked the quiet features as Sam and Sandy eased down the wagon.

"Whisky, Sam."

The girl sat cross-legged, her father's head in her lap, one hand smoothing his forehead while the other felt under his vest and shirt, above his heart.

"He ain't gone yit," she announced.

The old miner's teeth were tight clenched, but there were gaps in them through which the whisky Sandy administered trickled.

"Daddy! Daddy!"

It might have been the tender agony of the cry to which Patrick Casey's dulling brain responded, sending the message of his will along the nerves to transmit a final summons. His body twitched, he choked, swallowed, opened gray eyes, filmy with death, brightening with intelligence as he saw his daughter bending over him, the face of Sandy above her shoulder. The gray eyes interrogated Sandy's long and earnestly until the light began to fade out of them and the wrinkled lids shuttered down.

Another swallow of the raw spirits and they opened flutteringly again. The lips moved soundlessly. Then, while one hand groped waveringly upward to rest upon his daughter's head, Sandy, bending low, caught three syllables, repeated over and over, desperately, mere ghosts of words, taxing cruelly the last breath of the wheezing lungs beneath the battered ribs, the final spurt of the spirit.

"*Molly — mines!*"

"I'll look out for that, pardner," said Sandy.

The eyelids fluttered, the old hands fell away, the jaw relaxed, serenity came to the lined face, and no little dignity. For the first time the girl gave way, lying prone, sobbing out her grief while the two cowmen looked aside. The bay horse began to groan and writhe.

"Got to kill that cavallo," said Sam in a whisper.

"Wait a minute." The girl had quieted, was kneeling with clasped hands, lips moving silently. Prayer, such as it was, over, she rose, her fists tight closed, striving to control her quivering chin — doing it. She looked up as the shadow of a buzzard was flung against the cliff by the slanting sun.

"We got to bury him, 'count of them damn buzzards."

"We'll tend to that," said Sandy. "Ef you-all 'll take the dawg on up to the hawsses...."

"No! I helped to bury Jim Clancy, out in the desert, I'm goin' to help bury Dad. It's goin' to be lonesome out here — " She twisted her mouth, setting teeth into the lower lip sharply as she gazed at the desolate cliffs, the birds swinging their tireless, expectant circles in the throat of the gorge.

"Dad allus figgered he'd die somewheres in the desert. 'Lowed it 'ud be his luck. He wanted to be put within the sound of runnin' water — he's gone so often 'thout it. But — " She shrugged her thin shoulders resignedly, the inheritance of the prospector's philosophy strong within her.

"See here, miss," said Sandy, while Sam crawled into the wagon in search of the dead miner's pick and shovel that now, instead of uncovering riches, would dig his grave, "how old air you?"

"Fifteen. My name's Margaret — Molly for short — same as my Ma. She's been dead for twelve years."

"Well, Miss Molly, suppose you-all come on to the Three Star fo' a spell with my two pardners an' me? You do that an' mebbe we can fix yore daddy's idee about runnin' water. We'd come back an' git him an' we'll make a place fo' him under our big cottonwoods below the big spring. I w'udn't wonder but what he c'ud hear the water gugglin' plain as it runs down the overflow to the alfalfa patches."

Molly Casey gazed at him with such a sudden glow of gratitude in her eyes that Sandy felt embarrassed. He had been comforting a girl, a boyish girl, and here a woman looked at him, with understanding.

"Yo're sure a white man," she said. "I'll git even with you some time if I work the bones of my fingers through the flesh fo' you. Thanks don't amount to a damn 'thout somethin' back of 'em. I'll come through."

She put out her roughened little hand, man-fashion, and Sandy took it as Sam emerged from the wagon with the tools. The bay mare groaned and gave a shrill cry, horribly human. Sam drew his gun, putting down pick and shovel.

"Got any water you c'ud spare?" asked the girl. Sandy handed her his canteen.

"Use it all," he said. "Soon's it's dark, it'll cool off. We'll git through all right."

He picked up the tools and moved toward Sam as the bay collapsed to the merciful bullet. The girl washed away as best she could the stains of blood and travel from the dead face while Sandy sounded with the pick for soil deep enough for a temporary grave.

The body would have to lie on the ledge over night, nothing but burial could save it from marauding coyotes, though the wagon might have baffled the buzzards. The two set to work digging a shallow trench down to bedrock, rolling up loose boulders for a cairn. The whirring chorus of the cicadas drummed an elfin requiem. Now and then there came the chink of bit, or hoof on rock, from the waiting horses in the broken road. The sun was low, horizontal rays piercing the flood of violet haze in the cañon. Across the gorge the cliff, above the wash of shadow, glowed saffron; a light wind wailed down the bore. Lizards flirted in and out of the crevices as the miner was laid in his temporary grave, the girl dry-eyed again.

She had brought a little work box from the wagon, of mahogany studded with disks of pearl in brass mountings. Out of this she produced a handkerchief of soft China silk brocade, its white turned yellow with age. This she spread over her father's features, showing strangely distinct in the failing light.

"I don't want the dirt pressin' on his face," she said.

From the dead man's clothes Sandy and Sam had taken the few personal belongings, from the inner pocket of the vest some papers that Sandy knew for location claims.

"Want to take some duds erlong to the ranch?" he asked Molly. "We can bring in the rest of the stuff later. Got to shack erlong, it's gittin' dark. Brought an extry hawss with us. Can you ride?"

"Some. I ain't had much chance."

"Don't know how the mare'll stand yore skirt. If she won't Pinto'll pack you."

"I'll fix that." She clambered into the wagon. Before she came out with her bundle they piled the cairn, a mask of broken rim-rock heavy enough to foil the scratching of coyotes.

It looked to Sandy as if the girl had changed into a boy. The slender figure, silhouetted against the afterglow, softly pulsing masses of fiery cloud above the top of the mesa, was dressed in jean overalls, a wide-rimmed hat hiding length of hair.

"I reckon I can fool that hawss of yores now," she said. "I gen'ally dress thisaway 'cept when we expect to go nigh the settlements or a ranch where we aim to visit. We was makin' for the

Two-Bar-P outfit, where Grit came from when he was a bit of a pup. I expected that's where he was headin' for when I sent him off after help, but you come instead."

"I was wonderin' how he come to make the ranch," said Sandy. "You see we-all bought the Two-Bar-P, though I never figgered old Samson 'ud ever own a sheepdawg. He might give one away fast enough."

"Grit was sent him for a present by a man who summered at the ranch an' heerd Samson say he wanted a dawg," said the girl. "He was a tenderfoot when he come, an' when he left, 'count bein' sick. Samson didn't want to kill the dawg an' didn't want to keep him, so he gave him to Dad an' me when I was ten years old. Are you ready to start?"

She had avoided looking toward the grave, purposely Sandy thought, talking to bridge over the last good-by, the chance of a breakdown. Suddenly she pointed down the cliff.

"Wait a minute," she cried and disappeared, sliding and leaping down like a goat, reappearing with her hat half filled with crimson silk-petaled cactus blooms, scattering them at the head of the cairn.

"Seemed like there jest had to be flowers," she said as, with Grit nosing close to his mistress, they mounted to the road. The gray mare made no bother and soon they were riding down toward the strip of Bad Lands. Sandy let the collie go afoot for the time.

The glory of the range departed, the cliffs turned slate color, then black, while a host of stars marshaled and burned without flicker. The wind moaned through the trough of the cañon as they rode out on the plain. Up somewhere in the darkness the buzzards came circling down, to settle on the ledge beside the carcasses of the two horses.

It was close to midnight when they reached the home ranch, riding past the outbuildings, the bunk-house of the men where a light twinkled, the cook shack, the corrals, up to the main house. There they alighted. All about cottonwoods rustled in the dark, the air was sweet and cool, not far from frost. Molly Casey shivered as she moved stiffly in her saddle. Sandy lifted her from the saddle and carried her up the steps, across the porch, kicking open the door of the living-room where the embers of a fire glowed. There was no other light in the big room, but there was sufficient to show the great form of Mormon, stowed at ease in a chair, asleep and snoring.

Sam struck a match and lit a lamp. He struck Mormon mightily between his shoulders.

"Gawd!" gasped the heavyweight partner. "I been asleep. But there's a kittle of hot water, Sandy. Where's the — what in time are you totin'? A gel or a boy?"

"This is Miss Molly Casey," said Sandy gravely, setting down the girl. "Miss Casey, this is Mr. Peters. Mormon, Miss Molly is goin' to tie up to the Three Star for a bit."

Mormon, a little sheepish at the suddenly developing age of the girl as she shook hands with him, recovered himself and beamed at her. "Yo're sure welcome," he said. "Boss hired you? Cowgirl or cook?"

Sandy noticed the girl's lips quiver and he slipped an arm about her shoulders. He was not woman-shy with this girl who needed help, and who seemed a boy.

"Don't you take no notice of him an' his kiddin'," he said. "We'll make him rustle some grub fo' all of us an' then we-all 'll turn in. I'll show you yore room. Up the stairs an' the last door on the right. Here's some matches. There's a lamp on the bureau up there. Give you a call when supper's ready."

He led her to the door and gave her a friendly little shove, guessing that she wanted to be alone.

"The kid's lost her father, lost most everything 'cept her dawg," he said to Mormon. "Thought we might adopt her, sort of, then I thought mebbe we'd hire her — for mascot."

"Lost her daddy? An' me hornin' in an' tryin' to kid her! I ain't got the sense of a drowned gopher, sometimes," said Mormon contritely.

"She's game, plumb through, ain't she, Sam? Stands right up to trouble?"

"You bet. Mormon, open up a can of greengages, will ye? I reckon she's got a sweet tooth, same as me."

Molly Casey was not through standing up to trouble. They coaxed her to eat and she managed to make a meal that satisfied them. Then she got up to go to her room, with Grit nuzzling close to her, her fingers in his ruff, twisting nervously at the strands of hair.

"Do you reckon," she asked the three partners, "that Dad knows he fooled me when he told me to jump? If I'd known he c'udn't git clear I'd have stuck — same as he would if I was caught. Do you reckon he knows that — now?"

"I'd be surprised if he didn't," said Sandy gravely. "You did what he wanted, anyway."

She shook her head.

"If I'd been on the outside, he w'udn't have jumped, no matter how much I begged him. I didn't think of the brake. Don't seem quite square, somehow, way I acted. Good night. What time do you-all git up?"

"With the sun, soon's the big bell rings," said Sandy. "Good night."

She looked at them gravely and went out.

"Botherin' about playin' square in jumpin'," said Sandy. "That gel is square on all twelve eidges. Sam, slide out an' muzzle that bell. She'll likely cry herself to sleep after a bit but she'll need all the sleep she can git. No sense in wakin' her up at sun-up."

"How'd you come to know so much about gels?" asked Mormon.

"Me? I don't know the first thing about 'em," protested Sandy.

"No more'n any man," put in Sam. "'Cept it's Mormon. He's sure had the experience."

"Experience," said Mormon, with a yawn, "may teach a man somethin' about mules but not wimmen. Woman is like the climate of the state of Kansas, where I was born. Thirty-four below at times and as high as one-sixteen above. Blowin' hot an' cold, rangin' from a balmy breeze through a rain shower or a thunder-storm, up to a snortin' tornado. Average number of workin' days, about one hundred an' fifty. Them's statistics. It ain't so hard to set down what a woman's done at the end of a year, if you got a good mem'ry, but tryin' to guess what she is goin' to do has got the weather man backed off inter a corner an' squealin' for help. They ain't all like Kansas. My first resembled it, the second was sorter tropic — she run off with a rainmaker an' I hear she's been divorced three times since then. Mebbe that's an exaggeration. My third must have been born someways nigh the no'th pole. W'en she got mad she'd freeze the blood in yore veins.

"No, sir, that feller in the po'try who says, 'I learned about wimmen from 'er,' was braggin'. Now, this gel of Casey's 'pears like what her dad 'ud call a good prospect, but you can't tell. Fool's gold is bright enough but you can't change it to the real stuff no matter how you polish it."

"Ever see the sour-milk batter Pedro fixes fo' hot cakes?" asked Sam.

"Sure I have. What's that got to do with it?" demanded Mormon.

"That's what you've got sloppin' inside of yore haid 'stead of brains. Yore disposition concernin' wimmen is gen'ally soured. You 'mind me of the man from New Jersey who come out west to buy a ranch. A hawss throwed him five times hand-runnin'. He ropes a steer that happens to run into the bum loop he was swingin' an' it snakes him out'n the saddle. A pesky cow chases him when he was afoot, a couple calves gits a rope twisted round his stummick an' lastly a mule kicks him into a bunch of cactus. Whereupon he remarks, 'I don't figger I was calculated for runnin' a cattle ranch,' sells out an' goes back to herdin' muskeeters in New Jersey.

"Mormon, you warn't calculated to handle wimmen. This li'l' gel is game as they make 'em, an' I reckon she's right sweet if she on'y gits a chance. Leastwise, I see several signs of pay dirt this afternoon an' evenin' as I reckon Sandy done the same. She's been trailin' her dad all over hell an' creation, talkin' like him, swearin' like him, actin' like him. Never see nothin' different. All she needs is a chance."

"What's the idee in pickin' on me?" asked Mormon aggrievedly. "She's as welcome as grass in spring. They ain't no one got a bigger heart than me fo' kids."

"No one got a bigger heart, mebbe," said Sam caustically. "Nor none a smaller brain. All engine an' no gasoline in the tank!"

"She's an orphan," went on Sandy. "She ain't got a cent that I know of. The claims her old dad mentioned ain't no good because, in the first place, they'd have been worked if they was; second place, they're over to Dynamite an' the sharps say Dynamite's a flivver. All she has in sight is the dawg. Some dawg! Comes in from the desert an' takes us out to her an' Pat Casey — him dyin'. Ef it hadn't been fo' the dawg, she'd have stayed there, to my notion. Got some sort of idee she'd deserted ship ef she hadn't stuck till it was too late fo' her to crawl out of that slit in the mesa. She's fifteen an' she's got sense. I figger we better turn in right now an' hold a pow-wow with the gel ter-morrer."

"Second the motion," said Sam.

"Third it," said Mormon.

And the Three Musketeers of the Range went off to bed.

Molly came down next morning in the faded blue gingham. Sandy marked how worn it was and marked an item in his mind — clothes. He smiled at her with the sudden showing of his sound white teeth that made many friends. She was much too young, too frank, too like a boy to affect him with any of his woman-shyness. He did not realize how close she was to womanhood, seeing only how much she must have missed of real girlhood.

Molly had a snubby nose, a wide mouth, Irish eyes of blue that were far apart and crystal clear, freckles and a lot of brown hair that she wore in a long braid wound twice about her well-shaped head. She was a combination of curves and angles, of well-rounded neck and arms and legs with collar-bones and hips over-apparent, immature but not awkward.

None of the three partners observed these things in detail. All of them noted that her eyes were steady, friendly, trusting, and that when she smiled at them it was like the flash of water in a tree-shady pond, when a trout leaps. Grit, entering with her, divided his attentions among the men, shoving a moist nose at last into Sandy's palm and lying down obedient, his tail thumping amicably, as Sandy examined the tape protectors.

"You lie round the ranch for a day or so," he told the collie, "an' you'll be as good as new."

"Fo' a sheepdawg," said Mormon, "he sure shapes fine."

Molly's eyes flashed. "He don't *know* he's a sheepdawg," she protested. "He's never even seen one, 'less it was a mountain sheep, 'way up against the skyline. Samson liked him. Don't you like him?"

"I like him fine," Mormon answered hurriedly. "Fine!"

"Ef you-all didn't, we c'ud shack on somewheres. I c'ud git work down to the settlemints, I reckon. I don't aim to put you out any. I've been thinkin' erbout that. 'Less you should happen to want a woman to run the house. I don't know much about housekeepin' but I c'ud l'arn. It's a woman's job, chasin' dirt. I can cook — some. Dad used to say my camp-bread an' biscuits was fine. I c'ud earn what I eat, I reckon. An' what Grit 'ud eat. We don't aim to stay unless we pay — someway."

There was a touch of fire to her independence, a chip on the shoulder of her pride the three partners recognized and respected.

"See here, Molly Casey," — Sandy used exactly the same tone and manner he would have taken with a boy — "that's yore way of lookin' at it. Then there's our side. You figger yore dad was a pritty good miner, I reckon?"

"He sure knew rock. Every one 'lowed that. They was always more'n one wantin' to grubstake him but he'd never take it. Figgered he didn't want to split any strike he might make an' figgered he w'udn't take no man's money 'less he was dead sure of payin' him back. Dad was a good miner."

"All right. Now, yore dad believes in them claims. The last two words he says was 'Molly' and 'mines.' I give him my word then and there, like he would have to me, to watch out for yore interests. My word is my pardners' word. I'm willin' to gamble those claims of his'll pan out some day. Until they do, ef you-all 'll stay on at the Three Star, stop Mormon stompin' in from the corral with dirty boots, ride herd on Sam an' me the same way, mebbe cook us up some of them biscuits once in a while, why, it'll be fine! Then there's yore schoolin'. Yore dad 'ud wish you to have that. I don't suppose you've had a heap. An' you sabe, Molly, that you swear mo' often than a gel usually swears."

She opened her eyes wide. "But I don't cuss when I say 'em. An' I don't use the worst ones. Dad w'udn't let me. I can read an' write, spell an' cipher some. But Dad needed me more'n I needed learnin'."

"But you got to have it," said Mormon earnestly. "S'pose them claims pan out way rich and you git all-fired wealthy? Bein' a gel, you sabe clothes, di'monds, silks, satins an' feather fuss. You'll want to learn the pianner. You'll want to know what to git an' how to wear it. Won't want folks laffin' at you like they laffed at Sam, time he won fo' hundred dollars shootin' craps an' went to Galveston where a smart Alec of a clerk sells him a spiketail coat, wash vest an' black pants with braid on the seams.

"Sam, he don't know how to wear 'em, or when. His laigs sure looked prominent in them braided pants. Warn't any side pockets in 'em, neither, fo' him to hide his hands. Sam's laigs got warped when he was young, lyin' out nights in the rain 'thout a tarp'. That suit set back Sam a heap of money an' it ain't no mo' use to him than an extry shell to a terrapin."

He grinned at Molly with his face creased into good humor that could not be resisted. She laughed as Sam joined in, but the determination of her rounded chin returned after the merriment had passed.

"If you did that — took my Daddy's place," she said, "why, we'd be pardners, same as him an' me was. When the claims pan out, half of it'll have to be yores. I won't stay no other way."

The glances of the three partners exchanged a mutual conclusion, a mutual approval.

"That goes," said Sandy, putting out his hand. "Fo' all three of us. When the mines are payin' dividends, we split, half on 'count of the Three Star, half to you. Providin' you fall in line with the eddication, so's to do yore dad, yo'se'f an' us, yore pardners, due credit when the money starts comin' in. Sabe?"

"I don't sabe the eddication part of it," she answered. "Jest what does that mean? I don't want to go to school with a lot of kids who'll laf at me."

"You don't have to. As pardners," Sandy went on earnestly, "I don't mind tellin' you that the Three Bar has put all its chips into the kitty an', while we figger sure to win, we can't cash in any till the increase of the herds starts to make a showin'. Not till after the fall round-up, anyway. So yore eddication'll have to be put off a bit. Meantime you'll learn to ride an' rope an' mebbe break a colt or two, between meals an' ridin' herd on the dirt. When you start in, it'll be at one of them schools in the East where they make a speshulty of western heiresses. How's that sound?"

"Sounds fine. On'y, you've picked up Dad's hand to gamble with. Mebbe it ain't yore game, nor the one you'd choose to play if it wasn't forced on you."

"Sister," said Sam, "yo're skinnin' yore hides too close. Sandy 'ud gamble on which way a horn-toad'll spit. It's meat an' drink to him. We won this ranch on a gamble — him playin'. He gambles as he breathes. An' whatever hand he plays, me an' Mormon backs. Why, if we win on this minin' deal, we're way ahead of the game, seein' we don't put up anythin' in cold collateral. It's a sure-fire cinch."

"Sam says it," backed Sandy. "One good gamble!"

Molly's eyes had lightened for a moment, losing their gloom of grief they had held since the shadow of the circling buzzards in the gorge had darkened them. She fumbled at the waistband of her one-piece gown, working at it with her fingers, producing a golden eagle which she handed to Sandy.

"That's my luck-piece," she said. "Dad give it to me one time he cleaned up good on a placer claim. Nex' time you gamble, will you play that — for me? Half an' half on the winnin's. I sure need some clothes."

The glint of the born gambler's superstition showed in Sandy's eyes as he took the ten dollars.

"I sure will do that," he said. "An' mighty soon. Now then, talk's over, all agreed. Sam an' me has got some work to do outside. Won't be back much before sun-down. Mormon, he's goin' to be middlin' busy, too. Molly, you jest acquaint yorese'f with the Three Star. Riders won't be back till dark. No one about but Mormon, Pedro the cook, an' Joe. Rest up all you can. I'm goin' to bring yore dad in to runnin' water."

Tears welled in Molly's eyes as she thanked him. Again Sandy saw the girlish frankness change to the gratefulness of a woman's spirit, looking out at him between her lids. It made him a little uneasy. The men went out together, walking toward the corral.

"Sam an' me's goin' to bring in what's left of Pat Casey, Mormon. Wagon's kindlin', harness is plumb rotten. Ain't much to bring 'cept him, I reckon. We'll take the buckboard, with a tarp' to stow him under. Up to you to knock together a coffin an' dig a grave under the cottonwoods an' below the spring. Right where that li'l knoll makes the overflow curve 'ud be a good spot. Use up them extry boards we got for the bunk-house. Git Joe to help you. No sense in lettin' the gel see you, of course."

"Nice occupation fo' a sunny day," grumbled Mormon, but, as the buckboard drove off, he was busy planing boards in the blacksmith's shop, with the door closed against intrusion.

Mid-afternoon found him with the coffin completed. He rounded up the half-breed to help him dig the grave, first locating Molly in a hammock he had slung for her in the shade of the trees by the cistern. He had furnished her with his pet literature, an enormous mail-order catalogue from a Chicago firm. It was on the ground, the breeze ruffling the illustrated pages, lifting some stray wisps of hair on the girl's neck as she lay, fast asleep, relaxed in the wide canvas hammock, her face checkered by the shifting leaves between her and the sun.

Mormon could move as softly as a cat, for all his bulk. There was turf about the cistern, he had made no sound arriving, but he tiptoed off, his kindly mouth rounded into an O of silence, his weather crinkled eyes half-closed.

"She's jest a baby," he said, half aloud, as he passed beyond the trees to where Joe waited with pick and spade.

The soil was soft and clear from stone. An hour sufficed to sink a shaft for Pat Casey's last bed. Mormon carefully adjusted the headboard he had fashioned from a thick plank, to be carved later when the lettering was decided upon. This done he buckled on the belt he had discarded, from which his holster and revolver swung. Sandy carried two guns, his partners one, habits of earlier, more stirring days, toting them as inevitably as they wore spurs, though there was little occasion to use them on the Three Star, save to put a hurt animal out of misery, or kill a rattlesnake.

Moisture streamed from Mormon's face, patched his clothes as the heat and his exertions temporarily melted some of his superfluous adiposity. Joe, his mahogany face stolid as a wooden carving, rolled a cigarette.

"I sure hate to see a nameless grave," said Mormon.

"Si, Señor," Joe's amiability agreed.

"You go git a dipper. I'm drier'n Dry Crick. Fetch it full from the spring." The half-breed ambled off. Mormon wiped his face with his bandanna. Suddenly his big body stiffened. He heard Molly's voice from the cistern, frightened, then storming in anger. Mormon ran at a sprinter's gait from the cottonwoods, along a side of the corral, through the trees bordering the cistern. The girl was out of the hammock, facing a man in riding breeches and puttees, his face concealed for the moment by his hands. A sleeve of the girl's frock was torn away, the outworn fabric in streamers. The man's hands came down and Mormon recognized him for Jim Plimsoll, owner of the Good Luck Pool Parlors, in the little cattle town of Hereford, where faro, roulette, chuckaluck and craps were played in the back room, owner also of a near-by horse ranch. There was blood on his face, the marks of finger nails.

Plimsoll jumped for the girl, caught her by one arm roughly. She struggled fiercely, silently, striking at him with her free fist. Mormon's gun flashed from its sheath as he shouted at the man. Plimsoll wheeled, releasing Molly. His dark face was livid with rage, a pistol gleamed as he plucked it from beneath the waistband of his riding breeches. The turf spatted between his feet as Mormon fired.

"Got the drop on ye, Jim! Nex' shot'll be higher. Shove that gun back. Now then," as Plimsoll sullenly obeyed, "what in hell do you figger yo're doin'?" Mormon's jovial face was tense, his voice stern and cold, he stood crouched forward a little from the hips, legs apart, his gun a thing of menace that seemed to be alive, snaky.

"Keep still," he ordered, walking toward the pair, his gun covering Plimsoll, the cheery blue of his eyes changed to the color of ice in the shade, the pupils mere pin-pricks. Molly glanced at him once, fingers caressing her bruised arm.

"He kissed me while I was asleep, the damned skunk!" she flared. "I'd sooner hev rattlesnake-pizen on my lips!" She stopped rubbing the arm to scrub fiercely at her mouth with the back of her hand.

"It ain't the first time I've kissed you," said Plimsoll. "Yore dad didn't stop me from doin' it. I didn't notice you scratching like a wildcat either. Where's your dad? And where do you come in on this deal between old friends?" he demanded of Mormon.

"Her dad's dead," said Mormon simply. "Molly is stayin' fo' a spell at the Three Star. Sandy Bourke, Sam Manning an' me is lookin' out fo' her, an' we aim to do a good job of it. Sabe?"

Plimsoll's thin-lipped mouth sneered with his eyes.

"Gone in for baby-farming, have you, or robbing the cradle? Who's playing the king in this deal? I — — " The leer suddenly vanished from his face, the tip of his tongue licked his lips. Mormon's gun was slowly coming up level with his heart, steady as Mormon's gaze, finger compressing the trigger.

"The law reckons you a man — so fur," said Mormon. "Yore pals 'ud pack a jury to hang me fo' shootin' the dirty heart out of you, but — ef you ever let out a foul word or a look about that gel, I'll take my chance of their bein' enough white men round here to 'quit me. There ought to be a bounty on yore scalp an' ears. You hear me, Jim Plimsoll, I'm talkin' straight. Now git, head yore hawss fo' the short trail to Hereford an' keep travelin'. Pronto!"

Plimsoll's pony was standing under the trees and the gambler turned and, with an attempted laugh, swaggered toward it.

The threat to his personal safety, his desire to fling a sneer at Mormon, seemed to have halted any correlation of the statement concerning the death of the girl's father until now.

"If that's true about your dad," he said, "I'm sorry. How did he die?"

Sensing the hypocrisy of the shift to sympathy, the girl took a step forward. Mormon's pupils contracted again; his finger itched to press the trigger it touched.

"It's none of yore business," said the girl. "You git."

Plimsoll's eyes shifted to Mormon's big body, stiffening to the crouch that prefaced shooting. He faced toward the trees again, flinging his last words over his shoulder.

"None of my business? I don't agree with you there, you little hell-weasel. Your father and me had more than one deal together. You and I may have to do business together yet, Molly mine!"

Molly's teeth showed between her parted lips, her fingers were hooked. Mormon anticipated her indignant leap. His gun spurted fire, the expensive Stetson broadrim seemed lifted from Plimsoll's hair by an invisible hand. With the report it sailed forward, side-slipped, landed on its rim, perforated by a steel-nosed thirty-eight caliber bullet.

"I give you last warnin'," roared Mormon.

Plimsoll sprang ahead like a racer at the starter's shot, snatched at his hat, missed it, let it lie as he ran on to his horse, mounted and went galloping off. Mormon holstered his gun and swung about to Molly, standing with crimson cheeks, blazing eyes and a young bosom turbulent with emotions.

"I wisht you'd killed him. I wisht you'd killed him!" she cried. "I wisht I had a gun — or a knife! I hate him — hate him — *hate him*! When he says he was ever in a deal with Dad, he lies. Dad stood for him and that was all. He purtended to be awful strong for Dad, purtended to be fond of me, jest to swarm 'round Dad, for some reason. Brought me a doll once. I was thirteen. What in hell did I want with a doll?" she panted. "I burned the damn thing that night in the fire. He kissed me an' Dad seemed to think I owed it him for the doll. I nigh bit my lip off afterward. I wisht yore first shot had been higher, or yore second lower, Peters."

"Call me Uncle Mormon, Molly. I had all I c'ud do not to make it plumb center, li'l' gel, but the jury'd ring in a cold deck on me if I had. He's sure some snake. But we'll take care of Jim Plimsoll, yore Uncle Mormon, with Sam an' Sandy."

Patting Molly's shoulder, Mormon smiled at her with his irresistible grin, and she reflected it faintly as she tucked in the remnants of her torn sleeve.

"That's the on'y dress I got till Sandy Bourke wins me some money," she said. "You sure are quick, Uncle Mormon, when you git inter action. An' you can shoot some."

"I reckon I coil up tight, between times, like a spring. Used to be pritty light an' limber on my feet oncet. As for shootin', I wish Sandy 'ud been here. He'd have shot both the heels off that fo'-flusher, right an' left, 'thout you ever see his hands move. I ain't so bad, Sam's better, but we had to throw a lot of lead in practise. Sandy shoots like he walks or breathes. It comes natcherul to him, like Sam's ear fo' music. I've allus 'lowed Sandy must hev cut his teeth on a cartridge."

His arm around her shoulder, purposely chatting away, Mormon led Molly toward the ranch-house, waving off the half-breed who came toward them, his dipper of the spring water half emptied in the excitement. Plimsoll's horse was stirring up a dust-cloud on the way to Hereford, other puffs, far-away toward the range, proclaimed that the buckboard was on its way with its funeral freight.

The body of the old prospector was lowered into the grave with the last of the daylight. The raw scar of the grave was covered with turfs Mormon ordered cut by the half-breed. Molly Casey walked away alone, her head high, the corner of her lower lip caught under her teeth, eyes winking back the tears. It was the headboard that had forced her struggle for composure. Mormon had marked on it, with the heavy lead of a carpenter's pencil.

PATRICK CASEY
lies here
where the grass grows
and the water runs. He
looked for gold in the desert
and found death.
Buried June 10,
1920

"Ef that suits you," he told Molly, "they's a chap over to Hereford who's a wolf on carvin'. My letterin's punk. When yore mines pay you c'ud have it in stone."

"You-all are awful good to me," was all she could trust herself to say. Each of the Three Musketeers of the Range felt a tug to take her in his arms and comfort her. Instead they looked at one another, as men of their breed do. Sam pulled at his mustache. Mormon rubbed the top of his bald head and Sandy rolled a cigarette and smoked it silently.

Molly ate no supper that night. Before dawn Sandy thought he heard the door of her room open and soft footfalls stealing down the stairs. When he went later to the spring he found the grave covered with the wild blooms that the girl had picked in the dewy dawn.

CHAPTER IV
SANDY CALLS THE TURN

It was a week after Plimsoll's dismissal from the Three Star premises, that one of the riders, coming back from Hereford with the mail, brought rumors of a new strike at Dynamite. Neither of the partners paid much attention to a report so often revived by rumor and as swiftly dying out again. But the man said that Plimsoll had stated that he expected to go over to the mining camp in the interests of claims located by Patrick Casey in which he had a half-interest, by reason of having grubstaked the prospector.

"There's the thorn under *that* saddle," said Sandy to Mormon. "That's what Jim Plimsoll meant by his 'deal.' I don't believe he'd stir up things unless he was fairly sure there was something doin' oveh to Dynamite. He may be wrong but he usually tries to bet safe."

"Molly's father located Dynamite, didn't he?"

"So she tells me. Hopeful, as he called it. Seems he picked up some rich float. This float was where a dyke of porphyry comes up to the surface an' got weathered away down to the pay ore. Leastwise, this was her dad's theory. He told her everything he thought as they shacked erlong together, I reckon, an' she remembers it. He figgers this sylvanite lies under this porphyry reef, sabe? Porphyry snakes underground, sometimes fifty feet thick, sometimes twice that, an' hard as steel. Matter of luck where you hit it how fur you have to go. Cost too much time an' labor an' money for the crowd that made up the rush to stay with it, 'less some one of them hits it at grass roots an' stahts a real boom atop of the rush. They don't an' Hopeful becomes Hopeless. Me, I got fo'-five chances to grubstake in that time, but I'm broke. I reckon Casey's claims, which is now Molly's claims, is the pick of the camp. Not much doubt, from what I pick up, that he was sure a good miner. One of the ol' Desert Rats that does the locatin' fo' some one else to git the money.

"Molly ses her dad never grubstaked. She don't lie an' she was close to the old man. Mo' like pardners than dad an' daughter. Plimsoll smells somethin'. Figgers there's somethin' in the rumor an' stahts this talk of bein' pardners with Casey 'cause there's a strike. Me, I'm goin' to take a pasear to town soon an' I'll have a li'l' conversation with Jim the Gambolier."

"Count me in on that," said Sam.

"Me too," said Mormon.

"Can't all three leave the ranch to once," demurred Sandy.

The half-breed came sleepily round the corner of the ranch-house and struck at the gong for the breakfast call. The vibrations flooded the air with wave after wave of barbaric sound and Joe pounded, with awakening delight in the savage noise and rhythm, until Sandy, after yelling uselessly, threw a rock at him and hit him between the shoulders, whereupon the light died out of his face and he shuffled away.

With the boom of the gong, daylight leaped up from the rim of the world. In the east the mountains seemed artificial, sharply profiled like a theatrical setting, a slate-purple in color. To the west, the sharp crests were luminous with a halo that stole down them, staining them rose. With the jump of the sun everything took on color and lost form, plain and hills swimming, seeming to be composed of vapor, the shapes of the mountains shifting every second, tenuous, smoky. The air was crisp, making the fingers tingle. The riders came from their bunk-houses, yawning, sloshing a hasty toilet at a trough with good-natured banter, hurrying on to the shack, where Joe tendered them the prodigious array of viands provided by Pedro, who waited himself on the three partners and the girl, at the ranch-house. The smell of bacon and hot coffee spiced the air. Sam, twisting his mustache, led the way.

"Smells like somethin' in the line of new bread to me," he said. "Bread or — it ain't *biscuits*, Molly?"

"Sure is." Molly came in with a plate piled high with biscuits that were evidently the present pride of her heart. "Made a-plenty," she announced. "Had to wrastle Pedro away from the stove an' I ain't quite on to that oven yet, but they look good, don't they?"

"They sure do," said Sandy, taking one to break and butter it. The eagerness with which his jaws clamped down upon it died into a meditative chewing as of a cow uncertain about the quality of her cud. He swallowed, took a deep swig of coffee and deliberately went on with his biscuit. Mormon and Sam solemnly followed his example while Molly beamed at them.

"You don't *say* they're good?" she said.

"Too busy eating," said Sandy. And winked at Sam.

Molly caught the wink, took a biscuit, buttered it, bit into it.

Camp-bread and biscuits, eaten in the open, garnished with the wilderness sauce that creates appetite, eaten piping hot, are mighty palatable though the dough is mixed with water and shortening is lacking. As a camp cook, Molly was a success. Confused with Pedro's offer of lard and a stove that was complicated compared to her Dutch kettle, the result was a bitter failure that she acknowledged as soon as her teeth met through the deceptive crust.

Molly was slow to tears and quick to wrath. She picked up the plate of biscuits and marched out with them, her back very straight. In the kitchen the three partners heard first the smash of crockery, then the bang of a pan, a staccato volley of words. She came in again, empty-handed, eyes blazing.

"There's no bread. Pedro's makin' hot cakes." Then, as they looked at her solemnly: "You think you're damned smart, don't you, tryin' to fool me, purtendin' they was good when they'd pizen the chickens? I hate folks who *act* lies, same as them that speaks 'em."

"I've tasted worse," said Mormon. "Honest I have, Molly. My first wife put too much saleratus an' salt in at first but, after a bit, she was a wonder — as a cook."

Molly, as always, melted to his grin.

"I ain't got no mo' manners than a chuckawaller," she said penitently. "Sandy, would you bring me a cook-book in from town?"

"Got one somewheres around."

"No we ain't. Mormon used the leaves for shavin'," said Sam. "Last winter. W'udn't use his derned ol' catalogue."

"I'll git one," said Sandy. "Here's the hot cakes."

They devoured the savory stacks, spread with butter and sage-honey, in comparative silence. There came the noise of the riders going off for the day's duties laid out by Sam, acting foreman for the month. Sandy got up and went to the window, turning in mock dismay.

"Here comes that Bailey female," he announced. "Young Ed Bailey drivin' the flivver. Sure stahted bright an' early. Wonder what she's nosin' afteh now? Mormon — an' you, Sam," he added sharply, "you'll stick around till she goes. Sabe? I don't aim to be talked to death an' then pickled by her vinegar, like I was las' time she come oveh."

A tinny machine, in need of paint, short of oil, braked squeakingly as a horn squawked and the auto halted by the porch steps. Young Ed Bailey slung one leg over another disproportionate limb, glanced at the windows, rolled a cigarette and lit it. His aunt, tall, gaunt, clad in starched dress and starched sunbonnet, with a rigidity of spine and feature that helped the fancy that these also had been starched, descended, strode across the porch and entered the living-room, her bright eyes darting all about, needling Molly, taking in every detail.

"Out lookin' fo' a stray," she announced. "Red-an'-white heifer we had up to the house for milkin'. Got rambuncterous an' loped off. Had one horn crumpled. Rawhide halter, ef she ain't got rid of it. You ain't seen her, hev you?"

"No m'm, we ain't. No strange heifer round the Three Star that answers that description." Sam winked at Molly, who was flushing under the inspection of Miranda Bailey, maiden sister of the neighbor owner of the Double-Dumbbell Ranch. He fancied the missing milker an excuse if not an actual invention to furnish opportunity for a visit to the Three Star, an inspection of Molly Casey and subsequent gossip. "You-all air up to date," he said, "ridin' herd in a flivver."

"I see a piece in the paper the other day," she said, "about men playin' a game with autos 'stead of hawsses — polo it was called — an' another piece about cowboys cuttin' out an' ropin' from autos. Hawsses is passin'. Science is replacin' of 'em."

"Reckon they'll last my time," drawled Sandy. "I hear they aim to roll food up in pills an' do us cattlemen out of a livin'. But I ain't worryin'. Me, I prefers steaks — somethin' I can set my teeth in. I reckon there's mo' like me. Let me make you 'quainted with Miss Bailey, Molly. This is Molly Casey, whose dad is dead. Molly, if you-all want to skip out an' tend to them chickens, hop to it."

Molly caught the suggestion that was more than a hint and started for the door. The woman checked her with a question.

"How old air you, Molly Casey?"

The girl turned, her eyes blank, her manner charged with indifference that unbent to be polite.

"Fifteen." And she went out.

"H'm," said Miranda Bailey, "fifteen. Worse'n I imagined."

Sandy's eyebrows went up. The breath that carried his words might have come from a refrigerator.

"You goin' back in the flivver?" he asked, "or was you aimin' to keep a-lookin' fo' that red-an'-white heifer?"

Miranda sniffed.

"I'm goin', soon's as I've said somethin' in the way of a word of advice an' warnin', seein' as how I happened this way. It's a woman's matter or I wouldn't meddle. But, what with talk goin' round Hereford in settin'-rooms, in restyrongs, in kitchens, as well as in dance-halls an' gamblin' hells where they sell moonshine, it's time it was carried to you which is most concerned, I take it, for the good of the child, not to mention yore own repitashuns."

"Where was it *you* heard it, ma'am?" asked Sam politely.

"Where you never would, Mister Soda-Water Sam-u-el Manning," she flashed. "In the parlor of the Baptis' Church. I ain't much time an' I ain't goin' to waste it to mince matters. Here's a gel, a'most a woman, livin' with you three bachelor men."

"I've been married," ventured Mormon.

"So I understand. Where's yore wife?"

"One of 'em's dead, one of 'em's divorced an' I don't rightly sabe where the third is, nor I ain't losin' weight concernin' that neither."

"More shame to you. You're one of these women-haters, I s'pose?"

"No m'm, I ain't. That's been my trouble. I admire the sex but I've been a bad picker. I'm jest a woman-dodger."

Miranda's sniff turned into a snort.

"I ain't heard nothin' much ag'in' you men, I'll say that," she conceded. "I reckon you-all think I've jest come hornin' in on what ain't my affair. Mebbe that's so. If you've figgered this out same way I have, tell me an' I'll admit I'm jest an extry an' beg yore pardons."

"Miss Bailey," said Sandy, his manner changed to courtesy, "I believe you've come here to do us a service — an' Molly likewise. So fur's I sabe there's been some remahks passed concernin' her stayin' here 'thout a chaperon, so to speak. Any one that 'ud staht that sort of talk is a blood relation to a centipede an' mebbe I can give a guess as to who it is. I reckon I can persuade him to quit."

"Mebbe, but you can't stop what's started any more'n a horn-toad can stop a landslide, Sandy Bourke. You can't kill scandal with gunplay. The gel's too young, in one way, an' not young enough in another, to be stayin' on at the Three Star. You oughter have sense enough to know that. Ef one of you was married, or had a wife that 'ud stay with you, it 'ud be different. Or if there was a woman housekeeper to the outfit."

"That ain't possible," put in Mormon. "I told you I'm a woman-dodger. Sandy here is woman-shy. Sam is wedded to his mouth-organ."

The flivver horn squawked outside. Miranda pointed her finger at Sandy.

"There's chores waitin' fo' me. I didn't come off at daylight jest to be spyin', whatever you men may think. You either got to git a grown woman here or send the gel away, fo' her own good, 'fore the talk gits so it'll shadder her life. I ain't married. I don't expect to be, but I aimed to be, once, 'cept for a dirty bit of gossip that started in my home town 'thout a word of truth in it. Now, I've said my say, you-all talk it over."

Sandy went to the door with her, helped her into the machine. It shudderingly gathered itself together and wheezed off; he came back with his face serious.

"She's right," he said.

"Mormon," said Sam, "it's up to you. Advertise fo' Number Three to come back — all is forgiven — or git you a divo'ce, it's plumb easy oveh in the nex' state — an' pick a good one this time."

"We got to send her away," said Sandy. "Me, I'm goin' into Herefo'd to-night. I aim to git a cook-book, interview Jim Plimsoll an' then bu'st his bank. One of you come erlong. Match fo' it."

"Bu'st the bank what with?" asked Sam.

Sandy produced the ten-dollar luck-piece and held it up.

"This. Mormon, choose yore side."

"Heads."

Sandy flipped the coin. It fell with a golden ring on the floor. "Tails," said Sandy inspecting it. "You come, Sam. Staht afteh noon. Oil up yore gun."

"I knowed I'd lose," said Mormon dolefully. "Dang my luck anyway."

It was a little after seven o'clock when Sandy and Sam walked out of the Cactus Restaurant, leaving their ponies hitched to the rail in front. They strolled down the main street of Hereford across the railroad tracks to where the "Brisket," as the cowboys styled the little town's tenderloin, huddled its collection of shacks, with their false fronts faced to the dusty street and their rear entrances, still cumbered with cases of empty bottles and idle kegs, turned to the almost dry bed of the creek. The signs of ante-prohibition days, blistered and faded, were still in place. Light showed in windows where fly-specked useless licenses were displayed. Back of the bars a melancholy array of soda-water advertised lack of interest in soft drinks. The front rooms held no loungers, but the click of chips and murmurs of talk came from behind closed doors.

Sandy stopped outside the place labeled "Good Luck Pool Parlors. J. Plimsoll, Prop." The line "Best Liquor and Cigars" was half smeared out. He patted gently the butts of the two Colts in the holsters, whose ends were tied down to the fringe ornaments of his chaps. Sam stroked his ropey mustache and eased the gun at his hip. Sandy pushed open the door and went in. A man was playing Canfield at a table in the deserted bar. As the pair entered he looked up with a "Howdy, gents?" shoving back a rickety table and chair noisily on the uneven floor. The inner door swung silently as at a signal and Jim Plimsoll came out. He stiffened a little at the sight of the Three Star men and then grinned at Sam.

"How was the last bottle, Soda-Water?" he asked. "You didn't have to change your name with Prohibition, did you? Nor your habits."

"Main thing that's changed is the quality of yore booze — an' the price, neither fo' the better," said Sam carelessly.

"We ain't drinkin' ter-night, Jim," said Sandy. "Dropped in to hev a li'l' talk with you an' then take a buck at the tiger."

Plimsoll's eyes glittered.

"Said talk bein' private," continued Sandy.

Plimsoll threw a glance at the man who had been posted for lookout and he left with a curious gaze that took in Sandy's guns.

"Sorry I was away from the ranch, time you called," said Sandy, sitting with one leg thrown over the corner of the table. "Hope to be there nex' time. I hear you-all claim to have an interest in Pat Casey's minin' locations, his interest now bein' his daughter's?"

"That any of your business?"

"I aim to make it my business," replied Sandy.

For a moment the two men fought a pitched battle with their eyes. It was a warfare that Sandy Bourke was an expert in. The steel of his glance often saved him the lead in his cartridges. Jim Plimsoll was no fool to wage uneven contest. He fancied he would have the advantage over Sandy later, if the pair really meant to play faro — in his place.

"I grubstaked him for the Hopeful-Dynamite discovery," he said.

"Got any papeh showin' that? Witnessed."

"You know as well as I do that papers ain't often drawn on grubstaking contracts. A man's word is considered good."

"Pat Casey's would have been, I reckon," said Sandy.

"I've got witnesses."

"Well, we'll let that matteh slide till the mines make a showin'. Meantime, there's talk goin' on in this town concernin' the gel an' her livin' at Three Star. I look to you to contradict that so't of gossip, Plimsoll, from now on."

Plimsoll flushed angrily.

"Who in hell do you think you are?" he demanded. "Who appointed you censor to any man's speech?"

"A *man's* speech don't have to be censored, Plimsoll. An' I reckon you know who I am."

"You come here looking for trouble, with me?"

"I never hunt trouble, Jim. If I can't help buttin' into it, like a man might ride into a rattlesnake in the mesquite, I aim to handle it. Ef I ever got into real trouble, an' it resembled you, I'd make you climb so fast, Plimsoll, you'd wish you had horns on yore knees an' eyebrows."

Plimsoll forced a laugh. "Fair warning, Sandy. I never raise a fuss with a two-gun man. It ain't healthy. You've got me wrong in this matter."

"Glad to hear it. Then there won't be no argyment. Game open?"

"Wide. An' a little hundred-proof stuff to take the alkali out of your throats. How about it?"

"I don't drink when I'm playin'. I aim to break the bank ter-night. I'm feelin' lucky. Brought my mascot erlong."

"Meaning Sam here?"

All three laughed for a mutual clearance of the situation. Sandy had said what he wanted and knew that Plimsoll interpreted it correctly. They went into the back room amicably after Plimsoll had recalled his lookout.

There was little to indicate the passing of the Volstead Act in the Good Luck Pool Room, where the tables had long ago been taken out, though the cue racks still stood in place. The place was foul with smoke and reeked with the fumes of expensive but indifferently distilled liquor. Hereford — the "brisket" end of it — had never been fussy about mixed drinks. Redeye was, and continued to be, the favorite. A faro and a roulette game, with a craps table, made up the equipment, outside of half a dozen small tables given over to stud and draw poker.

Some fifty men were present, most of them playing. Many of them nodded at Sandy and Sam as they walked over to the faro layout and stood looking on. Plimsoll left them and went back to a table near the door, where his chair was turned down at a game of draw. He started talking in a low tone to the man seated next to him. The first interest of their entrance soon died out. The dealer at faro went on imperturbably sliding card after card out of the case, the case-keeper fingered the buttons on the wires of his abacus and the players shifted their chips about the layout or nervously shuffled them between the fingers of one hand.

Sandy knew the dealer for Sim Hahn, a man whose livelihood lay in the dexterity of his slim well-kept fingers and his ability to reckon the bets; swiftly to drag in or pay out losings and winnings without an error. His face was without a wrinkle, clean-shaven, every slick black hair in place, the flesh wax-like. He held a record — whispered, not attested — of having more than once beaten a protesting gambler to the draw and then subscribing to the funeral. As he came to the last turn, with three cards left in the box, he paused, waiting for bets to be made. His eyes met Sandy's and he nodded. Three men named the order of the last three cards. None of them guessed the right one of the six ways in which they might have appeared. Hahn took in, paid out, shuffled the cards for a new deal. Sam nudged Sandy, speaking out of the corner of his mouth words that no one else could catch.

"The hombre Plimsoll's talkin' to is 'Butch' Parsons. He's the killer Brady hired over to the M-Bar-M to chase off the nesters."

Sandy said nothing, did not move. As the play began he turned and looked at the "killer" who had been named "Butch," after he had shot two heads of families that had preempted land on the range that Brady claimed as part of his holding. Whatever the justice of that claim, it was generally understood that Butch had killed in cold blood, Brady's political pull smothering prosecution and inquiry. Butch had a hawkish nose and an outcurving chin. He was practically bald. Reddish eyebrows straggled sparsely above pale blue eyes, the color of cheap graniteware. His lips were thin and pallid, making a hard line of his mouth. He packed a gun, well back of him, as he sat at the game. Meeting Sandy's lightly passing gaze, Butch sent out a puff of smoke from his half-finished cigar. The pale eyes pointed the action, it might have been a challenge, even a covert insult. Sandy ignored it, devoting his attention to the case-keeper.

The jacks came out early, three of them losing, showing second on the turn. A dozen bets went down on the fourth jack to win. Sandy placed the luck-piece on the card, reached for a "copper" marker, and played it to lose.

"That's a luck-piece, Hahn," he said. "If it loses, I'll take it up." Hahn gave him an eye-flick of acknowledgment. He was used to mascots. Sandy watched the play until at last the jack slid off to rest by the side of the case, leaving the winning card, a nine, exposed. Sandy alone had won. The luck-piece had proved its merit.

In twenty minutes Sam borrowed a stack from Sandy's steadily accumulating winnings and departed for the craps table. He wanted quicker action than faro gave him. Luck flirted with him, never entirely deserting him. And Sandy won until the news of his luck spread through the room. The gamblers began to get the hunch that the Three Star man was going to break the bank. Not all at the faro layout attempted to follow his bets. Plimsoll's roll had never yet been very badly crimped. With the peculiar paradox of their kind, while they told each other that Plimsoll's game was square, they held the secret conviction that Hahn's fingers would manipulate the case in an emergency so that the house would win. And they waited feverishly for the time to come when such a show-down would arrive.

Sandy did not have many chips in front of him, but there were five small oblongs of blue, markers representing five hundred dollars apiece. Hahn laid the fingers of his right hand lightly across the top of the case, the fingers of his left hand curled about it. It had come down to the last turn of the deal again. Every player and onlooker knew what the three cards were — a queen, a five and a deuce. The checking-board showed that the queen had lost twice and won once, the five had won three times and the deuce had won twice and lost once. Most of the players shifted their bets accordingly, the queen to win, the five and deuce to lose. Hahn still waited.

"Goin' to call th' turn?"

All eyes shifted to Sandy. No one else was going to try to name that combination. If the order of the three cards were named correctly the bank would pay four to one. If Sandy staked all on his call he would win over ten thousand dollars. Plimsoll would have to open his safe. Hahn did not have that amount in his cash drawer.

The rest — save Sam, now close behind Sandy, with ninety dollars winnings cashed-in — watched Sandy enviously and curiously. Hahn was a wonder. The case might be crooked, the spring eccentric. Plimsoll himself was looking on. Butch Parsons stood beside him for a second and then strolled into the front room. Another man followed him.

Sandy shoved the markers across the board, followed by his chips. Apparently aimlessly, he hitched at his belt and the two Colts with their tied-down holsters swung a little to the front, their handles just touching his hips.

"Deuce — queen — five, I'm bettin'," he said. *"An' deal 'em slow."* His voice drawled and his eyes lifted to Hahn's and rested there.

Hahn had been mechanically chewing gum most of the evening. Now his cheek muscles bulged more plainly and the end of his tongue showed for a second between his lips. His right hand dropped and he drew out a deuce. Eyes shifted from Sandy to Plimsoll, to Hahn. Little beads of moisture oozed out on the dealer's forehead. Plimsoll's black brows met. Sandy's face was placid. Breaths were indrawn as Hahn paid out and raked in on the card, his left hand covering the top of the case.

The atmosphere was charged with intensity. Plimsoll's dark eyes were boring through the dealer's lowered lids.

"Move yo' fingehs, dealer, an' reveal royalty," drawled Sandy. "The queen wins!" His hands were on his hips, fingers touching the butts of his guns, his eyes burned. For all its drag there was a ring to his voice.

Hahn shot one swift look at him and removed his hand. The queen showed. The room gasped. Plimsoll clapped Sandy on the shoulder.

"You did it," he said. "Broke the bank when you called that turn. Game's closed and the drinks on the house. How'll you have it?"

The crowd made way as Plimsoll walked across to his safe, twirled the combination, opened the doors and took out a stack of bills.

"Bills from a century up," said Sandy. "The odds and ends in gold — for the drinks."

The excitement was dying down. The man from the Three Star had won and had been paid. Plimsoll's game was square. A few, reading the slight signs of Hahn's nervousness, still held some doubts, but the games were closing. The drinks were brought. Two men lounged out into the front room after they had tossed theirs down. Sandy slipped the folded bills into the breast pocket of his shirt in a compact package.

"See who went out?" asked Sam in his side whisper.

"Yep. Saw it in the glass of that picture. We'll go out the back way. Not yet." He shouldered his way through the congratulating crowd, Sam close behind him, into the front room. It was empty. The short end of Sandy's winnings still provided liquor. For a moment they were alone. Plimsoll had not followed them. Sandy swiftly socketed the bolt on the inside of the front door, turned the key and slid that into his pocket.

"Now we'll go out the back way," he said. "I ain't strong fo' playin' crawfish, Sam, but I ain't keen on bein' potted in the dark. I'll bet what I got in my pocket Butch is huggin' the boards to one side of this shack. I got too much money on me to be a good insurance risk."

Sam chuckled. Plimsoll met them just inside the door.

"Makin' a short cut," said Sandy. "Good night."

As the pair went out at the rear, Plimsoll jumped into the front room. Sam, closing the back door behind them noiselessly, heard the gambler cursing at the bolted door. Silently as a cat, he covered the short distance between the house and the arroyo of the creek and disappeared, merged in its shadow. Sandy joined him and they made their way swiftly along the bottom, climbing the bank where the railroad bridge crossed it, striking off for the main street, lit by sputtery arc-lamps, making for their ponies, still standing patiently outside the all-night restaurant.

"No sense in runnin' our heads into a flyin' noose," said Sandy. "Plimsoll owns the sheriff. Married his sister. We'd be wrong whatever stahted. They'd frisk me of my roll an' we'd never see it ag'in, less we made a runnin' fight of it. Wondeh how much eddication costs nowadays, Sam? What you laffin' at?"

"Butch an' the rest of Plimsoll's gunmen holdin' up the shack, waitin' fo' us to come out, while Plim is huntin' that key."

"Don't laff too hard till we git home," said Sandy. "It's eleven miles to the Three Star."

They mounted, swung their horses and loped off toward the bridge across the creek. There were two spans, one built since the advent of automobiles, the other ancient, little used. They headed for the latter. Passing the end of the street they saw nothing out of the ordinary. The door of the "Good Luck" was open, shown by a square of light. A group stood outside. Sandy and Sam rode off, the ponies' hoofs silent in the soft thick dust; moving shadows in the twilight, merging with the dark.

CHAPTER V
IN THE BED OF THE CREEK

The old bridge, utilized only by wheels with metal tires these days, and by riders, opened a short-cut to the road leading to the Three Star, a way hardly to be distinguished from the plain. Sandy was minded to get back to the ranch as soon as possible with his winnings. Five thousand for Molly, five thousand for the Three Star, that was the agreement, the custom, and he knew the girl's breed well enough to have no hesitation in making the split as he would with a man. The next thing to do was to pick out a school for her. There Sandy was at a loss. He mulled it over as he rode, his outer senses playing sentinels to his consciousness.

He had deliberately avoided trouble for reasons he considered quite sufficient, but annoyance pricked him that he had been forced to slide out the back way from Plimsoll's, for all the odds against him. If it had been his own money — a sudden flash of future responsibilities as Molly Casey's guardian illumined his thought — if the luck-piece had not been hers, the play for her future welfare, he would have set his own marvelous coordination against Butch and the others in a shooting match, as he had done other times, in other places. Sam, he knew, was wondering a little at their strategic retreat.

But the old days were going, law and order were beginning to supersede the old methods of every man to his own judgment and action. Hereford had a sheriff who was not above suspicion, but the majority of the people had little use for him and this term of office would be his last.

Sandy could not quite gauge Plimsoll's actions in tamely paying over the winnings and he looked and listened, noting every movement of Pronto moving free-muscled beneath him, for some sign of alarm — perhaps a rifle-shot out of the mesquite. They were not the best of targets, Sam and he, riding fast in the thick dusk under the stars. The road was almost invisible, the plain unsubstantial, though the far-off mountain ranges showed plainly cut, with a curious trick of seeming always to shift back as the observer advanced. Little winds blew in their faces, cool and sweet from the desert, charged with spice of sage.

The ponies struck the loosened planks of the bridge clop-clop, springing forward into a gallop as their riders touched heels to flanks. The pinto was the quicker to get into his stride. Just past the center of the bridge Sam saw Sandy's mount jump like a startled cat into the air. He saw Sandy pliant in his seat; marked against the starry sky. Then came a spurt of red flame from the far bank — to the right — another — and another — from the left. A bullet hummed by him and his own horse slid stiff-legged, plowing the planks, hind feet flat from hoof-points to fetlocks as the pony whirled away from the yawning gap in the bridge, where boards had been pried away in the preparation, of the ambush.

Helpless for the moment until he got his bearings and his pony gained solid footing, Sam automatically whipped out his gun, cursing as he saw Sandy slide from the saddle, clutch at the rim of the gap, drop down to the bed of the creek, while Pronto, frantic at the loss of his master, leaped the opening and fled with clatter of hoof and swinging stirrup into the desert.

Sam, wild with rage at the thought of Sandy shot, scrambling in bloody sand below him, flung himself from the roan as more bullets whined, whupping into the planks. One seared his upper arm, another struck the saddle tree as he vaulted off, slapping the roan on the flanks, yelling at it as it gathered, leaped the gap and followed Pronto.

"You damned, cowardly, murderin' pack of lousy coyotes!" swore Sam mechanically, as he knelt on the edge of the gap and tried to pierce the blackness, listening fearfully for a groan. He had not fired back. There was nothing to fire at but clumps of blurred growth. The shots had been too sudden, the shying of the horses too confusing for location.

He kneeled over the rim of the last plank, turned, caught with his hands, revolver thrust back into its holster, swung, dropped. A hand closed about his ankle, pulled him down sprawling on the soft sand.

"I'm O. K.," whispered Sandy, and Sam's heart leaped. "Only plugged the rim of my hat. I faked a fall to fool 'em. Snake erlong down the crick bed. Here's where we git even." Sam knew that ring in his partner's voice, low though it was, and his blood tingled. The high crumbly banks of the creek, gouged out by winter rains and cloud-bursts, were set with brush. Immediately above the bridge were the stripped trunks of cottonwoods, stranded in a flood. Peering through the boughs, they saw stooping figures running along the bank. A man called from the lower side of the bridge, a shot was fired harmlessly. The hunters in view raced back.

"Think they saw us," whispered Sandy. "They'll hear from us, right soon." He led the way back, crossing to the town side beneath the bridge, keeping half-way up the bank, close under the stringers of the bridge, crawling between bushes on his belly, Sam with him. Now they could see no gunmen but occasionally they caught a whisper, the slight sound of moving brush.

There was only a trickle of water in the bed of the creek. Here and there were small bars of bleached shingle and larger boulders. Sandy found a stone imbedded in the bank, loosened it, squatted on his haunches and passed it to Sam, taking a gun in each hand.

"Chuck it into that sunflower patch," he said with his mouth close to Sam's ear. "Then fire at the flashes." Sam pitched the stone through the darkness. It fell with a rustle, chinked against a rock. Instantly there came a fusillade from the opposite bank, four streaks of fire, the bullets cutting through the dried stalks, the marksmen evidently hunting in couples.

Sandy, crouching, pulled triggers and the shots rattled out as if fired from an automatic. Beside him, Sam's gun barked. Each fired three times, Sandy shooting two-handed, flinging six bullets with instinctive aim while the bed of the creek echoed to the roar of the guns and the air hung heavy with the reek of exploded gases. Then they rushed for the top of the bank, wriggling behind the cover of bushes, lying prone for the next chance.

One yell and a stream of curses came from across the arroyo. Two indistinct figures bent above a third, lifted it, hurrying back toward a clump of willows. The fourth man trailed the others, his oaths smothered, running beside the two bearers, his hand held curiously in front of him, dimly seen.

"They're through. That's enough," said Sandy. "We ain't killers."

"Got two of 'em," said Sam. "Good shootin', Sandy! I reckon I missed clean. I fired to the left."

"The man who's down is Butch," said Sandy. "I'd know his figger in a coal shaft. I've a hunch the other was Hahn. Hit him somewheres in the hand; spile his dealin' fo' a while. Let's git out of this. They've quit."

"Wonder if Plimsoll was with 'em. How about the hawsses? Can you whistle Pronto back?"

"Reckon so."

They walked toward the bridge and crossed it, passing the gap on the side timbers. Plimsoll's men had departed with their casualties. Sandy whistled shrilly through his teeth. After a minute he repeated the call.

"Sure hate to hoof it to the ranch," said Sam. "Mebbe the shots stampeded 'em. Better not try to borrow hawsses in town, I figger."

"No. Pronto ain't fur. Yore roan'll stick with him. That pinto of mine is half human. I've sent him ahead before. Ef I'd yelled 'Home' he'd have gone. Shots w'udn't have scared him. Made him stand by — like Molly."

"Got yore money safe?"

"Yep."

There came a sound of pounding hoofs. Then that of others, coming from the town.

"Better load up, Sam," said Sandy grimly, "we ain't out of this yet. That'll be Jim Plimsoll's brother-in-law, likely."

"Here come our ponies."

As yet they could see nothing advancing, but a horse whinnied from the plain lying between them and the Three Star road.

"Pronto," said Sandy, shoving cartridges into his guns.

A body of mounted men had come out from town and ridden fast upon the bridge. The foremost stopped with an exclamation at the missing boards. All wheeled in some confusion and slid their horses down into the arroyo to scramble up the bank again and spur for Sam and Sandy just as the pinto and the roan, curveted up to their masters. The two cowmen leaped for their seats, Sandy temporarily sheathing one gun. They faced the townsmen who formed a half-circle about them.

"You, Sandy Bourke an' Sam Manning, stick up yore hands!"

"You got good eyesight," returned Sandy. "What's the idee? Ef you shoot, don't miss, I'm holdin' tol'able close ter-night."

His tone was almost good-humored, tolerant, full of confidence.

"You was shootin' in town limits. May have killed some one. Ag'in' the law to shoot inside the Herefo'd line. I'm goin' to take you in."

"You air?" Sandy's drawl was charged with mockery. "How about the Herefo'd men who stahted the fireworks? Ef you want our guns, Sheriff, come an' take 'em. First come, first served."

There was no forward movement. A man swore as his horse began to dance.

"You go back an' tell Jim Plimsoll to do his own dirty wo'k, if he's got any guts left fo' tryin'. Me, I'm goin' home."

The sheriff and his hastily gathered band of irregular deputies, working in the interests of Plimsoll, knew, with sufficient intimacy to endow them with caution, the general record of Sandy Bourke and Soda-Water Sam. None of them wanted to risk a shot — and miss. Sandy would not. Even a fatal wound might not prevent him taking toll. Sam was almost as dangerous. They were politicians rather than fighting men, every one of them. And they were tolerably certain that Plimsoll had ambushed the two from the Three Star. His methods were akin to their own. The sheriff blustered.

"I ain't through with you yit, Sandy Bourke. I know where to find you."

"You-all are goin' to have a mighty hard time findin' yo'se'f afteh election, Sheriff, as it is. The cowmen ain't crazy about you. They might take a notion to escort you out of the county limits."

"You're inside the town line. I — —"

"I won't be in two minutes. Git out of our road," said Sandy, his voice freezing in sudden contempt. He roweled Pronto and, with Sam even in the jump, they galloped through the half-ring without opposition. Horses were neck-reined aside to let them pass. The wind sang by them as they tangented off from the road. A shot or two announced the attempt of some to save their own faces, but no bullets came near the pair. The fusillade was sheer bravado.

Pronto and the roan went at full speed, bellies low to the plain that streamed past, the manes whipping the hands of their riders, springing on sinews of whalebone through soapweed and mesquite, spurning the soil with drumming hoofs, night-seeing, danger-dodging, jumping the little gullies, reveling in the rush. Sandy and Sam sat slightly forward, loose-seated, thigh-muscles and knees feeling the withers rather than pressing them, balancing their own limber bodies to every movement of the flying ponies.

A late moon climbed out of the east and scudded up the sky, silvering the distant peaks. For almost a mile they rode at top speed, then they settled down to a lope that ate up the miles — a walk at the end of three — then lope and walk again, until the giant cottonwoods of the Three Star rose from the plain, leaves shimmering in the moonlight, the ranch buildings blocked in purple pin-pointed with orange — the pin-points enlarging, resolving into two lighted windows as they passed shack and barn and rode into the home corral at last, to unsaddle, wipe down the horses and dismiss them for the time with a smack on their lathery flanks, knowing they would be too wise to overdrink at the trough, promising them grain later.

Mormon tiptoed heavily out on the creaking porch with a husky, "Hush!"

"What fo'?"

"Molly's asleep. 'Sisted on waitin' up for you."

"Well, we're here, ain't we?" demanded Sam. "Me, I got a scrape in my arm an' some son of a wolf spiled my saddle. Sandy, he sorter evened up fo' it."

"Bleedin'?" asked Mormon.

"Nope. Tied my bandanner round it. Cold air fixed it. Shucks, it ain't nuthin'! Sandy's got a green kale plaster fo' it. Come to think of it, I got ninety bucks myse'f."

"You won?"

"Did we win? Wait till we show you."

Molly met them as they went in, her eyes wide open, all sleep banished.

"Was it a luck-piece?" she demanded.

Sandy produced the package of bills, divided it, shoved over part.

"Your half," he said. "Five thousand bucks. Bu'sted the bank. An' here's the 'riginal bet." He showed the gold eagle, put it into her palm.

"Served me, now you take it," he said. "I'll git you a chain fo' it. It's sure a mascot — same as you are — the Mascot of the Three Star."

She looked up, her eyes, cloudy with wonder at the sight of the money, shining at her new title. They rested on Sam's arm, bandaged with the bandanna.

"There's been shootin'," she said. "You're hit. Oh!"

"More of a miss than a hit," replied Sam.

Molly turned to Sandy. Anxiety, affection, something stronger that stirred him deeply, showed now in her gaze.

"*You* hurt?"

"Didn't hardly muss a ha'r of my head. Jest a li'l' excitement."

"Tell me all about it."

Sandy gave her a condensed and somewhat expurgated account to which she listened with her face aglow.

"I wisht I'd been there to see it," she said as he finished.

"It warn't jest the time nor place fo' a young lady," said Sandy. "Main p'int is we got the money for yo' eddication, like we planned."

The light faded from her face.

"Air you so dead set for me to go away?" she asked.

"See here, Molly." Sandy leaned forward in his chair, talking earnestly. "You've got the makin' of a mighty fine woman in you. An' paht of you is yore dad an' paht yore maw. Sabe? They handed you on down an', if you make the most of yo'se'f, you make the most of them. Me, I've allus been trubbled with the saddle-itch an' I've wanted the out-of-doors. A chap writ a poem that hits me once. It stahts in,

"I want free life an' I want free air,

An' I sigh fo' the canter afteh the cattle,

The crack of whips like shots in battle;

The melly of horns an' hoofs an' heads
That wars an' wrangles an' scatters an' spreads,

The green beneath an' the blue above,

An' dash an' danger an' life....

"Somethin' like that. I mayn't have got it jest right, but that's *me*. The chap that wrote that might have writ pahts of it jest fo' me. He sure knew what he was writin' erbout. It's called *In Texas, Down by the Rio Grande*. I've been there. Arizony ain't much differunt."

"It's called *Lasca*," put in Sam. "I seen it in the movies. Had the po'try strung all through it. It was a love story. This Lasca, she — — "

Mormon put a heavy foot over Sam's and he subsided.

"So you see I lost out on a heap," said Sandy. "An' I'm a man. I can git erlong with less. But fo' a gel, learnin's a grand thing. An' there's the big cities, an' theaters, fine clothes an' fine manners. Like livin' in another world."

"Where they wear suits like Sam's spiketail," said Mormon. "I mind me when I was to Chicago with a train of steers one time, the tall buildin's was higher than cañon cliffs. On'y full breath I drawed was down on the lake front where they was a free picter show in a museum. Reg'lar storm there was out on the lake; big waves. Wind like to curl my tongue back down my throat an' choke me."

"Who's hornin' in now?" asked Sam. "Go on, Sandy."

"But," said Molly, wide-eyed, "that's the life *I* like. I mean out here. I don't want to be different."

"Shucks," said Sandy. "You won't be. Jest polished up. Skin slicked up, hair fixed to the style, nails trimmed an' shined. Culchured. Inside you'll be yore real self. You can't take the gold out of a bit of ore any more than you can change iron pyrites inter the reel stuff. But, if the gold's goin' to be put into proper circulation, it's got to be refined. Sabe?"

"I ain't refined, I reckon," said Molly with a sigh. "I don't know as I want to be. I can allus come back, can't I?"

"You sure can."

"An' there's Dad. He's where he wanted to be. I w'udn't want to go away from him."

"He'd want you to make this trip, sure," said Sandy. "An' that settles it. You go off to bed an' dream on it. We got to figger out where you go an' that'll take some time an' thinkin'. I'm some tired myse'f. I've been out of trainin' lately fo' excitement. Sam, I'm goin' to soak that place on yore arm with iodine. Good night, Molly."

She got up immediately, went to Mormon and to Sam and gravely shook hands, thanking them.

"You-all are damned good to me," she said. Opposite Sandy she hesitated, then threw her arms round his neck and kissed him before she ran from the room, with Grit leaping after her. Sandy's bronzed face glowed like reflecting copper.

"Some folks git all the luck," said Mormon.

"There you go," bantered Sam, stripping his arm for the iodine. "You been married three times, reg'lar magnet fo' the wimmin, an' you grudge Sandy pay fo' what he done. Me, I helped, but I ain't grudgin' him. Though I sure envy him."

"Yes, you helped an' left me to home to count fingers."

"Shucks! You matched for it, didn't you? An' didn't you have yore li'l' session with Plimsoll all to yorese'f. What's eatin' you? You want to be a five-ringed circus all to yorese'f an' have all the fun. Ef that stuff heals like it smahts, Sandy, I'll say I'm cured now."

"It don't amount to much, Sam," said Sandy. "Yore flesh allus closed up quick. What you goin' to do with yore ninety dollars?"

"I thought of buyin' me a new saddle. Mine's spiled. Couldn't trust that tree fo' ropin' now. But I figger I'll buy me a fine travelin' bag fo' Molly. Loan me yore catalogue, Mormon, so's I can choose one."

So, bantering one another, they bunked in.

CHAPTER VI
PASO CABRAS

They did not make butter on the Three Star.

Since the arrival of Molly an unwilling and refractory cow had been brought in from the range and half forced, half coaxed to give the fresh milk that Mormon insisted the girl needed. Until then evaporated milk had suited all hands. But butter — to go with hot cakes and sage-honey — was an imperative need for the riders. Riders demanded the best quality in the "found" part of their wages and the three partners supplied it. The butter came over weekly from the Bailey ranch to be kept under the spring cover for cooling. Usually the gangling young Ed Bailey brought it over in the crotchety flivver. When Sandy saw the sparsely fleshed figure of Miranda Bailey seated by the driver he winced in spirit. This second visitation looked like mere curiosity and gossip and offset the opinion he had begun to form of the spinster — that she was sound underneath her angularities and mannerisms.

It was twilight. The three partners and Molly were on the ranch-house porch after supper, and there was no escape. Sam slid his harmonica into his pocket silently and Mormon groaned aloud as the rattlebang car chugged up and was braked, shaking all over until the engine was shut off. Ed Bailey crossed his legs and rolled his cigarette. No one at the Three Star had ever seen him alight from the car, Mormon insisted he ate and slept in it. Miranda nodded at the three partners, who rose as she came up the steps.

"You sure need some new clothes, child," she said to Molly. "You got to have 'em. I heard you was shot," she went on to Sam. "That sling ain't right. You should have it fixed so yore wrist is higher'n yore elbow. Who's tendin' it?"

"It's healin' fine," said Sam. "I'm pure-blooded an' my flesh allus heals quick."

Miranda sniffed.

"I reckon prohibition helps some," she retorted. "Now then, I come on business. Sandy Bourke, you ain't any of you the legal guardian of that child, air you?"

"Nothin' illegal in what we're doin', I reckon."

"I didn't ask you that. You-all ain't got papers?"

With the question she wriggled her eyebrows, shifted her glance and generally twisted her features in what Sandy interpreted plainly enough as a suggestion that Molly should be eliminated from the talk. He did not agree with the spinster. It was Molly's prime affair and he knew that she would resent being treated too childishly in regard to her own concerns. Sandy had gentled too many high-spirited fillies and colts not to have found out that methods that apply to well-bred quadrupeds are generally coefficient with humans. He shook his head slightly at Miss Bailey's signaling.

"Jest what's the idea?" he asked. "Some one figgerin' on makin' her stay at the Three Star unpleasant? Fur as jest gossip is concerned, it don't have any weight with none of us an' there ain't no sense in mentionin' it."

"'Pears you ain't givin' me over an' above credit for sense," said Miranda, a bit grimly. "This ain't gossip. Ef you're bound the gel is to sit in with her elders I'll go right ahead. I got a lot of chores to do yet, deliverin' butter, an' the car's actin' up uncertain. Here 'tis. I got it direct from my brother who's heard the talk that's goin' round. You've run foul of Jim Plimsoll — or he foul of you, which is more likely. Plimsoll an' Eke Jordan, the sheriff, are like two peas in a pod. The sheriff's got the inside of local politicks, so fur. When we wimmen git to votin' this fall things is goin' to be different. Right now, he's in. He an' the courts of this county are all striped the same way. Reg'lar zebras. Penitentiary pattern 'ud match their skins. Mebbe some of 'em ought to be wearin' it.

"Now for the meat of the nut. They're figgerin' on gettin' control of the gel away from you-all. They'll use argymints for the general public that she's too young to be keepin' house for three unmarried men, leastwise three men who ain't livin' with their wives." She looked pointedly at Mormon. "They'll rouse up opinion enough for a change. They'd like to app'int a guardian of their own kidney. Mebbe we can block that if one of us comes out an' offers to take her. I'd be glad to, for one, an' do the right thing by her."

Molly walked over to Sandy's chair and stood behind it, her eyes widening, her breath beginning to come quickly.

"There's some talk about her father's claims over to Dynamite lookin' up. Party of easterners over that way lately, nosin' around to find out owners, lookin' up assessment work an' so on. Talk of a boom. I reckon Plimsoll's twigged that. Lawyer Feeder, who run for state senator an' whose record's none too dainty, is in cahoots with Jordan an' Plimsoll. Ed heard they figger on goin' before Judge Vanniman, one of their crowd, to get an order of court. She's a minor. They can git her away from you. If we crowd them too hard for them to app'int one of their own ring — an' they're figgerin' on Plimsoll, he claimin' to be her father's partner — they'll likely have her put in some institution. An' it's goin' to be done right sudden. I w'udn't wonder, from all I hear, but what they're over here ter-morrer with a court order. An' you can't fight the courts 's long as they're in authority, the way you fought Jim Plimsoll."

Molly stepped out, eyes flashing, fists clenched, talking passionately. "I won't go with 'em. I'll run away. They can't take me. Jim Plimsoll is a damned liar. You won't let 'em take me?" She turned to Sandy, her arms stretched in appeal.

"No, Molly, I won't. Will we, boys?"

"You can bet everything you got an' ever hope to own we won't," said Sam.

"That goes for me," echoed Mormon, but he scratched his fringe of hair in some perplexity.

"Talk don't beat an order of the court," said Miranda Bailey. "Mebbe I seem sort of vinegary to you, child, but I'm not a bad sort. My brother Ed has got somethin' to say in this community an' I'm likely to control a few votes this fall myself. I figger if you came home with me to-day we c'ud manage to git you placed with us. There's been tattle about you stoppin' here. You're fifteen — an'...."

"Some folks is jest plumb rotten," flared Molly. "I'm no kid. I ...*oh, if* Dad was alive!"

Sandy stood up and slid an arm about her shaking shoulders. She wheeled and buried her head on his shoulder, sobbing.

"We're powerful obliged to you, Miss Bailey, for what you told us," said Sandy. "I'm right sure you'd give Molly a fine home, but we got other plans an' we aim to carry 'em out. Plimsoll's a skunk an' I'll block his game about the mines ef they amount to anything. Molly's goin' east for her eddication. She's got plenty money to git the best that's goin' an' she's goin' to have it."

"Then you better git her 'cross the county line before many hours are over." Miranda Bailey recognized something better than mere decision in Sandy's voice, she was not the leading suffragist of the county for lack of brains. But there was true regret in her voice as she went on. "I'm sorry she don't cotton to the idee of comin' over to our place. A woman needs a woman's company." At the diplomatic concession to her maturity Molly gave the spinster a mollified glance. Miss Bailey climbed into the machine.

"You aim on takin' her out of the county to the railroad ter-morrer?" she asked. "What school is she goin' to?"

"We ain't settled all the details," said Sandy. "But we'll do that all right. We'll git ready soon's we can. Meantime, we'll keep our eyes peeled ter-morrer against any order from Hereford."

"Want to use this car? I'll bring it over early. Ed can drive it."

The gangling youth for the first time showed an intelligent interest in anything outside of his cigarette.

"Fo' time's sake, aunt," he said, " 'twouldn't be no manner of good if it come down to a runnin' chase. Nearest depot's fifty mile' across the county line. Racin' this car ag'in' the sheriff's 'ud be like matchin' a flea ag'in' a grasshopper. Dern it, she's balked ag'in." He wrestled with the crank, conquered it and the machine shivered like a hunting dog while his aunt adjusted spark and gas. She nodded to him to start and they moved off, Miranda waving a farewell as she called out, "Good luck!"

"Some sport!" announced Sam. "That's the kind of woman you sh'ud have married, Mormon."

Molly, excited now, demanded audience.

"When do we start?" she asked eagerly. "Will you wait till they come out from Hereford?"

"I got to think out things a bit, Molly," said Sandy. "I figger we'll git a start on 'em, ef you can git ready. In the mornin'."

"I haven't got much to take."

"We'll buy you an outfit."

"Horseback?"

Sandy looked at her with puckered eyes.

"Can't tell you what I ain't sure of myse'f," he drawled. "One thing is sure, you got to tuhn in an' git a good rest. Ef we slide out it won't be all a pleasure trip. I reckon Plimsoll means business. An' he's sure got the county machinery behind him right now."

"I can take Grit?"

"W'udn't want to leave us somethin' to remember you by?" asked Sandy. "Somethin' to help make sure you'll come back?"

"I'd allus come back, to visit Dad," she said. "But Grit...? I don't want to leave Grit."

"It 'ud be a hard trip fo' him this way, Molly. I ain't sure about the regulations at them schools. I reckon the best way w'ud be fo' you to make arrangements fo' him to come on afteh you git there."

Molly regarded Sandy soberly, her fingers twining through the dog's mane.

"You'd be good to him — same as you air to me? Oh, I'm jest plumb mean to ask you that. I know you w'ud. He's goin' to be jest as lonesome as me for a bit, ain't you, Grit? He allus slep' with me, cuddlin' up, an' — — " She gulped, straightened.

"Good night," she said. "Come, Grit."

The three men sat silent for a moment or two after she left.

"She's sure a stem-winder," said Mormon presently. "How you goin' to fix to git her away, Sandy? Plimsoll'll be hotter'n a bug on a hot griddle."

"I got a plan warmin' up," said Sandy. "Nearest to the county line is west through the Cabezas Range. Only two gaps, Paso Cabras, an' the Bolsa."

"But the Bolsa...." started Sam.

Sandy checked him.

"I know. Listen! I aim to git to the railroad an' then me an' Molly'll make for New Mexico."

"Huh!"

"You guessed it, Mormon. For the Pecos River an' Boville an' the Redding Ranch. I reckon Barbara Redding'll handle the thing. She'll git Molly her outfit an' she'll know all about the right schools."

Mormon brought his hand down on Sam's thigh with a sounding whack.

"Dern me, ef he ain't the wise ol' son of a gun," he cried delightedly. "Sure!"

"It's the thing," assented Sam, rubbing himself, "but you don't have to break my laig over it. Sandy, you sure use yo' brains."

Barbara Redding, once Barbara Barton of the celebrated Curly O, was a bright star in the mutual firmament of the Three Star partners. They had all worked together on the Curly O in the old days. Sandy had been foreman there. Once he had rescued Barbara Barton from horse rustlers with a grudge against her father and once again he had rendered her even greater service when members of the same crowd kidnapped her two-year-old son whom Barbara Redding had brought on a visit to his grandfather. Sandy had trailed alone and brought in the "li'l' son of a gun," as he styled the youngster. There was little that Barbara Redding and her husband, wealthy rancher, would not do for Sandy.

"I've got an itch to give Plimsoll an' his pals a run fo' their money," went on Sandy. "An' here's the way I figger to do it, in the rough. See what you all think of it."

Subdued guffaws rose from the porch in through the open window of the room where Molly Casey lay wide awake, the dog beside her. Presently she heard the martial strains of Sam's harmonica, cuddled under his big mustache, played one-handed. He was playing an air that he had dedicated to Sandy. Vaguely it comforted her.

"They're *good*," she said to Grit. "An' they've figgered out something or they w'udn't be actin' thataway. You an' me got to be game."

Sandy smoked his cigarette and Mormon lolled in his chair, while Sam breathed out his melody into the night that was very still and very quiet, with the great white stars burning rayless. The tune swelled triumphantly.

Behold El Capitan, Notice his misanthropic stare,

Look at his independent air;

And match him if you can,

He is the champion beyond compare.

It was a tribute to the strategy of Sandy Bourke, the D'Artagnan of the Three Musketeers of the Range, whereof Mormon was surely Porthos, if Sam was hard to recognize as Aramis. "One for all and all for one" was their motto, and neither Mormon nor Sam doubted for an instant that Sandy would win. Sandy, smoking cigarette after cigarette, was not so sure but equally complacent.

Next morning, breakfast over before the sun was well above the peaks, while desert birds were still rising, twittering shrill welcome to the dawn, Sandy went about humming snatches of cowboy songs just above his breath as he oversaw the arrangements for the exodus that was to be; not so much a flight, as a deliberately calculated laying of a trail for the pursuit. So might an old dog fox, sure of his speed and wisdom, trot leisurely across a field in full sight of the pack. Sandy had no intention of waiting until the lawhounds arrived, he needed a start against the handicap of high-powered cars. He was in high humor as the buckboard was greased, a team of buckskins given a special feed and a rub-down, and various articles gathered for transportation. Among these were a spool of barbed wire and a dozen fence posts.

"I'm a rollickin', rovin' son of a gun
Of a roamin' gambolier;"

sang Sandy, lights dancing in his gray eyes. Sandy was not old — a little short of thirty — but he was generally mature, suggesting deliberation of mind if not of action. This morning youth was his, rollicking, devil-may-care youth that showed in his walk, the set of his shoulders, his smile.

His spirit was infectious. Four riders, jumping to his orders, tossed badinage among one another like a ball. Mormon and Sam, seated on the top rail of the corral fence, openly admired their partner.

"Like old times, Mormon?" suggested Sam.

"Sure is. I reckon we'll have some fun 'fore the day's out. Sandy can cert'nly scheme out the scenarios."

"The what?"

"The scenarios," repeated Mormon loftily. "I got that out of a moving pitcher magazine down to Hereford. It's the word fo' the plot of the story. Sabe?"

"Huh! I reckon them movin' pitcher shooters 'ud have to move some to git all that's movin' this trip. Got yore gun oiled up, Mormon? Here's Molly."

Molly came out on the porch carrying a small grip packed with her few belongings, Grit beside her. Sandy nodded to her, busy giving instructions to two riders. Mormon and Sam waved and she went over to them, swinging up to the rail beside them.

"Jim," said Sandy, "I want you should ride out to'ards Hereford an' hide out atop of Bald Butte. You don't need to stay there any later than noon. Take a flash-glass with you. If any of the sheriff's crowd comes erlong, any one who looks like he might be servin' papers, sabe, you flash in a message. Make it a five-flash fo' anything suspicious, a three-flash fo' any one shackin' this way, even if you figger they're plumb harmless."

"Seguro, Miguel." With the slang phrase, Jim, an upstanding young chap, despite his horse-bowed legs, walked over to the bunk-house for flash-mirror and gun, came back to his already caught-up and saddled horse, turned stirrup and set foot in it, caught hold of mane and horn, beat the quick swirl of his pony sidewise with the fling of leg over cantle and went streaming off for the Bald Butte in a cloud of dust. Sandy called to Buck Perches, oldest of his riders, whose exposed skin matched the leather of his saddle.

"Buck, ef any visitors arrives while we're gone, you entertain 'em same as I w'ud. I w'udn't be surprised but what Jim Plimsoll 'ud be moseyin' erlong, with Sheriff Jordan an' mebbe one or two mo'. Mo' the merrier. They'll be lookin' fo' me an' Miss Molly with some readin' matter that's got a seal to the bottom of it. We won't be to home. You'll be the only one to home 'cept Pedro an' Joe. They've got their instructions to know nothin'. They ain't supposed to know nothin'. You — you've stayed to the ranch to do some fixin' of yore saddle. Started, but come back when yore cinch bu'sted. Sabe? All the rest of the riders is on the range 'tendin' business. When they left, an' when you left with 'em, me an' Mormon an' Sam, with Miss Molly, was all here. So you supposed. Don't let 'em think yo're planted to feed 'em info'mation."

Buck nodded, solemn as an image, his dark eyes twinkling a little.

"I'm real pleasant to the sheriff an' sort of indifferent to this here Plimsoll person?" he suggested.

"Let 'em size up the thing fo' themselves. They'll find Pronto in the corral, also Sam's roan, which they know is our usual mounts. If they don't sabe the buckboard's gone, which they probably will, knowin' this outfit fairly well, an' the sheriff not bein' a dumbhead; lead up to it. Then you might horn it out of Pedro that he thinks we started erbout ten o'clock an' leave it to them to foller trail. It'll be plain enough. We'll take care of the rest. Up to you, Buck, to act natcherul."

"I'll sure do that. I sabe the play."

"Then we'll light out soon's we're packed. Mormon, git the grub an' water aboard. Sam, help me with the rest of the truck. Got yore war-bag, Molly?"

"I haven't said good-by to Dad, or Grit," she said.

Sandy nodded. "Reckon you'd like to do that alone. Suppose you take Grit with you to the spring an' then leave him up in yore room."

"He knows I'm goin'. I told him last night, but he knew it 'thout that." Molly spoke in a monotone. She was pale and her eyes showed lack of sleep but she had fought the thing out with herself and she was going to be game. She gave Sandy her grip and walked off toward the cottonwoods. Grit nosed along in her shadow, his muzzle touching her skirt.

It was a big load for the buckboard with Mormon and Sam in the back seat crowded by the piled-up baggage, with Sandy driving and Molly beside him, flushed a little with growing excitement. But the buckskins were sinewed with whalebone and used to desert work. They surged forward at the word, tightening the tugs in an eager leap and settled down to a fast trot, out across the prairie. The riders, with the exception of Buck, and Jim, who was already close to the butte, which was midway between the ranch and Hereford, loped off, two and two, to their work, not to return until sun-down.

It was still cool, the dust rose about them in eddies as they crossed the slowly descending slope of the sink that presently mounted again toward the far-off range. There was no apparent road, but Sandy chose a compass course between the sage for the first few miles, then skirted the mesquite. Sam leaned forward once when the buckskins had been pulled down to a walk and spoke to Molly.

"See that notch in the range?" he asked, "oveh to the no'th, where the shadder's blue. That's Paso Cabras, the Pass of the Goats. Some says it's named 'cause the cliffs is fair lousy with goats, some 'cause on'y a goat can make the climb. County line's five mile' out on the plain beyond the pass. Railroad two mo', at Caroca."

"Are we goin' through the pass?" she asked Sandy.

"Well, I'll tell you this much, Molly. If we sh'ud decide to go that way an' strike the pass afore the sheriff catches up with us, he'll have to foller afoot or go clean round the mesa. The Goat's Pass ain't no place fo' an automobeel, nor an airyplane neither. Don't believe there's a level spot wider'n five foot or bigger than that much square."

Either Mormon or Sam sat always with neck twisted, watching for a flash-signal from the butte that stood up clearly in the crystal atmosphere, sometimes distorted, changing hue from chocolate to indigo, never seeming to get any farther away, just as the mesa range never seemed to get any closer. Sometimes Molly relieved them as lookout, but hour after hour passed without sign.

Close to noon they reached a watering hole, with water none too cool or sweet, but still welcome. There the buckskins were unhitched, rubbed down and, after they had cooled off, given water and grain. Save for sweat marks, they showed little sign of the grueling trip through the soft dirt. A strip of lava, half a mile of ancient flow, lay between them and the long up-slope of the desert to the mesa. As they ate lunch in the shadow of some barrel cactus, Sandy suddenly gave a grunt of satisfaction, pointing with outstretched forefinger to the butte. Five flashes had flickered up. They were repeated. Jim had signaled a suspicious party on their way to Three Star. The sheriff was out with his papers.

"We got five hours' staht," said Sandy. "Made close to thirty mile'. They've got thirty-five to make. Take 'em mo'n two hours, countin' questions with Buck. Good enough. See anything of the boys, Sam? They ought to be showin' up. I told 'em noon."

"On time," announced Sam. The two riders who had last talked with Sandy rode out of a straggling thicket of cactus and skirted the lava flow. Each led a spare horse, unsaddled.

Sheriff Jordan had a high-powered car purchased, not so much from the fees of his office as with his perquisites, a word covering a wide range of possibilities, all of which the sheriff made the most of. He was proud of his car and proud of his ability to run it anywhere at record-breaking speed. It carried an extra water container that could be mounted on the running board for desert work, an extra gasoline and oil supply, there were always extra tires strapped on, extra spark plugs handy and his batteries were always well charged.

"I aim to make her efficient," said Jordan, "bein' she represents my office. That's me. If I needed me an airyplane, I'd get me one to hunt the outlaws out of cover, an' I'd run it myself, an' run it right. That's me, Bill Jordan!"

Boaster though he was, there was little doubt as to Jordan's efficiency or his courage. He brought in the criminals he went out to get, some alive, some dead; prosecuted the first with zeal and collected the rewards with alacrity. The trouble was that he did *not* always go out after certain individuals, who were outside the law, as interpreted by the people, but inside it, as protected by the political ring to which Jordan, with other prominent officials, belonged.

Jordan had taken up his brother-in-law's grievance with the greater zest since he had a half-interest in Plimsoll's Good Luck Pool Parlors, a share that had cost him good money. On top of that had come Sandy's flouting of him on the bridge in front of the sheriff's own followers. He had to save his face, politically as well as personally.

To secure papers bringing Molly Casey within the jurisdiction of the court was not a difficult matter, but it was not so easy to get them at an early hour, since court was not in session and the judge none too eager to arise of a morning. But Jordan knew nothing of the visit of Miranda Bailey to the Three Star and he pressed matters with no special expedition, though he characteristically wasted no time.

Armed with the necessary warrant, backed by an assurance that, unless some extraordinary howl went up, the girl would be given into the custody of Jim Plimsoll as guardian, by virtue of his claim to partnership with her father, the sheriff, Plimsoll and two others, all three deputized for the occasion, started the car from Hereford at a quarter of twelve, after an early lunch. They passed the butte where Jim lay prone atop without noticing the flashes he shot into the sky. At a few minutes after twelve they reached Three Star where Buck, seated on the porch, his saddle astride a sawhorse, stitched away at a cinch.

Buck played his part well, allowing Jordan to ferret out information to his own satisfaction. It appeared plain that all three partners had taken flight with the girl in the buckboard. Sandy's pinto and Sam's roan were in the corral. Jordan overlooked one thing, the counting of saddles, though that would not have been an easy determination.

"Some one tipped this thing off," he said sternly to Buck. "Who was it?"

"Meanin' this visit's offishul?" asked Buck. "What's it fo', Sheriff? Moonshine or hawss stealin'?" He spoke in a jesting note, his weathered face impassive as the shell of a walnut, but Plimsoll scowled, noting the turn of Buck's bland countenance in his direction for the first time. It was whispered that the brands on Plimsoll's horse ranch were not those usually known in the county, nor even in the counties adjoining. There were rumors, smothered by Plimsoll's stand with the authorities, of bands of horses, driven by strangers, arriving wearied — and always by night — at his corrals.

"It don't matter — to you — what it's for," answered Jordan. "I'll overhaul 'em an' bring 'em back. Crossin' the county line won't do 'em any good with this warrant. Ef they try hide-out tactics or put up a scrap, it'll be kidnappin' an' that's a penal offense."

Buck whistled.

"Thought you wasn't goin' to let me know," he said. "It's the gel."

"Who's been here to tip it off?" asked Jordan.

Buck looked at him serenely, took a plug of chewing from his hip pocket, took his knife, opened it deliberately and slowly cut off a corner of the tobacco.

"Search me," he drawled. "Me, I don't stay up to the house."

Jordan, temporarily discomfited but still confident of bringing back his quarry, marked the trail of the buckboard in the alkali soil, noted the hoof-prints of the diverging riders and nodded with the semi-smile and half closed-eyes of conscious superiority. He had already elicited apparently reluctant information from Pedro as to the four passengers in the buckboard. Buck had been more reticent. To the sheriff Buck's reticence betokened desire to cover the fugitives. He fancied that Pedro's testimony was the result of Jordan's own cleverness in cross-questioning. Joe resorted to "no sabes."

"You 'tendin' ranch?" Jordan asked Buck, at last.

"Yep. Till I git fresh orders."

"I'll bring you back those orders, also yore bosses, before sun-down."

Buck permitted himself his first grin.

"You'll have to go some," he said. "Goin' to bring 'em back in irons? Figgerin' on abduction?"

Jordan gave no hint of how Buck's shaft might have targeted his intentions, but climbed into the car and started it. The powerful machine went lunging through the soft dirt, following the blurry trail of the buckboard's iron tires, throwing up dust as a fast launch churns spray.

After leaving the Three Star all semblance of road vanished. The alkaline soil was almost as fine as flour, and deep. This and the fear of losing the trail kept the machine down to a limit that would have been ridiculous on a real road but represented fast work on the desert. The water boiled in the radiator from the heat of the toiling engine and Jordan stopped, replenished, reoiled. Reaching the lava strip where the buckboard had halted for water and the noon meal, they found the trail skirting the flow toward the south. The main mass of the mesa, broken up into gorges, gaps, stairway cliffs, marked by purple shadows, scanty in the early afternoon but gradually widening, was about fifteen miles away. Jordan braked his car. He ignored the water in the spring. His spare supply was still ample and was distilled, not alkaline.

He turned to one of his deputies.

"Which way do you figger they're headin', Phil?" he asked. "Is there a cut or a pass through the mesa?"

"Dam'fino. Mesa's all cut up, but it's sure a Godforsaken country. Nothin' but rock an' clay an' cactus. No one ever goes there. I reckon I know as much of this country as most an' I sure never explored the dump. One thing's sure an' certain. Them fellers from the Three Star usually know where they are headin'. Trail's plain."

"Sure is." But Jordan scratched his head a trifle doubtfully. If Sandy Bourke and his chums had been tipped off, this trail was a little too plain to be true. Presently, as the machine plowed on south, they struck a patch of desert where the rock surfaced out and showed no trace of hoof or tire. Jordan stopped the car and the four got out, casting around, expecting that this outcropping had been used as a device to throw off the pursuit. Fairly fresh horse droppings showed that the buckboard had held to its course and, the rock passed, the trail showed plain again, curving in toward the broken wall of the mesa, leading toward a cleft that was plainly distinguishable.

"That's Bolsa Boquete," announced the deputy named Phil. "I never went through it."

"What's it mean — the name?"

"Boquete's gap. Bolsa's money — not jest the same as dinero. It's the word they have on the bank winders down in Mexico. Exchange."

"Money Gap? That don't tell us a thing," said Jordan. "But I'll bet my star they've gone through it all right. We ought to be not much more'n an hour behind them."

"They're on about us getting the papers," said Plimsoll. He had not said much on the trip so far. "Too much talk nowadays. You can't whisper in a dugout but what the news is all over the county inside of twenty minutes. Bourke sabes that getting the girl out of the county won't do any good; he aims to get her out of the state and any Arizona court or sheriff jurisdiction. He's the brains of the outfit. We've got to get her, Jordan."

"You ain't tellin' me a thing I don't know, Jim. But there's one thing you *can* tell me. Is that tip you got about Dynamite a sure one?"

Plimsoll, sitting beside Jordan, flashed him a look of contempt.

"Do you think I'm chasing this girl because I'm stuck on her? One of the party with this eastern crowd dropped into my place and talked. Showed some samples and I had a good look at them. He happened to leave a bit or two behind and I had them assayed. Here is where I get back the money I put up to grubstake Casey."

Jordan gave him a grin of derision.

"You an' yore grubstake," he jeered.

Plimsoll said nothing more.

As they neared the gap, translated by Phil in the unconsciousness that Bolsa had two meanings in Spanish, Jordan slowed up.

"No shootin' in this deal," he warned. "Come to a show-down, Bourke won't buck the law soon's we show papers. So long's he ain't been notified the court is makin' a ward of the girl they ain't done nothin' wrong. But — if he resists, that's different."

"I ain't goin' to be awful anxious to start shootin'," said Phil. "They done some pretty shootin' at the bridge that time. Sandy Bourke's a two-handed lead flinger an' Soda-Water Sam's no slouch. Neither's Mormon. Me, I'll be peaceable 'less it's forced on me otherwise."

They entered the split in the mesa. The cliffs shimmered in the heat, their outlines fuzzy. Branched and pillared cactus showed in gray-green reptilian growths. The soft earth, through which here and there the volcanic cores of the range were thrust, seemed as if it could supply the paint shops of a nation with almost any hue desired, ready for mixing with oil or water. Waves of heat beat between the walls of the cleft. The floor was fairly smooth, swept clean by occasional cloud-bursts, save for the skeleton of a tree and another of a too-far wandering steer, both blanched white as the alkali-crusted boulders. It was nearly level going and the car pounded along, all the occupants looking for trail sign. The mesa corridor, nowhere more than thirty feet wide, twisted and snaked, three hundred feet of sheer wall on either side topped by sloping cliffs mounting far higher toward the actual top of the mesa.

"Keep an eye peeled for rain, Phil," said Jordan, "I'd sure hate to get caught in here with a cloud-burst."

"Right," answered Phil. "I c'ud see better if I had a drink. Plimsoll, you got somethin' on the hip, ain't you?"

Plimsoll produced a bottle and the four of them drank the fiery unrectified, unstamped liquor. Ahead was an abrupt turn. Jordan slowed. Making the curve, a fence stretched across the gorge, reaching from wall to wall, a four-strand barrier of barbed-wire, strung on patent steel posts. Jordan braked with emergency. The sight of such a fence in such a place was as unexpected as the sun-dried carcass of a steer would be on Broadway. Plimsoll and Jordan cursed, the former in pure anger, the latter with some appreciation of the stratagem for delay.

"We can tear it down quicker'n they fixed it," he said. "I've got a pair of nippers in the tool kit. They can't have driven in those posts deep. Come on."

A voice floated down to them.

"You leave that fence alone, gents. *If* you please. I went to a heap of trouble puttin' up that fence. It's *my* fence."

They looked up, to see Mormon seated on the top of a great boulder that had land-slipped from the cliff into the gorge. From thirty feet above them he looked down, amiably enough, though there was a glint of blued metal in his right hand.

"Hello, Jim Plimsoll," he went on. "I ain't seen you-all fo' quite a while. You fellers out fo' a picnic?"

Jordan advanced to the foot of the rock, producing his papers.

"I have a bench warrant here to bring into court for the appointment of a proper guardian, the child Molly Casey, she being a minor and without natural or legal protectors. I've got yore name on these papers, Mormon Peters, as one of the three parties with whom the girl is now domiciled. I warn you that you are obstructing the process of the law by yore actions. You put up that gun an' come down here an' help to pull down this fence, illegally erected on property not yore own. Otherwise you're subject to arrest."

"That is sure an awful long speech fo' a hot day," said Mormon equably. "But I don't sabe that talk at all. Molly Casey ain't here, to begin with. Nor she ain't been here. An' I don't sabe no obstruction of the law by settin' up a fence in a mesa cañon to round up broom-tails."

One of the deputies snickered.

"Broom-tails?" cried Jordan. "That's too thin. There's no mustangs hangin' round a mesa like this, 'thout feed or water." He flushed angrily. He was short-tempered and he was certain the fence was a ruse to gain time, with Mormon left behind to parley. It all seemed to point to Sandy Bourke making for the railroad.

"You never kin tell about wild hawsses, or even branded ones," said Mormon pleasantly. "Ask Plimsoll. He picks 'em up in all sorts of places."

Plimsoll cursed. Mormon still held his gun conspicuously, and he restrained his own impulse to draw. Jordan wheeled on the gambler.

"You keep out o' this, Jim Plimsoll," he said. "I'm runnin' this end of it. He's talkin' against time. You come down an' help remove this fence," he shouted up at the smiling Mormon, "or I'll start something. It ain't on yore property and it's hindering the carrying out of my warrant."

"It ain't on a public highway neither," retorted Mormon. "But I'll come down. Don't you go to clippin' those wires an' destroyin' what *is* my property." He slid down the rock and commenced to unbend the metal straps that held the wire in place. Jordan and one of his men followed suit with pliers from the motor kit. The job took several minutes.

"You'll come along with us," said Jordan. "You lied about the girl comin' this way. I've a notion to take you in for that. But I reckon you can go back in the buckboard with yore partners."

"Reckon I'll travel in the buckboard, when you catch up with it," said Mormon. "But I'll come erlong with you fo' a spell — of my own free will. I don't see no harm in takin' the gel visitin' anyway," he concluded as he took an extra seat in the tonneau.

Jordan made no answer but started the engine. The gorge began to narrow perceptibly, its floor slanted upward and the machine labored with a mixture that constantly needed more air. The way zigzagged for half a mile and then they came to a second fence. No buckboard was in sight. Beyond the wire the pitch of the ravine showed steeper yet, as it mounted to a sharp turn. Leaning against a post stood Soda-Water Sam, smoking a cigarette, his gun holster hitched forward, the butt of the weapon close to one hand. Jordan and his men leaped out as the car stopped, Mormon following more slowly.

"Afternoon, hombres all," said Sam. "Joy-ridin'?"

Jordan wasted no more explanations.

"You take down this fence," he fairly shouted.

"What fo'?"

"Ask yore partner."

"Sheriff claims we're cumberin' the landscape with our li'l' corral, Sam," said Mormon. "He's got a paper that gives him right of way, he says. Seen anything of Molly Casey?"

"Not for quite a spell. Go easy with them wires, Sheriff. Price of wire's riz considerable."

The second barrier down and the car through, Jordan ordered Sam to get in the car.

"Jump, or I'll put the cuffs on you," he said.

"Not this trip," replied Sam coolly. "No sense in my climbin' in there. Me an' Mormon's through with our li'l' job. We'll go back in the buckboard. It's round the bend. I was jest goin' to hitch up."

Jordan glared unbelievingly, yet Sam's words carried conviction.

"Yo're sure goin' to have trouble turnin' yore car right here," Sam went on imperturbably. "Kind of mean to back down, too. It's worse higher up. Matter of fac' the gap peters out jest round the turn. This is Bolsa Boquete. Bolsa means purse, Sheriff, one of them knitted purse nets. Good name for it. Look for yo'self, if you don't believe me."

Jordan and Plimsoll strode on up the pitch. Mormon followed, Sam stayed with the two deputies. Around the bend stood the buckboard with the buckskins in a patch of shadow under a scoop in the ending wall that turned the so-called pass to a box cañon.

"I told you the gel warn't erlong," said Mormon. "She and Sandy was with us fo' a spell. But they're goin' visitin' an' they shifted to saddle way back, out there by the spring beside the lava strip."

Mormon's bland smile masked a sterner intent than showed in his eyes. Jordan, furious at being outwitted, dared not provoke open combat. He had nothing on which to make arrest of the two Three Star partners and he was far from sure of his ability to do so under any circumstances. Mormon hitched up the buckskins, but followed the sheriff and the scowling, silent Plimsoll back to the car.

"See that notch, way over to the no'th?" said Mormon, bent on exploiting the situation to the full. "I reckon Sandy and the gel's shackin' through there about now. Hawss trail only. 'Fraid you won't catch him, Sheriff. They aim to ketch the seven o'clock train at Caroca. It's the on'y pass over the mesa. If Sandy had knowed you wanted him he might have waited. Why didn't you phone? Ninety mile' around the mesa, nearest way, an' it must be all of five o'clock now, by the sun."

He stopped, puzzled by the change in the sheriff's face. Chagrin had given place to exultation.

"Catch the seven o'clock train at Caroca?" said Jordan. "Thanks for the information, Mormon. That schedule was changed last week when they pulled off two trains on the main line. The train leaves at nine-thirty an', if I can't make ninety miles in four hours an' a half, I'll make you a present of my car. Stand back, both of you. No monkey business with my tires. Cover 'em, boys. The law's on my side, you two gabbing word-shooters."

He handled the car wonderfully, backing and turning her, and, while Mormon and Sam stood powerless, the former crestfallen, the latter sardonically gazing at his partner, the machine went tilting, snorting down the gorge.

"You sure spilled the beans, Mormon," said Sam finally. "I'd have thought them three wives of yores 'ud have taught you the vally of silence."

"I ain't got a damned word to say, Sam. But I'd be obliged if you'd kick me — good. Use yore heels, I see you got yore spurs on."

CHAPTER VIII
THE PASS OF THE GOATS

In the throat of the gorge the sun shone red on the tawny cliffs. The trail, a scant four feet wide at its best, with crumbled, weathered margin, crept along the face of the cliff above a deep cañon where the night shadows had already gathered in a purple flood, slowly rising as the rays of the setting sun shifted upward, not yet staining the summit.

It was close to seven o'clock. Sandy's lean face was anxious. The girl drooped in her seat tired from the long climb, not yet inured to the saddle. The horses traveled gamely, sure-footed but obviously losing endurance. Every little while they stopped of their own accord, their flanks heaving painfully in the altitude.

Sandy had only once crossed the Pass of the Goats and that was years before. There had been washouts since then. Several times they were forced to dismount and lead the nervous beasts, Sandy doing the coaxing, helping Molly over the difficult places. He rode a mare named Goldie and the girl a bay with a white blaze that Sandy had chosen for the mountain work and which had been brought to them at the lava strip.

The mare halted, neck stretched out, turning it to look inquiringly at her master. A sharp incline lay ahead, the path little better than one made by the goats for which the pass was named. Behind, Molly's mount followed suit, blowing at the dust. Sandy patted the mare's neck and dismounted.

"It's late, ain't it?" asked Molly. "Will we miss that train?"

"There's others," answered Sandy. "Or, if there ain't any mo' ter-night, we'll hire us a car an' keep movin'. Yo're sure game, Molly;" he added admiringly, "you must be clean tuckered out."

She shook her head with an attempt at a smile.

"I'll be glad when we start goin' down, fer a change," she admitted, looking into the gloomy trough of the cañon through which the night wind soughed.

"I'll tighten up yore cinches," said Sandy. "Worst of the climb's jest ahead. Then we start to drop down t'other side. You don't have to git off. Trail's bound to be better once we git atop the mesa and start down. Mesa's right narrer, as I remember. T'other side's away from the weather. There's a cañon with oak trees an' a stream of water." He tugged at the leathers, his knee against the bay's ribs as she grunted.

"You ain't much furtheh to go, li'l' hawss," he chatted on. "Downhill all the way soon an' then a drink to wash out yore mouth an' the best feed in Caroca fo' the pair of you."

"Gits dark mighty quick up here," said the girl.

A great cloud was ballooning above them, like a dirigible that had lost buoyancy and was bumping along the mesa ridge. Its belly was black, its western side ruddy in the sunset. Sandy viewed it apprehensively. In superficial survey the mesa seemed much like the stranded carcass of a mastodonic creature left behind when the waters departed from these inland seas. A hard skeleton of igneous rock, with clayey soil for flesh, riven and seamed and pitted, crumbling and dusty in the sun, ever disintegrating with wind and water and frost. Under a rain the trail was slimy as a whale's back. The cloud was soggy with moisture. Bursting, it would send torrents roaring down every ravine, wash out weathered masses of earth, sweep all before it as it gathered forces and rushed out on the desert, leaving the main cañons carved a little richer, the surface of the soil on the sink a little deeper, against the time when men should control these storm waters or bring the precious fluid up from underground reservoirs and make the desert blossom like the rose.

Where Molly and Sandy rode they were exposed to the first drench of a cloud-burst. Deeper in the pass, where the flood would be confined, their chance for escape would be infinitesimal. Even on the heights it would be precarious unless they could cross the remainder of the up-trail before the inevitable downpour.

Sandy examined his own cinch and tightened it before he mounted. And he whispered something in the mare's ear that caused her to lip his sleeve.

"Let yore hawss have his own way, Molly," he said. "I'm lettin' Goldie do the pickin' fo' the lead. Ready?"

It was growing cold in the deepening twilight, the belt of sunshine was rapidly climbing toward the topmost palisades with the purple shadows in the gorge mounting, twisting and eddying in skeins of mist, twining up toward them. One spire ahead glowed golden. The cloud drifted down upon it, glooming and glowing on its sunset side. The crag pierced it, ripped it as it glided along, like the knife of a diver in the belly of a shark. A cold wind blew from the riven mass. Then came the hiss of descending waters. There was neither thunder nor lightning, only the steady rush of the rain that glazed the slippery trail, hid the opposing cliff from sight, sheeting it with dull silver, pounding, pitting, beating at them as they plodded doggedly on, almost blinded, trusting to the instinct of their horses.

Through the steady patter began to sound the savage voice of torrents falling over cliffs, rapids rising and surging in deep gorges. The wetness and the cold sapped Molly's vitality. She shivered, her flesh seemed sodden, her hands and wrists began to puff and she saw their flesh was purple in the fading light. She rode with hands on the saddle horn, her head bowed, water streaming from the rim of her Stetson, the thud of the rain on her tired shoulders heavy as shot. The bay slipped, lurched, scrambled frantically for footing, hind feet skidding in the clay, haunches gathering desperately, heaving beneath her to the effort that brought him back to the trail. She saw Sandy ahead, dimly, like a sheeted ghost, twisted in his saddle, watching her. From the hips down he was a part of the mare he rode, from waist up he was in such exquisite balance while keeping his individuality apart from the horse that, despite her present misery and a presentiment of coming evil that was beginning to encompass her, Molly realized what a magnificent rider he was, and clung to his strength and skill, sensing the comforting power of his manhood.

To her right was the cliff, slimy with water, the trail so narrow that now and then her elbow dug into the soft stuff. To the left was blackness out of which mists ascended, writhing, like steamy vapors, the rain pelting into the gulf, far, far below; the thunder of augmenting waters. Masses of broken cloud swept on above their heads, purple and crimson and orange as they streamed across the summit like the tattered banners of a routed army. The light rayed upward at an acute angle. In a few moments it would be dark. But they were close to the top. The mare already stood on a level ledge of side-jutting rock, a horizontal protuberance that marked the extreme height of the Pass of the Goats, from which one could look down into the cañon of the oaks and the unfailing stream.

Sandy heard a cry from Molly and saw, through the curtain of the falling rain, the wide-flared nostrils of her horse, its eyes protruding as the brute, with the ground slopping away beneath him, slid slowly down toward the gulf, the girl, her weight flung forward on the withers, her face white as paper, turning to him mutely for help. It was a bad moment. Sandy and his mount stood upon an island in a shifting sea. The whole cliff seemed working and crawling, slithering down.

He had no space to turn in, no chance to whirl his lariat, even for a side throw. There was no time to spin a loop. But his hand detached the rope, flying fingers found the free end as he pivoted in the saddle, thighs welded to the mare.

"Take a turn about the horn!" he shouted. "Hang to the end yo'se'f!" He sent the line jerking back, whistling as it streaked across the girl's shoulders. She clutched for it, with plenty of slack, snubbed it about the saddle horn, clung to the end, made a bight of it about her body.

Sandy spoke to the mare.

"Steady, li'l' lady, steady!" The rope was about his own horn; he thanked God that he had examined the cinches of Molly's saddle. The bay was cat-footed; with the help of the mare Sandy believed he could dig and scrape and climb to safety. It was the decision of a split-second and he did not dare risk dragging the girl from the saddle past the struggling horse.

He felt Goldie stiffen beneath him, braced against the strain she knew was coming. The taut lariat hummed, it bruised into Sandy's thigh. Behind, the bay snorted, struggling gallantly.

They were poised on the brink of death for a moment, two — three — and then the mare began to move slowly forward, neck curved, ears cocked to her master's urging, while the bay sloshed through the treacherous muck, found foothold, lost it, made a frantic leap, another, and landed trembling on the ledge. Sandy leaped from his saddle and caught Molly, sliding from her seat in sheer exhaustion and the revulsion of terror, clinging closely to him.

"It's all right, Molly darlin'," he said soothingly. "All set an' safe. Rain's oveh an' stars comin' out. We're top of the pass. We'll git down inter the cañon a ways an' then we'll light a fire an' warm up a bit, 'fore we go on."

She found her feet and cleared from his hold, gasping for recovery of herself.

"I'm all right," she said. "I was scared an' yet I knew you'd pull me out. I'm plumb shamed of myself. Jest like a damned gel to act that way."

"Shucks! You wasn't half as scared as the bay. Wonder did he strain himself?" He passed clever hands over the bay's legs, talking to it.

"Yo're all right, ol' surelegs. Right as rain." Goldie, the mare, stood stock-still with trailing lariat, watching them intelligently in the dusk that was growing quickly luminous as star after star shone through the flying wrack. A clean, strong wind blew through the throat of the pass. Sandy recoiled his lariat, gave Molly a hand to her foot to lift her to her saddle, mounted himself and they rode slowly down. The trail was in better shape this side, though half an inch of water still topped it. The turmoil of running waters far below burdened the night, but the danger from the storm was over.

Train time was long past. Sandy knew nothing of the change of schedule, but he was confident of winning clear. He knew a man in the little town they were aiming for whose livery stable was, in the march of the times, divided between horses and machines. There he expected to put up the horses until they could be returned to Three Star, and there he figured on hiring a car and a driver if, as he anticipated, there were no more trains that night. He believed that Mormon and Sam had delayed the sheriff. Probably the latter had given up the chase, but there was no telling. Jordan's best attribute was his pertinacity. They should lose no time in getting out of the state.

CHAPTER IX
CAROCA

As Sandy had promised, there was a wide-bottomed cañon where great oaks grew on the flats beside the unfailing stream. The trees were only vast shapes in the starlight, the long grass was wet and clinging, the creek spouted and tore along as Sandy led the way on the mare to a shelving bench, a place where he had camped once long before and, with his out-of-doors-man's craft, never forgotten. Molly was tired almost to insensibility as to what might be going on, soaked and chilled to limpness. Sandy got her out of the saddle and into a shallow cave in a sandy bank. The next thing she knew a fire was leaping and sending light and warmth into her nook.

She heard Sandy talking to his mare. Between the range rider and his mount there is always an understanding born of loneliness, close companionship and mutual appreciation. Sandy was certain that his ponies understood most of what he said, and they were very sure that Sandy understood them thoroughly.

"Used yore brains, you did, li'l' old lady," said Sandy. "Sure did. Can't do much fo' you now. There's a li'l' grain left fo' you an' the bay, an' we'll dry out these blankets a bit. Can't let you stay long or we'll git all stiffened up, but Chuck Goodwin, down to Caroca, he knows hawses an' he's a pal of mine. He'll fix you with a hot mash an', after that, anything on the menu from alfalfy to sugar. The pair of you. You bay, you, dern me if you ain't a reg'lar goat! A couple o' pie-eatin', grain-chewin', antelope-eyed, steel-legged cayuses, that's what you are!"

Molly listened drowsily to the affection in his voice. It was nice to be spoken to that way, she thought. Nice to be looked after. Her dad had been fond of her, but his words had lacked the silk, the caress that savored the strength, as it did with Sandy. She snuggled into the warm heat-reflecting sand like a rabbit in its burrow.

"Eat this, Molly, an' we got to be on our way." Sandy was handing her a cupful of hot savory stew, made for the trip, warmed up hastily, the best kind of a meal after their strenuous experience, though Sandy bemoaned its quality.

"Figgered you an' me 'ud eat on the Pullman ter-night," he said. "But this snack'll do us no harm. We'll git a cup of coffee in Caroca if there's a chance."

She gulped the reviving food gratefully, strength coming back with the fuel that gave both warmth and motive power. Soon they were jogging on down the wide trough of the cañon beneath the white, steady stars, through scrub oak and chaparral, the air sweet scented with wild spice, through slopes set with sleeping folded poppies and Mariposa lilies, past cactus groves, columnar, stately, mystic; the mesa slopes receding, its great bulk dim mass, the twin notches that marked the Pass of the Goats hardly discernible against the sky. They crossed a white road, unfenced but evidently a main source of travel though now deserted.

"County line runs plumb down the middle of the road," announced Sandy. "There's the lights of Caroca blinkin' away to the left. Too bad we missed the train. Sleepy?"

"Some," she admitted.

"Me too," lied Sandy companionably.

Coming down from the mesa he had talked with her about Barbara Redding, how welcome she would make Molly and what she would do for her. Molly had listened silently. Only once she had spoken.

"Why didn't you marry her 'stead of that Redding?" she asked.

Sandy laughed, whole-heartedly.

"Don't believe she'd have had me. Never figgered on marryin' anybody. I'm a privateerin' sort of a person, Molly, sailin' under my own colors, that means. I've allus had the saddle itch till Mormon an' Sam an' me settled down to the ranch. Never had time enough in one place to fool round the gels."

"Sam says yo're woman-shy?" queried Molly.

"Mebbe I am. But it ain't the way a dawg is gun-shy. Must be the horrible example Mormon's set up."

"Don't you like wimmen?"

"Sure do. Admire 'em pow'ful. Never met the one I'd want to tie to, that's all, Molly."

"None of 'em pritty enough?"

"Pritty? Shucks! Looks don't count so all-fired much. The woman I most admired was the wife of ol' Pete Holden, a desert prospector an' drifter, like yore dad, Molly. She was old an' tough an' wiry, like he was. I don't figger she'd ever have taken a blue ribbon in a beauty contest, but she was like first-grade linoleum, the pattern wore clean through an' the stuff was top quality. She'd drifted with Pete over most of Idaho, Colorado, Wyoming, Utah, Arizony, Nevada and paht of New Mexico an' Texas, an' she warn't jest his wife, she was his pal an' fifty-fifty partner. Pete said the on'y time he ever knew her to hold out on him was once in the Cañon Pintada when he woke up in the night and saw her pourin' water out of her canteen into his. Nothin' pritty about Kate Holden, but she was full woman-size from foot callus to gray ha'r, back to back with Pete all the time she wasn't standin' side of him."

"She warn't eddicated?" asked Molly.

"She was. Some thought it funny, for Pete was no scholar. I've listened with him, more'n once when she'd tell us things about plants and insects, or about the stars, things we'd never dreamed of. They say she c'ud play the pianny an' she sure c'ud sing. Ask Sam about that. But Pete was her man an' she was his woman, so they trailed fine together."

"I see," said Molly. "She loved him."

There was a peculiar quality to the tone of the girl's voice. It was not the first time that Sandy had noticed it, lately wondering a little, not realizing that his own observation was a recognition based upon response. Now he figured that the low softness of her speech was due to her tired condition and a little wave of tenderness swept him, blent with admiration of her pluck. Saddle-racked, nerve-tried, she had never murmured, never mentioned the trials of the trail.

They entered the little town, once a cattle station, now renamed in musical Spanish, Caroca, — A Caress — a spot where fruits were grown and shipped and flowers bloomed the year round wherever the water caressed the earth. Sandy rode the mare into the livery where the last skirmish between hoof and rim, iron and rubber tire was being fought, and called for "Chuck" Goodwin.

A stout man came out, not so heavy, not so big as Mormon, but sheathed in flesh with the armor of ease and good living. He peered up at Sandy, then let out a shout.

"You long-legged, ornery, freckle-faced, gun-packin' galoot, Sandy Bourke! Light off'n that cayuse, you an' yore lady friend. Where in time did you-all drop from?"

"Come across the mesa. Like to git washed across through Paso Cabras," said Sandy. "Miss Casey, let me make you 'quainted with Chuck Goodwin, one time the best hawss-shoer in the seven Cactus States, now sellin' oil an' gasoline at fancy prices, not to mention machines fo' which he is agent."

"Got a few oats left fo' yore hawsses, Sandy. Miss, won't you come inside the office? Where you bound, Sandy?"

"We was aimin' to catch the seven o'clock train east, makin' fo' New Mexico an' the Redding Ranch, where Miss Casey is to visit fo' a spell, but we found the trail bad an' a cloud-bu'st finally set us back so we quit hurryin' an' loafed in. Chuck, have you got a machine you c'ud rent us, with a driver?"

"You can have anything I got in the place with laigs or wheels, an' welcome. Goin' to the old Redding Ranch? Give my howdedo to Miss Barbara, or Mrs. Barbara as she is now. But — " He looked at the wall clock. "It's a quarter of ten. Yore train's been altered to suit main line schedules. She don't come through till nine-thirty an' she's gen'ally late makin' the grade. I ain't heard her whistle yet. I wouldn't wonder but what you can make it. Not that I'm aimin' none to hurry you."

The ex-blacksmith reached for the telephone and got his connection.

"Runnin' twenty minutes late," he announced. "Hop in my car an' we'll jest about make her. She don't do much more'n hesitate at Caroca when she's behind time."

He hurried them out on the street to where a car stood by the curb. Molly and her few belongings got in behind, Sandy mounted with Goodwin.

"You'll take good care of the hawsses, Chuck?" he said. "I'll probably be back for 'em myse'f in three-fo' days."

"Seguro." Goodwin stepped on his starter and the flywheel whirred to sputtering explosions. Another car came limping down the street, flat on both rims of one side, its paint plastered with mud, one light out, the other dimmed with mire. The driver called to Goodwin.

"Which way to the depot?"

Goodwin, his hand on the lever, foot on the clutch, was astounded to hear Sandy hissing out.

"Don't tell 'em. Scoot ahead full speed." Then, over his shoulder to the girl, "Crouch down there, Molly." Goodwin was still a man of action and he knew Sandy Bourke of old. Out came the pedal, the gears engaged and the car shot ahead, beneath a swinging arc light. Sandy's hat-rim did not sufficiently shade his face or Molly's action had not been swift enough. There came a yell and a string of curses from the crippled car which backed and turned and followed, its torn treads flapping.

Goodwin asked no questions of Sandy. If the latter wanted ever to tell him why he required a quick exit out of Caroca, or why he was followed, he could. If not, never mind. He slid his gears into high and dodged around corners recklessly. A red lantern showed ahead in the middle of the road. They crashed through a light obstruction of boards and trestles, overturning the lantern and plowed on over rough stones.

"I'm mayor," said Goodwin with a grin. "Breakin' my own rules but I figger that broken stone'll bother 'em some. We'll chance it."

They lunged through, regardless of tires and, behind them, the pursuing car rattled, lurched, skidded. A third tire blew out and as Goodwin swung a corner with two wheels in the air the sheriff's machine smashed viciously across the sidewalk, poking its crumpling radiator into a cottonwood.

"Brazen bulls!" shouted Goodwin. "There she blows! You got to run."

The depot was ahead, to one side of the road-crossing. The train, its clanging bell slowing for the stop, ground to a halt, the conductor swinging from a platform to glance at the "clear" board. He waved "ahead" as Sandy and Molly raced up and clambered to the platform from which the trainman had dropped off. Now the latter remounted while the train restarted, gathered speed.

"Where to?" he asked Sandy, surveying the pair of them curiously.

Sandy did not answer. He was watching four running figures coming down the street. A star flashed on the breast of one of them, a star dulled with mud. Goodwin had disappeared. Jordan pulled up, Plimsoll close behind him, and the depot building shut off Sandy's view.

"Where to?" asked the conductor again. "Got reservations?"

"Bound for Boville, New Mexico. On the El Paso and Southwestern. What's the charges? No reservations, but we rode fifty mile' across the mesa to make the train."

Sandy produced his roll and at the same time he grinned in the light of the conductor's lantern. And Sandy's smile was worth much more than ordinary currency. It stamped him bona-fide, certified his character. The conductor's profession made him apt at such endorsements.

"We take you to Phoenix," he said. "Change there for El Paso. I can give you a spare upper for the lady."

Molly, all eyes, tired though they were, was staring at the Pullman Afro-American, flashing eyes and teeth and buttons at her and even more at Sandy.

"Fine!" said Sandy. "Smoker's good enough fo' me. He's got a bed for you, Molly. See you in the morning."

He waited, countenancing her while she climbed the short ladder to the already curtained berth. Molly's system might be aquiver with wonder but she never showed loss of wits or poise. She might have traveled so a hundred times. Back of the curtain she curled up half-undressed but, even as Sandy registered to himself with a low chuckle: "She never turned a hair or shied."

He found the smoking-room empty and rolled cigarettes. Presently the conductor came in to go over his batch of tickets and accounts.

"Cattle?" he asked Sandy.

"Yes, sir. Three Star Ranch, nigh to Hereford."

"Business good these days? Beef's high enough in the city."

"It's fair in the main," answered Sandy. "Sometimes we seem right happy an' prosperous an' then ag'in," he added with a twinkle in his eyes, "we're jest a jump ahead of the sheriff."

"Boss," said the porter to the conductor, later, "Ah reckon that's a bad man fo' suah. Carryin' two of them six-guns. You figgah he's elopin' wiv that gal?"

The conductor surveyed his aide disdainfully.

"You've been seeing too many cheap picture-shows lately, Clem," he said. "Eloping with that young girl? I wouldn't hint it to him if I were you. Don't you know a he-man when you see one?"

Eight days passed before Sandy came riding back on Goldie, leading the bay, reaching the Three Star at the end of sunset. Mormon was in his chair with the one letter that Sandy had written on his lap. It was almost too dark to read it. Mormon's eyes were beginning to fail him at anything short of long distance but he knew the contents by heart, yet he liked to keep the letter near him as a dog loves a favorite bone long after all the nourishment from it has been absorbed. Mormon was still penitent. He knew that the sheriff had just failed to make the train, but he did not cease to blame himself for submitting Sandy and Molly to so close a chance, neither did Sam forget occasionally to remind him of his lapse of tongue.

Sandy pulled in the mare beyond the corral. He could hear the sound of Sam's harmonica and pictured him with the instrument cuddled up under his great mustache. Sam was playing *The Girl I Left Behind Me* and he managed to breathe a good deal of pathos into the primitive mouth organ.

"It's sure good to be home, Goldie," said Sandy. The mare whinnied. The bay nickered. Answers came back from the corral. Pronto, Sandy's first string horse, came trotting cross the corral, head up.

"Hello, you ol' pie-eater!" said Sandy. "You sure look good to me. C'udn't take you erlong this trip, son, but we'll be out ter-morrer together." Then he let out a mighty, "Hello, the house!"

Sam's lilt ceased abruptly. The riders came hurrying. Sam appeared, with Mormon waddling after, too swiftly for his best ease or grace of motion, both grabbing at Sandy, swatting him on the back as he off-saddled.

"Lemme go," said Sandy. "I'm hungry as a spring b'ar. Where's Pedro? Pedro, I'm hungry — *muy hambriento. Despachese Vd. Pronto! Huevos — seis huevos — fritos! Frijoles! Jamon! Cafe! Panecilos! Todo el rancho! Pronto!*"

"*Si, señor, inmediatamente.*" And, with a yell for Joe the half-breed, Pedro hurried away, grinning, to prepare the six fried eggs, the ham, the coffee, the muffins, everything in the larder!

His two partners watched him eat, plying him with food and then with question after question about the trip, about Barbara Redding and about Molly's going to school. Mormon made abject apology for talking too much and Sandy told how close a shave it had been.

"I don't cotton to playin' jack-rabbit to Plimsoll and Jordan's coyotes," said Sandy. "Speshully Plimsoll, who's at the bottom of the whole thing. Nex' time he may not have the law backin' him, an' I won't have to run. How's the sheriff?"

"Sort of tamed. They've been kiddin' him a mite. Seems he done some boastin' 'fore he started. His car's laid up fo' repairs. Jordan's layin' low. Miss Bailey, she's at the head of the Wimmen's League to gen'ally clean up politics an' the town, one to the same time. I figger the first thing their broom's goin' to locate'll be either Jordan or Plimsoll. They're sure goin' into all the dark corners an' under the furniture. She's a hustler an' she's thorough, is Mirandy Bailey."

"Where'd you learn all this, Mormon? Over to Herefo'd?"

"'Pears Miss Bailey's took a great interest — in Molly," said Sam, with a grin. "She's been over here twice to see if there was news. Mormon entertained her. He seems to be the fav'rite. Beats all how one man'll charm the fair sect, like honey'll bring flies, while another ain't ever bothered."

Mormon changed the trend of the conversation by demanding to know about the school.

"Molly's got an outfit Barbara Redding bought her," said Sandy. "Trunk an' leather grip, all kinds of do-dads. School costs fifteen hundred bucks a year. The rest of Molly's money is banked. Barbara picked out a school in Pennsylvania she said was the best. Here's an advertisement of it."

He handed the magazine leaf to Sam who read over the items with Mormon looking over his shoulder, forming the words with his lips. Sam read:

CORONA COLLEGE

"Developing School for Girls. Development of well poised personality through intellectual, moral, social and physical trainin'.

"Extensive Campus — (whatever that is) *— Elective Academic —* (Sufferin' Cows!) *— Domestic Science, Household Economics, Expression, Supervised Athletics.*

"Horseback Riding — (Huh, I never see an eastener yet who c'ud ride) *— Swimming, basketball, country tramping, dancing, military drill."*

Sam made heavy going of many of the words that left him in the dark as to their meaning. Sandy tried to elucidate, repeating the explanations Barbara Redding had given him.

"Campus is the College Field, Sam," he said.

"Then why in time don't they say so? Ain't they goin' to teach her to talk United States? I s'pose them things is all fine an' necessary fo' the female eddication but, dern me, if I can see where she's goin' to find time to eat an' sleep."

"It's been all-fired lonely with both you an' her gone," said Mormon. "An' the dawg ain't eat a mouthful, I don't believe. Mebbe you can coax him, Sandy. Set around an' howled like a sick coyote fo' fo'-five days — mostly nights. If the gel balks at all that line of stuff I'll stand back of her to quit an' come back to Three Star."

"An' have Jordan git her away an' put her under Plimsoll's guardeenship?"

"He c'udn't do that. Mirandy Bailey 'ud block him."

"He c'udn't do anything," said Sandy. "I got myse'f app'inted legal guardeen to Molly while we was in Santa Rosa, one day Barbara an' Molly was shoppin'. John Redding's lawyer fixed it up."

The months passed without especial incident at the Three Star. Sandy purchased a Champion Hereford bull for the herd out of the ranch share of the faro winnings. Other improvements were added, and the three partners seemed on the fair way to prosperity. Sandy's theory that better bred and better fed beef, bringing better prices, would pay, began to demonstrate itself slowly, though it would take three years before the get of the thoroughbred stock was ready for marketing.

Occasional letters came from Molly. Homesickness and unhappiness showed between the lines of the first epistles, despite her evident efforts to conceal them. Her ways were not the ways of the other girls who were *developing a well poised personality through intellectual, moral, social and physical training.* She apparently formed no friendships and it seemed that none were invited from her.

> "But I'm going to stick with it till I get same as the rest — on the outside, anyway," she wrote. "I don't know how some of them work inside. It ain't like me. But I've started this and you-all want me to go through so I will, though I get lonesome as a sick cat for the ranch. I don't swear any more — I got into awful trouble for spilling my language one time — and I can spell pretty good without hunting up every word in the dictionary. I reckon I'm a hard filly to break but then I was haltered late. I don't think it would be allowed for me to have Grit, so you'll have to look out for him and not let him forget me. I hope you won't do that yourselves. Some of the other girls are nice enough. It will be all right soon as we get to understand each other. Don't think I'm starting out to buck or that I'm unhappy, because I'm not."

"If she's happy, I'm a Gila lizard," said Mormon. "What's the sense of havin' her miserable fo' the sake of a li'l' book learnin'. She's gettin' to spell so I can't make out what she's writin' about."

At last Molly wrote that she had made the basketball team and won honors and favors. She gained laurels for Corona in swimming and tennis, and life went more merrily. Mormon looked up tennis outfits in his mail catalogue and sent for a book on the game, which he soon abandoned.

"You have to learn a foreign langwidge before you start to play," he said. "Leastwise a code. The langwidge ain't what you'd expect them to be handin' out in a young lady's college. All erbout deuce an' love. I'd a notion we'd fix up the game fo' her so she'd c'ud keep it up but I dunno. It sure ain't a fat man's game. It's a human grasshopper's."

CHAPTER XI
PAY DIRT

In September there was a killing in the Good Luck Pool Room, the murder of a stranger whose friends made such an investigation, backed by the real law-and-order element of Hereford, that the exposure brought about forfeiture of all licenses and a strict shutting down on gambling and illicit liquor. Plimsoll left Hereford for his horse ranch, deprived of the sheriff's official countenance, and Jordan began to worry about election.

One evening in early October a little body of riders came to the Three Star, all strangers to the county, men whose faces were grim, who cracked no jokes, whose greetings were barely more than civil. They were well armed and they acted like men of a single purpose.

"This is the Three Star, ain't it?" asked the leader of a cowboy, who nodded silently, taking in the appearance of the visitors.

"Bourke, Peters and Manning?"

"One and all," answered the Three Star rider. "Find 'em at chuck, I reckon. You-all are jest in time. If you aim to stay overnight I'll tend yore hawsses an' put 'em in the corral."

"You seem hospitable here."

The tone was half sarcastic.

"Rule of the ranch," replied Buck. "Folks arrivin' after sun-down, the same bein' strangers, is expected to pass the night, if they're in no hurry."

Sandy personally backed the invitation a moment later and steaks were being pan-fried as the men dismounted and lounged on the porch, awaiting their meal. The leader introduced himself by the name of Bill Brandon, claiming previous knowledge, without actual acquaintance, of Sandy, Mormon and Sam in Texas. Sizing each other up, man-fashion, eye to eye, appraising a score of tiny things that aggregated sufficiently to tip the mental scale, the crowd grew more familiar and welded with supper, exchanged anecdotes with digestion, to get confidential over the tobacco.

"We're out after a man who's been collectin' hawsses too primiscuous," said Brandon finally. "We know you gents by past reputation an' by what they say of you in Herefo'd. Also, by that last reckonin', I ain't figgerin' you as any speshul pal of the man we're tryin' to round up. I reckon you know who we mean. Jim Plimsoll, who owns what he calls the Waterline Hawss Ranch, sixteen miles east of you, more or less; an' who gits more fancy breeds out of the mangy cayuses he shows his breedin' mares an' stallions, than there is different fish in the sea. From all I can figger most of his mares must have fo' foals a year.

"Some of us are from this state — Mojave County — two of us from Nevada. Me, I'm from California. We've all been losin' hawsses off an' on an' we've final' got together an' compared notes. Seems most of the missin' stock sorter drifted across the Arizony line somewheres between Mojave City an' Topock. Most of 'em have been sold or passed on. All of 'em have been faked an' doctored more or less. Talk points to Plimsoll, so do some facts, but not enough. An' this Plimsoll has got some mighty close friends where they do the most good. You'd have to prove a damn sight more than we got to even sight a blank warrant."

"You been over to his ranch?" asked Sandy.

"Jest come from there. He's slick an' cool, is Plimsoll. We was supposed to be lookin' over hawsses for buyin', but he's careful who he sells to. We saw some. An' we recognized some. But you know how it is, Bourke, it ain't hard to change a hawss. Dock its foretop, do a little doctorin', an' how you goin' to prove it? I'll say this for the man, he's the finest brand-faker I've met up with. He suspicioned what we was after an' we didn't see all he had. But we're goin' to git him yet an', when we do, there won't be any more hawss-stealin' an' fakin' in Coconino County, Arizona. Hawss-stealin' was a hangin' matter when I first come west an' I reckon there's some feels the same way now. Speshully when the courts back up a man like Plimsoll. Lead's cheaper than rope, but somehow it ain't so convincin'."

Brandon changed the subject after he had spoken, but it was plain that he and his companions had not given up the matter; clear also that they were sure of Plimsoll's guilt and laying plans to trap him. They stayed until the next morning and departed.

"That man Brandon's got some trick up his sleeve to trap Plimsoll," said Sam, watching them ride off. "He ain't quite got it fixed up yet to suit himself but it's a good un."

"He's got brains," commented Sandy, rubbing Grit's ears. The collie had picked up since Sandy's return, sensing some connection with his mistress closer than that of Mormon and Sam. He would feed only from Sandy's hand and attached himself to the latter almost as permanently as his shadow. "So has Jim Plimsoll. I ain't hankerin' fo' another man to clean him up befo' I get my own chance. But that bunch sure mean business."

The incident was forgotten as the round-up days grew near, with frosty mornings when the mountains looked as flat as if they had been profiled from cardboard and stuck up along the horizon — until the lifting sun modeled them with shadows — with sweltering noons tapering slowly off to cool nights while horses raced after the flying cattle, driving and cutting out, and so to the corral brandings, where the three partners found their increase better than they had anticipated.

Molly was not to come home at Christmas after all. She formed a friendship, the first close one she had made, and Barbara Redding advised that the invitation extended by this new acquaintance to spend the holidays be accepted. There had been plans of a Christmas tree and a celebration, but the gifts were boxed and sent off. Others arrived from the East in exchange, a collar for Grit, a cigarette case for Sandy, a necktie for Mormon and a three-decked harmonica for Sam. There was a picture too, not so much of a girl but a young woman, a somewhat wistful look in her eyes, but a firm-lipped, resolute-chinned young woman for all that, who smiled out at them frankly and confidently. It was signed

> A Merry Christmas and a Prosperous New Year
> from the Mascotte of the * * *

Molly.

"I dunno about the merry Christmas," said Mormon. "We're prosperous enough, short of bein' profiteers. Molly's gettin' to be a good-looker, ain't she? Goin' to git it framed, Sandy?"

Snows fell, the temperature ranged down far below zero at times, winter gave reluctant place to spring until the last moment when it turned and fled and, far into the desert, myriads of flower-blooms sprang up overnight while everywhere the cactus gleamed in silken blooms in yellow and crimson.

One April night the Bailey flivver came charging up to Three Star, smothering itself in a cloud of dust that had not settled before there sprang out of it Miranda Bailey and the lanky Ed, temporarily charged with a tremendous activity. The cause of young Ed's galvanism was so strong that he actually won from his aunt as bearer of the news.

"Gold!" he cried. "They've struck pay dirt at Dynamite! Chunks of sylvanite that sweat gold in the fire. Assay thirty thousand dollars a ton. Whole streaks of it. Vein's twelve foot wide. The whole town's stampedin' by way of White Cliff Cañon. I'm goin'. Got a pick an' shovel in the car. Aunt Mirandy, she was bound we'd come this way. Mebbe we can pack you all in. But you got to hurry or they'll swarm over Dynamite like flies on a chunk o' liver!"

"It's true," backed Miss Bailey. "Folks over to Hereford have gone crazy. I caught a word or two that Plimsoll's to the bottom of the rush. Ed heard he got hold of some samples them easterners took an' had 'em sent away an' assayed. They turned out to be the big stuff. 'Course you can't depend on gossip, when folks are talkin' mines but, if it's so, Plimsoll's burned the wind to git first pick. An' he'll grab those claims of Molly's first thing. That's one reason I made Ed come this way. Thought you might like to come erlong, on'y he took the words out of my mouth."

"You goin'?" asked Mormon. There were two red splotches in Miranda's cheeks, a glitter in her eyes that suggested she had not escaped the gold fever.

"Sure am," she answered. "Ed Bailey Senior, he 'lows there's no sense in chasin' gold underground. Says he likes to see his prospects growin' up under his own eyes an' gazin' on his own land. I'm the adventurous one of the Bailey fam'ly, though you mightn't guess it to look at me," she said with a twitch of her lips. "Me an' young Ed here. He takes after me. Got the gamblin' germ in our systems. Want to git somethin' fo' nothin'," she went on with grim humor. "I reckon Ed's right but, land-sake, doin' the same thing, day in an' out — gits mighty monotonous. Bein' a woman, you're more tied than a man. I tried to work my extry energy out in politics but it all come my way too easy.

"Plimsoll ain't got much love for me. He figgers I lost him his license an' his brother-in-law sheriff his badge. He's right. I did. I figgered you'd not be anxious to let him have his own way about Molly's claims an' I 'lowed I'd like to be along an' see the excitement. Me an' Ed here'll stake off suthin' for ourselves. I'd jest as soon git some easy money as the rest of 'em. If I do I'll buy another car. This thing" — she surveyed the panting flivver contemptuously — "is nigh worn out and it's jest a tin kittle on wheels. Biles if you leave it out in the sun."

Sandy, after a swift word of apology, turned away toward the bunk-house. Mormon, with a sweeping salute from his bald head to his knees, voiced his opinion.

"Marm," he said, "you're a dyed-in-the-wool sport an' I'd admire to trail with you. But that kittle, as you call it, 'll sure bu'st its cinches with we-all ridin' it. I'm no jockeyweight, fo' one."

"It'll stand up. We've got to make time. I was wonderin' if we c'ud make it by the old road, where you found Molly? It's shorter than White Cliff Cañon an' we've lost time comin' out here."

Sam shook his head.

"No'm, c'udn't be done. There ain't no road. Las' winter 'ud finish what was left of it an' there was spots this side of where we found Casey where a wagon c'udn't have passed. We just made it with the buckbo'd. Ask Sandy."

Sandy, coming up, endorsed Sam.

"We'll have to go the long way," he said. "How are you off fo' grub? It'll be sca'ce an' high in Dynamite. Some of us may have to stay an' hang on to claims until they're recorded an' the new camp settles down. An' one of us sh'ud stay an' run the ranch," he added. At which his partners balked resolutely.

"We've got some food," said Miranda. "You might fetch along some canned stuff if you've any handy. Ed, you sure you got plenty ile, gas an' water? Better look her all over."

With orders to Buck, with some provisions, ammunition and a few tools, the hurried start was made. Mormon clambered to the front seat beside young Ed, Miranda Bailey sat between Sandy and Sam. Whatever lack of energy the lank Ed Junior displayed on his feet, he eliminated as a driver. The springs creaked, chirpings arose from various parts of the car as it ran, but he coaxed the engine, performed miracles at bad places in the road, nursed the insufficient radiator surface and kept the "kittle" at a simmer.

He judged grades, rushed them, conquered them, sometimes at a crawl, slid and skipped and jumped down slopes, negotiated curves on two wheels and brought them triumphantly through White Cliff Cañon, over the malpais belt, up and across a mesa and so to the far brink of it an hour before dawn without puncture, without a broken leaf in the springs, with shock absorbers still on duty and the cylinders performing full service.

Cold and raw as it was, the engine was hot and they halted to cool it. They could see a light or two glimmering at the foot of the mesa, something that had not shown in the deserted mining camp for many years. Miranda Bailey shivered as she got stiffly from the car.

"I've got some powdered coffee an' some solid alcohol," she announced. "We can all have somethin' hot to drink anyway. It won't take but a minute. Here's some cold biscuits we can warm up on that radiator. It's nigh as good as a stove."

The trio watched interestedly the capable way in which she got together the meal, adding sugar and evaporated milk to her coffee. Sam picked up the tin of solid alcohol after it had cooled off.

"It's too bad they can't fix up the real stuff that way," he said. "It 'ud sure make a hit. Canned Tom-and-Jerry, all ready for heatin'."

"And you called Soda-Water Sam," said Miranda Bailey.

"That title was give me in derision," replied Sam. "Me, I don't hesitate to say I like my licker. Likewise I can do 'thout it. They claim that I used to leave nothin' but the sody-water inter a saloon once I'd entered it. Which same is a calummy. Gittin' light in the east, ain't it, folks?"

Coffee-comforted, they made the down-road as the sun rose above the rim of the eastern range, so jagged it seemed trying to claw back the mounting sun. Ever in view below them lay the intermountain valley in which the camp had been located. Its floor was jumbled with hard-cored hills. There was little greenery. A few cottonwoods, fewer willows along the deep bed of a scanty stream. Under the sunrise the whole scene was theatrical with vivid light and shade. The crumpled ground, the deep-ridged hills, all seemed unreal, made up of papier-mâché, crudely modeled and painted, garish, unfinished. The effect was enhanced by the appearance of the one main street of the camp and the few scattering cabins on the hills, the ancient dumps in front of the lateral shafts where the weathered timbers sagged.

There were a few tents, some wagons and picketed horses, and there were a great many machines parked at will. But, from the height, it all looked like the miniature scene of a panoramic model, the houses cardboard, the horses and wagons toys of tin. The horses were the only moving objects, no smoke curled yet from the chimneys.

Here and there unbroken glass in the windows flung back the sun. A door opened and a midget in shirtsleeves came out, stretching arms, palpably yawning. Suddenly smoke jetted from a tumbled chimney, other puffs followed and steady vapors mounted. Ant-like men emerged from every house, gathered in little knots, busied themselves with the horses, hurried back to breakfasts. Faint sounds came up to the travelers.

"W'udn't think that place had been dead as a cemetery fo' years?" commented Sandy. "Stahted up overnight like an old engine. That's the hotel, with the high front. Furniture all in it an' in the cabins. Most of the fixtures left in the saloons, an' there was a plenty of them. Two hotels, five restyronts, seven gamblin' houses, twenty-two saloons an' the rest sleepin' cabins. That was Dynamite. When they git it dusted off and started up it'll run ortermatic."

"Cuttin' out the saloons," said Miranda.

"I'm not so sure of that," said Mormon, turning in his seat. "You-all want to remember, ma'am, that this is an unco'porated town an' that's there's allus a shortage of law an' order for a whiles wherever there's a strike, gold, oil or whatever 'tis. Eighty per cent. of the rush is a hard-shelled lot an' erlong with 'em is a smaller bunch that thrives best when things is run haphazard. There'll be licker down there, an' it'll sure be quickfire licker at that. If you warn't the kind you are," added Mormon, "I'd tell you that down there ain't no place fo' a woman?"

"Meanin'?" snapped Miranda Bailey. But there was a gleam in her eye that showed of a compliment accepted.

"Meanin'," said Mormon "that, ef you'll take it 'thout offense, you-all air plumb up-to-date. When wimmen took up the ballot I figger they wasn't on'y ready fo' equal rights, they knew how to git 'em. 'Side from the shootin' end of it, I'd say you was as well equipped as any man to look out fo' yore own interests."

"Thanks," replied Miranda. "I suppose you mean that as a compliment. Also I know one end of a gun from another an' I can hit a barn if it ain't flyin'. Ed, what you stoppin' fer?"

"Blamed if they ain't a puncture," said Ed as he put on the brakes. "We got a spare tire but 'twon't do to spile this 'un. We got to git back some time. Might not be able to buy a spare round here. I got to fix this."

"Fix it when you git down," said his aunt. "Put on the spare. I'm kinder nervous to git my claim staked. There's a sight of folks here. Look at 'em runnin' around like so many crazy chickens. Put on the spare, Ed, while we pile out. An' hurry."

The spare was soon adjusted and they rolled down to the valley and over the dusty road to the camp. Before they reached the main street a car passed them from behind with a rush, driver and passengers reckless, whooping as they rode, one man waving a bottle, another firing his gun into the air.

"That's the kind that'll figger to run Dynamite fo' a while," said Sandy. "I'll bet there ain't twenty old-timers in the camp — real miners, I mean."

The street was alive with changing groups, merging, breaking up to listen to some fresh report of a strike, or opinion as to the prospects. There were no women in sight. The men were of all sorts, from cowboys in their chaps, who had left the range for the chance of sudden wealth, to storekeepers from Hereford and other towns. Excitement reigned, no one was normal. Bottles passed freely. Among the crowd moved shifty-eyed men who had come to speculate. There were gamblers, plain bullies, swaggerers, with here and there a bearded miner, gray of hair and faded blue of eye, either moving steadily through the throng or held up by a little crowd to whom he declaimed with the right of experience. Some, it seemed certain, must be on their claims, but the bulk of the men who filled the street of the resurrected town, were those who prey upon the work and luck of others, camp-followers of the Army of Good Fortune.

Mormon's pronouncement that the town, after its long desertion, had automatically refunctioned, was not far wrong. Rudely lettered signs proclaimed where meals could be bought and boldly announced gambling.

KENO — CHUCKALUCK AND STUD
CRAPS AND DRAW POKER
THE OLD RELIABLE FARO BANK
J. PLIMSOLL, PROP.

read Sandy.

"He's here, lookin' fo' easy money, both ends an' the middle," he drawled. "W'udn't wonder but what we'd rub up ag'in' him 'fo' we leave."

"You'll want to go right through to Molly's claims, I suppose," said Miranda Bailey. "Do you know where they are?"

"I can soon find the location," replied Sandy. "But there ain't any extry hurry. They've been recorded. They'll keep. We'll git us some real hot grub at one of these restyronts an' listen a bit to the news. Find out where is the most likely place fo' you an' yore nevvy to locate."

"Ain't you afraid Plimsoll or some one'll have jumped those claims?" asked the spinster.

"W'udn't be surprised. But there's allus two ways to jump, Miss Mirandy. In an' *out*. Let's try Cal Simpson's Place. I knew him when he was runnin' a chuck-wagon. He's sure some cook if it's him."

They pressed through the crowded street to the sign. Next door to the cabin that Simpson had preempted on the first-come-first-served order that prevailed, was one of the olden saloons. Through door and window they could see the crowded bar with bottles and tin mugs upon the ancient slab of wood. Over the door the inscription:

ROCKY MOUNTAIN GRAPEJUICE
MULE BRAND
TWO KICKS FOR ONE BUCK

Some looked curiously at Miranda Bailey, but the sight of her escort checked any familiarity. Covered with dust from their ride, guns on hip, the three musketeers did not encourage persiflage at the expense of their outfit and they passed unchallenged into the eating-house where a stubby man with a big paunch shouted greetings at Sandy.

”You ornery son of a gun! *An’* Mormon. This yore last, Mormon. No? I beg yore pardon, marm. I c’ud have wished Mormon ‘ud struck somethin’ sensible an’ satisfactory at last. It’s his loss more’n your’n. What’ll you have, folks? I’ve got steak an’ po’k an’ beans. Drove over some beef. More comin’ ter-morrer. I’ll have a real mennoo by the end of the week. Steak? Seguro! Biscuits an’ coffee.”

He shouted orders to a helper and hurried off to pan-broil the steaks. To the order he added some fried potatoes.

“They ain’t on the bill-of-fare,” he said. ”Try ‘em, marm. Hope you strike it lucky, Sandy. Damn few — beggin’ yore pahdon, miss — damn few of this crowd ever had a blister on their hands. It ain’t like the old days when the sourdoughs made a strike. They worked their own shafts. This bunch specklates on ‘em. A claim’ll change hands twenty times between now an’ ter-morrer night.

“Rush is over fo’ the mornin’. I’ll sit in with you, if you don’t mind. I got my steak in that pan.”

“What’s the indications?” asked Sandy, after Simpson had rejoined them.

“Big. Look here. White gold!” He pulled out a piece of tin white mineral with a brilliant metallic luster, sparkling with curious crystals. “Sylvanite — twenty-five per cent, gold an’ twelve an’ a half silver. Veined in the porphyry. There’s a young assayer come in last night. He ‘lows it’s sylvanite, same as they have over to Boulder County in Colorado. He comes from the Boulder School of Mines. He’s a kid, but I w’udn’t wonder but he knows what he’s talkin’ about. Some calls it telluride. But it’s gold, all right, an’ there’s a big vein of it close to the surface on the knoll east side of Flivver Crick.”

They passed the heavy mineral from hand to hand, examining it with eager curiosity. Simpson rambled on.

”Over five hundred in camp an’ more comin’ all the time. The rush ain’t started yet. Goin’ to be an old-time boom, sure. Bound to make money ef you don’t hold on too long. Peg you out a claim or two ‘long that east bank, Sandy. Don’t matter ’ef she’s located or not, you can sell it fo’ mo’n you’ll ever git out of it by workin’ it.

“This man Plimsoll aims to make him a fortune,” he continued. “He’s got a gang of bullies with him who’re stakin’ out the best claims an’ jumpin’ others. He’s runnin’ a game wild. He’s here to clean up. I tell you, Sandy, the sheriff ought to be on the job on the start of a rush like this. But he’s t’other end of the county, they tell me, an’ likely he won’t hear of it for three-four days. And by that time she may have blew up ag’in,” he closed pessimistically. “Blew up once, did Dynamite. This may be jest a flash in the pan, a grass-root outcrop. That’s the way she started when old man Casey drifted in an’ his burro kicked up pay-ore. Damn — dern — few of this crowd’ll ever stop to run shaft or tunnel. Though this young assayin’ feller talks big about folds an’ uplifts, synclines an’ anticlines. Claims the po’phyry is syncline. You got to catch it where the fold is shaller or else dig half-way to China. You still in the cow business, Sandy?”

So he chatted until fresh customers came in and claimed his skill and steaks. Miranda Bailey and her companions finished the meal and started out.

The Casey claims were on the east side of the creek, Sandy knew. The old prospector’s lore, or instinct, had been unfailing. It remained to see if his marks and monuments had been respected. Molly had said that the assessment work had been done, and she had so described the place in a narrow terrace of the hill that Sandy felt sure of finding them without trouble.

He pointed out a sign over the door of a shack ahead, white lettered on black oil cloth:

CLAY WESTLAKE.
ASSAYER — SURVEYOR AND
MINING ENGINEER.

A knot of men were milling about the place.

"Doin' a trade already," said Sam. "Must have brung that sign erlong with him. Smart, fo' a youngster. Simpson said he was a kid. How 'bout seein' him befo' Miss Bailey an' Ed here stake their claims? I'm aimin' to mark out one fo' me, same time."

"Also me," said Mormon.

Guffaws suddenly rose from the little crowd by the assayer's sign. A deep voice boomed out in bullying tone, followed by silence, then more laughs. Sandy leaned to Mormon.

"You keep her an' young Ed back," he said. "Trouble here, I figger."

Mormon nodded, stepping ahead, blocking Miranda's progress in apparently aimless and clumsy fashion while Sandy, his hands dropping to his gun butts, lifting the weapons slightly and, releasing them into the holsters once again, lengthened his stride, walking cat-footed, on the soles of his feet, as he always did when he scented trouble. Sam, easing his own gun, lightly touched his lips with the tip of his tongue and followed Sandy with eyes that widened and brightened.

"Bullyin' the kid, I reckon," he said to Sandy as they went. Sandy did not need to nod before they reached the half-ring that had formed about a young chap in khaki shirt, riding breeches and puttees, whose fair hair was curly above a face tanned, and resolute enough. Yet he was clearly nervous at the jibes of the crowd and the actions of the man who faced him, heavy of body, long of arm, heavy of jowl; a deep-chested, broad-shouldered individual whose head, cropped close, tapering in a rounded cone from his bushy eyebrows, helped largely to give him the aspect of a professional wrestler, or a heavyweight prizefighter. He carried a big blued Colt revolver, and the way he spun the weapon on the trigger guard showed familiarity with the weapon.

The young assayer had no holster to his belt, seemingly no gun. His clean shaven jaws were clamped tight so that the muscles lumped here and there, and he fronted the unsympathetic crowd and the jeering bully with a courage that was partly born of desperation.

"Mining engineer!" read the bully. "Smart, ain't he, for a curly-headed kid! Engineer? Peanut butcher 'ud suit better. Looks like a movie pitcher actor, don't he? Mebbe he's a vodeville performer. I'll bet he is, at that. What's yore speshulty, kid? Singin' or dancin'. Or both."

He flung a shot from the gun into the ground between the young man's feet.

"Show us a few steps, you powder-faced dood! Mebbe we'll let you stay in camp if you amuse us."

Sandy and Sam had elbowed their way lightly through the ring and the former turned to the man beside whom he happened to stand.

"What's the idea?" he asked.

"The young 'un good as told Roarin' Russell he didn't know what he was talkin' about. Chap asked the kid's opinion on a bit of ore an' he give it. It didn't suit Russell."

"It didn't, eh? Now, that's too bad," drawled Sandy. The other looked at him curiously. Sandy's drawl was often provocative. Russell's gun barked again.

"Dance, damn ye! An' sing at the same time; blast you for a buttin' in tenderfoot! Won't, eh?"

The victim, game but despairing, flung a look of appeal about him. To give in meant to become the laughing-stock of the camp, to have its ribaldry follow him, to be laughed out of the camp, branded as a coward. Yet to resist was a challenge to death. The bully had been drinking, the gleam in his eyes was that of the killer, a man half insane from alcohol.

"Up with yore hands! Up with 'em, or I'll shoot the knuckles off of 'em! I'll make a jumpin'-jack of you or I'll shoot yore...."

The first syllable of the intended volley of foulness was barely out when Sandy, stepping forward, touched the bully on the shoulder. Russell whirled as a bear whirls, gun lifting.

"Lady back here in the crowd," said Sandy quietly.

For a second Russell gasped and stared and, as he stared, the cold hard look in Sandy's eyes told him the manner of man who had interrupted him. But this man's guns were in the holsters, Russell's weapon was in hand though its muzzle was tilted skyward. The crowd, thickening, waited his next move. He had been stopped in his baiting. He saw no woman back of the big bulk of Mormon, keeping Miranda well away, not seeing what was going forward.

"To hell with the lady!" shouted Russell. At his back was only the unarmed assayer. This lean cold-eyed interferer was a hardy fool who needed a lesson. He swept down his gun, thumb to hammer. Two guns grew like magic in Sandy's hands. Russell read a message in Sandy's glance, he heard the gasp of the crowd. With his own gun first in the open the stranger had beaten him to the drop and fire. He felt the fan of the wing of death on his brow. His gun flew out of his fingers, wrenched away by the force of impact from Sandy's bullet on its muzzle, low down, near the cylinder. Dazed, he watched it spinning away, his hand numb.

"Back up to that door, you! Back up!" Sandy's voice was almost conversational but it was profoundly convincing. The bully obeyed him, standing at the door in the place of the assayer, who stepped aside, feeling a little sick at the stomach, Sam bracing him in friendly fashion by one elbow.

"I won't shoot *yore* knuckles off," said Sandy, "pervidin' you keep yore fingers wide apaht, an' don't wiggle 'em. Spread 'em out against the wood, bully man!"

His face whitening from the ebb of blood to his cowardly heart, Roarin' Russell opened his fingers wide, judging implicit obedience his greatest safety. Sandy did not move position, he hardly seemed to move wrist or finger as his guns spat fire, left and right, eight shots blending, eight bullets smashing their way through the door between the "V's" of the bully's fingers while the crowd held their breath for the exhibition.

Sandy quickly reloaded, quickly but without obvious haste. He did not return the guns to their holsters and he paid no attention to the admiring comments of the crowd.

"Who is he? Two-gun man! They say his name's Sandy Bourke."

"You-all interfered with a friend of mine," said Sandy. "It ain't a healthy trick. An' you ain't apologized to the lady. I don't know how Westlake feels about it, but you've sure got to apologize to the lady."

The assayer, bewildered at Sandy's assumption of friendship, waved his hand deprecatingly. Russell's eyes rolled from side to side toward his still elevated hands.

"You can lower 'em if you can't talk with 'em up," said Sandy. "I'm waitin' fo' that apology, but I'm in a bit of a hurry."

"I didn't see no woman," mumbled the bully, crestfallen.

"I told you there *was* one," said Sandy. "I don't lie, even to strangers. You're sorry you swore, ain't you?"

"You're quicker'n I am on the draw with yore two guns," retorted the goaded Russell. "I c'ud lick you one-handed 'thout guns — or any man in this crowd," he blustered in an attempt to halt his departing prestige.

"You-all had a gun in yore hand when we stahted in," said Sandy equably. "You're sorry you swore — *ain't* you?"

The repeated words, backed by the cold gaze, the ready guns, were merciless as probes.

"I apologizes to the lady," growled Russell.

"Now, that's fine," said Sandy. "Fine! Westlake, will you come erlong with me fo' a spell?"

He made his way through the opening group. Sam followed with the assayer who now began to realize that Sandy's interference had established a friendship that would continue protective. They met Mormon, almost purple in the face from suppressed feelings. Young Ed Bailey eyed Sandy with awe and new respect. Miranda Bailey's attempt to learn exactly what had happened was thwarted by Sandy's presentation of Westlake. During the introduction Mormon slipped away. Roaring Russell was endeavoring to readjust his swagger when the stout cowboy met him.

"I was with the lady," said Mormon. "Consequent I c'udn't git here sooner. You said you c'ud lick any one in the camp one-handed, guns barred. Now I don't like the way you apologized, sabe? It warn't willin' enough, nor elegant enough, nor spontaneous enough. Ter-night, after I git through showin' the lady around the diggin's, I'll meet you where you say for fun, money or marbles, an' argy with you barehanded. Thisaway."

He slapped Russell on the cheek. The bully roared and the crowd stepped back. Mormon, with the surprising alertness he showed in action, for all his bulk and weight, sprang back, poised for strike or clutch. Miranda Bailey came with a rush and stepped between the two men. Russell foresaw a laugh at his expense and curbed himself, the sooner for his new-found consideration for Sandy's gunplay.

"You ought to be ashamed of yoreselves, both of you," exclaimed the spinster. "I'll have no one fightin' over me. I can take care of myself."

"Yes, m'm, I reckon you can. I reckon we are ashamed," said Mormon meekly, as the crowd roared in laughter that died away before the evenly swung gaze of Sandy, backed by Sam. Russell slipped off and the men dispersed. Miranda addressed Mormon.

"I'll not have you fighting with that hulkin' brute on my account," she said. "Do you understand?"

Mormon gulped. He seemed summoning his courage, gripping it with both hands.

"Marm," he said desperately, "you can't stop me."

The spinster gasped, met his eyes, flushed and turned away. Sam nudged Mormon with elbow to ribs.

"You dog-gone ol' desperado," he said in a whisper. "I didn't think you had it in you. That the way you treated the first three?"

"No, it ain't," said Mormon, mopping his forehead. "And she ain't the same kind they was, neither. Come on, or we'll lose 'em."

"It was mighty decent of you to take me under your protection," said the young engineer to Sandy. He made hard going of the last word but shot it out with a snap that left his jaw advanced. Sandy told himself that he liked the clean-cut, well-set-up Westlake.

"Shucks," he answered, "I reckon you w'udn't have much trubble protectin' yo'self, providin' terms was any way nigh even. That Roarin' Russell throwed down on you, figgerin' you packed no gun, seein' there was none in sight.

"I sabe that kind of hombre. Since he was knee-high he's always had an aidge on most folks, 'count of his size an' weight. But that ain't enough, he's got to have somethin' on the other man 'fo' he tackles him. He plays all his games with an ace in a hold-out. Which shows him fo' a man who figgers he ain't equal to tacklin' another 'thout he knows he's got the best of it. He thinks he's one hell of a wrastler an' rough-an'-tumble man but, if he ever mixes with Mormon, it's goin' to be a bull an' b'ar affair — an' Mormon'll do the tossin'."

Westlake looked somewhat dubiously at Mormon's girth.

"Don't jedge a man by the size of his waistband," said Sandy. "Mormon's fooled mo'n one. He's hog fat, to look at, but if you was to skin him you'd find mighty li'l' fat an' a heap of muscle. Got flesh like an Injunrubber ball, has Mormon. Minute Roarin' Russell finds he ain't got a walkover he'll begin to quit. That sort does, ninety-nine out of a hundred. The yaller jest natcher'ly oozes out of 'em. How'd your fuss come to staht?"

"A man was showing Russell and some others a piece of quartz picked up round here. It had nothing in it but some mica and galena, but Russell had given it as his opinion that it was the gold-bearing rock of the region. I told them I thought they would find that in the porphyry and Russell asked me what the hell I knew about it? That's how it started. I don't know how it would have finished if you hadn't taken a hand and said I was a friend of yours. That saved my face. I came to the strike because I thought there would be a chance of getting in on the ground floor in new diggings and I hated to be driven out of it by having to dance for a bully and a bully's crowd. I don't know that I *would* have danced. It's hard to weigh the odds when a gun has been fired at you, but I figured he wouldn't shoot to kill."

"Might have crippled you," said Sandy. "If I'd been you I'd have danced."

"You would?"

"I sure would. No sense in argy'in' with a gun an' a boozy bluffer at the other end of it. He'd put up his bluff an', feelin' sure you c'udn't hurt him, he'd have carried it through. Any time a man has the drop on me I raise my hands — or my feet, 'cordin' to orders. I've spent a deal of time practisin' so it's hahd to beat me to the draw. Trouble was, ef you-all don't mind my sayin' so, you horned in. You give out information gratis. You had yore sign up fo' minin' engineer. Chahge fo' what you know, son, an' yo' customers'll be grateful. Give 'em a slug o' gold free an' they'll chuck it at a perairie dawg befo' they've gone fifty yards."

"Do you know anything about mining, Mr. Bourke?"

"Sandy is my name to my friends. A cowman with a mister to the front of his name seems to me like a hawss with an extry bridle. No, sir, I don't. Do you?"

Sandy's eyes twinkled as he put the quiz. Westlake laughed.

"I hope so. I think so. Mining is bound to be more or less of a gamble. A first-class mining engineer could tell you where you ought to find the gold in a certain region, but he couldn't guarantee that there would be any. Experience counts a lot, of course, but I do know something about sylvanite, or white gold. I've seen its big field over in Boulder and Teller Counties, Colorado. They call it graphic gold, sometimes, because the crystals are very frequently set up in twins and branch off so that they look like written characters. The crystals are monoclinic and occur in porphyry almost exclusively. It is a mixture of gold and silver telluride and it's also called tellurium. Named after Transylvania where it was first found. There's some in Australia."

"I'm much obliged," said Sandy. "I've learned a heap."

Westlake looked at him suspiciously, but Sandy's face was grave as that of the sphinx.

"The porphyry dykes here are in syncline," the engineer went on. "They dip toward each other from both sides of the valley and form loops or folds. If you imagine an onion sliced in half you catch the idea. Call every other layer porphyry, with rock and other dirt between. The bottom of a loop may be deep down or it may be missing altogether, ground away when the valley was gouged out by a glacier. There may be other loops beneath it. Some portions of the loops come to the surface on the hillside and you can guess at their dip. But — the gamble lies in this. The ones that are exposed may or may not carry the gold-bearing veins. You might hit it at grass roots and find a lot of it. Or you might go down deep sinking through the hard porphyry for nothing. Science says that the tellurium crystals are in the porphyry dykes and that these dykes lie in syncline, perhaps two or three, nested one under the other."

"Gosh," ejaculated Miranda Bailey. "It sure sounds like a lottery to me. I wonder c'ud we hire you to p'int out a likely place for us to locate?" They had left the one street by this time and were making their way slowly along the western slope of the valley. Men worked at creaky and shaky old windlasses or appeared and disappeared at the mouths of lateral shafts, repairing the ancient timbers, wheeling out rubbish. Once or twice they heard the dull boom of a shot where dynamite was trying to split the rock and uncover a lead. On several of the claims were groups, the members of which made no pretense at mining, but lolled about, playing cards or pitching dollars at a mark. These were speculators, holding to sell. Stakes with papers in clefts, piles of stones at the corners, showed the boundaries of the claims.

"If you think my judgment is any good," said Westlake, "you're welcome to it. I could be more certain of helping you when it comes to assaying or developing a mine. Are you-all taking up claims? Do you want to align them, or do you want to pool interests and locate here and there where the chances look good?"

"Miss Bailey an' her nephew are goin' to take a chance," said Sandy. "Me an' my two partners are lookin' for claims located by the man who first discovered the camp. They can't get away an' we'll see Miss Mirandy settled first."

"Me, I aim to take up a claim," said Mormon. "So does Sam."

"Who's goin' to work it?" asked Sandy. "You-all forget that we agreed when we went into the ranchin' business together not to go into speculations on the side 'thout mutual consent. From what I can make out from Westlake's talk speculation is a mild term fo' lookin' fo' gold. I don't consent, by a long shot. We got Molly's claims to look after with our interest in 'em, an' I've a hunch that's goin' to occupy all our time we got to spare. What does Roarin' Russell do in the camp," he asked Westlake, seemingly irrelevantly, "or ain't he shown yet?"

"He is a sort of bouncer, or capper for that gambling joint run by Plimsoll."

Sandy nodded. "I ain't surprised. Plimsoll's figgerin' that he'll get a big chunk of whatever's dug out, 'thout takin' any chances on diggin'. W'udn't wonder but what he figgers to run the camp, mo' ways than one, with a few bullies like Roarin' Russell to help him."

"This Casey," said Westlake, "who made the original strike, did he take out much?"

"As I understand it," replied Sandy, "he hits the porphyry where it's shaller, or worn off, like you said. An' he finds rich pay stuff right away, enough to start the camp. Quite a few works on that outcrop an' then it peters out. Casey sabed a bit about synclines, I reckon, fo' he kept faith in the camp, on'y he realized it 'ud take a heap of money to develop, meanin' to dig through the porphyry, I suppose. Now they've found some mo' of that float ore that the first crowd overlooked. Reckon that'll peter out too, after a while. But capital may come in on this second staht. Some eastern folk were lookin' over the place a while back. Took samples an' Plimsoll got wise to what they amounted to."

"And he hasn't taken up any claims?" said Westlake. "Despite his gambling investment, I should have thought he would."

"He's got an interest in one or two, I fancy, or thinks he has," said Sandy dryly.

Westlake halted and took a small steel hammer from his pocket with which he struck off a fragment of rock protruding from the ground. The cleavage showed purple. He walked slowly along for some fifty feet, kicking the soil with his foot, breaking off other samples to which he put his tongue.

"Taste good?" asked Sam.

"Not bad, if you're looking for mineral. They've got a distinct flavor all their own, but I wetted them to show the color up more plainly. Here is the outcrop of a syncline reef. It may carry gold and it may not, but it's wide enough, it's near the surface and it's as good a place as any. It dips deeper lower down, but I imagine you'll find it floating out again on the other side of the valley. Runs like the ribs of a ship, with the valley the hull. And the ship's rail, the gunwale in the rim-rock that outlines the auriferous deposit."

Sandy, glancing across the valley to where the engineer pointed, nodded his head. "Your judgment goes with Casey's," he said. "Right across from here is where he located his claims, I take it. How about it, Mormon? Fits the description to a T."

"Sure does," assented Mormon. "Thar's the notched boulder half-way up the hill, the three-forked dead pine on the ridge. If you locate here, marm," he said to Miranda, "an' we-all make a strike, we'll be on the same vein, I reckon."

"It's all Greek to me," said the spinster. "How do we locate? I've come this far, an' I'll see the thing through to some sort of finish. Me an' young Ed'll camp here. I figger we can git the car up. It's gone through worse places. There's water down there in the crick. We've got grub. When it's gone we can buy more. How many claims can we take up an' what's the size of 'em, Mr. Westlake?"

The three partners left Miranda and the engineer measuring off and setting up their monuments at the corners of the claim. Young Bailey started for the faithful flivver. They started directly down the sidehill, making for the valley, in silence, like men with business ahead of them that called for action rather than words.

"Figger that tent is on them claims of Molly's and our'n?" asked Sam, as they paused before they tackled the eastern slope. "Looked like it was to me."

"Me too," said Mormon.

"I wouldn't wonder," agreed Sandy. "Here's the situation, as I sabe it. Plimsoll met up with Pat Casey from time to time. Molly said so. There's other witnesses to that. Plimsoll'll use some of them to swear that he grubstaked Casey. They'll be some of his own crowd. No doubt Plimsoll got the location of the claims from the old records an' these buckaroo pals of his, who are roostin' on said location, knew jest where to go an' stahted out well in front with their outfit. I don't reckon we'll find Plimsoll up there, though we ain't seen him so far this mo'nin', but I'll bet our best bull ag'in' a chunk of dogmeat that they're on his pay-roll."

"Shucks, it don't make no difference whose pay-roll they're on," said Mormon. "They're claim-jumpers an', like you said, Sandy, a jump can be made two ways. Let's go look 'em over."

The tent was pitched on the hillside where the grade was too steep to permit of level ground enough for more than the actual floor space. The brown duck erection strained at the guy ropes of its upper side where the stakes had been driven deep into the soil. The chimney of a small stove came through the top of the cloth, guarded by a metal ring. Outside were boxes, saddles, an ax, kettles and pans, a portable grill and other camping equipment. The tent flaps were open and showed cots on which blankets and clothing were roughly spread. On two of these beds men sprawled asleep. Five others were seated on boxes about a boulder that looked like porphyry outcrop. Its surface was flat enough to serve as a table. The five were playing poker. One was bearded and seemed the old-time miner. All boasted stubble on their chins, two wore mustaches. One was bald. Their clothes varied, from the miner's faded blue overalls, high boots and flannel shirt, to soiled khaki and laced prospector's footwear. One thing they all had in common, cartridge belts and guns, in plain view. Taken together they were not a prepossessing lot, playing their game in silence, looking up with a scowl and movements toward gun butts at the visitors. Two burros cropped at the scanty herbage above the tent. A demijohn stood between two of the box seats.

"I've seen that tent afore," whispered Sam to Sandy. The latter nodded.

"Campin' out, gents?" he asked amiably.

"No, we ain't. These claims are preempted. Trespassers ain't welcome. You're invited to move on."

"That's a new name fo' it," said Sandy pleasantly. "New to me. Preempted."

"What in hell are you driving at?" asked the other. "This is private property."

"Property of Jim Plimsoll?"

"None of yore damned business."

There was a movement in the tent. One of the men got up from his cot and stood yawning in the entrance, one hand on the pole. The other snored on. Sandy, with Mormon and Sam, stood just above the group on the narrow bench that furnished the floor for the tent. They had little doubt that the jumpers knew who they were, though they recognized none of them by sight. There was a hesitancy toward action that might have been born out of respect to Sandy's two guns or a foreknowledge of his reputation in handling them, aside from the armament of his partners. Sandy's hands rested lightly on his hips, his thumbs hooked in his belt, fingers grazing the butts of his guns. There was a smile on his lips but none in his eyes. His tone and manner were easy.

"Saw his stencil on the tent," he said. "J. P. in a diamond. Same brand he uses fo' his hawsses. Or mebbe you found it."

His drawling voice held a taunt that brought angry flushes of color to the faces of the men opposing him, yet they made no definite movement toward attack. It seemed patent that Sandy Bourke was testing them. Trouble was in the air, two kinds of it: on the one side hesitant belligerency; on the other — cool nonchalance. Sandy, with his smiling lips and unsmiling eyes, stood lightly poised as a dancing master. Mormon and Sam were tenser, crouched a little from the hips, elbows away from their sides, hands with fingers apart, ready to close on gun butts, standing as boxers stand or distance-runners set on their marks.

The man who stood in the tent door kicked at his sleeping companion and roused him to sit on the side of his cot and stare sleepily out, gradually taking in the situation. There were seven against three but, when the odds are so big and the minority faces them with a readiness and an assurance that shows in their eyes, on their lips, vibrates from their compacted alliance, the measure is one of will, rather than physical and merely numerical superiority, and the balance beam quivers undecidedly. The bearded miner, with the rest, looked shiftily toward the man who had done the speaking, the bald-headed one, whose khaki and nail-studded boots were belied by the softness and puffiness of his flesh, the sags and wrinkles beneath his eyes and under his double chins. He had little gray-green orbs that glittered uneasily.

"I'm giving you men two minutes to clear out of here," he said. "No two-gunned cow-puncher can throw any bluff round here, if that's what you're trying to do."

Sandy laughed joyously. The smile was in his eyes now.

"If I figger a man's throwin' a bluff," he said, "I usually figger to call him, not to chew about it. Me, I pack two guns fo' a reason. Once in a while I shoot off all the ca'tridges from one an' then I don't have to reload. Now, *I'm* talkin'. These claims are duly registered in the name of Patrick Casey, his heirs an' assigns. Here's the papers. The assessment work is all done. Pat's daughter owns 'em now. We're representin' her. An' I'm servin' you notice to quit. We'll take the same two minutes you was talkin' of. They must be nigh up now, though I didn't see you lookin' at yo' watch. I'm lookin' at my Ingersoll an' I give it sixty seconds mo'. Then staht yore li'l' demonstration, gents, providin' I don't beat you to it." He started to roll a cigarette with hands skilful and steady. Back of him Sam and Mormon stood like dogs on point, watchful, unmoving, but instinct with suppressed motion.

"The girl may be his heir," said the bald-headed man, "but Plimsoll is assignee. Plimsoll staked him an' these claims are half his. The girl can put in her share to the title later, if they amount to anything. She ain't of age."

"So J. P. was hirin' you to do his dirty work," said Sandy, his voice cold with contempt. "You go back to him, the whole lousy pack of you, an' tell him from me he's a yellow-spined liar. Git! Take yore stuff with you or send back fo' it. Now, git off this property."

If a man can make movements with his hands so swiftly that they are covered in less than a tenth of a second, ordinary human sight can not register them. He has achieved the magician's slogan — *the quickness of the hand deceives the eye.* It takes natural aptitude and long practise, whether one is juggling gilded balls or blued-steel revolvers. Sandy could, with a circling movement of his wrists, draw his guns from their holsters and bring them to bear directly upon the target to which his eyes shifted. Glance, twist of wrist, arrest of motion, pressure of finger, all coordinated. One moment his hands were empty, his glance carelessly contemptuous, the veriest movement of a split-second stop-watch and the gun in his right hand spat fire, the gun in his left swung in an arc that menaced the five card players.

The other two were struggling beneath the crumpled folds of a collapsed tent, wriggling frantically like the stage hands who simulate waves by crawling beneath painted canvas. Sandy had shattered the pegs that held up the upper corners of the tent on the slope, had cut the cords of the remaining guys on that side and the structure had swayed and collapsed.

Sam and Mormon had lined up now with Sandy. There was no mistaking their intention to use their guns. But the exhibition had been quite sufficient. With one accord the five raised their hands shoulder high and began to shuffle down the hill, regardless of their equipment, which, having been paid for by Plimsoll, they regarded as of much less value than the necessity for departure.

"Come out of that," commanded Sandy to the two wrigglers. "Git a move on."

The faces that appeared were ludicrous in their expressions of dismay and appeal. Their owners came out like dogs from a kennel who expect to be kicked as they emerge. One of them had taken off his boots for better sleeping and he hobbled uneasily in his socks.

"Take along yore booze," said Sandy.

The bootless one looked furtively at the demijohn, still like a wary cur who snatches at and bolts with a stray bone. Then the pair set off at a jog trot after the rest.

"I wonder," said Sam, "if that was good whisky?"

Sandy looked at him reproachfully. "Sody-Water," he said, "I'm plumb disappointed in you an' yore cravin'. Smell it an' see."

His gun exploded. The man with the demijohn gave a curious hop, skip and jump. The demijohn jerked in his hand but seemed intact. The bullet, smashing through the wickerwork, had shattered the container but the tough willow twigs preserved the shape. Two more shots and there was a tinkle of broken glass. The last bullet had clipped the neck. It was too close shooting for the sockless one and the whisky was dripping fast through the weave, bringing a reek of crude liquor to Sam's twitching nostrils. The claim-jumper dropped what was left of his burden and went hopping on, acquiring stone bruises with every leap.

"Scattered like a bunch of coyotes," said Sam.

"Sure did," agreed Sandy. "Minute they stahted talkin', 'stead of shootin', I knew they was ready to stampede. They'll beat it to Plimsoll an' we'll see jest how much sand he's got in his craw."

"Not enough to keep him from skiddin' on a downgrade," said Mormon. "Sandy, that's cruelty to animals, sendin' that hombre off 'thout his boots after you took away his licker. I've got tender feet myse'f as well as a soft heart. Help me with this tent a minute, Sam."

Together they raised the fallen canvas enough to discover the boots, which Mormon hurled down-hill after the limping one, who was far in the rear of his companions. He turned at Mormon's shout and he stopped, fearful at the act of kindness, crawled up the slope and retrieved his footwear, pulled them on and scurried off.

A distant shout reached them from the other side of the gulch. By position, rather than actual recognition, Sandy guessed the figure that of Westlake. The firing must have sounded only a little louder than cork poppings, but evidently the engineer had sized up the retreating men and the collapsed tent. Sandy waved to him in assurance that all was well and the other waved back in understanding.

"Think Plim'll show?" asked Sam.

"Got to — or quit," said Sandy. "That bunch of jumpers he got together'll spill the beans unless he makes some play. It's plumb evident he wants these partickler claims. I don't believe he's hirin' men just to make us peevish. 'Sides, he didn't know fo' sure we were comin'. Might have figgered we'd trail the news of the rush, but I'll bet a sack of Durham against a pinch o' dirt that he's fairly sure that old man Patrick Casey picked him some first-class locations. We got one card that'll upset him considerable, my bein' the legal guardeen of Molly."

"A heap he cares fo' legal or not legal," said Sam.

"That's jest what he *will* do, now he ain't standin' in with the crowd that hands out the law, Sam. He might try to make it a show-down right here an' drive us out of the camp or leave us tucked away stiff in some prospect hole. But there's a lot of decent material drifted in an' it w'udn't be hard to beat him to that play an' organize a camp committee fo' the regulation of law an' order till such time as the camp proves itself an' is established. Once big capital gits stahted in here the law'll be workin' right along hand in hand with the development. Let's take a pasear an' look at Casey's workings."

Patrick Casey had run in a tunnel from the face of his discovery. Weathered porphyry float showed on the dump whose size suggested greater depth to the tunnel than they had expected. Its mouth had been closed by timbers fitting closely into the frame of the horizontal shaft, forming, not so much a door, as a barricade, that had been firmly spiked to heavy timbers. This had been recently dismantled and then replaced, as recent marks on the weathered lumber showed. Sandy looked at these places closely, frowning as he gave his verdict.

"Some one monkeyin' with this inside of the last month," he announced. "The nails ain't rusted like the old ones an' the chips are fresh. Like as not it was that bunch of easterners. They'd figger the camp was abandoned an' consider themselves justified as philanthropists into bu'stin' open anything that looked good — like this tunnel. A man w'udn't go to the trouble of timberin' up if he didn't think he had somethin' inside that was goin' to turn up high cahd some day. 'Course the capitalist, if he found somethin' that looked good, 'ud hunt up the owner in the registry an' make him an offer. But it w'udn't be a half interest in the mine. He'd say he was thinkin' of developin' half a mile away an', if he bought cheap enough, he might make an offer. Yes, sir," Sandy went on, warming to his own theory, "it w'udn't surprise me if this warn't the mine they sampled which Plimsoll finds out is the real stuff an' clamps on."

"Well," said Mormon, "we'll have a chance to ask him in a minute. He's comin' up with that crowd of his rangin' erlong an' their ha'r liftin'. Thar's that ungrateful skunk I chucked the boots at. Plim don't look over an' above pleased the way things are breakin'. Looks as amiable as a timber wolf with his tail in a b'ar trap."

The three partners met the jumpers, now headed by Plimsoll, on the border of the claims. The gambler's face was livid. He had boasted and lashed himself into a bullying confidence that he knew was inadequate to meet the situation he could not avoid. Hatred of the men who had balked him more than once served him better.

"You four-flushers get off this ground," he blustered. "You're claiming to represent Molly Casey's rights after you've kidnaped the girl and sent her out of the state. It won't get you anywhere or anything. I've got a half interest in these claims and I've plenty of witnesses to prove it."

"I don't believe yore witnesses are half as vallyble as they might have been before politics shifted in Herefo'd County," said Sandy. "You ain't got a written contract an' it w'udn't do you a mite of good if you had, fur as I'm concerned. Because I've been duly an' legally app'inted guardeen to Casey's daughter Molly an' I'm here to represent her interests, likewise mine. I've got my guardianship papers right with me."

"A hell of a lot of good they'll do you in this camp," sneered Plimsoll. "Representin' *her* interests. I'll say you are, an' your own along with 'em." A laugh from his followers heartened him. "If the camp ever hears the yarn of your running off with the girl and now, with her tucked away, coming back to clean up, I've a notion they'd show you four-flushers where you've sat in to the wrong game. Why...."

Something in Sandy's face stopped him. It became suddenly devoid of all expression, became a thing of stone out of which blazed two gray eyes and a voice issued from lips that barely moved.

"I've got a notion, too, Plimsoll. A notion that it 'ud be a good day's work to shoot you fo' a foul-mouthed, lyin', stealin' crook! You sure ain't worth bein' arrested fo', an' there ain't no open season fo' two-laigged coyotes of yore sort, so I'll give you yore chance. You've called me a fo'-flusher twice, an' the on'y way to prove a fo'-flush is to call fo' a show-down. I'm doin' it."

The words came cold and even, backed by a grim earnestness that imprinted itself on the lesser manhood of the jumpers as a finger leaves its print in clay. They shifted back a little from Plimsoll, circling out as they might have moved away from a man marked by pestilence. He stood trying to outface Sandy, to keep his eyes steady. His lips were tight closed, still he could not help but open his mouth to a quickened breathing, to touch the lips with a furtive tongue that found the skin peeling in tiny feverish strips.

"You pack yore gun under yore coat flap," said Sandy. "I don't know how quick you can draw but I aim to find out."

He handed one of his own guns to Mormon, announcing his action lest Plimsoll might mistake it.

"Now then," he went on, "I once told you I looked to you to stop any gossip about Molly Casey. Same time Butch Parsons an' Sim Hahn got huht. You don't seem able to sabe plain talk an' I'm tired of talkin' to you, Jim Plimsoll. Me, I'm goin' to roll me a cigareet. Any time you want to you can draw. I'm givin' you the aidge on me. If you don't take that aidge, Jim Plimsoll, I'm givin' you till sun-up ter-morrer mornin' to git plumb out of camp. An' to keep driftin'."

Deliberately Sandy took tobacco sack and papers from the pocket of his shirt, his fingers functioning automatically, precisely, his eyes never shifting from Plimsoll's face, measuring by feel the amount of tobacco shaken into the little trough of brown paper. While he rolled the cigarette the sack swung from his teeth by its string.

The group gazed at him fascinated. Plimsoll's face beaded with tiny drops of sweat, his hands moved slowly upward toward his coat lapels, touched them as Sandy twisted the end of the cigarette, stayed there, shaking slightly with what might have been eagerness — or paralysis. For the look in the steel gray eyes of Sandy Bourke, half mocking, all confident, spurred the doubts that surged through the gambler's chance-calculating mind, while he knew that every atom of hesitation lessened his chances.

His own hands were close to his chest. His right had but a few inches to dart, to drag the automatic from its smooth holster. Sandy's hands were high above his belt, rolling the cigarette. They had four times as far to go. But Plimsoll knew that if anything went wrong with his performance, if he failed to kill outright, that nothing would go wrong with Sandy's shooting. The mention of Butch and Sim Hahn did not compose him. He had had the stage all set that time and Butch had been shot down, Sim Hahn's capacities as a crooked dealer had been spoiled for ever. But — if he did not take his chance and, failing it, did not leave camp....

He felt cold. The temperature of his own conceit, the mercury of the regard of his bullies, was falling steadily. The nervous sweat was no longer confined to his face. The palms of his hands were moist, slippery....

"Gimme a match, Sam." Sandy's voice came to Plimsoll across a gulf that could never be bridged. He watched the flame, pale in the sunshine, watched it lift to the cigarette and then a puff of smoke came into his face as Sandy flung away the burnt stick and turned on his heel. Murder stirred dully in Plimsoll's brain at the sneers he surmised rather than read on the faces of his followers. His defeat was also theirs. But the moment had gone. He knew he lacked the nerve. Sandy knew it and had turned his back on him.

His prestige was gone. His boon companions would talk about it. Mormon gave Sandy back his second gun and Sandy slid it into the holster. He exhaled the last puff of his cigarette before he spoke again to Plimsoll.

"Sun-up, ter-morrer. You can send fo' yore stuff here any time you've a mind to. Fo' a gamblin' man, Plimsoll, you're a damned pore judge of a hand."

Plimsoll strode off down the hill alone. The men who had come with him hesitated and then crossed the gulch. They had severed connections with the J. P. brand for the time, at least. The three partners walked back toward the tunnel.

"I saw the carkiss of a steer one time," said Sam, "that had been lyin' on a sidehill fo' quite a spell. The coyotes an' the buzzards had been at it, an' the wind an' weather had finished the job till there warn't much mo'n hide an' some scattered bones. Mebbe a li'l' hair. But that carkiss sure held mo' guts than Jim Plimsoll packs."

"He ain't through," said Mormon. "You didn't ought to give him till sun-up, Sandy. Sun-down 'ud have been better. He's a mangy coyote, but he's got brains an' he'll addle 'em figgerin' out some way to git even."

"I w'udn't wonder," answered Sandy. "Me, I'm goin' to do a li'l' figgerin' too."

"We got to stay on the claims," said Sam. "If they happened to think of it they might heave a stick of dynamite in our midst afteh it's good an' dahk. A flyin' chunk of dynamite is a nasty thing to dodge, at that."

He spoke as dispassionately as if he had been discussing a display of harmless fireworks. Sandy answered in the same tone.

"I don't think it likely, Sam. Camp knows, or will know, what's been happenin'. If dynamite was thrown they'd sabe who did it an' I don't believe the crowd 'ud stand for it. Jest the same it 'ud sure surprise me if we didn't git some sort of a shivaree pahty afteh nightfall. I w'udn't wonder if Jim Plimsoll forgets to send fo' that tent an' stuff of his. Hope he does."

"What do we want with it?" demanded Mormon.

"Nothin', with the stuff. We'll set it out beyond the lines come dusk. But the tent'll come in handy. We didn't bring one erlong."

Sam and Mormon both looked at him curiously, but Sandy's face was sphinx-like and they refrained from useless questioning.

"Here comes young Ed," announced Sandy as they gained the tunnel. "He's totin' somethin' that looks to me as if it might be grub."

"Won't offend me none ef it is," said Mormon. "I'm hungrier'n a spring b'ar an' all our stuff's oveh with Mirandy Bailey."

"She's sure one thoughtful lady," said Sam. "What you got, Ed?" he queried as the gangling youth came up.

"Beans, camp-bread an' coffee. Aunt Mirandy, she 'lowed you-all might not want to leave the claim so she sent this over to bide you through. You been havin' some trouble, ain't you?" he asked, his eyes gleaming with interest. "We heard somethin' that sounded like shots an' Mr. Westlake saw the first bunch go away. He said you waved to him it was all right. Aunt, she 'lowed you c'ud look out fo' yourselves. Then the second bunch come erlong."

"Jest wishin' us luck, son," said Sandy. "How's everything with you?"

"I bet it warn't good luck they was wishin'," grinned Ed, squatting down on his haunches and rolling a cigarette. "We're gettin' on fine. Got some dandy claims, I reckon. One for maw an' one fo' father, right alongside Aunt Mirandy's an' mine. It 'ud be great if we sh'ud all strike it rich, to once, w'udn't it?"

"Great!" agreed Sandy, munching beans with gusto. "Don't you think you ought to be gettin' back, 'case some one might take a notion to them claims of yores? 'Pears to me it's up to you, Ed, to protect yore aunt. Westlake can't stick around with you all the time. He's got his business to attend to."

Young Ed straightened.

"I'll look out for her all right," he said. "But you don't know Aunt Mirandy over well or you'd know she can do her own protectin'. You bet she can. 'Sides, the men who've got claims nigh us come over an' told her they'd see she wasn't interfered with none. Said they'd heard some bully had sworn at her an' the real miners in camp warn't goin' to stand anything like that. Nor no claim-jumpin'. They're goin' to organize, they say. Git up a Vigilance Committee."

"Good!" said Sandy. "That means the decent element aims to run things. We'll help 'em. It'll be easier with Plimsoll out of camp."

"Figger he'll go?" asked Sam.

"I w'udn't be surprised if he listened to the small voice of reason," answered Sandy. "You tell yore aunt we're much obliged fo' the grub, Ed. One of us'll be over afteh a bit an' tote our things across. We'll camp here fo' a bit an' sit tight. I'd do the same, if I was you, Ed, spite of yore friends. I don't doubt fo' a minute but what yore aunt is plumb capable of lookin' out for herself, but you see, she's a woman an' yo're a man, an' it's you folks'll be lookin' to."

The lad flushed with pride under the hand that Sandy set in chummy fashion on his shoulder.

"I'll do that," he said, and, picking up the emptied utensils he had brought he started off down and across the gulch.

"No sense in encouragin' him to hang around us," said Sandy. "There's apt to be fireworks round here most any time between now an' ter-morrer mo'nin'. Plimsoll'll shack erlong about sun-up — providin' he ain't able to call the tuhn on us befo'. Mormon, if you'll go git our blankets an' outfit, Sam an' me'll fix up those bu'sted guy ropes an' shift the tent."

"You don't aim fo' us to sleep in it, do you?" asked Mormon.

"Don't believe we'd rest well if we tackled it. But it mightn't be a bad scheme if we give the gen'ral idee that we *are* sleepin' in it. I put a lantern in the car when we stahted. Fetch that erlong too, will you, Mormon?"

It was late afternoon before Mormon reappeared, bearing a camp outfit, part of which was carried by Westlake. Sandy and Sam had repitched the tent on fairly level ground of the valley bottom. The claim boundaries ran to within fifty yards of the little creek named Flivver and the tent-pins were set almost on the border-line. The ground was sparsely covered with scrub grass, shrubs and willows, the space about the tent clear of anything higher than clumps of bushes and sage.

Mormon's eye brows went up at the location with which Sandy and Sam, seated cross-legged on the ground, one smoking, the other draining low harmonies through his mouth organ, appeared perfectly satisfied.

"Why on the flat?" asked Mormon. "There's a heap of cover round here where they might snake up afteh dahk an' sling anythin' they minded to at us, from lead to giant powdeh!"

"Wal," drawled Sandy, flicking the ash from his cigarette, "it's handy to watch, fo' one thing, an' yore right about that coveh, Mormon. That's why we chose it. Sam an' me had a heap of trouble pickin' out this place. Finally we found jest what we wanted, didn't we, Sam?"

"Sure did."

Mormon set down his load and took off his hat to scratch his head perplexedly. Then his face lightened as he looked up-hill.

"You figger on settin' the lantern in here afteh dahk," he said. "An' watchin' the fun from the tunnel."

"Pritty close, Mormon. Come inside, you an' Westlake, an' I'll show you suthin'."

They followed him into the tent and came out again laughing.

"No matteh what happens," said Sandy, "an' I'm hopin' fo' the worst, it ain't our tent. You been up to the main street this afternoon, Westlake?"

"Yes. There's a lot of talk loose about the trouble between you and Plimsoll's crowd. Factions for both sides and a lot of onlookers who are neutral and just waiting for the excitement. I saw Roaring Russell but he passed me up. He might not have known me. He was pretty well drunk. He's talking big about taking you apart, Mr. Peters. He claims to have been a champion wrestler at one time."

"You don't say so," said Mormon. "Me, I was the champeen wrastler of the Cow Belt, one time. Had the belt to prove it till I lost it at draw poker. I've got hawg fat sence then, but I don't believe I've softened any. An' the booze he's tuckin' away is mighty pore stuff fo' trainin'. But I ain't long on walkin'," he added. "B'lieve I'll sit me down a spell. I'll make fire an' git supper if you want to take Westlake up to the tunnel."

Westlake carefully inspected the tunnel, the float and the contents of the dump.

"I wouldn't wonder if Casey was running this as a drift to follow a good lead," he pronounced. "It looks better to me than any part of the camp I've inspected. I'll assay these samples for you, if you've no objection. I've got a lot of orders back at my shack already. My customers told me that they'd put a flea in Russell's ear that the camp assayer was not to be interfered with, so there is some value in an education, you see."

Sandy nodded. "You pack a gun?" he asked.

"No. I've got one, but I don't carry it. My practise with firearms has been with larger calibers."

"War?" asked Sandy.

"Yes. I was in the artillery. Is there anything else I can do? Get you some supplies? I'm coming back to have supper with Miss Bailey and her nephew."

"Not a thing," said Sandy. "Much obliged." He watched the engineer swing away.

"There's a good man for you," he said to Sam. "Well set up and able to handle himself. I like his ways first-rate."

"Me, too," said Sam. "He'd make a good match fo' Molly, when she comes back with her eddication, w'udn't he?"

Sandy stopped in his stride suddenly, so that Sam halted and regarded him curiously.

"Twist yo' foot?" he asked. "High heels is all right fo' stirrups but they're tough on hill climbin'."

"No. I was jest thinkin'. Nothin' that amounts to shucks. Gettin' dahk. We better git outside of our supper an' sneak up to the tunnel soon's it gits dusk enough to light the lantern."

CHAPTER XIII
A ROPE BREAKS

The lantern, turned down, dimly illumined the tent and revealed the figures of three men seated about some sort of rough table. The flap was drawn and fastened. Occasionally a figure moved slightly. No passer-by would have guessed that the three partners were ensconced in the black mouth of the tunnel, ramparted by the dump heap, watching for developments they were fairly sure would start with darkness. Every little while Sandy twitched a line that was attached to a clumsy but effective rocker he had contrived beneath one of the dummies they had built from the stuff that Plimsoll had not reclaimed.

"Don't want to work the blamed thing too much," he said. "Might bu'st it. It's on'y the one figger but I'll be derned if it don't look natcherul."

After which they all relapsed into silence, restrained from smoking for fear of a telltale spark or casual fragrance carried by the wind. It was a dark night, the hillsides stood blurry against a blue-black sky in which the stars glittered like metal points but failed to shed much light. Later, much later, toward morning, a moon would rise.

Here and there on the slopes bright spots or glows of fire marked the occupied claim-sites. From the camp itself there came a murmur that sometimes swelled louder under the dull flare that hung over the lower end of the valley; reflection and diffusion from the gasoline lights and acetylene flares used by the owners of the eating-houses, the bars and gambling shacks, all open for business during miners' hours, which meant two shifts, of night and day.

From the mouth of the tunnel the three watched the march of the stars, the wheel of the Big Dipper around its pivot, the North Star; marking time by the sidereal clock of the heavens, each with a variant emotion.

Mormon shifted his position more frequently than the others. None of them was especially comfortable, but Mormon wanted to keep as limber as possible, he was afraid of stiffening up, thinking always of his challenge to Roaring Russell. Slow to anger, Mormon, when his rage mounted was slow of statement. What he said he meant. The insult to Miranda Bailey while under his escort chafed him as a saddle chafes a galled horse. It had to be wiped out at the earliest moment and, singularly enough, the spinster was not particularly prominent in the matter. It was not a personal question; the insult had been offered to womanhood, and Mormon was ever its champion and its victim.

Sam, cut off from tobacco and melody, bunkered down with his back against a frame timber and looked at the tall lean figure of Sandy silhouetted against the stars, wondering why Sandy had stopped so abruptly when the names of Westlake and Molly Casey had been coupled. It wasn't like Sandy to move or halt without definite purpose, Sam reasoned. "I suppose he figgers Molly too much of a kid," he told himself. "If these claims pan out she'll be rich. Likewise, so will we." His thoughts shifted to dreams of what he would do when they were wealthy. Very far beyond the purchase of an elaborate saddle and outfit, a horse or two he coveted, the finest harmonica to be bought, he did not go. That Sandy might have felt a tinge of jealousy toward young Westlake was furthest from his conjectures.

As for Sandy, he had lost his mental orientation. Something had happened, something was happening within him and he could not tell the process nor name it. He was as a man who goes out into the darkness amid rooms and passages with which he considers himself familiar and suddenly — there comes a door where should be space, or space where there should be a window — and he is lost, his senses betray him, for the moment he is completely fogged, all bearings lost, possessed with the blankness that accompanies the flight of self-confidence.

He could see very plainly in mental vision the picture that Molly had sent to the Three Star, now framed and given the place of honor on the table of the ranch-house living-room. The picture of a girl in whose eyes the fleeting look of womanhood, that Sandy had now and then seen there and which had thrilled him so strangely, had become permanent. That she was something so vital she could not be dismissed from the life of the Three Star, from his own life, by sending her to school whence she would return almost a stranger, by making her an heiress, Sandy recognized. He had deliberately given her his hand to help her out of the rut in which he had found her and now, with the swift series of tableaux conjured up by Sam's suggestion of her and Westlake together, lovers, Sandy realized the gap that was widening between Molly and him. If she was out of the rut would she not now regard him as in another of his own from which there was no up-lifting?

To Sandy, Westlake seemed little more than a likable lad, placing him at about twenty-three or four. He felt immeasurably older, harder, though there were not more than six years between them — seven at the most. Even that made him almost twice the age of Molly. With this twist of his reverie he realized that Molly was no longer to be considered as a girl. Toward the little maid he had poured out protectiveness, affection and, while his vials were emptying, she had crossed the brook. Into what had his affection shifted with the changing of Molly to womanhood?

Sandy Bourke, knight of the roving heel, had never attempted to find solution for his attitude toward women. It was neither wariness nor antipathy. His life, drifting from rancho to rancho, sometimes consorting with the rougher side of men careless of conventions, had been, in the main, not unlike the life of a hermit, with long periods when he rode alone under sun and stars with only his horse for company.

There were months of this and then came swiftly moving periods of relaxation in a cattle town where men unleashed the repressions and let pent-up energies and appetites have full sway. Sandy loved card chances where his own skill might back what luck the pasteboards brought him in the deal. Drinking bouts, the company of the women with whom many of his fellows consorted, never appealed to him. His reservations found outlet in gambling or in the acceptance of some job where the danger risks ran high, where success and self-safety hung upon his coolness, his keen sense, his courage and his skill with horse and lariat and gun. A life as apart as a sailor's, more lonely, for he was often companionless for months.

So far he had never felt lack of anything, least of all lately, with the two men he liked best in active partnership with him, with a maturing interest in the development of his ranch and his grade of cattle by modern methods. But, to have Molly not come back, or, returning, to have her wooed and won, entirely absorbed by some one like Westlake, struck him with a sense of impending loss that amounted to a real pain, difficult of self-diagnosis. Westlake was worthy enough. A good mate for Molly, climbing up the ladder of education and culture to stand where the engineer, well-bred, well-mannered, now stood, the two of them to go on together....

"Shucks!" muttered Sandy. "And he ain't even seen her picture. I must have been chewin' loco weed."

"What say?" asked Sam.

"I'm goin' to take a li'l' look-see," said Sandy. "I reckon they're tryin' to git warmed up an' decide on what they'll do round here. No tellin' how long they may take or what kind of deviltry that camp booze may work 'em up to. I'm pritty certain no one saw us sneak out of the tent afteh dahk."

If they had been seen no attempt might be made to dislodge them from the claims. Sandy did not believe such effort would turn out to be a shooting match, — unless the defenders started it, — but something more underhanded. The flinging of a dynamite stick, if the throwers felt certain of not being caught, was a possibility if enough crude whisky had been absorbed. In all probability the crowd of ousted men were making themselves conspicuous in the camp during the earlier hours of the evening in view of a needed alibi. Nothing might happen until midnight and the long vigil was not comfortable. Sandy vanished from the tunnel mouth, sinking to the ground, instantly indistinguishable even to Sam and Mormon. There was nothing to tell whether he had gone up-hill or down. The momentary cessation of the cicadas' chorus was the only warning that a human was abroad.

"Have a chaw?" Mormon whispered presently, after he had changed his pose.

Sam took the plug tobacco and bit into it gratefully.

"I sure hate stickin' around, waitin'," he said under his breath. "Allus makes me plumb nerv'us."

"Same here," answered Mormon. "Reckon it's that way with most men. Sandy don't show it, 'cept by goin' out on a snoop."

"He can see, smell an' hear where we'd be deef, dumb an' blind," said Sam. "Wonder what time it is? We've been here all of two hours already 'cordin' to them stars."

"What time does the moon rise?" asked Mormon.

"'Bout half past three or so. You figgerin' on wrastlin' Roarin' Russell by moonlight, after we git through down here?"

"I've got a hunch this is goin' to be a busy night, plumb through till sun-up," said Mormon. "An', when I meet up with Roarin' Russell it ain't goin' to be jest a wrastlin match, believe me. It's goin' to be a free-fo'-all exhibition of ground an' lofty tumblin', 'thout rounds, seconds or referee. When one of us hits the ground it'll likely be fo' keeps."

"I ain't seen you so riled up in a long time, old-timer. An' I'm backin' you fo' winner, at that. Jest the same, me an' Sandy'll do a li'l' refereein' fo' the sake of fair play."

"I can hear you two gossipin' old wimmin gabbin' clear up to the top of the hill an' down to the crick," added a third voice as Sandy glided in, materializing from the darkness.

"Anythin' doin'?" asked Sam.

"No, an' there won't be long as you air yo' voices. You play like an angel on that mouth harp of yores, Sam, but you talk like a rasp. Mormon booms like a bull frawg."

They settled down again to their watch. The Great Bear constellation dipped down, scooping into the darkness beyond the opposing hill.

"Pritty close to midnight," said Sam at last. "What's the..."

Sandy's grip on his arm checked him, all senses centering into listening.

The three stared blankly into the night, while their hands sought gun butts and loosened the weapons in their holsters. Out of the blackness came little foreign sounds that they interpreted according to their powers. The tiny clink of metal, the faint thud of horses' hoofs, an exclamation that had barely been above the speaker's breath floated up to them through the stillness. The glow of the lantern showed through the tent wall.

"Two riders," mouthed Sandy so softly that Mormon and Sam swung heads to catch his words. "Came up the valley t'other side of the crick. Both crossed it above the tent. Reckon they're visitin' us. One of 'em's comin' this way."

They crouched, breathless now, listening to the soft padded sounds that told of the approach of man and horse. These ceased. Still they could see nothing. Then there came a sharp shrill whistle, answered from the levels. Followed instantly the thud of galloping ponies going at top speed, parallel, one between the watchers and the tent as they saw the swift shadow shade the glow for an instant, the other between the tent and the creek. There was a sharp swishing as of something whipping brush.

"Yi-yi-yippy!" The cries rang out exultant as the horses dashed by the tunnel. The light in the tent wavered, went out. There was a shout of surprise and dismay, a *twang* like the snapping of a mighty bowstring and then came the whoops of the trio from the Three Star as they realized what the attempt had been and how it had failed.

Two riders, trailing a rope, had raced down the valley hoping to sweep away the tent, to send its occupant sprawling, its contents scattered in a confusion of which advantage would be taken to chase the three off their claims, taken by surprise, made ridiculous.

Sandy and Sam, searching for a convenient tent site, had happened upon a mass of outcrop, overgrown by brush. Over this they had pitched the tent, using the rock for table, propping their dummies about it. If dynamite was flung it would find something to work against. They had not anticipated the use of the rope to demolish the canvas any more than the two riders had expected to bring up against a boulder. The impact, with their ponies spurred, urged on by their shouts to their limit, tore the cinches of one saddle loose, jerked it from the horse and catapulted the unprepared rider over its head, flying through the air to land heavily, while his mount, unencumbered, frightened, went careering off leaving its breathless master stunned amid the sage.

As the cinches had given way at one end, the line itself had parted at the other. The second pony had stumbled sidewise, rolling before the man was free from the saddle. They could hear it thrashing in the willows, the rider cursing as he tried to remount while Sandy ran cat-footed down the hill, leaving Mormon and Sam to handle the other. If there had been assistants to the raid they had melted away, willing enough to join in a drive against men yanked from their tent, defenseless, but not at all eager to face the guns of those same men on the alert, the aggressive.

Mormon and Sam found their man groaning and limp.

"Don't believe he's bu'sted anything," announced Sam, "'less he's druv his neck inter his shoulders. Got his saddle, Mormon?"

"Yep. Want the rope?"

They trussed their captive with the lariat still snubbed to his saddle-horn. Down in the willows there was a flash, a report, a scurrying flight punctuated by an oath almost as vivid as the shot. Sandy came up the hill toward them.

"Miss him?" asked Mormon.

"It was sure dahk," said Sandy, "and I hated to plug the hawss. So I only took one shot to cheer him on his way. He was mountin' at the time an' it was a snapshot. I aimed at the seat of his pants. I w'udn't be surprised but what he's ridin' so't of one-sided. Who you got here? Tote him down-hill. I don't believe they bu'sted the lantern. We'll take a look at him."

Sandy retrieved the lantern from the collapsed canvas and lit it. Mormon and Sam took the senseless man down to the creek where they attempted to revive him by pouring hatfuls of the icy water on his head. He was a black-haired chap, sallow of face, clean-shaven. His clothes were those of a cowman.

"Looks a heap like a drowned rat," said Mormon. "It's Sol Wyatt, one of Plim's riders oveh to his hawss ranch. He got fired from the Two-Bar-Circle fo' leavin' his ridin' iron to home an' usin' anotheh brand. Leastwise, that's what they suspected. Old Man Penny giv' him the benefit of the doubt an' jest kicked him out of the corral. If he'd had the goods on him he'd have skinned him alive an' put his pelt on the bahn do' fo' a warnin'."

"The damn fool rode a single-fire saddle fo' a job like that," said Sam. "No wonder it bu'sted. He's sniffin', Sandy; what we goin' to do with him?"

"Take him up inter camp, soon's he's able to walk an' hand him over to Plimsoll with our compliments. They figgered they'd make us all look plumb ridiculous with bein' flipped out of the tent. Then they'd have had the crowd on their side erlong with the la'f, way it usually goes. Don't drown him, Mormon, he don't look oveh used to water, to me."

Wyatt opened a pair of shifty black eyes to consciousness and the light of the lantern and immediately closed them again, playing opossum. Sam prodded him gently in the ribs.

"Wake up, Sol," he said. "Come back to earth, you sky-salutin' circus-rider. You sure looped the loops 'fore you lit. Serves you right fo' usin' a one-cinch saddle. Git up!"

Wyatt gasped and sat up, grinning foolishly.

"What happened?" he asked.

"Nothin'," answered Sandy. "Jest nothin'. Who was your buckaroo friend on the otheh end of the rope?"

"I dunno. Never saw him before to-night."

"Pal of Jim Plimsoll?"

"I dunno. Nobuddy I know. Nobuddy you know, I reckon."

"I'll know him likely next time I run across him," said Sandy. "He's packin' a saddle brand I put on him." His voice was grimly humorous, he recognized Wyatt's obstinacy as something not without merit. "How's yore haid?"

"Some tender."

"It ain't in first-rate condition or you w'udn't be drawin' pay from Plimsoll. Yore saddle's here, yore hawss went west. Ef you want to leave the saddle till you locate the hawss, you can git it 'thout any trouble any time you come fo' it. Or you can pack it with you now. We're goin' up to camp."

"Figger it's safe to leave yore claims now?" asked Wyatt cheerfully.

"I don't figger we'll be jumped ag'in befo' mornin'," replied Sandy. "Ef we are, why, we'll have to start the arguments all over."

"I w'udn't be surprised," said the philosophic Wyatt, gingerly pressing his head with his fingertips, "but what there is a gen'ral impression 'stablished by this time that you three hombres from the Three Star are right obstinate about considerin' this yore property."

"You leavin' camp with Plimsoll in the mornin'?" Mormon asked casually.

"I heard some rumor about his hittin' the sunrise trail," said Wyatt. "Ef he goes, I stay. I'm a li'l' fed up on Jim Plimsoll lately. He pulls too much on his picket line to suit me. Ef he's got a yeller stripe on his belly, I'm quittin'. Some day he's goin' to git inter a hole that'll sure test his standard. Me, I may be a bit of a wolf, but I'm damned ef I trail with coyotes. I'll leave my saddle. Any of you got the makin's? I seem to have lost most everything but my clothes. I shed a gun round here somewheres."

"You can have it when you come back fo' yore saddle, Wyatt," said Sandy. "Where was you an' yore unknown pal goin' to repo't back to Plimsoll?"

Wyatt grinned in the lantern light.

"Ef we trailed inter his place an' made a bet on the red over to the faro table he'd sabe everything went off fine an' dandy. He w'udn't figger we'd show at all if it didn't come off. An' we w'udn't have."

"There was one or two mo' staked out in the brush, 'less my hearin's gone back on me," said Sandy. "Seemed to me I heard 'em makin' their getaway. I suppose you don't know their names, either?"

"No, sir, I sure don't. An' I don't imagine they'll be showin' up at Plimsoll's right off. It was a win-or-lose job. Pay if it was pulled off. Otherwise, nothin' doin'. You hombres treated me white. There's a lot who'd have plugged me full of lead an' death. I was on yore land. Ef you force me to walk into Plimsoll's Place ahead of you I ain't resistin' none, an' I shall sure admire to watch Plim's face when he sees you-all back of me."

He took the trail ahead of them, hands in his pockets, his cigarette glowing. Behind him walked Sandy. Wyatt finished his smoke and started to hum a tune.

> "Oh, I'm wild an' woolly an' full of fleas,
>
> I'm hard to curry below the knees.
>
> I'm a wild he-wolf from Cripple Crick,
> An' this is my night to howl.
>
> "I ain't got a friend but my hawss an' gun,
>
> The last kin shoot an' the first kin run,
>
> An' I'm a rovin' son-of-a-gun,
> An' this is my night to howl."

"He's a cool sort of a cuss," said Sam to Mormon. "I reckon he's a bad actor, but there's sure somethin' erbout the galoot I like. He ain't over fond of Plimsoll, that's a sure thing, if he is workin' fo' him. Wonder why?"

"They tell me," replied Mormon, "thet Plimsoll's apt to be fond of the other feller's gal. He ain't satisfied with what he can pick for himself. T'otheh feller's apple allus has a sweeter core.

I w'udn't wondeh but what that was the trouble. Plim ain't got any mo' respect fo' wimmen than hell has fo' fryin' souls."

"Uh-huh! He w'udn't go round pickin' a scrap with Roarin' Russell on their account, fer instance?"

Mormon paid no attention to the friendly gibe. As they entered the street of the camp, largely deserted, though there was every evidence of crowds forgetting time in the drinking and gambling shacks, Sandy moved up even with Wyatt and locked arms with him.

"I ain't goin' ter make no break," said Wyatt. "Here's Plim's. Jest you let me go in ahead through the door. I've seen you use your guns. I ain't suicidin'."

They allowed him to go in first, unescorted. Their plans held no further reprisal against Wyatt.

Plimsoll's place was crowded. There were more onlookers than actual players though the tables were fairly well patronized. Many of those who had seats were only cappers for the game. The majority of the men who had rushed to the new strike had not brought any great sums of money with them, or, if they had, reserved its use for speculation in claims rather than the slimmer chances of Plimsoll's enterprises. In a few days, if the camp produced from grass roots, as was expected and hoped, Plimsoll would gather in his harvest. A garnering in which Sandy had sadly interfered.

Plimsoll had set up a working partnership with a man who had brought moonshine and boot-legged whisky to the camp, occupying the next shack to the gambling place. For convenience of service extra doors had been cut and a rough-boarded passageway erected between the two places. The fever of gambling provided thirsty customers for the liquor dealer, and the whisky blunted the wits of the gamblers and gave the dealers more than their customary percentage of odds in the favor of the house. It was a combination that worked both ways. Waiters impressed into service from camp followers, crudely took orders and delivered them. There were no mixed drinks, no scale of prices. And there was no question of license. The will of the majority ruled. The gold-seeking reduced things to primitive methods, men to primitive manners.

Plimsoll himself presided over the stud-poker table, dealing the game. He showed nothing of the nervousness that crawled beneath his skin. He awaited the result of his play with Wyatt and the latter's companions. If he could make Sandy, Mormon and Sam ridiculous, he would achieve his end, but he hoped for bigger results. Wyatt and his fellow rider had been detailed to ride down the tent that had been reported occupied by the Three Star owners. That part of the plan had been suggested by Wyatt out of the sheer deviltry of his invention. Plimsoll had enlisted others of his following, none too fearless, to loiter in the brush and, in the general confusion, fire to cripple and to kill.

Plimsoll had learned of the visit of the men who had come with Bill Brandon to investigate Plimsoll's methods of running the Waterline Horse Ranch. He had learned, through the leak-age that always occurs in a cattle community, that Brandon claimed to be an old acquaintance of Sandy and his partners. So he had told his men who had come with him to the camp from the Waterline Ranch that the Three Star outfit was a danger to all of them, undoubtedly acting as spies for Brandon, and that they should be eliminated for the general good. But there was none of them, from Plimsoll down, who had any fancy to stand up against the guns of Sandy, or of Mormon and Sam, when the breaks were anywhere nearly even.

So Plimsoll dealt stud and collected the percentage of the house, watching his planted players profit by their professionalism and by the little signs bestowed upon them by Plimsoll that tipped them off as to the value of the hidden cards. Plimsoll, with his ejection from Hereford, the advent of woman suffrage, the coming of Brandon and other irate horse owners, had begun to realize that his days were getting short in the land. He looked to the camp for a final coup. If he held the Casey claims and sold them, as he expected to do, to an eastern capitalist to whom he had telegraphed some days before, he might reestablish himself. Sandy's prompt arrival and subsequent events had crimped that plan and he fell back upon all the crooked tactics that he possessed in gambling. And now, if Wyatt....

He was dealing the last card around when Wyatt came in and his eyes lit up. Then his face stiffened, the light changed to a gleam of malevolence. Following Wyatt were the three partners, taking open order as they came through the entrance, about which the space was clear, Sandy in the middle, Mormon on the right flank and Sam on the left. The two last smiled and nodded to one or two acquaintances. Sandy's face was set in serious cast. The players at Plimsoll's table turned to see what caused the suspension of the game, others followed their example. The Three Star men were known personally to some of those in the room. The story of what had happened during the day had buzzed in everybody's ears, from Roaring Russell's discomfiture to Plimsoll's failure to hold the claims and the eviction notice served on him by Sandy.

The phrase "you'll see me through smoke," held a grim significance that touched the fancy of these gold gatherers, men of the cruder types for the most part. The issue between Sandy and Plimsoll was the paramount topic, they wanted to see the two men face to face and size them up. There was no especial sympathy with one or the other. There were other gamblers to provide them with excitement. Mormon's challenge of Russell was a sporting event that appealed to them more directly and there were many possessed of a rough chivalry that appreciated the heavyweight cowman's taking up the cudgels on behalf of a woman. But that was sport, this was a business matter, a duel, with Death offering services as referee.

Chairs edged back, the standing moved for a better view-point, the room focussed on Plimsoll, Wyatt and the three cow-chums. Then Wyatt stepped aside. There was a malicious little grin on his face. Mormon's suggestion as to his private grudge against Plimsoll was not without foundation. Wyatt had been glad to find excuse for severing relations with the gambler. He had done his best and failed, but his failure was not bitter.

The partners walked between the tables toward Plimsoll who sat regarding them balefully, his teeth just showing between his parted lips, cards in midair, action in a paralysis that was caused by the concentration forced by Sandy's even gaze, by the same sickening conviction that his manhood shriveled in front of Sandy and that Sandy knew it. Oaths against Wyatt rose automatically in his brain like bubbles in a mineral spring, together with the consciousness that Wyatt, if not allied against him, was no longer for him, that his chosen tools lacked edge. The placing of bets ceased, there was no sound of clicking chips, the roulette dealer held the wheel, expectant, dealer and case-keeper at the faro bank halted their manipulations, the presiding genius of the craps layout picked up the dice. Tragedy hovered, the shadow of its wing was on the dirt floor of the rude Temple of Chance.

"The chaps you sent up to move yore tent an' truck didn't make a good job of it, Plimsoll," drawled Sandy. "I reckon they warn't the right so't of help. Ef you-all are aimin' to take that stuff erlong with you I'd recommend you 'tend to it yorese'f. It's gettin' erlong to'ards sun-up, fast as a clock can tick."

Silence held. Sandy stood non-committal, at ease. His conversation with Plimsoll might have been of the friendliest nature gauged by his attitude. His hands were on his hips. Back of him, slightly turning toward the crowd, were Mormon and Sam, smilingly surveying the room. But not one there but knew that, faster than the ticking of a clock, guns might gleam and spurt fire and lead in case of trouble. It was all being done ethically enough. They did not know exactly what the entrance of Wyatt meant, but Sandy's talk gave them a hint and his poise was correct, without swagger, without intent to start general ruction. It was up to Plimsoll.

"I'll attend to my own business in my own way," said the gambler, knowing the room weighed every word. It was a non-committal statement and a light one, but it passed the situation for the moment. His eyes shifted to Wyatt, shining with hate, the whites blood-flecked by suppressed passion.

Sandy pulled out a gunmetal watch.

"I make it half afteh one. 'Bout three hours to sunrise, Plimsoll. I'll be round later." He turned his back on the gambler and sauntered toward the door. Before the general restraint broke Mormon put up his hand.

"I figger Roarin' Russell ain't in the room," he said. "Ef he happens erlong, some of you might tell him I was lookin' fo' him. An' I'm goin' to keep on lookin'," he added.

There was a laugh that swelled into a roar of approval in the general reaction.

"Good for you!" A dozen phrases of commendation chimed and jangled. A few followed the three out into the street, among them, Wyatt.

"I got a hunch it ain't extry healthy fo' me in there," he said. "A gamblin' parlor where I ain't welcome to stay or play makes no hit with me. I'll help you-all find Russell."

The search was not an easy one. Russell had been seen freely in the makeshift saloons and other places on both sides of the street. It seemed, from what they could glean and put together, that he had stopped drinking when he had arrived at a certain point in his boasting and had announced his intention of sobering up before he "took the bloody, hog-bellied cow-puncher apart, providin' the latter showed." This suited Mormon, who wanted fairly to whip a live opponent, not fight a staggering drunkard. But they could not find him. They had several volunteer assistants who proved useless. Sam began to yawn.

"I ain't sleepy, I'm hungry," he said. "Let's go get us a steak oveh to Simpson's. If he's gone to bed we'll rout him out. Won't be the first time he turned out to cook me a meal. A shot of that Rocky Mountain grapejuice w'udn't go so bad. Mormon, a feed 'ud round you out. Roarin' Russell has crawled in somewheres an' died of heart failure. Come on, hombres."

Simpson was awake and dressed and on the job. His place was almost as well filled as it had been the first time they entered it. In the first seethe of the gold excitement no one seemed to get sleepy, while appetites developed. Word had preceded them that Mormon Peters was looking for Roaring Russell and their entrance caused more than a ripple of interest. Simpson came bustling forward to serve them.

"Good thick rare steak's what you want, ain't it? Fine fightin' food. Me, I'm takin' in a few bets on you, Mormon. 'Member the time you got a hammerlock on that long-horned gent from Texas with the Lazy Z outfit? I cleaned up on you that time an' this'll be a repeater. This same Roarin' Russell has been tellin' the camp what a rip-snortin', limb-loosenin', strong-armed galoot he is, an' some of 'em have swallered it. They ain't seen you in action, Mormon, an' I have. You'll jest natcherly chaw him inter hash. I'm bettin' there won't be enough of him left to stuff a Chili pepper after you git through."

"I ain't as limber as I was, Alf," said Mormon deprecatingly. "Make my steak thick, will you? Have you seen anything of the Roarin' gent?"

"Not personal. He don't eat here. There was a friend of yores in a while ago who seemed to be sort of keepin' tabs on him. That young assayer Russell started to bulldoze when Sandy took a hand. Said he'd be in ag'in later. 'Peared to think you was bound to show before mornin'."

Simpson went to the back of his shack and started the steaks. A waiter brought over drinks of the Rocky Mountain grapejuice with the information that they were "on the house."

"It ain't the hooch we're sellin'," he said. "This is private stock, hundred proof." He eyed Mormon professionally as he hung about the table, setting out the battered cutlery and tin plates that Simpson provided. "They was offerin' two to one on Roarin' Russell a little while ago," he volunteered. "I think I'll take up a piece of their money."

"This ain't a prize-fight, it's a privut quarrel," said Mormon as he smelled the fiery stuff in the glass, sipped it and then swallowed it in one gulp. "That's prime stuff."

"You'll have one hell of a time keepin' it privut, mister," said the waiter. "They tell me there's nigh to six hundred folks in the camp an' there won't be many more'n six missin' when you two meet up. You want to watch out for Russell's pals, though; they ain't the gentlest bunch in the herd. But I reckon you can handle 'em," he said, turning to Sandy. "I saw you handlin' your hardware this mornin' an' you sure can juggle a gun."

A call from another of the makeshift tables claimed his attention. Simpson came hurrying with the meat, biscuits and coffee. He sat down with them, offering more drinks which they refused.

"Slack right now," he said, "but I sure have done a whale of a business to-day. If this keeps up I don't want no claims. They're tellin' me you give Plimsoll till sun-up to git out of camp, Sandy. I don't figger there'll be any argyment. He's yeller as the yolk of a rotten aig. Hell w'udn't take him in, he ain't fit to be fried. Gittin' rid of him an' his crowd'll sure purify the air in this camp. Times ain't like they used to be. This ain't the frontier any more and a few bad men can't run a strike to suit themselves. If the camp's no good it'll peter out like it did afore; if it amounts to anything, we'll have a police station on one end of this street, a fire station at t'other an' streetcars runnin' down the middle, inside of a month. Plimsoll's gettin' a bum name in this county. The wimmin are ag'in' him. An' I tell you, gents, we hombres 'll have to watch our steps or they'll be takin' our vote away from us next thing you know. It's a lucky thing for us that men is in the majority in this section. Here's yore friend now."

Westlake came through the door, looked round, saw them and came over.

"Russell is down at the Chinaman's eating shack by the bridge," he announced. "He's been drinking black coffee to sober up on. He's got some of his own sort with him. I think they're nearly ready to come up-street. He knows you are in camp and looking for him."

"Then we'd better be shackin' erlong," said Mormon, mopping up gravy with half a biscuit. "I w'udn't want to keep him waitin'."

Outside, it was apparent that the whole camp was waiting for the appearance of the two principals in an event that was not to be allowed to be dealt with purely as a personal encounter. The waiter's estimate was a fair one. The moon had risen, sailing round and fair and mild of beam from behind the eastern hills, making pallid by comparison the artificial flares. The one street was packed with men, not all of whom were sober. The crowd thickened every moment from outlets of the gambling shacks and saloons. All other business and pleasure was forgotten with the swift word passing to say that the cowman who had slapped the bully in the face and challenged him that morning to a catch-as-catch-can, free-for-all contest, was now in Alf Simpson's Chuck House while his opponent, in the cold range of enforced, semi-sobriety, was in Su Sing's Hashery, the pair about to emerge.

This was to be better than any gunplay, a gladiatorial combat to delight the hearts of frontiersmen. And they warmed to it. All day there had been rumors busy of the clash, of the matters involved. Garbled versions of the truth ran excitement up to hot-blood heat. The town had stayed up for developments. Bets had been made on Plimsoll's backing down at sunrise; on the cowman, Mormon; on the bully, Russell.

The affair with Plimsoll at sun-up was likely to be short and sharp. Men who knew the three from the Three Star Ranch spread their opinions. The prime event was the scrap. Russell was, or had been, a professional wrestler and held fame as a rough-and-tumble fighter. Mormon had once beaten all comers for the Cow Belt. The spectators swarmed like bees and buzzed as busily. They came in from the claims, warned by their friends. They greeted Mormon with a shout and one bulk of them surged down toward the bridge over Flivver Creek, escorting the three partners and Westlake, Simpson and his help with them. More were milling up-street from Su Sing's place, Russell in their midst. Where the two factions met, the principals kept apart by the crowd, a broad-shouldered giant with the voice of a bull and a beard that crimped low on his chest, harangued the multitude from a wagon-box. They halted to listen, like a crowd at a fair.

"Gents all," bellowed the big man. "There's been some tall talkin' done to-day between two hombres who have agreed to see which is the best man, in man fashion, usin' the strength an' skill that God gave 'em, without recourse to gun, knife or slungshot. Roarin' Russell, champeen wrastler, allows he can lick any man in camp. Mormon Peters, champeen holder of the Cow Belt, 'lows he can't. That's the cause an' reason of the combat. Any other reason that has been mentioned is private between the two principals an' none of our damned business."

The crowd roared in approval of the speaker's style and the force of his breezy delivery. He had touched their chivalry in thus delicately alluding to the episode of the insult and apology to the only woman in camp.

"Therefore," he went on, and the word slipped round that he was Lem Pardee, wealthy rancher and ex-representative of the state, "such an affair appealin' to every red-blooded male among us, it behooves us to see it brought off in due form, fair an' square to both parties, in a bare-fisted settlement — an' may the best man win."

More howls went up, dying as he held up his hand.

"There's level ground below the bridge with free seats an' standin' room for all on both sides. The moon graces the occasion an' provides the proper illumination. I move you that a referee be appointed to discuss fightin' rules with Roarin' Russell an' Mormon Peters, to settle all side bets, with power to app'int a committee to keep the side lines an' take up a suitable purse for the winner. Referee will give the decision, if necessary, an' settle all disputes."

Shouts that drowned all others nominated Pardee as chief official. He accepted the choice with a wave of his hand and, glancing about him, rapidly picked five men as his committee. Two of them he did not know by name but selected from his judgment of men, and his choices met with general approval.

"The principals will choose their own seconds," he said. "Not more than three to each man, to act only in that capacity and in no way to interfere. That's all."

In two factions the crowd moved down the slant of the street, turned aside at the bridge and, as Pardee indicated the level space on the nigh side of the creek that trickled down the gulch like quicksilver in the moonlight, ranged themselves about the natural arena while the committee established the side lines and the referee conferred with Mormon, Russell and their seconds in the open. Sandy and Sam appointed themselves corner men for Mormon, and Sandy asked Westlake to make the third. A roulette dealer from Plimsoll's and a bartender ranged themselves alongside Russell, together with Plimsoll himself. Pardee eyed the group.

"There's bad blood between you two," he said to Plimsoll and Sandy. "I understand you've got your own grudges. You'd better keep clear of this. And I'm tellin' you both this," he added. "This camp is in the rough-and-ready stage, but there's enough of us who've got together to see it's goin' to be run decent an' regular. We're goin' to establish fair play and order, from now on. We don't expect to run no man's affairs so long's they don't interfere with the general welfare of the camp, but, if there's any dirty work pulled off, the man that spills the dirt is goin' to be interviewed pronto. Things are goin' to be run clean. We ain't goin' to give this camp a bad name at the start."

"Suits me," said Sandy. "My blood's runnin' cool enough, Pardee."

"I'm not talkin' personal, 'cept so far as this bout is concerned. You two had better stay out of it."

Sandy stepped back and Plimsoll, after a few whispered words to Russell, followed suit.

"You men want another second apiece?" asked Pardee. "Or are two enough?"

"The Roarin' gent," said Mormon, "made his brags an' I took it up. Me, I don't know nothin' about Queensbury rules an', though the camp seems to have arranged this affair to suit itself, I didn't bargain for no boxin' match, nor no wrastlin' match either. It's either he can lick me, man to man, or I lick him. An' a lickin' don't mean puttin' down shoulders on a mat. If a man goes down, t'other lets him git up, if he can. Bar kickin', bitin', gougin' an' dirty work, an' to hell with yore seconds an' yore rounds. This ain't no exhibition. It's a fight!"

He spoke loudly enough for most of the crowd to hear, and they cheered him till the hills echoed.

"That suit you, Russell?" asked Pardee sharply.

Russell, stripping to the waist, belting himself, stood forward.

"Suits me," he said. "Suit me better to cut out all this talk an' get this over with. It won't take long."

He was a formidable-looking adversary. In the moonlight certain signs of puffiness, of dissipation, did not show, save for rolls of fat about shoulders and paunch. He was powerfully built, his chest matted with black hair, his forearms rough with it. Taller than Mormon, he had all the advantage of reach. He sneered openly at his opponent.

"One thing more," said Mormon. "We ain't fightin' fo' a purse. Roarin' knows what we're fightin' fo'. A private matter. But we'll put up a stake, if he's agreeable. Loser leaves the camp."

"When he's able to walk. You slapped my face this morning. This evens it."

Russell lashed out suddenly, his hand open, striking with the heel of his palm for Mormon's jaw. Mormon sprang back, warding off, but it was Pardee who struck aside Russell's blow and sent him reeling back with a powerful shove.

"Strip down," he said to Mormon. "Both of you keep back of your lines till I give the word. Sabe?" He scored two lines in the dirt with the toe of his shoe and waved them behind the marks.

"No rounds to this affairs," he called to the crowd. "Fair fightin', foul holds and punches barred. Everything else goes. Man down allowed ten seconds. That's my ruling," he added to the two men.

Mormon looked clumsy as a bear as he waited for the word. He was far stouter than Russell. His bald pate, with its reddish fringe of hair, looked grotesque under the moon. The bulge of his stomach seemed a strong handicap in agility and wind. Yet his flesh was hard and, where the tan ended on neck and forearms, it held a glisten that caused the knowing ones to nod approvingly. There was strength in his back, big muscles shifted on his shoulders and his arms were bigger than Russell's, if shorter, corded with pack of sinew and muscle. As he toed his line, swaying from side to side, arms apart, the left a little forward, he moved with a lightness strange to his usual tread. Russell crouched a little, his long arms hanging low, knees bent. The two lines were about six feet apart.

They faced each other in a silence of held breath on all sides. Pardee stood to one side, equally between them. His arm went up.

"Ready?" he asked. "Let her go!"

A great sigh went up as the two fighters leaped forward. Both seemed about to clinch, to test their prowess as wrestlers. Murmurs went up from back of Mormon where his fanciers had ranged themselves. "Russell's got too many tricks for him," men told each other and then gasped.

Mormon had landed, light as a dancing master, despite his bulk, had stooped, turned in a flash with his right hand clamped about the right wrist of Russell, bowing his back, heaving with all his might.

Russell, shifting at the last second from a clutch, seeing Mormon charging, swung a vicious uppercut. He made the mistake of underestimating Mormon, thinking him slow-witted. He found his wrist in a vise, his arm twisted, bent down across the thick ridge of the cowman's shoulder, the powerful heave of Mormon's back. His own impetus served against him. Mormon shifted grips, he cupped Russell's elbow with his right palm and crowded all his energy into one dynamic effort of pull and hoist. Russell went over his head in a Flying Mare as the crowd stood up and yelled.

Surprised off his feet, Russell's experience served him in good stead as they left the ground. Mormon's trick had scored, but it was an old one and had its counter-move. As he landed, legs flexed, he twisted, grabbed Mormon's arm with his free one and jerked him forward, hunching a shoulder under the cowman's stomach. The pair of them rolled together on the ground, struggling and clubbing, while the spectators shouted themselves hoarse and smote each other great blows. Pardee, stepping warily, watched the writhing pair.

Russell, wiser at this game, contrived leverage, twisting Mormon, and pinned his arms in a scissors grip while he battered at his face and Mormon writhed to get away from the reach of those long arms. The soft dust clouded about them and their grunts came out from it as they struggled. Once, with Mormon striving to open the leg grip, jerking away from the flailing blows, they rolled perilously near a clump of prickly pear on the verge of their little arena and a universal cry of warning went up.

The two heard nothing of it in their hammer and tongs affair, the superheated blood, stoked by passion, surging through their veins.

Mormon felt the pressure of Russell's thigh-muscles closing relentlessly, clamping down on his chest, shutting off oxygen. His energy waned, his limbs grew heavy, nerveless, his brain clogged and dulled. He set his chin well down into his neck to save his jaw, but his right cheek was pounded, one eye closing. It was only a matter of moments before he must relax and then Russell would pin him down with one arm and send in the final smashing blow. He felt himself suffocating, sinking — the noise of roaring waters dinned in his ears.

He lay on his back, Russell on his side, one leg below, one leg above Mormon's body, bending at the hips in his efforts to reach the cowman's jaw. He bent a fraction too much, the scissors grip shifted imperceptibly and the message of that weakening of the chain flashed to Mormon's hazy brain. With every muscle taut in one supreme convulsion he managed to twist sidewise, back to Russell, opening the grip that now compressed shoulders instead of chest and back. He got a breath of air, dust-laden but blessed. His chest expanded, strength flowed in, he forced his arms apart, rolling over on Russell, crushing him into the soft earth with his weight. Another wriggling twist and he faced his man, bringing his mighty back into play to break clear. He got a forearm across Russell's Adam's apple, regardless of the blows that smashed into his face. He hammered home one jolt hard to the jaw and, as Russell's body grew limp, dragged himself from the relaxing hold and crouched on hands and knees, wheezing, spent, gulping air to his flattened lower lungs that refused to function.

Now he could hear the shouting of the crowd, a clatter of yells. He saw Russell's head move, his eyes opening in the moonlight. Mechanically Mormon stood up, swaying, bruised, one eye useless. Pardee began counting over Russell, according to the ruling he had made.

Russell rolled over on his face. It looked as if he was not going to try to get up. This was not how Mormon had wanted the fight to end, in a technical knockout, with his man beginning to come back and he not allowed to finish him.

Pardee had put in the clause, "Man down allowed ten seconds, with the other on his feet," merely to make a better, longer fight of it from the spectator's standpoint. It was supposed to be the sporting thing to do, but Mormon, blood-flushed, brain-dull, had no thought of ethics at that moment. Russell was lifting himself to knees and elbows, crouching as Mormon had done, watching his opponent, listening to the count. He was going to get up. He *was* up at nine, stooping, groggy, his long arms hanging low, and a shout went up from his backers as Pardee stepped aside.

Russell began to back away, to describe a half-circle, right forearm across his chest, left arm extended, both in slight motion. Mormon stood like a baited bear, slowly revolving to face Russell, wary of a feint to draw him out. There were smears of blood on Russell's arms, on his face, dark in the moonlight. Mormon's whiter skin showed greater defacement. There was a mouse swelling above his eye, the lids were clamping.

The ring of spectators was almost silent now, leaning forward, watching. Little jerky sentences passed between them.

"Russell's goin' to box." "He can beat the cowman at that game." "Cut him to ribbons. Blind him first."

The man in the crowd was right. Mormon knew little of boxing, but he knew enough to throw a cushion of sturdy arm across his jaw, the left elbow crooked, nose buried in it, eyes — one eye — indomitable above it. And the blunted elbow like a ram, as he ducked and Russell's straight right slid over his bald pate. He was far faster, lighter on his feet than Russell dreamed. The bully still underestimated his man, but woke to vivid and just appraisal as Mormon's elbow smashed against his collar-bone, left forearm clubbing his nose, starting spurts of blood, right fist coming up like a piston in short-armed, jolting upper-cuts.

Desperately Russell clutched, failed; held, clung, half tumbling into a clinch. Mormon's arms were about him, underneath, binding him with hoops of steel, compressing. He lost his footing, began to rise and he back-heeled in an outside click. They both went down together side by side in a dog-fall. Mormon loosed his arms as he rolled atop, got astride of Russell, strove to gather and control the arms that thrashed and smote.

Something jagged crushed against Mormon's temple. It seemed as if the skull split open and a jagged, red-hot probe searched through his brain. He threw up his head in agony, his chin exposed, but instinct still awake to fling out both hands, catch the oncoming blow, his fingers clamping deep about the wrist above the hand that held the rock — some ore fragment tossed away by an old-timer — that Russell had found in the dirt, and used in unfair, murderous intent.

The maddening pain of first impact died to a throb as the blood poured down, seeming to leave his brain clear, cold with a rage that responded to a deep disgust of the bully who was now at his mercy. For, with the rage came absolute conviction that this was the end of the fight.

He screwed unmercifully, flesh and sinews and the small bones of the wrist, until Russell shrieked through his swollen mouth at the anguish of it and dropped the rock. Pardee, hovering near, seeing all, picked it up and slipped it into his pocket as Mormon pinned down Russell's arm with his left knee and swung left and right in sledge-hammer blows to the jaw of the face that tried in vain to dodge the knockout. As if a galvanic current that had simulated life had suddenly been shut off, Roaring Russell's body lost all energy, it seemed to flatten, lay without a quiver.

Mormon got on his feet and stood to one side while Pardee counted off the seconds that were only a grim parody. Russell's brain was short-circuited. There was not even a tremor of his eyelids. Pardee knelt, felt pulse and heart. Then he beckoned to the loser's seconds.

"Come and get your man," he told them. "He's through for this evening."

Pandemonium broke loose as the crowd broke formation and surged down. Four men packed off Roaring Russell, limp and sagging between them. Pardee exhibited the chunk of ore, stained with Mormon's blood, while Sandy, Sam and Westlake ramparted Mormon from enthusiastic admirers and pushed down to the creek where he washed his hurts with the stinging icy water and stiffly put on his clothes.

"Knew he was licked and figured he might get away with it," declared Pardee. "Lucky it didn't split his head open." Murmurs gathered force against the bully's methods.

"Cut out the lynching talk, boys," cried Pardee. "The man's been beaten up. I wouldn't wonder if his jaw was bu'sted. His nose is. Let him go; we'll see that he leaves the camp as soon as he can hobble." He broke through to Mormon, being assisted into his coat by Sandy. "How are you standing up, old bearcat?" asked the referee. "I thought he had you nipped once but you walloped him."

"Me? I'm jest about standin' up, an' that's all," said Mormon, gingerly feeling certain places on his face. "I sure thought it was my brains oozin' when he swiped me with that rock. But my bone's pritty solid in the head, I reckon. I don't mind tellin' you-all I'm feelin' a good deal like a bass drum at the end of a long parade, but I believe it's all on the outside. And I ain't entered for any beauty show — at present."

"Eleven minutes of straight fighting by the watch," said a man.

Mormon looked at him humorously, and one-eyed.

"Seemed mo' like 'leven hours to me." He caught sight of Simpson, holding out a flask. "Now that's what I call a friend," he started, his hand outstretched. Then it dropped and a blank look came over his face.

"Let's git out of this," he murmured to Sandy. "Dern me if I didn't plumb forgit about any chance of her showin' up."

"Here's where you git called a hero," said Sam. "She knows what you've been fightin' erbout. More'n that she's been in the crowd for the last five minnits of the scrap. That right, Westlake?"

"Yes. I saw her come into the crowd with young Ed. She wants to thank you, Mormon. No use dodging it."

Young Ed was maneuverin' through to their side.

"Aunt wants to see you," he announced with a grin. "We heard the row down here, an' she sent me to see what it was. When I didn't hurry back she trailed me. Great snakes, Mormon, but you sure whaled him!"

"Huh!" Mormon said nothing but that mystic monosyllable until they reached the place where Miranda Bailey stood apart from the crowd who deferentially gave her room, whispering her supposed share in the recent event. She did not look much like the heroine of a romance, neither did Mormon resemble a hero. Her somewhat worn but wholesome face was set in forbidding lines, but Westlake and Sandy fancied they saw the ghost of a twinkle in her eyes. She greeted Mormon as if he had been a disgraced schoolboy.

"What have you been fightin' about?" she demanded.

But, like Russell, she underestimated Mormon. His one working eye was innocent of all guile as he looked at her.

"Fightin' fo'? Jest fo' the fun of it, marm."

She surveyed him grimly and then her features softened.

"I reckon yo're too tough to get hurt much," she said. "I can fix up that eye. I sh'ud think a man of yore age 'ud have more sense than fightin' at all in front of a crowd of hoodlums who ought to be asleep, 'stead of disturbin' the whole camp, let alone for sech a ridicklus reason."

"I didn't think the reason ridicklus," said Mormon, and the spinster's lips twitched.

"What he wants is a lancin' an' a chunk of raw beef," put in Simpson, with a sympathetic wink at Mormon that suggested more pungent remedies in the background. "Come up to my place."

There may have been some thought of trade from the many who would want to see the victor at close range. Mormon hesitated, all slowly moving toward the bridge. Men were staring toward the mesa whence came a high-powered car, rushing at high speed, magnificently driven, taking curve and pitch and level with superb judgment. Its lights flamed out on the night. It turned and came on, stopping on the bridge, blocked by the crowd that made slow opening for it. The driver, in chauffeur's livery, sat immobile, controlling the car, his worldly-wise, blasé face like a mask. Two men were in the tonneau. One of them leaned forward, looking at the crowd, a square-jawed man, clean-shaven but for the bristle of a silver mustache beneath an aggressive nose, above a firm hard mouth and determined chin. The mintage of the East was stamped upon his features. He was a man accustomed to sway, if not to lead. His companion was as plainly as eastern product, but his manner was subordinate though his face that, alone of the three, seemed to hold a measure of fearful wonder at the turbulent throng of men, was shrewd enough.

"I'm looking for a man named Plimsoll," said the first of these two, his voice an indication that he was accustomed to a quick answer. "He wired me about some claims. Where'll I find him?" He made no question concerning the crowd, his eyes passed casually over Mormon's damaged countenance, over the procession that bore Russell, sack-fashion. Here was a man who, at any hour of the twenty-four, was primed for business and for profit.

Yet he could not fail but see that his question charged the crowd with some emotion he could not fathom. The night was spent, it was getting close to dawn. The issue between Sandy Bourke and Plimsoll, crowded aside for the moment, was now paramount. Some craned for sight of the two-gun man, others glanced toward the eastern sky. The stars seemed to be losing their brilliance, the golden moon turning silver, the high horizon, jagged with mountain crests, appeared to be gaining form and a third dimension.

"You'll likely find him at his place," answered a miner. "Up-street on the left. Name's outside."

They let the car go on in a lane that was pressed out of their ranks. They fell in behind or alongside of it as it passed slowly up the street. One or two of the bolder got on the running boards unchecked. The easterner who was looking for Plimsoll took in the situation as something beyond his present range, accepting it. Sandy turned to Mormon.

"You better see Miss Mirandy up to her claim," he said, his voice casual enough. Mormon started an appeal but it died unvoiced. The spinster knew nothing of the clash impending between Sandy and the gambler, neither did her nephew, who, the excitement of the fight over, yawned and went off with his aunt and Mormon.

"I'll bring you up that chunk of meat, Mormon," whispered Sam. "An' I'll bring you somethin' stronger, same time."

"Don't bring it all on yore breath," Mormon whispered back. "If I hear any shootin' I'll come back lopin'."

"There won't be any shootin'," said Sam. "You go soak that eye of yores in Mirandy Bailey's sage tea. Me 'n' Sandy, we'll handle Plimsoll." Then Sam broke clear from Mormon and hurried after Sandy and Westlake.

Sandy walked up the street without hurry and, as they had made way from the car, men gave him space. The nearer he got to Plimsoll's place the more room they allowed him. They melted away from the car on all sides, leaving it clearest between the machine and the entrance to the gambling shack. The chauffeur preserved his bored look and carved attitude. His face was lined with lack of sleep and the strain of driving at high speed over unknown mountain roads, powdered gray with dust. He seemed almost an automaton. The man with the square face looked alertly about him at the crowd, giving place to the lean tall man walking leisurely up the street, high lights touching the metal of the two guns that hung in holsters well to the front of his hips. Sandy's face was serene, but there was no mistaking the fact that the star performer of the moment had come upon the stage. Five paces back of him strolled Sam, his eyes dancing with the excitement that did not show in Sandy's steel-gray orbs. Westlake followed to one side, by the advice of Sam.

The stranger saw that Sandy walked lightly, on the balls of his feet, with a springy tread. He appraised his face, frown-lines appeared between his eyebrows and he half rose in his seat. Then the door of the cabin opened and the man who had volunteered to find Plimsoll emerged.

"He's comin' right along," he announced.

It was Plimsoll's way — the professional gambler's way — to play his cards until he knew himself beaten. He had been hoping for the arrival of this man. He represented capital, the development of the camp into a mining town, the movement of money, the boom of quick sales. With his backing — once the camp understood what it meant to all of them — he might turn the tables on Sandy Bourke. The protection of Capital was powerful.

He came out licking his lips nervously, with a swift survey that took in the setting of the stage prepared for his entrance. His eyes, shifting from the big machine, as if drawn by something beyond his will, focused on the figure of Sandy, easy but sinister in its capacity to avoid all melodrama. Half-way between door and car he halted.

"Plimsoll?" said the stranger. "I am Keith."

The light was perceptibly changing. Faces of men came out of the shadows, pale but visible. The lights of the machine changed from yellow to pale lemon, the flares outside the cabins, the illumination of the windows altered. High up, a tiny fleck of cloud caught the fire of the as yet unseen sun, rolling on to dawn behind the range. Things seemed flat, lacking full definition, lacking shadow. In the east the sky showed gray behind the dark purple crests between which mists were trailing. Men shivered, half from cold, half from tension and lack of sleep.

"Plimsoll," said Sandy. "That peak oveh on Sawtooth Range is goin' to catch the light first. I'll call it sun-up when the sun looks oveh the mesa."

Plimsoll bared his teeth in a fox-grin. Sandy stood with his hands by his sides, covering him with his eyes. Plimsoll looked at the hands that he knew could move swifter than he could follow, he looked at the car with Keith gazing from him to Sandy, he sensed the waiting strain of all the men, waiting to see Sandy shoot — if he did not go, to see him crumple up in the dust, and — he looked at the peak on Sawtooth and his face grayed as the granite suddenly flushed with rose. His will melted, he turned and went inside his cabin. No one followed him, there was no one inside to greet him. His heart was filled with helpless rage, centered against Sandy Bourke. He knew the camp was against him, considering him outbluffed or outmatched. His horse, ready saddled, had been at the door since midnight. He mounted, dug spurs into the beast's flanks and went galloping madly up the slope that rose from the street gulch leading down to the main gulch of Flivver Creek. He was shortcutting for the mesa road, hate in his heart, his blood, his brain; poisoning hate that turned all his secretions to gall. His plans for wealth had been blocked by a man he dared not face. Before Sandy Bourke his spirit flinched as a leaf shrinks and curls from flame. The forced acknowledgment of it was an acid aggravation. He raked his horse's flanks with his rowels and the spirited brute, pick of all Plimsoll's horse herd, tore up the hillside to suit the mad humor of his master, who was permeated with the venom of a man who knows his deeds at once evil and futile, a venom that was bound to spread until the infection mastered him, body and mind and soul, steeped them in a devil's brew that permitted of no other thought but what was dominated by the mad desire to get even.

Some one caught sight of the galloping horse and rider lunging along in a cloud of dust that showed golden as the sun rose and looked over the mesa. He raised a shout that was joined in by the rest, that reached the flying Plimsoll as the view-halloo reaches the fox making for its earth.

The man named Keith called to Sandy Bourke who, for the moment, still stood alone, now rolling a cigarette. He was the only man in the close vicinity of the car and he turned at the sound of Keith's voice.

"You-all talkin' to me?" he inquired mildly.

"I would like to know," said Keith in a manner which he appeared struggling to invest with humor, "exactly what is the idea of this theatrical, moving-picture episode?"

Sandy smiled back at him.

"Look like film stuff, to you?" he asked in his drawl. "Surely is movin' pictures to Plimsoll, though it's hell on the hawss. You can let it go at that, if you like. Li'l' western drama entitled *To Be Shot at Sunrise*."

The crowd began to gather closer, curious to find out the reason for the swift advent of the car, the desire to see Plimsoll.

"You were ready to shoot at Plimsoll?"

"I was ready. I didn't figger there was goin' to be much shootin'."

"It looks to me as if you've driven the man out of camp and, as I've come all the way from New York to do business with him, driven the last two hundred miles in this car, I'd be obliged if you would tell me just what was the matter, Mr. — — ?"

"Bourke. Sandy Bourke."

The stranger had managed to muffle down his chagrin and resentment at the outcome of his trip. Of necessity he was a judge of men and it did not take him long to place Sandy. Keith was an adept at adapting himself to his environment.

"Sorry to have upset things fo' you," went on Sandy, "but this was a personal matteh between myse'f an' Plimsoll that had to be settled pronto an' permanent. I don't reckon how you've lost a heap, said Plimsoll bein' a crook."

"My name's Keith, Wilson Keith," said the other. "I don't know that that means much to you as I judge you generally belong to the range rather than the mining camp, but there may be a few in the crowd who know me. I am a mining promoter. Plimsoll had agreed to sell me his interest in certain claims which showed well in assay reports. They alone were insufficient to interest me. When he wired me the news of the general strike, the prospect of development opened and I came on. You seem to have blocked the deal. However, I suppose Plimsoll can be located later. Have you any idea where he might be found?"

"It w'udn't do you one mite of good," said Sandy. "Plimsoll didn't own those claims. Didn't have an interest in 'em. Tried to jump 'em, an' did the jumpin' himse'f. I've got an idea you might have been through here some time back. I heard some eastern folk had been samplin' ore an' I saw some signs up on the Casey claims. Those are the claims Plimsoll tried to sell you, I reckon, for cash, figgerin' on the deal goin' through quick. He 'lowed he'd grubstaked Casey, which was a plumb lie. Casey had a constitutional objection about bein' grubstaked, an' he had none too much use fo' Plimsoll. Plimsoll's got nothin' to prove his end. From now on he won't try to. The claims belong to Molly Casey, the same bein' my legal ward."

"Ah!" Wilson Keith's eyes grew keen and cold. "Have you any interest in them yourself, Mr. Bourke?"

"Me an' my two partners of the Three Star Ranch own one-half interest, equal with Molly," said Sandy easily. His eyes matched those of the promoter and held them for a second or two.

The thought passed through Keith's mind that Sandy's interest, and that of his partners, might have been obtained from the girl under false pretenses, but he was very far from a fool and, among the things he saw in Sandy's eyes, it was clearly written that here was a man who was both absolutely fearless and absolutely honest. He had not seen many such.

"I'll be glad to talk with you later," he said. "Just now I'm ravenous. Any place to eat? And does the camp get up early or just go to bed late?"

The remark raised a laugh in the crowd, now milling good-naturedly about the machine.

"Want to buy any more claims?" asked a voice.

"I might. I've looked over the ground once, I may as well admit, and I've had an expert report upon it. I'd like to have a talk with all of you after I've had some coffee. This is a camp where it will take a great deal of money, of labor and of time to develop it, whether you try to drill and blast yourselves, or pool your interests and install machinery. Did you say which was the best place to eat, Mr. Bourke?"

Sandy recommended Simpson's and pointed it out. Keith, the man with him, his secretary, and the chauffeur, got out and walked stiff-legged to their coffee. The crowd once more had sleep discounted by excitement. Keith had shrewdly said just enough. The seed that he had planted in the suggestion that they pool interests fell in such rich ground that it began sprouting immediately.

Sandy introduced Sam as his partner, Westlake as a mining engineer and assayer. Keith gave Westlake a shrewd appraising glance, and a nod.

"I'm too sleepy myse'f to talk business," said Sandy. "My two pardners are in the same boat. So, if you-all want to look oveh the camp ag'in, Mr. Keith, an' talk business with any one you find awake an' willin', I'll prob'bly see you befo' nightfall. You know where the claims are."

Keith stood for a moment in the door of Simpson's, looking after Sandy.

"A fairly slick article, the man with the two guns, Blake," he said to his secretary. "But he's straight."

"And mighty hard to bend," added Blake with a yawn.

The chauffeur ate apart, devouring enormous quantities of food with as much emotion as a hopper taking in grain. Keith talked matters over with Blake, not because he valued his secretary's opinion, able as he was in his appointed duties, but because it helped Keith to clarify conditions in his own mind.

"There were only a few old-timers in the crowd, Blake," he said. "The rest of them will want to be going back to wherever and whatever they came from as soon as they find this is not a placer proposition. A heap of people heard of a gold rush and think it's always a Tom Tiddler's Ground, like washing out the rich sands of Nome. They'll be glad to sell and take shares for cash."

"Ought to change the name of the camp," suggested Blake. "Dynamite is known as an exploded prospect."

"Thought of that," said Keith. "This is damned good coffee. I'll have another cup....How about Casey Town, after the original discoverer who always believed in the place, but lacked the money for development and wouldn't take in a partner? Picturesque and good stuff for the prospectuses. You might send off some stuff about that, Blake, work in this Sandy Bourke and Plimsoll affair and find out what this all-night racket was about. Good, lively publicity stuff we can use again later on. Romance of Casey's daughter. Wonder where she is?"

He lapsed into silence, swallowing his third cup of coffee in gulps. Blake, who admired his employer's successes, whatever he thought of his methods, did not interrupt him. Keith was planning a campaign, figuring out the best bait for gulls.

Sandy and his companions found Mormon asleep on the Bailey claims. Miranda brewed coffee, and they told her the news of Plimsoll and the arrival of Keith.

"It's too bad you didn't run Plimsoll out of the county, or the state," remarked the spinster. "He'll not rest until he does you some sneakin' injury, soon as he figgers out what'll do you the most harm."

"An' him the least risk," remarked Sam.

"Since the excitement is temp'rarily over," said Miranda dryly, looking at where Mormon snored beneath blankets, "I reckon we better all foller his example. If that man Keith wants to buy my claims I'm willin' to sell. Milkin' is more in my line than minin', I've decided. I had a fool idea we'd pick up nuggets, top of the ground. From what Mr. Westlake tells me, you got to put out a lot of money before you even find out whether you're goin' to see the color of gold."

"Let's hold a pow-wow before we turn in," said Sandy. "Westlake, what do you know about Keith? Anything?"

"I've heard of him. I imagine he started out as a promoter rather than a developer. He has made some lucky strikes. There is no doubt but that he can float this proposition on a large scale, induce others to put money into it. The least likely-looking properties he'll put on the market and tie them up with the reports of any strikes he, or others, may make. He'll put the camp on a working basis. If the gold's here that will be a sound one. You see, Miss Bailey, not every porphyry dyke is going to have a gold lining."

"Do you figger it w'ud pay best to sell him outright or let him form a company?" asked Sandy.

"For your claims, or these of Miss Bailey and her nephew?"

"All of 'em. Didn't you say they were all on the same syncline?"

"Yes. You really want to go by my opinion? I am not too experienced."

"You know a darn sight mo' about it than we do. I'm not takin' Keith's opinion on anything he wants to buy. He's tipped his hand already in showin' how far an' fast he came here. Probably had Plimsoll tied up on an option or he w'udn't have said 's much as he did."

"Then — there is no doubt in my mind that Patrick Casey picked the best side of the gulch. The indications are in sight there. This side the exposed reef may have been ground down below the sylvanite. There are glacial signs all around here. I would say sell these for cash, holding out on price until Keith refuses to offer more. He'll come back for a final bid. But let him organize with your claims."

"The Molly Casey Mine? With fifty-one per cent. of the shares, if we can't get more?"

"He'll squeal like a pig before he grants that," said Westlake. "But he'll have to come through to your terms. Those claims are the big bet of this camp, and he knows it."

It would have surprised Keith had he known how accurately the young engineer he had glanced at and dismissed as almost an amateur at the game, followed the trend of his scheming. There is not much variation in the methods of Mining Promotion, and Westlake was an observer and a conserver of the pith of what he had seen.

"Fifty-one per cent., an' the name's Molly Casey, then," said Sandy. "What's more, you're to be consulting engineer or whatever they call the fat job, Westlake. I'm dawg-tired. Sam, let's you an' me shack over to our claims. We'll leave Mormon where he is till he gits his sleep out, if you've no objection, marm?"

Sandy, Sam and Mormon returned to the Three Star with the papers drawn and signed and the shares of stock issued that gave twenty-six per cent. of the Molly property to her and twenty-five to the three partners. Keith returned to New York with his forty-nine per cent. to weave his plans for the full development of the claims he had acquired.

While he lacked the controlling interest, there was always, he fancied, a chance of division between the four who held control. Either he could get the girl to vote apart from the three partners or he might split them some way or another. But, wisely, he did not count on this. And he took up the task of exploitation with zest, Blake, primed with material and notes gathered on the spot, a ready and expert assistant.

When Wilson Keith made up his mind there was money in a plan — money for Wilson Keith — he lost no time in planning and carrying out all details. He loved the excitement of the gamble, he loved to evolve some play for which he could pat himself upon the back and tell himself how much cleverer he was than the public, swimming up to his golden-baited hooks like so many fish. Thornton, expert mining engineer, believed the prospects good for the new camp at Casey Town; but Keith, with Blake, who was a wizard at publicity, delighted most in the way it lent itself to exploitation.

Blake, nosing here and listening there, while Keith satisfied himself as to the legality of Sandy's guardianship of Molly and the powers that had been granted him to look after all her interests, assuring himself of the speciousness of Plimsoll's claim for grubstake interest. Blake, weaving fact into fiction, compiled the romance of Molly Casey, daughter of the wandering prospector, Patrick Casey; her father's trail-chum by mountain and desert; the death of Casey, the rescue of Molly, the strike at Dynamite.

Much about Sandy's part in it all Blake did not use. He learned little and said nothing of Plimsoll's attempt to get the girl under his control, of the wild ride across the county line. Blake's general canniness concentrated wherever his personal interests were concerned and he had made up his mind that Sandy Bourke was a man whom it would not pay to offend. He might never see the story in print, then again he might, and Blake, very likely, would return to Casey Town once in a while with Keith.

But it was a good story. A Sunday feature story if he could strengthen it a little. If the mine made the girl a millionairess it would carry the yarn as sheer news, but Blake wanted the story to help to carry the mine, to bring in the money from the outside to exploit Casey Town and the Keith holdings.

Keith had the capital and was willing enough to put it into developing the Molly Mine if necessary, but it was a business principle of his never to use his own money when he could get hold of some one else's. His stock in the Molly Mine he meant to hold on to, not to sell, but, with the profits from the sale of his promoter's shares of the "Groups," he expected to mine the Molly claims.

He had turned his eyes toward oil of late, scenting quick turns and this took money. His wife took more, his son, just out of college, took all that he could get. Mrs. Keith seemed to regard her husband's bank-account much as the wife of a farmer might regard the spring in the meadow. With the extravagance of the post-war period, the advance in prices, the amounts she spent were staggering even to Keith, who set no limits on his own ability to make money. To suggest retrenchment would not merely have had small effect upon his wife, but any curtailment would infallibly hurt the standing of the Keith investments. New York was full of people with money to invest. Profiteering, easy-come money, a lot of it. Easy-go money, too, when the profiteers, still dazzled by their riches, totally unconscious of real values, would meet Keith, thinking their money an open sesame to equality with such financiers.

Then Keith entertained them, taking them to his clubs — not his best — to his home where he dazzled them, fogged them in an atmosphere where they were ill at ease though striving to cover it; Keith, drawing them aside when the time was ripe, would tell them of their shrewdness, confess a liking, almost an admiration for them — and let them in on the ground floor.

There were the many who could not be touched personally and, for these, Blake prepared the literature and laid his schemes for real newspaper publicity. Submitting them to Keith, the latter approved. Mrs. Keith was to look Molly up at her school, take her into the Keith home on vacations, introduce her into the social whirl. The right newspapermen would see her, meet her, get the story from Blake of her romantic childhood, with photographs of the Western Heiress in the Park on Horseback. There would be drawings by staff artists of the way she and her father appeared wandering through the desert, discovering the claims, her father's grave, anything to round out the human interest. Moreover, she could be introduced to the right people, that was Mrs. Keith's end of it.

Then would come the prospectuses with these extracts of the best paragraphs, tied up with views of Casey Town, with engineers' reports, with semi-scientific stuff about sylvanite, a masterpiece of romance and fiction, peppered with fact. The whole to be titled *White Gold*.

Advertisements, headed *White Gold*, offering the shares. Personal letters to those on the carefully selected lists of *Preferred Investors*. Offices of the Casey Town Mining Company with alluring specimens behind glass cases, with models of mining machinery and of sections of mines, framed maps and drawings, blue-prints, a chunk of sylvanite ore in a railed-off enclosure with the legend of its marvelous value. Many, most, of these lures, had done service in previous enticements of Keith, but they still held good. They were a good deal like the fake mermaids, the skulls and odds and ends in the window of a palmist, all bait, of better quality, more deftly arranged and displayed, part of the fakir's kit, bait for goldfish. Also brass rails, fine rugs, mahogany furniture, a ticker, busy and pretty stenographers.

Blake submitted his clever campaign, worthy of better things, and Keith approved of it. That the partners of the Three Star as fifty-one per cent, owners, or Molly Casey herself with them, should be consulted or informed, never entered his head.

Of course there was always a chance of the investors realizing heavily if Casey Town turned up big production. Keith hoped it would. Provided he made all the money he wanted, he was always willing to have others get hold of some, especially when he would be regarded by them as the benefactor who had given them the golden opportunity. He would reap the major harvest, and success would open up the way for other fields — perhaps in oil. Keith had some associates who rather scoffed at his gold-mining promotion as out-of-date. Oil was quicker, more in the public eye. Every time the price of gasoline or kerosene went up the American automobile-owning public thought of oil, they were primed perpetually toward its possibilities.

But Keith was still in gold. He knew all the technique of that branch of speculation and Blake's campaign was carried out most successfully. Mrs. Keith descended overwhelmingly upon Molly at her school, chauffeur and footman on the driving seat of her luxurious sedan; gasped a little when she saw that Molly was a beauty, could be made an unusual one with the right dressing, the right setting.

Her brain, which was keen enough in business matters, told her that she could improve her husband's program of using Molly as an attraction to bring investors to the Keith residence. It might be a good thing — Mrs. Keith was quick at dealing with the future — if her son, Donald, fell in love with Molly, the heiress. She wrote to the Three Star Ranch, to Sandy Bourke, guardian of Molly Casey, without Molly's knowledge. Sandy read the letter aloud to his partners.

Dear Mr. Bourke:

I feel that I should write this letter to you although I have never met you, rather than my husband, since the question is one that a woman can handle better than a man, — that only a woman can understand and appreciate.

I have seen your Molly and she has entirely captivated me. She is really wonderful, with wonderful possibilities. She is more than pretty, she is talented and she possesses character in a marked degree that sets her aside from the rest. It is this difference, this broadness of view, perhaps a certain intolerance of conventionality, that make me feel that, much as it has done for her, and that has been largely due to her own endeavors, this school, or any school, is not the place for her best development.

I want to take her into my home, Mr. Bourke. She is practically a woman grown, much more so than the girls with whom she associates. This, I suppose, is due to her early experiences. There she would be under my own eye, which will be a maternal one, and she can have private tutoring in what she still lacks. I think she feels the need of the companionship and advice of an older woman, rather than that of the girls at the school.

I wish I could talk with you personally about this. Letters are such inadequate things. But I know, from Mr. Keith, that you have her interests at heart — and so have I. I shall dearly love to have her with me. I have, of course, said absolutely nothing to her about this plan before I hear from you, but I feel confident from what I have seen of her, that she will be happier in a home, with some one, who, however poorly, may take the place of the mother she must have missed all these years.

Let me hear from you soon. If my health and other matters permit, I must try to come out with Molly before very long. Mr. Keith has seen this letter and approves of my suggestion to have Molly with us.

Most sincerely yours,

Elizabeth Vernon Keith.

It was a clever letter. There were several touches about it that almost amounted to genius. The hints of Molly's unhappiness so cleverly suggested, the mother suggestion, the need of companionship and advice from an older woman, Molly's intolerance of conventionalities, all went home; though it was some time before the trio entirely absorbed the meaning of the glossy phrases and glib vocabulary. The letter passed about in silence after Sandy had read it, Sam and Mormon plowing through the maze of the fashionable script.

"Reckon she's right," said Mormon. "Molly's different. She had a mighty hard time of it along with her old man, compared to what them soft-skinned snips must have had. Stands to reason she c'udn't be like 'em, any mo' than Sam c'ud be easy in his spiketail suit, or me handin' ice-cream at a swarry. Not that Molly 'ud make no breaks, but their ways w'udn't be her'n, most of the time. How 'bout it, Sam?"

"This Mrs. Keith must live high," said Sam. "She w'udn't be botherin' about Molly if she didn't see a heap of promise in her. I mind me it must be tough to be herded inter a corral where you got to learn all over ag'in how to handle yore feet an' hands, not to mention forks. This Keith woman's spotted Molly ain't easy at school. The other gals like her, but they ain't her style. She's range bred an' free. Those other fillies have been brought up in loose boxes. They probably don't mean to hurt her feelin's none, but I 'low they snicker once in a while if Molly forgets the right sasshay. An' Molly's proud as they make 'em. Sounds good to me. What you think, Sandy? It's up to you as her guardeen."

"It sure sounds good," said Sandy. "Seems like this Mrs. Keith must be a pritty fine woman to think of takin' Molly into her own home. I reckon Molly must have changed a good deal. I'd be inclined to put it this way; if Molly cottons to the idea, let her hop to it."

"Mirandy ain't brought over the butter yet," put in Mormon, with a glance at his partners that was half shamefaced. "Why not git her opinion? Takes a woman to understand a woman. She'd sabe this letter a heap bettern' we c'ud."

Sam winked covertly at Sandy and shoved his tongue in his cheek.

"That's a good idea, Mormon," said Sandy.

"Never did find out jest what happened to that last wife of your'n, did ye, Mormon?" asked Sam.

"Never did."

"That's too bad."

"Why?"

"Gen'ral principles." Sam said no more but took out his harmonica, ever in one hip pocket, and crooned into it. A jiggly-jazz edition of *Mendelssohn's Wedding March* strained through the curtains of Sam's drooping mustache.

"Speakin' wide, the weddin' cake of matrimony has been mostly mildewed for me," said Mormon reflectively, "but there was one thing about my last wife I sure admired. Uncommon thing in woman an' missin' in some men."

Sam, eager for chaffing, fell.

"What was that, Mormon? I heerd she was a good cook."

"It warn't her cookin', though that was prime when she was in the humor. But she sure c'ud attend to her own business, an' there's damn few can do that. Sandy's one of the few. I can't call another to mind jest now."

Sam grinned.

"You sure had me that time, ol' hawss. An' the mildew on the weddin' cake warn't none of yore fault. That sort of pastry's too rich for me to tackle. I used to wonder why they allus put frostin' on weddin' cake. I reckon it's a warnin' — or else sarcasm."

"Ef you ever git roped thataway, Sam, you're goin' to fall high an' hard," said Mormon. "You'll come to consciousness hawg-tied an' branded."

"That the way it was with you?"

"Yep. I've allus had an affinity fo' the sex. I ain't like Sandy. Nature give him an instinct ag'in' 'em, as pardners. He was bo'n lucky."

But Sandy had gone out. Sam and Mormon trailed him and saw him walking toward the cottonwood grove with Grit at his heels.

"He thinks a heap of Molly," opined Sam. "I reckon he sure hates to lose her, if he is woman-shy. 'Course Molly was jest a kid. But I don't fancy she'll take the back-trail once she gits mixed up with the Keith outfit."

"I ain't so plumb sure of that," returned Mormon. "Molly's bo'n an' bred with the West in her blood. She'll allus hear the call of the range, like a colt that's stepped wild. He'll drink at the tank, but he ain't forgettin' the water-hole."

Sam glanced at Mormon curiously. It wasn't often Mormon showed any touch of what Sam characterized as poetical.

Sandy, under the cottonwoods where the spring bubbled, so near the old prospector's grave that perhaps the old-miner lying there could, in his new affinities with Nature, hear its flow, was thinking much the same thing Mormon had expressed, hoping it might be true, chiding himself lest the thought be selfish.

A granite block stood now as marker for Patrick Casey's resting-place, carved with the words that Mormon had chalked on the wooden headstone. A railing outlined the grave, and the turf within it was kept short and green. Sandy squatted down and rolled a cigarette, smoking it as he sat cross-legged. Grit, as was his custom, leaped the railing lightly and lay down above the dust of his dead master, head couched on paws, turned a little sidewise, his grave eyes surveying Sandy.

"Miss her, ol' son? So do I. Mebbe she'll come back to see us-all. She sure did seem to belong."

Memories of Molly flickered across the screen of his mind: Molly beside her father by the broken wagon, climbing to get the cactus blossom for his cairn; Molly at the grave; Molly giving him the gold piece; the wild ride across the pass and the race for the train and a recollection that was freshest of all, one he had not mentioned to his partners; the touch of Molly's lips on his as he had bade her good-by. The kiss had not been that of a child, there had been a magic in it that had thrilled some chord in Sandy that still responded to that remembrance. He never dwelt on it long, it brought a vague reaction always, stirred that strange instinct of his that had branded him as woman-shy, kept him clean. Part of it was intuitive desire for freedom of will and action, as the wild horse shies at even the shadow of a halter that may mean bondage, however pleasant. Part of it was reverence for woman, deep-seated, a hazy, never analyzed feeling that this belief might be disappointed.

Miranda, alone in the flivver, a new car of her own, bought with money paid by Keith for her claim, was at the ranch-house when Sandy returned. Miranda and young Ed Bailey, accepting Westlake's advice, had sold for cash, getting fifteen thousand dollars to divide between them, refusing more glittering offers of stock. It was a windfall well worth their endeavor and they were amply satisfied. Young Ed had promptly gone to Agricultural College, putting in part of his money to buy new stock and implements for his father's ranch, in which he now held a half partnership. Miranda, Mormon and Sam were talking about this when Sandy came up.

"It sure made a man of young Ed overnight," said the spinster. "He thought it out all by himse'f an' nigh surprised us off our feet. He was sort of ganglin', more ways than one, an' we feared the money 'ud go to his head. Which it did, as a matter of fact, but it was a tonic, 'stead of actin' like an intoxicant. We're plumb proud of him.

"Mr. Westlake was over day before yesterday," she went on. "Goin' on through to the East fo' a consultation with Mr. Keith an' his crowd. Said to say he was mighty sorry he c'udn't git out to the Three Star, but he only had a couple of hours before his train. He says things is boomin' up to Casey Town. There's been some good strikes, one in the claim nex' but one to ours. Keith's goin' to start things whirlin', I reckon."

"Mebbe he'll see Molly," suggested Sam. "Though of course she ain't to Keith's house yet."

"How's that?" asked the spinster eagerly.

"We are waitin' fo' Sandy to show you the letter," said Sam.

Miranda read the letter through twice, folded it and held it in her lap for a few moments.

"Want my opinion on it?" she asked finally.

"Yes," said Sandy. "If the mines are goin' to produce big she'll likely be rich. She went east to git culchured up. Seems like the school idea might not have been the best, after all."

"I don't know. I don't rightly git the motive back of this writin'. It ain't been sent without one. Mebbe she's just taken a fancy to Molly, mebbe she's a woman that likes to do kind things and thinks Molly'll pay well for bein' taken up. I don't mean in money but, if Molly didn't have a show of bein' rich, an' warn't pritty, which she is, I ain't certain Mrs. Keith 'ud be so eager. I guess it's all right but, somehow, it don't hit me as plumb sincere. Still … I reckon my opinion is like that gilt hawss top of Ed's barn," she ended with a smile. "It was set up too light, I reckon, an' it was allus shiftin', north, south, east an' west, when you c'udn't feel a breath of wind on the level. I ain't got a thing to pin it to, but I feel there's something back of it, like a person's rheumatic spot'll ache when rain's comin'."

"You'd vote ag'in' it?" asked Sandy.

"No-o. I w'udn't."

"I figgered on puttin' it up to Molly."

"That's a good idee. An', as her guardeen, I'd suggest that Mrs. Keith lives up to that half-promise of hers an' make it a condition she brings Molly out here inside of six months. That'll give time for a fair trial an' you can see right then fo' yoreself how it's workin'. Long's she goin' to have teachers she can't lose much."

"That's a plumb fine idee," said Mormon, looking triumphantly at his partners.

It ran with Sandy's own wishes and he subscribed to it. Sam endorsed it as well, and a letter was sent east that night, containing the proviso of Molly's return and another that Molly should bear all her own expenses of tuition and living. All this to hang upon Molly's own desire to make the change.

When Molly's letter came there appeared no doubt as to her willingness. She admitted that she had been sometimes "lonesome" at the school. One page was devoted to her anticipations of coming back to visit Three Star:

> I may stay; there are lots of new and lovely things here, but I miss the mountains and the range terribly. Also Grit. Please tell him I have not forgotten him. You might draw cards to see who will kiss him on the end of the nose — for me. It is a very nice nose. High man out.
>
> Lovingly, MOLLY.
>
> P. S. There are three other people I miss just as much as I do Grit, but, being quite grown up, I can not send them the same message, though it would be awfully funny to see you delivering it to each other. Maybe, when I come, I'll be so glad to see you, I'll do it myself.   M.

"I'll kiss no dawg," declared Sam. "I like a dawg first-rate, like I do a hawss, on'y not so much, but I'm a hell-singed son of a horned-toad if I'd ever kiss one."

"It's two to one you don't have to," said Mormon. "If you're a sport you'll do as Molly asks an' draw cards fo' the privilege. It's a sure-fire cinch she'll never give you one of them salutes she hints at when she comes home ef she knows you backed out. Wait till I git the cards."

It was plain to Sandy that Sam and Mormon, despite Sam's protest, took Molly's pleasantry in earnest and he made no comment as Mormon deftly shuffled the deck and riffled it out over the table. He picked a jack, Mormon a three of clubs and Sam an eight of hearts. Sam whooped at sight of Mormon's card.

"Hold on, Molly said 'High man out.' That's Sandy. You an' me got to draw again. Ain't that so, Sandy?"

"Sure is," said Sandy gravely. "You hollered too soon, Sam. Prob'ly crabbed yore luck."

Both chose their cards and drew them to the edge of the table, face down, taking a peep at the index corners.

"Bet you ten dollars I got you beat," said Mormon cheerfully.

Sam turned up his card disgustedly. It was the deuce of spades.

"Oh, hell!" he exclaimed. "Now I got to kiss a dawg!"

At his voice and face Mormon and Sandy bent double with laughter that brought water to their eyes and nearly sent Mormon into convulsions. Sam surveyed them with gloomy contempt.

"Laf, you couple of ring-tailed snakes in the sage!" he said bitterly. "I'm stuck an' I'm game, but if either of you ever whisper a word of it to a livin' soul, outside of Molly, I'll plumb scalp, skin an' silence both of you. *Kiss a dawg!* Hell's delight!"

They started to follow him, still weak with laughter, but he threatened them with his gun and they fell back in mock alarm while Sam went round back of the corral and they heard him whistling for Grit. When he reappeared, straddling along on his bowed legs, his good humor had returned.

"How's he like it?" asked Mormon.

Sam grinned at him.

"You bald-headed ol' badger, you, he acted plumb like yore wives must have, when I salutes him on the snoot. Licks my nose first an' then curls up his tongue an' licks off his own. Wipes out all trace of the oskylation pronto an' thorough. Most unappreciative animile I ever see."

"I'll tell you straight out that none of my wives ever acted thataway," started Mormon, and the laugh swung at his expense.

"I didn't mind the operation so much," Sam confided to them, "when I figger out that I was just handin' it on fo' Molly, an' that she owes me one, whether she decides to salute you two galoots or not."

Molly's letters were prime events at the Three Star. She wrote every week telling of life at the Keiths'. Miranda made up the quartet to read them. Molly wrote:

> It is full of excitement, this life at the Keiths', and they are just lovely to me. There is a lot of company always at the house and every one seems to be enjoying himself, but somehow it strikes me as not quite real. I want to be back where nobody pretends.
>
> I go automobiling a good deal, with Mrs. Keith and once in a while with Donald, but I'd give anything, sometimes, for a good gallop through the redtop and sage and rabbit-brush on my pony. I can go riding here, but it is in the Park and you should see the saddle! Imagine a real saddle with the cantle taken away, the horn gone, the pommel trimmed down to almost nothing, no skirts to it, just pared to the core. And the poor horse bob-tailed and roach-maned, taught to go along with its knees high, like a trained horse in a circus. High-school gaited, they call it.

There was more talk of dinners and dances, of receptions and theaters, with mention of Donald Keith here and there, chat of new clothes, kind words for the elder Keiths. "Don't think I've changed," she said. "I'm the same Molly underneath even if I have been revamped and decorated."

The famous *White Gold* prospectuses and advertisements duly followed the news stories. Three Star saw no copies of the last, nor, it seemed, did Molly. Neither did prospectuses or advertisements come their way, for that matter. Casey Town boomed with some bona-fide strikes that sent Keith's stocks soaring high. The porphyry dyke at the Molly Mine began to yield rich results almost from the first and dividends were paid in such quantities as to stagger the Three Star outfit who saw themselves in a fair way to become rich. All over the barren hills, where the first futile shafts had been driven and abandoned, buildings sprang up like mushrooms, housing machinery, sending up plumes of white smoke that tokened the underground energies. The Keith properties were being developed with much show of outlay, prices jumping at every report from the Molly Mine or other successful developments. None of the investors in these Keith undertakings knew that he owned forty-nine per cent of the shares of the Molly and of none other, save for the space between issuing them and selling them.

The three partners held consultation as to their disposal of the checks that were sent them.

"Molly, she's gettin' the same amount we're splittin' both ways," said Sam, "but somehow it don't seem right to me the way we come in. It was her dad's mine. He found it. All we did was to find her — an' Grit done that. The dawg ought to have a gold collar an' we might accept a gold plated collar-button, apiece, that's the way it sizes up to me."

"The gal w'udn't promise to go to school 'less we shared even-Steven," said Mormon.

"She didn't know how much money she c'ud use then," demurred Sam. "Now she's bein' shown how to spend it. It ain't that she'd kick, but some might think we'd taken advantage of her. Darn me if I don't feel thataway myse'f."

"I see it this way," said Sandy. "I've done a heap of thinkin' over the matter. I don't believe that Molly has changed — still she might be influenced by folks who w'ud look at it that she made the deal when she was a minor an' we c'udn't enfo'ce it. Bein' her guardeen, I'm responsible fo' what she makes an' what she loses. Jim Redding fixed up things in that line. He an' Ba'bara Redding understand it all but others mightn't. I'm plumb sure that if we-all didn't take the money Molly 'ud pull out her picket-pin an' say we wasn't playin' fair an' square with her. It was a deal an', at the time, I had no mo' idee the mines w'ud pan out than I have that Sam's laigs'll grow straight. I figger we can do this. We can use the money, keepin' account of it, puttin' it into stock an' improvements that'll pay fo' themselves long befo' Molly comes of age an' my guardeen papers play out. That way we'll have the benefit of the capital an' keep it ready to turn over to her if she ever needs it. I don't believe she'll ever take one red cent of it. It was a gamble with her an' she's a thoroughbred sport. To my mind, she'd sooner be slapped in the face by us than have us try an' wiggle out of the deal. But, in case anything ever turns up, or she gits married, we'll have it handy."

"Figger she's goin' to marry that young Keith? She writes a heap of Donald's this an' Donald doin' that. I'd like to take a slant at him. I sure hate to think of Molly hitchin' up with a tenderfoot."

"What put that in yore head?" Sam asked Mormon.

"Mirandy was wonderin' whether Ma Keith 'ud like to keep Molly's money in the family. Mirandy's allus 'spicioned a motive to that invite."

"Shucks! She asked her befo' the mine made a showin'. An' every dollar Molly makes, Keith makes five or six, out of the sale of them shares. But I subscribe to Sandy's scheme on these here dividends of ours."

"Count me in," said Mormon. And so the affair was settled.

Of Plimsoll little was heard. The gambler had deserted that now unpopular profession, since suffrage ruled, and stayed close to his horse ranch. It lay alone, and few visited it save Plimsoll's own associates. Rumors drifted concerning Plimsoll's remarkable herd increase of saleable horses but, unless proof of actual operation was forthcoming, there was small chance of pinning anything down in the way of illegal work. There was always the excuse of having rounded up a bunch of broom-tail wild horses to account for growing numbers, and, if he stole or not, Plimsoll left the horses of his own county alone. No neighbor was injured and though stories of wild happenings at the horse ranch were current it was considered nobody's business. Wyatt once, staggering out of some blind pig in Hereford, still existent despite the suffrage sweeping, babbled in maudlin drunkenness of his determination to get even with Plimsoll for stealing his sweetheart. For Wyatt, for the sake of the girl, had gone back to Plimsoll's employ. The new sheriff took Wyatt's guns away and locked him up overnight in the "cooler," letting him go in the morning, soberer and more silent.

"But," said the sheriff to his cronies, "some day there'll be one grand shoot-up an' carry-out at Plimsoll's. Wyatt's sore clean through."

"He ain't got the sand in his craw to make a killing," said one of the listeners. "Sandy Bourke backed him off the map to Casey Town."

"Just the same, he's got something in his craw," replied the sheriff. "He may not shoot Plimsoll, but he's primed to pull something off first chance he gets. I spoke to him about what he's been firing off from his mouth the night before an' he shuts up like a clam. 'I was foolish drunk,' he says, but there was a look in his eyes that was nasty. If Plim's wise he'll get rid of Wyatt. He knows too much an' he's liable to tip it off."

"Wyatt an' Plim's both of 'em side-swipers," returned the other. "They'd throw dirt but not lead. Plumb yeller as a Gila monster's belly. Plimsoll told it all over the county he'd tally score with Sandy Bourke. Has he? He ain't even bought him a stick of chalk."

"He ain't had the chance he's lookin' for. That's all that's holding Plimsoll. Same way with Wyatt. Two buzzards of a feather, they are."

Thoughts of Plimsoll and his revenges did not bother Sandy's head. The "old man" of the Three Star — bearing the cowman's inevitable title for the head of the management, whether young or old, male or female — carried out his long cherished plans for additional water-supply, for alfalfa planting, for registered bulls and high-grade cows. Now that there was money in sight the success of the ranch was assured. He studied hard, he got in touch with the state experimental developments, he subscribed for magazines that told of cattle breeding, he sent soils for analysis and young Ed, coming home from his first term, found, somewhat to his chagrin, that Sandy was far ahead of him in both the theory and practise of ranching.

The days multiplied into weeks and the weeks into months. Sandy received one letter from Brandon that seemed to presage another visit across the line. It was terse, characteristic of the man.

My Dear Bourke:

We are still losing three-and four-year-olds, and the evidence points plainly to their drifting over toward Plimsoll. We have traced up some of the links leading from this end. To be quite frank, the authorities of your own county do not seem over-disposed to bother in the matter, and we are taking things in our own hands. We have set a trap for Jim Plimsoll and have hopes he will walk into it if he is the guilty party.

If it springs and catches him you'll probably see us over your way again — after we have concluded our business with J. P. There are some of us old-timers — and I believe you are of our way of thinking or I would not write asking you to do this favor for me — who look at horse-stealing just as it used to be looked at — and dealt with. To be plain, we have been losing a lot of valuable animals and we are all considerably "riled."

The favor I want of you is to tip me off if Plimsoll appears about to leave the country. We have had a tip that he expects to do so before long. If you get wind of this a wire would be much appreciated by me.

Sincerely yours,

W. J. Brandon.

Have been hearing fine things about the way things are being run along modern lines on the Three Star. More power to you. Good stock *always* pays.

Sandy filed the letter. There was a room in the ranch-house that was now fitted up as an office, known to the riders of the Three Star as the "Old Man's Room." Sandy had even contemplated a typewriter, but given it up for the time being after talking it over.

"I don't believe I c'ud ever learn to ride one of those contraptions," he said. "I tried it once an' the wires bucked my fingers off reg'lar. But I sure hate writin' longhand."

"Why not import one of them stenographers?" suggested Mormon.

"Sure," jeered Sam. "Why not? Then you c'ud put in yore spare moments gentlin' a hawss fo' her an' pickin' wild flowers, until Mirandy Bailey persuades her the climate is too chilly. But I'll bet Molly c'ud handle that end of it prime, if she was back."

"I w'udn't wonder," said Sandy.

There was a lot of interjected talk about what Molly might say or do. With the founding of the Three Star Ranch the lives of the partners had changed a good deal. They held responsibilities, they owned a home and they lived there. None of them, since they were children, had ever known the close companionship of a young girl. Mormon's matrimonial adventures had been foredoomed shipwrecks on the sands of time, his wives marital pirates preying on his good nature and earnings. Molly had leavened their existences in a way that two of them hardly suspected and the yeast of affection was still working. Each hung to the hope that she might return to the ranch again to stay and each felt that hope was a faint one.

When, at last, there came the news, from Molly herself and from Mrs. Keith, that Keith was coming out to make inspection of his Casey Town properties, that he was traveling in a private car with his son, with Molly and her governess-companion, and that the two latter would get off at Hereford for a visit to the Three Star, Sandy went about with a whistle, Sam breathed sanguine melodies through the harmonica and Mormon beamed all over. The illumination was apparent. Sam told him he looked "all lit up, like a Chinee lantern" and Mormon beamed the more.

Molly's letter was primed with delight. Mrs. Keith's contained regrets that her physicians did not think the journey would be best for her to undertake in the present state of her health, which meant that she feared possible discomforts en route and imagined the ranch as a place where one was fed only on beans, sourdough bread, bull meat and indifferent coffee.

> "You will find Miss Nicholson most efficient and amenable," she penned. "She has done remarkably well with your ward. I believe my husband expects to stay in your vicinity about a month and we have decided to make a holiday of it for Molly, so far as lessons are concerned. She can resume her studies on her return to New York. I regret exceedingly not being able to make your personal acquaintance. But, if ever you come east, we shall hope to see something of you."

Miranda Bailey sniffed at this letter openly.

"I hope they ain't spiled the child," she said. "I wonder what's the matter with the Nicholson teacher woman?"

"What do you mean?" asked Mormon.

"She says she's amenable. I ain't sure of the word, but I believe that means thin-blooded or underfed. My sister's niece by marriage was that way till they fed her cod-liver oil an' scraped beef. 'Pears to me as if all the companions an' governesses was that kind of folk. I suppose they hire out cheaper account of not bein' overstrong."

"You can search me," answered Mormon. "Ask Sandy, he's browsin' through the dikshunary reg'lar these days. Gettin' so it's hard to sabe half he tells you."

Sandy had to look up the word. "Liable to make answer," he read out.

"One of the snippy kind, back-talkin' an' peevish," said Miranda. "I can't bear 'em."

"That's the legal meaning," said Sandy. "I reckon this is it — submissive."

"Halter-broke. That's more likely. That's the kind that Keith party w'ud pick. I ain't ever seen her nor don't hope nor expect to, but that's the kind she'd pick. No backbone. Molly'll twist her round her little finger. Wonder how old she is?"

"The word you meant was anemic, Miss Mirandy," said Sandy, turning a leaf in the dictionary. "They sound about the same."

"There's too many words anyway," she replied. "Folks don't use mo'n a hundredth part of 'em an' git along first-rate. I don't see why they print 'em." Miranda did not show to the best advantage during the rest of her visit. She snubbed Mormon severely when he offered to get water for her car. "I've fetched an' carried for myself long enough not to want to be waited on," she said. "An' I don't need water anyway." She drove off and had to bail from an irrigating ditch before she was half-way to her destination. Whereupon she took herself to task.

"Miranda Bailey, there's no fool like an old fool," she said aloud, with sage-brush and timid prairie dogs for audience. "What you want to do is to keep sweet. Now git on." The final adjuration was to her car, to which she always spoke exactly as if it was a horse.

"What do you suppose made her so cantankerous?" Mormon inquired after she had driven round the corral. "Reckon you got her sore bawlin' her out about usin' the wrong word, Sandy. A woman's sensitive about them things."

Sam smote Mormon between the shoulders before Sandy could make answer.

"Fo' a man who's had yore experience, you're deef, blind, dumb an' lost to all sense of touch or motion," he shouted. "Remember what I said about the stenographer? Mirandy's jealous of the Nicholson woman. Plumb jealous! You better wear blinders while she's here, Mormon. If she's a good-looker, Gawd help you! Mirandy won't."

CHAPTER XVI
EAST AND WEST

When Miranda Bailey heard the news she announced her determination of coming over to the Three Star to prepare for the visitors.

"I reckon my reputation'll stand it," she said, "seein' I'm older than two of you an' the third is still a married man. That spineless governess'll be writin' back to the Keith woman about everything she sees, eats, sits or sleeps on. Pedro's cookin' is enough to give any easterner dyspepsy. The whole house wants reddin' up, it ain't been swept proper fo' a year."

Abashed, the partners gave her full sway. They lived on the porch in their spare waking moments, they ate cold victuals, and the lives of Pedro and Joe were made miserable. But the ranch-house was scoured from top to bottom. Miranda's car brought over curtains for the windows, flowers for the window-sills, odds and ends that made the place look homely, cheerful, inviting. Pedro was given lessons at the stove that he at first took sulkily but, being praised and his wages raised, took pride in.

"He'll do," vouchsafed Miranda at last, the evening before the arrival. "He's no hand at cookies or doughnuts an' never will be, but I'll bring them over from time to time. He can make a pie an' biscuit an' he can broil meat. I've taught him to mash his pertaters with milk 'stead of water an' to put butter in his hot cakes. I'm stayin' over till supper ter-morrer to see everything has a good staht."

"She's stayin' over to git a good look at the Nicholson party," Sam said to Mormon. "All this ain't jest for Molly."

"There's nothin' between Miss Mirandy an' myse'f," replied Mormon with dignity. "She's a wonderful housekeeper."

"She sure is. Me, I'm so I'm afeard to come into my own house, it's so golderned clean. If that third wife of yor'n...."

The long-suffering Mormon turned upon his partner. They were seated on the broad top rail of the breaking corral, waiting the call to supper. Mormon clutched Sam by his collar and jerked him off the rail, catching the slack cloth of his pants at the seat, holding him firmly gripped and bending him across his padded lap. Despite Sam's kicks and squirms, he paddled him unmercifully and then dropped him sprawling into the corral.

"I ain't done that to you, Sam Manning," he said sternly, "fo' five-six years. An' you've got too all-fired fresh. Nex' time I'll do it in front of Mirandy, you ornery, bow-laiged, hornin'-in son of a lizard."

Sam said nothing. His face, as he stooped somewhat painfully, was fiery red. He took hold of a post to help himself up, pretending disability. On the post a horsehair lariat hung from the snub of a lopped-off bough of the tree that made the heavy stake. He fumbled with this while Mormon shook with laughter like a great jelly. The next moment the lariat came flying, circling, settled down over Mormon's head, over his body and arms. Sam, working like a jumping-jack, took a quick turn, flung a coil about Mormon's legs and in a few seconds, had him trussed helplessly to the rail.

"Paddle me, you overgrown buzzard, will you? There you roost till Mirandy comes to look for you."

Mormon pleaded and Sam pretended to be inflexible. At last they came to a capitulation. Mormon promised to keep his hands off Sam, and the latter vowed he would gibe no more about Mormon's matrimonial affairs, past, present or future.

"An' don't *look* nothin', neither," added Mormon as Joe glided into sight and grunted his message.

"Grub piled. Squaw she say hurry."

For the life of him Sam could not resist a side glance of mirthful suggestion at Miranda's tendency to issue orders. Mormon did not notice it.

"There's room for five — supposed to be — in my car," said Miranda. "An' there's four of us an' six to come back. The other car's in use. How we goin' to manage it?"

"Mormon c'ud take the Nicholson party on his lap, if she ain't too finicky," suggested Sam. This was hewing close to the line, and Mormon glared at him while the spinster sniffed.

"Molly'll ride in with me," said Sandy. "I'm goin' over early on Pronto an' take the white blazed bay along that Molly rode over the Goats' Pass."

"Ride in?"

"She wrote she was jest waitin' fo' the minute she c'ud climb into a real saddle, astride a range-bred hawss," said Sandy.

"She won't be dressed for it, travelin' on the train," said Mirandy.

"I've got a hunch she will," Sandy answered simply. "They got their own private car. If she ain't, why, Sam can ride the bay back. But me an' Pronto, the bay an' Grit are goin' thataway."

There were certain tones of Sandy's voice that gave absolute finality to his statements. He used them on this occasion. The argument dropped. In a way Sandy was making the matter a test of Molly. If she was as anxious as she wrote to "fork a bronco," if she understood Sandy and he her, she would feel that he would be waiting with her mount for her to return to the ranch western fashion. If not, it meant that she was out of the chrysalis and had become, not the busy bee that belongs to the mesquite and the sage, but a gaudier, less responsible flutterer among eastern flower-beds.

The bay with the white blaze had been groomed by Sandy until his hide was glossy and rich as polished mahogany, while the blaze on his nose shone like a plate of silver. His dark mane and tail had been braided and combed until it crinkled proudly, the light shone from his curves as he moved, reflecting the sky in the high-lights. Hoofs had been oiled and Sandy had attended to his shoeing. The bay had been up for a month and fed until he was almost pampered, save that Sandy took the excess pepper out of him every morning.

A new saddle came from Cheyenne, most famous of all cities for making of saddles that are tailor-made, the leather carved cunningly into arabesques of cactus design, bossed and rimmed here and there with silver, the pattern carried over into the tapideros that hooded the stirrups, even into the bridle. It was a masterpiece of art craft, that saddle, "made for a lady to ride astride," and it cost Sandy an even quarter of a thousand dollars.

Sam and Mormon knew of the grooming of the horse but, when the saddle, cinched above a Navajo blanket, smote their vision, they blinked and complained. They too had gifts for the homecomer, but Sandy's outshone them as a newly minted five-dollar gold piece does a silver coin.

"If that don't win her to stay west there ain't no use a-tryin'," declared Sam as Sandy mounted and rode away, leading the bay. Grit, newly washed also, sorely against his will, since he did not know the occasion of the bath at the time of suffering it, went bounding on pads of rubber, leaping up, tearing ahead and back, a shuttling streak of gold and silver.

Miranda's caravan started an hour later, she driving, Mormon and Sam in the back, each dressed in his best, minus chaparejos and spurs, but otherwise most typically the cowboy and therefore out of place — and feeling it — as they sat stiffly in the leatherette-lined tonneau. Miranda was in starched linen, destitute of all ornament, a dark red ribbon at her throat the only touch of color, looking extremely efficient and, as Sam whispered to Mormon, "a bit stand-offish." He wanted to add, "count of the Nicholson party," but dared not.

The train rolled in majestically, the private car gleaming with varnish and polished glass and brass, with a white-coated darky flashing white teeth on the platform as the fussy local engine took the detached luxury to the side-track designated for its Hereford location. There, forewarned by the agent, much of Hereford assembled to witness the arrival of the magnate who had helped to place them more definitely on the map and increased their revenues as supply depot for Casey Town. The flivver was parked and Miranda, Mormon and Sam made one group a little ahead of the others, recognized by the crowd as privileged. Sandy sat Pronto, talking to the restive bay, proudly conscious of its new trappings and the remarks of the onlookers.

If Wilson Keith, clad in tweeds tailored on Fifth Avenue, a little portly, square-faced, confident, a trifle condescending, typified the East, Sandy was the West. A good horse is the incarnation of symmetry, grace and power. Sandy, erect in the saddle, lean and keen, matched all of Pronto's fitness. Man and mount both eminently belonged to the land, shimmering with sage, far-stretching to the mountains, a land that demanded and bred such a combination.

Sandy's clean-shaven face was sharp with obstacles faced and overcome, his eyes held clean fine spirit, his jaw showed determination and the good lines of his mouth belied obstinacy. He wore the regalia of his cow-punching holidays, soft-collared shirt of blue, silk bandanna of dark weave in lieu of tie, leather gauntlets, leather chaps, fringed and buttoned with leather and trimmed with disk of silver, silver spurs on his high-heeled boots, trousers of dark gray stripe, a quirt with the handle plaited in black and white diamonds of horsehair dangling from one wrist, and the blue Colts in the twin holsters. He could not avoid being picturesque, yet there was nothing of the masquerader, the moving-picture cowboy. He held the eye, even of Hereford, but only because they liked to gaze upon a good man on a good horse. His body responded to every shift of Pronto, jigging impatiently, showing off, pretending to be afraid of the panting locomotive, body shining like metal of bronze and aluminum, his nostrils pink as the inside of a shell, ears twitching, rider and mount one in every movement. Grit stood with plumy tail erect and waving gently, ears up, red tongue playing between white teeth, his eyes like jewels; braced on his feet, tiptoe on his pads, watching the parking of the private car with now and then a glance of inquiry at Sandy.

Keith stood by the railing of his platform, the darky ready with the dismounting stool. He surveyed the crowd affably, with the poise of a successful candidate assured of welcome, waving his hand in demi-salute to Sandy, Sam and Mormon, lifting his hat graciously to Miranda Bailey. The man and the car emanated prosperity. Yet, for all the booming of Casey Town, the finding of pay-ore, the sale of shares, Keith's present financial status was not all that he trusted it might be within a short time. It was part of the technique of his profession to assume a mask and manner of financial success, and of late he had worn these until at times they jaded him, but they were well designed, well worn, and no one doubted but that Wilson Keith was a man of ready millions.

Keith was essentially a gambler. He knew that those who bought his shares were largely tinctured with the same spirit that exists, more or less, in almost every man. They were amateurs and Keith the professional, that was the main difference. The average man likes to believe himself lucky. Keith was no exception. He knew the prevalence of the trait and traded upon it. Also he knew the gold mining game from prospect to prospectus and possible profit. But the expert faro-dealer, after his trick is over, is apt to take his wages to the roulette wheel of an opposition house and buck a game that his experience tells him is, like his own, run with the percentages against the player.

Keith had dallied with oil, had speculated, plunged, been persuaded to invest heavily. He was beginning to have a vague fear of not being so certain as he would have wished as to which end of the line he had taken, that of the baited hook, or the end that was attached to the reel that automatically plays the fish.

He sold gold and he was buying oil. More, he was sinking wells, infected with the fever of the game, whereas, with his own mines, he was cool with the poise of the physician who takes count of a pulse. Others, partners with him in new enterprises in the petroleum field, were making sudden fortunes. His turn had not come yet, but they assured him that his ventures promised even more than those that had enriched them. Faster than gold came out of Casey Town, Keith used it in Oklahoma and Texas. He had come west to view his resources, to strain them to the utmost, to overlook the ground with the eye of the past-master of promotion, who could conjure up visions of wealth from the barest indication of pay-ore, trusting to find inspiration for further flotation on his return to New York, his market-place, "fresh from the field of operations."

The engine uncoupled and panted off, leaving the car at rest on the spur-track. The fox-faced secretary came out, held the door open. Some one followed Molly Casey. Sandy surmised it must be Donald Keith, but he had sight for nothing except the slender figure whose radiant face, between a Panama hat and a dustcoat of pongee silk, shone straight at him. It was Molly, but a glorified Molly, woman not girl. The freckles had gone, the snub nose had become defined, the eyes of Irish blue seemed to have deepened in hue back of their smudgy lashes. The wide mouth was the same, scarlet and soft as cactus blossom, smiling, opening in a glad cry....

"Sandy!" Her arms went out toward him in greeting over the brass railing. Then Grit, catapulting from ground to platform, with frantic yaps of welcome, fairly bowled over the darky with his mounting block and bounded up into Molly's embrace. There was confusion on the platform for a moment with Grit as the nucleus. Another person had come out, evidently Miss Nicholson. She was neither undernourished nor thin, she was medium-sized and her bones were well covered. She had the general appearance of a white rabbit and the manners of a maternally intentioned but none too efficient hen. "Amenable" described her in one word. The darky was bringing out kitbags and suit-cases, piling them on the ground. Sam tackled him and showed him the flivver.

"There's a cupple of trunks," said the porter.

"We'll come back for them," Sam told him and helped him pile in the smaller baggage.

Keith descended first, Molly darted by his extended hand and ran straight to Sandy, who had dismounted.

"I'm going to hug you, and Mormon and Sam, as soon as we get home to the ranch," she cried. "Home! I'm so glad to be here. Pronto, you beauty, and my own bay, Blaze! Do you remember the trip over the mesa, Blaze? How did you know I wanted to ride to Three Star instead of drive?"

"Took a chance," said Sandy. "Do you?" The old woman-shyness had come over him, fighting with his knowledge of the child who had changed into a woman. And the pongee duster deceived him.

"Do I? Didn't I write you I was aching to fork a saddle? Look!"

She unbuttoned the duster with swift fingers and stripped it off, standing revealed in riding togs of smallest black and white checks, coat flaring out from the trim waist, slim straight legs in breeches and riding boots, a white stock about the slender, rounded neck. She gave one hand to Mormon, the other to Sam, gazing at her in admiration that was radiant and goggle-eyed.

"You're losing weight, Mormon," she said. "I believe you must be in love."

"I allus was, with you," gallantried Mormon.

"You stand aside, you human chuckawalla!" said Sam. "Miss Molly, you sure look good to sore eyes. An' I'm sure happy you're in my debt, if you ain't grown up too fur to pay yore dues."

"I always pay my debts, Sam. What do you mean?"

"It was me kissed the dawg," said Sam. "I give the animile somethin' I hadn't received."

Molly laughed at him reassuringly. Sandy, looking down at her, saw her eyes crinkle at the corners in the old way. Keith and his son joined them, coming from the car, the Amenable Nicholson hovering behind ingratiatingly.

"Glad to see you, Bourke," he said. "And you, Manning. You too, Peters. Meet my son, Donald."

The three partners shook hands gravely with the boy, appraising him without his guessing it.

"Glad to see you out west," said Mormon. "We'd sure admire to have you visit us fo' a spell."

"I was hoping for a bid," said young Keith. "Thanks. The car is here, or will be within an hour or two. Father shipped it ahead. Sims wired us it was at the junction. He will drive it over for us to go on to Casey Town as soon as he overhauls it. Then I'll run in from the mines, as soon as Dad can spare me."

"Donald has to get acquainted with a real mining property," said Keith affably. "Molly was certain you would have a horse for her, Bourke. Don't wait round for us. We have to get some supplies and we'll wait in my car till the machine comes. Er" — he looked around, and Miss

Nicholson fluttered up — "this is Molly's companion, Miss Nicholson. She goes with you to the ranch. How...?"

Sandy indicated the flivver and introduced Miranda Bailey, who had been directing the stowage of the grips and the proper subordination of the porter, who had not seemed appreciative of the flivver.

Molly held out a gloved hand for the reins of the fretful Blaze. Young Keith advanced with the proffer of a palm of her mounting. She shook her head at him.

"Blaze wouldn't know what you were trying to do, Don," she said. She turned the stirrup, set in her foot, grasped mane and horn and raised herself lightly, holding her body close to the bay's withers for a second as he whirled, then lifting to the saddle, firm-seated, with a laugh for Blaze's plungings.

"I see they didn't unteach you ridin' back east," said Mormon admiringly.

The pair rode out of the crowd that opened for them, with whispered comments upon Molly's appearance, or rather, her reappearance. There were few stings in the remarks; the girl's spontaneous gaiety, her absolute unconsciousness of effort or cause, her evident delight in her return and reunion with the Three Star partners, disarmed all criticism of her costume. The Amenable Nicholson clambered into the flivver beside Miranda Bailey. Sam, Mormon and the grips packed the tonneau, and Keith and his son were left standing by the private car.

Keith was soon surrounded with a crowd, making himself popular, flattering them until they finally went away convinced that they had all constituted a first-class reception committee to meet the illustrious, the energetic, good-fellow-well-met promoter and engineer of other people's fortunes.

Some of them were invited into the car for a private talk. It is certain that cigars were handed round and it was hinted that some private stock had found its way upon the car. When, three hours later, the big machine with Sims the chauffeur, imperturbable as ever, at the wheel, departed with the promoter and his heir, the name of Keith was, for a time at least, a household word in Hereford.

There was not much spoken between Molly and Sandy on the way back to the ranch. She seemed content to breathe in deep the herb-scented air and gaze at the mountains.

Sandy, riding a little to one side, a little back of her, so that he could see her better without appearing to stare, echoed, for the time, her happiness. It seemed to him as if this ride had been dreamed of by him, long ago, as if he had always known this was to happen, the gallop, side by side, the wind in their faces, their gaze toward the range, he and a woman who was all the world to him. Even the dog, leaping beside them as they loped, ranging when the pinto and the bay broke to a breathing walk, belonged in that picture. It was, he told himself, as if a boy had long cherished an illustration seen in a book and, suddenly, the beloved picture had become real and he a part of it.

This was Molly, the girl, who had sworn when she told them of her father's death. He could recall the tone of the words at will.

"The damned road jest slid out from under. He didn't have a hell-chance!"

Molly, who had put arms about his neck and kissed him good-by when she went to school — how long ago that seemed — and said, "Sandy, I don't want to go, but I'll be game."

Game! Sandy looked at the supple strength of her, so subtly knit in curves of graciousness, alert and upright in the new saddle, Panama hat in one hand, the better to get the wind full in her face, her cheeks flushed with the caress of it, the thick brown braids fluffing here and there; — she was the essence of gameness. He had quoted *Lasca* to her once — a line or two. More came to him now.

> To ride with me and forever ride,
> From San Saba's shore to Valacca's tide.

Molly, who had told him, the first time the woman-look had come into her eyes, "Yo're sure a white man. I'll git even with you some time if I work the bones of my fingers through the flesh fo' you. Thanks don't 'mount to a damn 'thout somethin' back of them 'em. I'll come through."

That Molly, and yet another Molly, swiftly maturing, with all life opening up before her to wider horizons than would have been hers if she had stayed back west.

> I want free life and I want free air,
> And I sigh for the canter after the cattle,
> The crack of whips like shots in battle,
> The mêlée of horns and hoofs and heads.

Pronto's hoofs beat out the cantering rhythm of the poem.

> That wars and wrangles and scatters and spreads,
> The green beneath and the blue above,
> And dash and danger and life and — —

He had stopped the quotation there before. Now he finished the stanza,

> — —and life and love

> And Lasca!

Only it was Molly! The knowledge swept over Sandy and left him tingling. Love came to him, the first, clean white flame of first love, burning like a lamp in the heart of a man. It was for this, he knew, that he had been woman-shy, that he had cherished his own thought of womanhood as something so rare a thought might tarnish it. First love, shorn of boy fallacies, strong, irresistible, protective, passionate. He closed his eyes and, for the first time in his life, touched leather, gripping the horn of his saddle as if he would squeeze it to a pulp.

Game and dainty, tender, true, a girl-woman, partner — what a partner she would make, western-bred...!

He checked himself there. She was western born but, what had the transplanting done? Would she ever now be satisfied with western ways? She would come to him, Sandy knew that. Whatever he asked her she would not refuse. But would that be fair to her? And he did not want her to come to him out of gratitude. He wanted her nature to fuse with his. Swiftly maturing as she had done, out of the ruggedness of her early years, she was still young in Sandy's eyes.

It seemed no time since he had taken her from her saddle and carried her, a tired heartsore child, in his arms. She must have a fair chance to see if the East, with all it could offer her of amusement and interest, would not outbid the claims of the West. He must wait and watch and hold himself in hand though his love and his knowledge of it thrilled through him, charging him as if with an electric current that strove to close all gaps between him and Molly, struggling ever, in mind and body, to complete the circle.

Molly reined up Blaze and turned in her saddle toward him, her eyes sparkling, the color of lupines damp with the dew of dawn. Their eyes met, the glance held, welded. For a moment the circuit was formed, polarity effected. For a moment Sandy looked deep and then Molly's eyes hazed with tenderness, with a yearning that made Sandy's heart constrict, that warned him his emotions were getting beyond control, his own eyes betraying him. He summoned his will. His face hardened to the effort, his eyes steeled. Molly's face flushed rose, from the line of her white linen riding stock up to her hair, then it paled, her eyes seemed to hold surprise, then hurt. Their expression changed, Sandy could not read it now as long lashes veiled them. He spoke with an effort, his voice sounded strange to himself, phonographic.

"How's the saddle?" he heard himself asking.

"It's wonderful. I'm not going to begin to thank you for it, now, Sandy."

"Glad to be back?"

She shook her head at him.

"No words for that, Sandy." Her eyes crinkled at him, with a hint of mischief, the old Molly looking out. "If you want to find that out, just you watch my smoke," she said, and set her heels sharply to the flanks of her mount. The astonished Blaze responded with a snort and a leap and cut loose his speed, Sandy after them on the pinto.

They got to the ranch ahead of the flivver by a scant margin. Miranda Bailey inducted Molly and her chaperon governess into the quarters she had helped prepare for them, Molly giving little cries of delight at the improvements she saw down-stairs. Miranda came down first and joined the partners.

"Molly is certainly sweet," she said. "She's grown into a woman an' she's grown away from the old Molly. Can't say as how she's affected none an' her speech an' manners is sure fine. That gel's natcherally got a grand disposition.

"The Nicholson person — her first name is Clarice — is well-meanin' enough. She ain't shif'less, but she ain't what you'd call practical. I reckon she does fine in teachin' Molly some things, but she'd be plumb wasted out West. She never saw a churn an' she'd likely die of thirst before she'd ever learn how to milk a cow. She's like the rest of 'em back East, I imagine, goes fine so long as folks can be hired to do everything fo' you. I'll say she never washed out anything bigger than a hankychif or cooked a thing larger'n an egg. An' she c'udn't boss a sick lizard. But she's easy to git along with, I suppose."

There was a certain complacency about the spinster's summing up of the Amenable Nicholson that made Sam wink covertly at Sandy, watching Mormon at the same time. Sam was convinced that, despite the handicap of a third wife, present whereabouts unknown, Miranda had made up her mind to marry Mormon and regarded all other women as possible rivals.

"That Donald is a good-lookin' lad," went on Miranda. "It must take him an awful waste of time to fix his clothes every time he puts 'em on. I don't know how smart he is inside, but he's got some of them movin'-picture heroes beat on appearance. I'm wonderin' what Molly thinks about him. As for his father, he's smart enough inside an' out. But he talks too much like a politician to suit me. I'm mighty glad we got cash for our claims. Keith's too slick an' smooth an' smilin' to suit me. So long as he had lots he'd give you some to help the game erlong but, when the grazin' gits short, he'll hog the range or quit it. That's my opinion. Or ruther, it ain't my opinion, for I ain't done a heap of thinkin' on it, it's the way I feel. Some apples sets my teeth on aidge before I know it, some victuals riles my stomach jest to mention 'em. I never c'ud abear castor-ile, jest the mention of it makes me squirmy. Keith affects me that way, on'y in my mind, well as in the pit of my stomach."

It was a lengthy diatribe from Miranda Bailey, accustomed as they were to hear her state opinions freely. The trio at Three Star had universally come to respect her decisions and also her intuitions and none of them had felt especially cordial toward Keith as a man, though they considered him good in his profession.

"The writer, Kiplin'," said Sandy, "wrote a poem about East an' West, sayin' that never the two c'ud meet. I reckon he meant White Man an' Yeller Man but, seems to me, sometimes they do breed mighty different east an' west of the Mississippi. The man in New York is sure a heap different from the man in Denver or San Francisco or Phoenix. Out here we reckon a man is square till we find him out different an', back East, they figger he's a crook till he proves he ain't — which is apt to be some job. I don't cotton to Keith myse'f, because he ain't my kind of a hombre. He don't talk my talk, or think my line of thought, any mo' than he wears the same clothes or does the same work. Give him a cow pony or strand me alongside one of them stock-market tickers an' we'd both look foolish. I'm playin' him as square till I find he ain't. Ef he tries to flamjigger Molly out of anything that's comin' to her by rights, why, I reckon that's one time the West an' East is goin' to meet — an' mebbe lap over a bit. So fur, he's put money in our pockets. Here's Molly...."

"I'm goin' home," said Miranda, as the girl entered the room. "I've got you started an' I'll run over once in a while to see how Pedro is makin' out."

She said good-by to Molly, who had swiftly changed out of her riding clothes into a gown that looked simple enough to Sandy, though he sensed there were touches about it that differentiated it from anything turned out locally. With the dress she looked more womanly, older, than in the boyish breeches. Miss Nicholson had made some changes also, but she had a chameleon-like faculty of blending with the background that preserved her alike from being criticized or conspicuous. As she shook hands with Miranda the two presented marked contrasts. Miranda was twentieth-century-western, of equal rights and equal enterprise; Miss Nicholson mid-Victorian, with no more use for a vote than for one of Sandy's guns. Yet likable.

"I'm going to Daddy's grave," said Molly, when Miranda had flivvered off. "I wish the three of you would come there to me in about ten minutes. Miss Nicholson, everybody's at home here. Please do anything you want to, nothing you don't want to. She rides, Sandy. And rides well. Can you get up a horse for her to-morrow?"

Miss Nicholson's face flushed, the suggestion of a high-light came into her mild eyes.

"I used to ride a good deal," she said. "But I have no saddle, no habit, and I am afraid — " She hesitated looking at them in embarrassment.

"Nicky, dear, you must learn to ride western fashion. With divided skirts, if you like. We can get you a khaki outfit in Hereford."

"I should like to try it," said Miss Nicholson, her face still flaming, the high-light quite apparent.

"Up to you, Sam," said Sandy. "I sh'ud think the blue roan w'ud suit."

"I'll have her gentled to a divvy-skirt this time ter-morrer," said Sam gallantly. "You've got pluck, marm — I mean, miss — an' once you've forked a saddle, you'll never ride otherwise."

Miss Nicholson gasped at Sam's metaphor and Mormon kicked him on the shin.

"What's the idea?" he demanded after Molly had gone out and Miss Nicholson had ensconced herself on the veranda with a book.

"You're plumb indelicut. You ought to be ashamed of yorese'f. You got to be careful round females, Sam Mannin', with yore expressions. Speshully one like this Nicholson party. She's a lady."

"Who in hell said she ain't?" demanded Sam. "Me — I guess I know how to treat a lady, well as the nex' man. I don't notice you ever made a grand success of it with yore three-strikes-an'-out."

Mormon disdained to reply. They went outside and, at the end of the ten minutes, walked together toward the cottonwoods. Grit was lying on the grave, and they saw Molly kneeling by the little railing. They advanced silently over the turf and stood in a group about her with their hats off and their heads bowed. Grit made no move and Molly did not look up for two or three minutes. Then she greeted them with a smile. There were no tear-signs on her face though her eyes were moist.

"I wanted to thank you all," she said, "and to tell you how glad I am to be back. I have met lots of people, of all sorts and kinds, but not one of them who could hold a candle to any of you three kind, true-hearted friends. I wanted to do it here where Daddy is in the place you gave him and made for him under the trees, close to the running water. I was only a girl — a kiddie — when I went away. I think I am a great deal older now, perhaps, than other girls of my age. And I realize all you have done for me. The only thing is, I don't know how to begin to thank you."

She went to Mormon and took hold of both his hands, her head raised, lips curved to kiss him. Mormon stooped and turned his weathered cheek, but Molly kissed him full on the lips. So with Sam, despite the enormous mustache. Then she came to Sandy, taller than the others, his face grave, under control, the eagerness smothered in his eyes, desire checked by reverence for the pure affection of the offered salute. He fancied that her lips trembled for a moment as they rested softly warm, upon his own. But the tremor might have been his own. He knew his heart was pounding against the slight touch of her slenderness that was manifest with womanhood. His arms ached with the restraint he set upon them, despite the presence of Mormon and Sam.

Grit surveyed the gift of thanks gravely, as a ceremony, as some ancient lineaged noble might have looked upon the bestowal of sacrament and accolade for honorably deserved knighthood. Perhaps it was that and the dog knew it. To Sandy, the little space about the grave, where the great cottonwoods waved overhead like banners, their trunks like pillars, the dappled carpet of the turf, with the sweet air blowing through the clearing and peeps of blue above through the boughs, was like a sanctuary. That the two others, men of rough life and free habit, yet of clean thought and decent custom, were touched with the same sensation, their eyes attested.

"I've brought some things for you," said Molly. "Just presents that I bought in shops. But I wanted to thank you out here where Daddy lies." She sought their glances, searching to see if they understood, satisfied.

"We're sure glad to git back the Mascot of the Three Star," said Mormon.

"An' the sooner you git through bein' eddicated an' come back fo' keeps, the better," amended Sam.

Sandy said nothing but smiled at her and Molly smiled back again.

"I think you have been my mascot rather than me yours," she demurred.

"Shucks!" said Mormon. "Yore mine, warn't it? He found it," he added, setting a brown big hand on the headstone. "You wait till you see what we bought with our share of the Molly Mine. Prime stock an' machinery. Look at the new corrals an' buildin's. Wait till you've gone over the place. An' we sure have been lucky with everythin'. I'll say you're a mascot."

"I've still got my lucky piece," she said and pulled out of her neck, suspended by the fine chain of gold, the gold piece with which Sandy had won the stake that had started her east. "Now show me all the improvements. We'll get Kate Nicholson. She's a first-class scout if you ever get her out of the shell she crawled into a long time ago when her folks suddenly lost everything they had. If we had a piano, Sam, she'd play the soul out of your body. Wait until she gets at the harmonium to-night. You and she will have to play duets, Sam, you on the three-decked harmonica I got for you."

"Aw, shucks!" protested Sam? "I'm no musician."

"You are," she said gaily. "You are my Three Wise Men of the West. You are all magicians. You took me out of the desert, you have made life beautiful for me. Don't dispel the illusion, Soda-Water Sam. I'd rather hear you play *El Capitan* than listen to the Philharmonic Orchestra."

"Whatever that is," answered Sam.

Molly's words were light but her eyes were frankly wet now and so were those of the three men.

"Come, Grit," she said, and the dog bounded to her, licking her hand, and so to the rest of them cementing the alliance in his own way.

"Some day!" speculated Mormon as they went to the ranch-house. He got a good deal into those two words, for all three of them.

In the week that followed the partners of the Three Star managed to find many hours for holiday-making. The ranch ran well on its own routine, and Molly was a princess to be entertained. Kate Nicholson emerged from her chrysalis and became almost a butterfly rather than the pale gray moth they had fancied her. Even Miranda revised her opinion. The Nicholsons, it came out, had been a family of some consequence and a fair degree of riches in South Carolina before an unfortunate speculation had taken everything. Kate Nicholson, left alone soon afterward, had assumed the role of governess or companion with more or less success and drifted on, submerged in the families who had used her services until Keith had secured her for the post with Molly when things had seemed particularly black. Now, riding with Molly, with Sam and Sandy for escorts, over the open range or up into the cañons, on picnics, the years slid off from her. She acquired color with the capacity for enjoyment, she developed a quaint gift of jest and she proved a natural horsewoman. Molly coaxed her into different modes of hair dressing and little touches of color. She laughed understandingly and talked spontaneously. Evenings, when they would return to the disconsolate Mormon, who bewailed openly his lack of saddle ease, they found, two nights out of three, Miranda Bailey, self-charioted in her flivver with offerings of cake and doughnuts to supplement Pedro's still uncertain efforts.

Molly chuckled once to Sandy.

"Miranda's a dear," she said. "I wish she'd marry Mormon. But Kate Nicholson is a far better cook than she is. Only she won't do anything for fear of hurting Miranda's feelings."

Yet the governess did cook on occasion, trout that they caught in the mountain streams, and camp biscuits and fragrant coffee when they made excursion, so deft a presiding genius of the camp-fire that Sam declared she belonged to Sageland.

"I love it," she answered, sleeves tucked to the elbow, stooping over the fire, her face full of color, tucking a vagrant wisp of hair into place.

"Not much like the East, is it, Molly?" Sandy would ask.

"Not a bit. Lots better."

"You must miss a lot."

"What, for instance, Sandy?"

"Real music, for one thing. Concerts, theaters. Your sports. Tennis and golf. The people you met at the Keiths'. Clothes, pritty dresses, dancin'."

"I love dancing," she said. "But not always the way they dance. Tennis and golf are poky compared to riding Blaze. I like pretty things, but I'm not crazy about clothes, Sandy. And lots of them are, back there. Grown-up women as well as the girls I knew. And they are never satisfied, Sandy. It isn't real there. Nobody seems to know each other. Anybody could drop out and not be missed. It is all a rush. It is good to be back — good."

She stopped talking, gazing into the fire. The nights at Three Star were crisp. It was as if cold was jealous of the land that the sun wooed so ardently and rushed upon it the moment the latter sank behind the hills. Sandy looked at her hungrily, wishing she would elect to sit there always, mistress of the hearth and of him.

"Young Keith'll be over soon, I reckon," he said presently. "He said he'd come. Like him, Molly?"

It was not jealousy prompted the suggestion, but Sandy had more than once contrasted himself with the youngster and his easy manners, his undeniably good looks, his youth, wondering how close he was to Molly's moods and ideals, making him typical of the East as against the West.

"He's a nice boy," she said. "He has always had things his own way. He's partly spoiled, I'm afraid. He'd have been a lot nicer if he had been brought up on a ranch. I've told him so."

"Why?"

"Life's quieter out here, Sandy. It's bigger somehow. Donald only pleases himself. He — they don't seem to have real families out East, Sandy. I don't quite mean that, but as I have seen them. The Keiths. They are kind but they don't belong just to each other. They have their own ways and none of them do anything together. He's been nice to me — Donald. So have Mr. and Mrs. Keith."

Sandy had no effort imagining Donald being nice to Molly, contrasted with the other girls who just amused themselves.

"I'd cut a pore figger at tennis, I reckon," he said. "Or golf."

"So would Donald breaking a bronco," she laughed. "He's keen to ride one, to see a round-up. Why, Sandy, they think life is wonderful out here. And it is."

He wondered how much of her enthusiasm was lasting, how much came of the affectionate gratitude she showed them constantly, how much she thought of the swifter life she was going back to presently at the end of the month — with one week gone out of the four. He wrestled with the temptation to ask her not to go back, or to have Miss Nicholson remain on the ranch to complete the education that was steadily widening — as he saw it — the gap between them.

Sandy was not ignorant. His speech was mostly dialect, born of environment. He wrote correctly enough, aided by the dictionary he had acquired. He had business capacity, executive ability, strong manhood. He read increasingly, his mind was plastic. But these things he belittled. And he was her guardian. Though he knew he might win her promise to stay easily enough, he did not wish to exercise his authority. It might be misunderstood, even by Molly herself, later. He could not force his hand in this vital matter, as he handled other things. And yet....

Sam had stopped playing, Kate Nicholson was weaving chords in music unknown to those who listened, save that it seemed to speak some common language that had been forgotten since childhood. The fire shifted, there was silence in the big room. Mormon sat shading his face, Miranda Bailey beside him, her knitting idle. Sam lounged in a shady corner near the harmonium. Grit lay asleep. It was infinitely peaceful.

There was the sound of a motor outside, the honk of a horn. The door opened and a man came in, gazing uncertainly about him in the half-light — Westlake.

"This is the Three Star, isn't it?" he asked, evidently puzzled at the group.

Sandy lit the big lamp as they all rose, Grit nosing the engineer, accepting him.

"Sure is," he said. "You know Miss Bailey, Westlake? Miss Keith an' Miss Nicholson, Mr. Westlake. They both know something about you. Come to stay, I hope."

His voice was cordial as he gripped Westlake's hand, though the remembrance of what Sam had said at the mining camp leaped up within him. Westlake and Molly! Here was a man who might mate with her, might suit her wonderfully well. Upstanding, educated, no lightweight pleasure-seeker, as he estimated Donald Keith. Here was a complication in his dreams of happiness that he had lost sight of. He saw the two appraising each other and approving.

"If you can put up with me, for a bit," said Westlake. "I've come partly on business, Bourke. I've left Casey Town."

He seemed to speak with some embarrassment, glancing toward Molly. Sandy sensed that something had happened with his relations with Keith.

"You're more than welcome," he said. "Any one with you?"

"No, I came over with a machine from the garage at Hereford," he said. "I'll get my things and send him back."

Sandy went outside with him and helped him with his grips. The machine started.

"Quit Keith?" asked Sandy.

"Yes, we had a misunderstanding. About my staying here, Bourke. It may be a bit awkward. Young Donald Keith intends coming over. I am sure he doesn't know a thing about his father's business affairs. But I have a strong hunch that Keith himself will be along later to offset any talk he thinks I may have with you. He'll figure I've come here. He doesn't know all that I have found out, at that. If it's likely to embarrass you or your guests in the least I'll go on to Denver to-morrow. I'm headed that way. I've got a South American proposition in view. Wired them yesterday and may hear at any minute."

"Shucks!" said Sandy. "Yo're my friend. Young Keith don't interest me, save as Molly wants to entertain him. I'm under no obligations to Keith himse'f. Yo're my guest an' we'll keep you's long we can hold you in the corral. As fo' Molly, you don't know her. If it come to a show-down between you an' Keith, with you in the right, there ain't any question as to where she'd horn in."

"I had no idea Miss Casey would be like — what she is," said Westlake, as Miranda Bailey, Mormon in attendance, came out of the house.

"Time fo' me to be trailin' back," said the spinster. "Moon's risin'. Good night, Mr. Westlake. See you ag'in before you go, I hope. I reckon you sure gave me good advice when you said to take cash fo' my claims."

She climbed into the machine which Mormon cranked. It moved off, Mormon watching it. Then Sam came out and joined them.

"Gels gone to bed," he announced. "What's Keith doin' up to Casey Town, Westlake?"

"It won't take long to tell you."

The four walked over to the corral and the three partners climbed on the top rail, ranch-fashion. Westlake stood before them.

"Practically all the gold found in Casey Town comes from the main gulch where the creek runs. The gulch was once non-existent. It is likely there was a hill there. Its nub was a porphyry cap, the rest of it was composed of layers of porphyry and valueless rock dipping downward, nested like saucers in the synclinal layers. Ice and water wore off the nub and leveled the hill, then gouged out the gulch. They ground away, in my belief, all the porphyry that held gold except the portions now lying either side of the gulch. That gold was distributed far down the creek, carried by glacier and stream. Casey found indications and worked up to where he believed he had struck the mother vein. He did strike it but it had been worn down like the blade of an old knife.

"It was the top layers that held the richest ore. Of those that are left only one carries it and that is the reef that outcrops here and there both sides of the gulch. This isn't theory. All strikes have been made in this top layer. Where they have sunk through to a lower porphyry stratum they have found only indications where they found anything at all. But the strikes were rich because sylvanite is one of the richest of all gold ores. They look big and they encourage further development and — what is more to the point — further investment. Some of the strikes have been on the Keith Group properties. They have boosted the stock of all of them.

"I have been developing these group projects. The value of group promotion, to the promoter, is, that as long as one claim shows promise, the shares keep selling. The public loves to gamble. Keith came back this trip and proposed to purchase a lot of claims that are nothing but plain rock, surface dirt and sage-brush. They are not even on the main gulch. He can buy them for almost nothing. But he does not propose to sell them for that. He was going to start another group. He ordered me to make the preliminary surveys. Later I was to plan development work, to make a showing for his prospectus.

"He knew one would have as much chance digging in a New York back-yard. I told him so. He has his own expert and, if he didn't tell him so too, he's a crook.

"Keith said he understood his business and suggested I should attend strictly to mine. I told him I understood mine and that it included some personal honor. I was hot. I suggested that wildcat development was not my business. He called me a quixotic young fool among other things, and I may have called him a robber. I'm not sure. Anyway, I quit.

"Now, Keith's kept me off from the properties as soon as they have been fairly started and I have been only consulting engineer for the Molly. I've been busy on preliminary work. The engineer he brought from New York has been in actual charge. That was all right. I'm comparatively a kid. But I know what is going on generally in Casey Town. There have been no more strikes, for one thing; the discoveries have all been in the one layer and they are gradually working out.

"Keith would rather develop a good property than a bad one. He has established himself, has a future to look to. He carries his investing clients from one proposition to another. He never has to risk his own money and he has been lucky. He has made money — lots of it. Now then, why does he start wildcatting?"

"Must need money," suggested Sandy.

"That's my idea. I believe he's been stung somewhere. I know he's been fooling with oil stocks. His mail's full of it. And I believe he's been bitten by the other fellow's game instead of sticking to his own."

"It's been done befo'."

"But that isn't all." Westlake brought down his right fist into the palm of his left hand for emphasis. "This comes from information I can rely on, from logical deductions of my own, from actual observation of conditions. Yesterday they closed up the stopes in the Molly. Boarded 'em over. This was done without consulting me. The superintendent talked some rot about not wishing over-production and pushing development. I heard of it after I had walked out of Keith's office, resigned, or fired. You can't issue an order like that without miners talking. I know most of them.

"Now then — there's no gold left back of the boarding in those stopes — practically none! The Molly is played out, picked like a walnut of its meat! If they do develop down to the second porphyry level they won't find anything to pay for the work. They have taken all the sylvanite out of your mine and *Keith is trying to cover up that fact.*"

Westlake stopped and eyed them. They took it differently. Mormon softly whistled. Sam slid out his harmonica, cuddled in beneath his mustache and played a little of the *Cowboy's Lament.* Sandy's eyes closed slightly. They glittered like gray metal in the moonlight.

"Keith can't help the mine peterin' out," he said. "Jest why is he hidin' it? So's he can sell new shares an' keep the price up of the old ones. So's he can unload?"

"Plain enough. Now the Molly Mine stock isn't on the market. It is all owned, as I understand, by Miss Casey and you three holding the controlling interest, Keith the rest. It's been paying dividends from the start. Keith will try to unload."

"He'll have to do it on the quiet or it 'ud have the same effect as if the news came out about the mine," said Sandy.

"True. He may try to sell it to you."

"Not likely. He doesn't expect us to have the money. We haven't. I take it he can't dump 'em in a hurry. That's why he's boardin' the stopes. If he don't trail over here in a day or so I'll shack over to Casey Town fo' a li'l' chat. I'd admire to go over the mine. Mebbe we'll all go. Might even call a directors' meetin'. Quien sabe? Much obliged to you, Westlake."

Westlake nodded. He understood that quiet drawl of Sandy's. If the li'l' chat came off, Keith would not enjoy himself, he fancied.

"The question is what move to make an' when to make it. If Molly is one thing she is game. We've got a good deal out of the mine an' it's all come so far from the sale of gold to the mint, I take it. We don't dabble in stocks. We're ahead. If the mine's gone bu'st she's done nicely by us, at that."

Back of Sandy's talk thoughts formed in his brain that held a good deal of comfort. Molly was no longer an heiress, if Westlake's news was true. And he did not doubt it. Molly would not have to go back East. Her relations with the Keiths would be broken. She had not spent all her share of the dividends. Keith held some portion of this. Just how much Sandy did not know. He had not held Keith to strict accountings, he had trusted him to bank the funds. That Molly had a banking-account, he knew. It might mean her staying west. The principal used on the Three Star was intact and would be turned over to her, if they could make her accept it, but it began to look as if Molly might remain, all things considered.

"I figger you're right about Keith trailin' over here to see if you've showed," Sandy went on. "That's the way I'd play him. As you say, he's got to git rid of his shares quietly an' he can't do it in a rush. I don't want to tell Molly she's bu'sted until we're plumb certain. An' Keith's got money of hers. We want to git that out of the pot befo' we break with Keith. He'll give us an openin' fo' a general understandin', I reckon. If he don't show inside of a couple of days I'll take a pasear over to Casey Town an' have a li'l' chat with him.

"Young Keith sabe his father's play?" asked Sandy.

"No." Westlake spoke decidedly. "He's not interested in mining. He's on the trip because his father holds the purse strings. He's a good deal of a cub, at present. I mean he don't show much inclination to use his brains. He's having a good time on easy money. He doesn't know the difference between an adit and an air-drill. Doesn't want to. Makes a show of interest, naturally, to stand in with his old man, but he puts in a good deal of time scooting round the hills in that big car of theirs, or going hunting. I heard he was trying to buck a poker game, but Keith's secretary heard that too and I imagine attended to it. It was not my province. He's a likable kid in many ways but he's just a kid."

"'Tw'udn't be fair to hold anythin' ag'in' him, 'count of his breedin'," said Sandy, "but colts that ain't bred right bear watchin'. Men an' hawsses, there's a sight of difference between thoroughbred an' *well* bred. I've known a heap of folks mighty well bred who didn't have much pedigree. So long's the blood's pure, names don't amount to shucks. Now tell us some about that South American berth of yours, Westlake."

Westlake rather marveled at the ease with which Sandy and his chums dismissed a matter that meant a material loss of money to them, but he had seen the light in Sandy's eyes and he knew his capacity for action when the moment arrived. The four sat up late, talking of mining in various ways and places.

"This Westlake hombre'll go a long ways," summed up Sam to Sandy after Westlake had turned in and Mormon had yawned himself off to bed. "He sure knows a heap, he don't brag, he's on the square an' he ain't afraid of work."

"A good deal of a he-man," assented Sandy. "Stands up on his hind laigs. He didn't come out of the same mold as Keith. Sam, you ain't a potenshul millionaire any longer, just plain ranchman. You can go to sleep 'thout worryin' how yo're goin' to spend yore dividends."

"That so't of worry won't tuhn my ha'r gray," retorted Sam, "though I wish you'd talk plain United States an' forgit the dikshunary. What I'm worryin' about is Molly."

"So'm I, Sam," said Sandy. "Good night."

That Westlake won approval from Molly, and also from Kate Nicholson, was patent before breakfast was over the next morning. A buyer came out from Hereford demanding Sandy's attention and he stayed at the ranch while the three and Sam went off saddleback. Westlake had expressed a desire to see the ranch and Molly had volunteered to display her own renewed knowledge of it. The buyer looked at the Three Star stock with expert eyes and made bids that were highly satisfactory.

"Better beef, better prices, that's the modern slogan," he said at the noon meal with Sandy and Mormon. "I see you believe in it. You can establish a brand for the Three Star steers, Mr. Bourke, just as readily as any producer of staple goods, and you can command your own market.

"I heard some talk in Hereford this morning of trouble at one ranch not far from here," he went on. "A horse ranch run by a man named Plimsoll. Waterline Ranch, I think they call it. I have a commission from a man in Chicago to look up some horses for him and I had heard of Plimsoll before, not over-favorably. I understand he is a horse-dealer rather than a breeder. And that he is not fussy over brands."

"He's got a big herd," said Sandy non-committally. "Claims to round up slick-ears."

"Slick-ears?"

"Same as broom-tails — wild hawsses. What was the trouble?"

"General row among the crowd, far as I could make out. Plimsoll shot at one of his men named Wyatt, I believe, and started to run him off the ranch. There were sides taken and shots fired."

"News to me," said Sandy. He was not especially interested in Waterline happenings so long as Plimsoll remained set. The buyer left and the rest of the day went slowly.

When the quartet returned, Molly and Westlake were obviously more than mere acquaintances. Sandy felt out of the running though Molly held him in the conversation. Kate Nicholson unconsciously intensified his mood.

"They make a wonderful pair, don't they?" she said to him. "Both Western, full of life and mutual interest."

Miranda Bailey, driving over, created a welcome diversion.

"I've brought a telegram out for you, Mr. Westlake," she said. "The operator phoned us to see if any one was coming over. Said you left word you were at the Three Star. Here it is. When you goin' to have your phone put into the ranch, Sandy?"

"Company promised to finish the party line next month," answered Sandy. "Held up for poles."

He answered with his eyes on the yellow envelope that Westlake, with an apology, was opening. The engineer read it and passed it to Molly. Sandy saw her face glow.

"That's fine!" she exclaimed. "But it means you've got to go. I'm sorry for that."

The relief that Sandy felt, and dismissed as selfish, was marred by the cordial understanding that had sprung up between the two. He wondered if they had discovered a real attachment for each other. Such things could happen in a flash. His view was apt to be jaundiced, but he did not realize that.

"I'll have to go first thing to-morrow," said Westlake. "I'm sorry, too. They've come up to my counter-offer, Bourke, and they want me to come on immediately. It means a lot to me. Everything," he added, with a smile that Molly returned.

"You'll write?" she said. "You promised."

Kate Nicholson looked at Sandy with arching eyebrows. She too appeared to scent romance, to approve of it. Miranda broke in.

"I'm sure glad it's good news," she said.

Sandy fancied she was about to ask about Keith. He knew her curiosity to be lively, though he thought her tact would appreciate the situation with regard to Molly. "I've got some of my own," she continued. "There's been trouble out to Jim Plimsoll's. He shot at Wyatt or Wyatt at him, I don't know which rightly. But there was sides taken an' a gen'ral rumpus. Several of his men quit or was run off the place. It's been a reg'lar scandal. Called the place the Waterline. Whiskyline w'ud have suited it better, I reckon. Plimsoll's aimin' to sell out, Ed heard. It'll be a good riddance."

"Whoever buys the stock is takin' a long chance," said Mormon. "Aimin' to sell, is he?"

"I'll have a telegram fo' you to take back, Mirandy," said Sandy. "You sendin' one, Westlake?"

"If you'll take it, Miss Bailey."

"Glad to."

Westlake and Molly were both standing. They moved toward the door and out to the moonlit veranda together.

"They seem to hit it off well, that pair," said Miranda.

Kate Nicholson murmured something about the kitchen and left the room to attend to some refreshments. She had gradually taken over supervision of Pedro and the results had justified Molly's praise of her qualifications as a housekeeper.

"Now tell me about Keith," demanded Miranda. "What's he been up to?"

Sandy told her.

"I ain't a mite surprised. That Westlake acts white. I liked him from the start. What are you goin' to do about Molly? You ain't told her yet?"

"No use spoilin' her holiday befo' we have to," said Sandy. "I'm goin' to talk with Keith first."

"It'll be a good thing in a way, mebbe," said Miranda. "Molly belongs out west where she was born an' brought up. I hope she stays," she added with a shrewd glance at Sandy that startled him into a suspicion that Miranda had guessed his secret.

Kate Nicholson returned and the talk changed. Westlake and Molly remained outside until the food was served. Then there was music. Through the evening the pair talked together, confidentially, apart from the rest. Miranda departed at last with the telegrams. Molly lingered as good nights were said.

"I've got something to tell you, Sandy," she said. "It's private, for the present," she added with a glance toward Westlake.

Sandy sat down by the fire with a sinking qualm. Molly perched herself on the arm of his chair, silent for a moment or two.

"It's a love story, Sandy," she said presently.

"Westlake?"

"Yes. He wanted me to tell you before he went. He's very fond of you, Sandy."

"Is he?" Sandy spoke slowly, rousing himself with an effort. "I think he's a fine chap. I sure wish him all the luck in the world." He fancied his voice sounded flat.

"I suppose you wondered why we were so chummy all the evening?"

"Yes. I wondered a li'l' about that." Sandy did not look at her, but gazed into the dying fire. He saw himself sitting there, lonely, woman-shy once more, through the long stretch of years, with a letter coming once in a while from far-off places telling of a happiness that he had hoped for and yet had known could not be for him; Sandy Bourke, cow-puncher, two-gun man, rancher, growing old.

"I was the first girl he had seen for a long while, you see," Molly was saying. "And he had to talk it over with some one. He told me about it first this morning and then the telegram came."

"Talkin' about what?"

"His sweetheart. Now he can marry her with this opportunity. She may sail with him. Isn't it fine? He showed me her picture."

"It's the best news I've heard fo' a long time," answered Sandy soberly.

"I'm sleepy," said Molly. "Good night, Sandy, dear."

She put her lips to his tanned cheek and left him in a maze. The dying fire leaped up and the room lightened. It died down again, but Sandy sat there, smoking cigarette after cigarette.

CHAPTER XVIII
DEHORNED

Miranda Bailey had offered to come in for Westlake with her car, but the train went early and he had refused. Molly drove him in the buckboard, his grips stowed behind, and Sandy saw them go with the old light back in his eyes. He gave Westlake a grip of the hand that made him wince.

"Bring her out to the Three Star sometime," he told him. "Mind if I tell Sam and Mormon, Westlake? They'll sure be tickled."

"I'd like them to know. And we'll come, when we can. Maybe we'll find you coupled by that time, Sandy. All three of you. And I hope we'll find Molly here."

"I hope so." Sandy fancied the last sentence more than casual.

"You can rely upon my information being correct," were Westlake's last words, spoken aside before he climbed into the buckboard and Molly flirted the reins over the backs of the team shooting off at top speed.

Sandy's mood had changed. He was in high fettle as he watched them go. The rider who was breaking horses for the Three Star surrendered his job that morning to the "old man."

Molly came back a little before noon, her eyes wide with excitement.

"Mr. Keith's in town," she said. "With Donald and his secretary, Mr. Blake. He asked me if Mr. Westlake had been here and he seemed annoyed when I told him I had just seen him off on the train. They all came from Casey Town in the big car. Has there been any trouble between Mr. Keith and Mr. Westlake?"

"The South American offer is a better chance than Casey Town," answered Sandy. "Mr. Keith may have been annoyed about that. His boy's along, you say? Is he comin' oveh to the ranch?"

"Yes. He wanted to come with me, to drive me out in the car, but I had the buckboard and I'd rather drive horses any day. So he'll be out a little later to take up your invitation. Mr. Keith has some business in Hereford. He and Mr. Blake will stay on their private car. He told me to tell you he would be out to-morrow to see you. Oh, here's a telegram for you."

"Thanks." Sandy tucked the envelope in his pocket. "Hop out, Molly, an' I'll put up the team."

"I'll help you. I haven't forgotten how to unhitch." Her nimble fingers worked as fast as Sandy's with buckles, coiling traces and looping reins. She led the team off to the drinking trough and fed each an apple, with Sandy looking at her, registering the picture that made such strong appeal.

"Goin' to take Donald Keith out fo' a real ride on a real hawss?" he asked her.

"Yes. To-morrow. He's keen to go. You'll come. And Sam and Kate?"

"I've got a hunch I'm goin' to be busy ter-morrer. Keith's comin', fo' one thing."

"I forgot. I wish you could come." The passing shadow on her face was sunshine to Sandy. Molly went into the house and he opened the telegram. It was from Brandon, as he expected.

> Thanks. Coming immediately. Was starting anyway. That trap worked. May need horses for eight. Will you arrange?
>
> BRANDON.

"It sure looks like a busy day ter-morrer," Sandy said half aloud. "Keith and Brandon — which means roundin' up Jim Plimsoll. Sam don't get to any picnic, either. He'll have to 'tend to the hawsses."

The Keith touring car arrived in mid-afternoon with young Keith at the wheel, the chauffeur beside him, grips in the tonneau. Donald Keith jumped out, affable, a little inclined to condescension at first toward everything connected with the ranch, including Kate Nicholson. The imperturbable driver left with the car. Young Keith's snobbery wore off as he inspected the corrals and the stock with eager interest and the riders with a certain measure of awe, which he transferred to Sandy on learning that he had broken two colts that morning.

"If they're broken, I must be all apart," he said, watching them plunge wildly about the corral at the sight of visitors. "I'd hate to try to ride one of them in Central Park. If I could stick on I'd be pinched for endangering the public. Wish I could have seen you bu'st them."

"There'll be mo' of it befo' you leave," said Sandy. His mood of the morning held. His generosity of feeling toward Keith's boy did not lessen when he saw how much the elder of the two Molly appeared. The youngster was spoiled, probably selfish, but he was distinctly likable.

"Know what time yore father expects to be out?" Sandy asked him, later.

"He didn't say. He's got some business to attend to. Some time in the forenoon, I imagine. I know he's figuring on getting back to Casey Town to-night. Molly, you haven't taken me out to see your father's grave. Won't you? You promised to." Sandy liked the lad for that. But it did not ameliorate his attitude toward the visit of Keith Senior.

That worthy arrived after lunch had been cleared the next day. Kate Nicholson busied herself to wait deferentially upon him and his secretary, the fox-faced Blake. Keith was brisk and brusk, breathing prosperity.

"I was detained in Hereford, Bourke," he said. "I haven't much time for anything but a flying visit. I promised Mrs. Keith I'd come over the first opportunity, and I wanted to see you. Donald's out with Molly, you say. I'll leave him with you on your invitation and pick him up when we go back east. That will be in about a week. Sooner than I expected. I'd like to spare a day to look over the ranch. I've heard fine things about it."

"Thanks," drawled Sandy laconically. "Glad to have a talk with you. Sam, Mr. Blake might like to see the hawsses gentled that came up this mo'nin'."

Keith raised his eyebrows but said nothing. Leaving Blake, Sandy led Keith to his office, rolled a cigarette, offered a chair to his visitor and smoked, waiting for the latter to open the talk.

"There are some papers for you to examine, as Molly's guardian," said Keith. "But Blake has them."

"We'll take them up later. Anythin' else?"

Keith looked sharply at Sandy's face. There was a certain grimness to it that reminded the promoter of the first time he had seen it. His own changed to a mask, expressionless, save for his eyes, holding suspicion that changed to aggressiveness. But the latter did not show in his voice which was smooth and ingratiating.

"Nothing of great importance. I hear Westlake has been over here, Bourke. We had a misunderstanding. Sorry to lose him, since you recommended him."

"He figgers he has a better job," answered Sandy.

"I'm glad he thinks so. He is young and lacks experience. His opinion clashed with that of my engineer-in-charge, an expert of high standing. Westlake was hot-headed and would not brook being overruled. There is no doubt but that he was mistaken. He is a valuable man, under a superior, but he is intolerant."

"He didn't strike me that way," said Sandy. "Me, I set a good deal on his opinion."

"I didn't imagine you knew much about mining, Bourke." Keith looked at his watch. "I'll really have to be going as soon as you have looked over those papers. Hadn't we better call Blake?"

Sandy looked out of the window. He saw Miranda Bailey's flivver halting by the big car, Mormon walking toward her, and wondered what had brought her over. So far he had not got the opening he wanted, unless he took up defense of Westlake more forcibly to introduce the matter. He was inclined to suggest a trip for himself to Casey Town to inspect the mine in company with Keith that night, but the coming of Brandon hampered him. He wanted to be on hand for that. Then he saw Mormon leave Miranda and come toward the office, bowling along at top speed.

"Excuse me a minute, Keith," he said. "My partner wants to see me."

Keith's face wore a scowl as Sandy stepped outside. His conscience was not entirely clear and he did not like the general atmosphere of the office. He scented antagonism in this rancher who called him Keith without the prefix. It was all right for him to omit it, but....He took out a cigar, bit off the end savagely and lit it.

"Mirandy wants to see you," panted Mormon. "She's found out somethin' about Keith that sure shows his play. He's been discardin'!"

The Keith chauffeur had wandered off to the corrals where Sam was showing Blake around. Miranda handed Sandy a long envelope.

"Hen Collins had an accident last night," she said. "Blew a tire on the bridge by our place an' smashed through the railin'. Bu'sted a rib or two an' was knocked out. We took him in. I'm sorry for Hen but it sure was a lucky accident. You see, Keith told him to keep quiet but Hen was grateful to Ed fo' takin' him in an' puttin' him to bed an' sendin' fo' the doctor. Don't open that envellup, that Keith weasel might be lookin'. I reckon you'll want to spring it on him sudden."

"Sure," said Sandy. "Spring what?"

"I'm flustered," admitted Miranda. "I usually talk straight. Now I'll start to the beginnin'. When Keith arrived on this trip he held quite a reception in his private car. Ed was there with the rest. He invited them up fo' cigars. Talked big about Casey Town an' gen'ally patted himself on the back. Said it was too bad all the stock of the Molly wasn't held in locally, but of co'se the pore promoter had to have somethin' fo' his money. He was real affable. Ben Creel asked him if he didn't want to sell some of his Molly stock an' they all laffed.

"This time, when he come back yesterday, he brings up the subject ag'in. He, an' that secretary of his who looks like a coyote. I don't know how many he saw or jest what he said, but this is what he told Hen. After he'd got Hen to lead up to it, mind you. That Casey Town was boomin' big an' that his own holdin's was nettin' him a heap. That he liked Hen fine an' had picked him out as a representative citizen. With a lot mo' slush, the upshot of which was that he lets him have a hundred shares of the Molly Mine at par. Hen was to say nothin' about it because, says Keith, if it got out he was sellin' stock, it would send down the price of the shares an' hurt Casey Town in general, Hereford some, an' you-all at the Three Star in partickler. I reckon he was plausible enough. Hen was sure tickled. He w'udn't have said a word about it on'y Ed picks these shares up out of the bed of the crick an' give them to Hen afteh he'd been fixed up.

"Ed went nosin' around Hereford this mo'nin'. He got eight men — their names is inside the envelope — Creel one of 'em — to admit they'd bought some shares. Mighty glad they was to have 'em. Ed didn't tell 'em anything different, but he come scootin' home at noon an' I borrowed Hen's certificut, seein' he was asleep. An' here it is."

"Mirandy," said Sandy, "I'll let Mormon tell you what we all think of you. You've sure dealt me an ace. Mormon, help Sam ride herd on the secretary. I'll be callin' you in after a bit. You'll stay, Mirandy?"

"I'll go visit with Kate Nicholson. I'm beginnin' to like her real well. Molly away?"

Sandy left Mormon to tell her and returned to the office. Keith eyed the envelope.

"Blake coming?" he asked.

"Not yet. When do we get another dividend from the Molly, Keith?"

Keith laughed.

"You're as bad as all the others," he said. "Sell a man stock, give him a dividend and he's like a girl eating candy. You had one just fourteen weeks ago."

Sandy nodded.

"I was askin' you about the *next*," he said, his voice still drawling but with a finer edge to it.

"Needing some ready money?"

"How about the dividend?"

"Why, that depends upon the output." Keith's voice purred but his eyes had narrowed. He watched Sandy like a card player who begins to think his opponent superior to first impressions.

"The output has been big. The Molly has been a bonanza, so far. I do not think it wise always to pay dividends according to the immediate production, however. It is better, as a rule, to average it, generally to develop the mine as a whole rather than work the first rich veins."

"That why you boarded up the stopes?"

Keith's face grew dark. The veins twitched at his temples.

"Look here, Bourke," he blustered. "You've been listening to some fool talk from that cub, Westlake. I know my business. You've got some stock in the mine, twenty-five per cent. I've put money and brains into it and I've got forty-nine per cent. Molly...."

"If you *had* fo'ty-nine per cent. I wouldn't be worryin' so much."

"What the devil do you mean?"

"I took you fo' a betteh gambler than to git mad," said Sandy. "I'll jest ask you a question on behalf of myse'f an' partners' twenty-five per cent., an' Molly's twenty-six, me bein' her guardian. Plump an' plain, is the Molly pinched out?"

Keith hesitated, struggled to control himself.

"Save me a trip over to Casey Town, mebbe," Sandy added.

"I got mad just now, Bourke, because of the interference of a man I fired for lack of common sense, experience and recognition of his superiors. Westlake is a hot-head and I suppose he has some idea of trying to get even with me by belittling me in your eyes and running down my management. I think I have shown my interests allied with yours. Mrs. Keith and I."

"She don't come into this. You didn't answer my question, Keith. How about it?"

"It's a damned falsehood."

"Then why are you sellin' your stock?"

The words came like bullets as Sandy whipped the certificate out of the envelope and slapped it smartly on the desk. Keith whitened, flushed again, recovered himself.

"If I was not friendly to you, Bourke, I should take that as a direct insult. I can understand that you believe in Westlake and take stock in what he told you. But he is a discharged employee. He has every reason...."

Sandy held up his hand.

"He's a friend of mine," he said. "Keith, I may not know the minin' game — as you play it. In some ways it's gamblin', like playin' poker. I've played that a heap. I can tell pritty well when a man's bluffin'. Mebbe you're losin' some of yore nerve lately. You show it in yore face. Yore eyes flickered when you said it was a 'damned falsehood.' I don't hanker to insult a man but — I don't believe you. An' here's this stock you sold. I've got the names of more you sold it to. Why?"

"A man in my position," said Keith slowly, "swings many big deals and sometimes he is pushed for ready money."

"I reckon that's the reason," said Sandy dryly. "Well, you've got to git it some other way. You've got to buy these stocks back, Keith. I control the big end of the stock in the Molly. If I have to go to the bother of gittin' an expert of my own, an' goin' to Casey Town to look back of those stopes, you're goin' to be sorry fo' it."

"I have a right to sell my stock."

"You ain't goin' to exercise that right, Keith. You may make a business sellin' chances to folks who like to buy 'em, but you can't sell Herefo'd folks paper when they think they're buyin' gold. I won't bunco my neighbors an' I ain't goin' to 'low you to do it with any proposition I'm interested in. You'll give me the money you got fo' the shares with a list of the men you sold 'em to an' I'll tell 'em the Molly is pinched out — as it is."

"You must be crazy, man! They wouldn't believe you. If you went round with a statement like that you'd lose every cent of your own and your ward's. You have no right...."

"Trouble is with you, you don't know the meanin' of that last word," said Sandy. "Right is jest what I aim to do. We'll put it up to Molly an' you'll see where she stands. We don't do business out west the way you do. We don't rob our friends or even try an' run a razoo on strangehs. I reckon the folks'll believe me. If they don't I'll give 'em stock of ours, share fo' share, to convince 'em until it's known the Molly has flivvered."

"You'll ruin the whole camp."

"Not to my mind. They'll git out what gold's left The Molly'll shut down. I'll git you to give me a statement 'long with the money an' the list fo' me to check up, sayin' you've jest had news the vein has petered out sudden — like it has. That's lettin' you down easy. They'll think you an honorable man 'stead of a bunco-steerer. I'm doin' this 'count of the fact you folks have looked out fo' Molly. An' I'm tellin' you, Keith, that, if Herefo'd folks knew you'd deliberately sold them rotten stock, you an' yore private car might suffer consid'rable damage befo' you got away. Out west folks still git riled over trick plays an' holdouts, hawss-stealin' an' otheh deals that ain't square. I'd sure advise you to come across."

Keith looked into the face of Sandy and, briefly, into his eyes, hard as steel. He made one more attempt.

"Let's talk common sense, Bourke. You're quixotic. The Molly is capitalized for a quarter of a million dollars. The stock can be sold at par if it's done quietly. I can dispose of it for you. There is no certainty that the mine will not produce richly when we strike through the second level of porphyry. There are plenty of people willing to buy shares on that chance after the showing already made. I tried to say just now that you have no right to throw away your ward's money, and you are a fool to throw away your own. People buy stock as a gamble."

"No sense in you talkin' any mo' that way, Keith. Mebbe you sell paper to folks who gamble on it, an' on what you tell 'em about the chances, makin' yore story gold-colored. Folks may like to git somethin' fo' nex' to nothin', but I won't sell 'em nothin' fo' somethin', neitheh will my partners, neitheh will Molly Casey. She's a western gel. Above all, I won't gold-brick my friends. I know the mine is petered out. You won't call my play about havin' an expert examine it, which same is no bluff. I believe in Westlake's report. We've had our share of the gold in it an', we won't sell the dirt. No mo' w'ud Pat Casey, lyin' out there by the spring, if he was alive."

"Suppose I refuse?" asked Keith, his square face obstinate. "I've done nothing outside the law."

"To hell with that kind of law! We make laws of our own out here once in a while. Justice is what we look fo', not law. We aim to trail straight. I reckon you'll come through. Fo' one thing I expect to have yore boy visit with us till you do."

The promoter's face twisted uglily and he lost control of himself.

"Kidnapping? A western method of justice. Not the first time you've been mixed up in it either, from what I hear. You don't dare...."

Keith stopped abruptly. Sandy had not moved, but his eyes, from resembling orbs of chilled steel, seemed suddenly to throw off the blaze and heat of the molten metal.

"Fo' a promoter yo're a mighty pore judge of men," he said. "I'm warnin' you not to ride any further along that trail. Yore son can stay here, or we can tell the Herefo'd folk what you've tried to hand to them. Yo're apt to look like a buzzard that's fallen into a tar barrel after they git through with you, Keith. Trouble with you is that you've been bullin' the market an' havin' it yore own way too long. Now you see a b'ar on the horizon, you don't like the view.

"When we bring up stock fo' shipment we sometimes have trouble with the longhorns. We've got a dehornin' machine fo' them. That's yore trubble, so fur as this locality is concerned. You need dehornin'. I can find out who you sold stock to easy enough, but I don't care to waste the time. An' if I do there'll be more publicity about it than you'd care fo'. Might even git back to New Yo'k. I'm givin' you the easy end of it, Keith, 'count of Molly. You an' me can ride into town in yore car an' clean this all up befo' the bank closes. We'll leave the money with Creel of the Herefo'd National. Then you can come back an' git yore boy."

"I don't remember the names. Blake took the record of them," said Keith sullenly.

"Then we'll have him in."

Sandy went to the door and hailed Sam and Mormon. They came to the office escorting Blake, whose fox-face moved from side to side with furtive eyes as if he smelled a trap.

"We want the list of the folks you unloaded Molly stock to," said Sandy.

Blake looked at his employer who sat glowering at his cigar end, licked his lips and said nothing.

"Speak up," said Sandy.

"There's a fine patch of prickly pear handy," suggested Sam. "Fine fo' restorin' the voice. Last time we chucked a tenderfoot in there they had to peel the shirt off of him in strips." He took the secretary by one elbow, Mormon by the other, both grinning behind his back as he shook with a sudden palsy in the belief that they meant their threat.

"Tell him, you damned fool!" grunted Keith.

"The stubs are in the car at Hereford depot," said Blake. "In the safe."

"Money there too? I suppose you cashed the checks?"

"I deposited them to my own account," said Keith. "Come on, let's get this over with since you are determined to throw away your own and your partners' good money, to say nothing of the girl's. She could bring suit against you, Bourke, with a good chance of winning."

He glanced hopefully at Mormon and Sam. They kept on grinning.

"Round up that chauffeur, Sam, will you?" asked. Sandy. "Tell him we're startin' fo' Herefo'd right off. You an' me can go over those accounts of Molly's same time we attend to the other business, Keith."

They went outside, Blake looking anxious and a trifle bewildered, Keith throwing away his cigar and lighting a new one, his face sullen with the rage he dammed. Kate Nicholson and Miranda Bailey were on the ranch-house veranda.

"Could I ask you to mail these letters, Mr. Keith? Two of Molly's and one of my own." Kate Nicholson advanced toward him, the letters in hand. With a spurt of fury Keith snatched at the letters and threw them on the ground.

"To hell with you!" he shouted, his face empurpled. "You're fired!" All of his polish stripped from him like peeling veneer, he appeared merely a coarse bully.

Sam came up the veranda in two jumps and a final leap that left him with his hands entwined in Keith's coat collar. He whirled that astounded person half around and slammed him up against the wall of the ranch-house, rumpled, gasping, with trembling hands that lifted before the menace of Sam's gun.

"I oughter shoot the tongue out of you befo' I put a slug through yore head," said Sam, standing in front of the promoter, tense as a jaguar couched for a spring, his eyes glittering, his voice packed with venom. "You git down on yo' knees, you ring-tailed skunk, an' apologize to this lady. Crook yo' knees, you stinkin' polecat, an' crawl. I'll make you lick her shoes. Down with you or I'll send you straight to judgment!"

"No, Sam, Mr. Manning — it isn't necessary," protested Kate Nicholson. "Please...."

Sam looked at her cold-eyed.

"This is my party," he said. "It'll do him good. I'll let him off lickin' yo' shoes, he might spile the leather. But he'll git them letters he chucked away, git 'em on all-fours, like the sneakin', slinkin', double-crossin' coyote he is. Crook yo' knees first an' apologize! I'll learn you a lesson right here an' now. You stay right where you are, Kate. Let him come to you."

Sam fired a shot and the promoter jumped galvanically as the bullet tore through the planking of the ranch-house between his trembling knees.

"I regret, Miss Nicholson," he commenced huskily, "that I let my temper get the better of me. I was greatly upset. In the matter of your services I was — er — doubtless hasty. It can be arranged."

He shrank at the tap of Sam's gun on his shoulder, wilting to his knees.

"She w'udn't work fo' you fo' the time it takes a rabbit to dodge a rattler," said Sam. "She never did work fo' you. It was Molly's money paid her. Kate's goin' to stay right here as long as she chooses an' I...."

Catching Kate Nicholson's gaze, the admiring look of a woman who has never before been championed, conscious of the fact that he had blurted out her Christian name and disclosed the secret of that touch of intimacy between them, Sam grew crimson through his tan. Kate Nicholson's face was rosy; both were embarrassed.

"Thank you, Mr. Manning," she said. "Please let him get up, and put away your pistol."

"Git up," said Sam, "an' go pick up them letters."

Keith, humiliated before his secretary and his chauffeur, the latter gazing wooden-faced but making no attempt at interference, gathered up the envelopes and presented them, with a bow, to the governess. He had recovered partial poise and his face was pale as wax, his eyes evil.

"I'll mail them, Miss Nicholson," said Sandy. "Let's go." He took Sam aside as the car swung round and up to the porch. "I'm obliged to you, Sam," he said. "It was sure comin' to him an' I've been havin' hard work to keep my hands off him. I've a notion he'll trail better now. If Brandon arrives befo' we git back, look out fo' him. Mormon'll help you entertain."

"Seguro," replied Sam. "Look at Keith. He looks like a rattler with his fangs pulled. I'll bet he c'ud spit bilin' vitriol right now."

"His cud ain't jest what he most fancies, this minute," said Sandy dryly. "Sorter bitter to chew an' hard to swaller. Sammy," Sandy's voice changed to affection, his eyes twinkled, "I didn't sabe you an' Miss Nicholson was so well acquainted."

Sam looked his partner in the eyes and used almost the same words for which he had just tamed Keith. But he said them with a smile.

"You go plumb to hell!"

Creel, president of the Hereford National Bank, a banker keen at a bargain, shot out his underlip when Keith, with Sandy in attendance, tendered him the money for all shares of the Molly Mine sold in Hereford, including his own.

"You say the mine has petered out?" he asked Keith, with palpable suspicion. Keith glanced swiftly at Sandy sitting across the table from him in the little directors' room back of the bank proper. Sandy sat sphinx-like. As if by accident, his hands were on his hips, the fingers resting on his gun butts. Keith did not actually fear gunplay, but he was not sure of what Sandy might do. Sam's bullet, that had undoubtedly been sped in grim earnest, had unnerved him. Sandy Bourke held the winning hand.

"That is the news from my superintendent," said Keith. "I wish I could doubt it. Under the circumstances, consulting with Mr. Bourke, who represents the majority stock, we concluded there was no other action for us to take but to recall the shares although the money had actually passed. Naturally, in the refunding, which I leave entirely to you, it would be wiser not to precipitate a general panic and to treat the matter with all possible secrecy."

"Humph!" Keith's suavity did not appear entirely to smooth down Creel's chagrin at losing what he had considered a good thing. He smelt a mouse somewhere. "There are only two reasons for repurchasing such stock," he said crisply. "The course you take is rarely honorable and suggests great credit. The second reason would be a strike of rich ore rather than a failure."

"I will guarantee the failure, Creel," said Sandy. "If, at any time, a strike is made in the Molly, I shall be glad to transfer to you personally the same amount of shares from my own holdin's. I'll put that in writin', if you prefer it."

"No," said Creel, "it ain't necessary." He glumly made the retransfer. Sandy viséed Keith's accounts and took Keith's check for the balance, placing it to a personal account for Molly. The check was on the Hereford Bank and it practically exhausted Keith's local resources.

As they left the bank a cowboy rode up on a flea-bitten roan that was lathered with sweat, sadly roweled and leg-weary. Astride of it was Wyatt, riding automatically his eyes wide-opened, red-rimmed, owlish with lack of sleep and overmuch bad liquor. Afoot he could hardly have navigated, in the saddle he seemed comparatively sober. He spurred over to the big machine as Sandy and Keith got in to return to the ranch, sweeping his sombrero low in an ironical bow.

"Evenin', gents," he greeted them, his voice husky, inclined to hiccough. "This here is one hell of a town, Bourke! They've took away my guns an' told me to be good, they're sellin' doughnuts an' buttermilk down to Regan's old joint, popcorn an' sody-water over to Pap Gleason's! Me, I tote my own licker an' they don't take that off 'n my hip. You don't want a good man out to the Three Star, Bourke?"

"I never saw a real good man the shape you're in, Wyatt. Sober up an' I'll talk to you."

Wyatt leaned from the saddle and held on to the side of the machine with one hand, his alcohol-varnished eyes boring into Sandy's with the fixity of drink-madness.

"Why in hell would I sober up?" he demanded. "Plimsoll, the lousy swine, he stole my gal, God blast him! He drove me off'n the Waterline, him an' the ones that hang with him. I'd like to see him hang. I'd like to see the eyes stickin' out of his head an' his tongue stickin' out of his lyin' jaws! I'm gettin' even with Jim Plimsoll fo' what he done to me." Wyatt's eyes suddenly ran over with tears of self-pity. "Blast him to hell!" he cried. "Watch my smoke!" He withdrew his hand and galloped up the street as Keith's car started.

The powerful engine made nothing of the few miles between Hereford and the Three Star and it was only mid-afternoon when they arrived. Molly and Donald Keith were still absent, there was no sign of Brandon. Sandy fancied that any wait would not be especially congenial to Keith, but the promoter was firm in his determination to take away his son from the ranch. While his resentment could find no outlet, it was plain that he and his were through with any one connected with the Three Star brand.

Acting without any thought of this, save as it simmered subconsciously, Sandy rejoiced that Molly would now stay. He intended to give her open choice — there was money enough left, aside from the capital used on the Three Star, to send her back east for a completion of education. Or to pay Miss Nicholson for remaining as educator. He surmised that Sam would persuade Kate Nicholson to stay in any event. Molly, returned, appeared so much the woman, that the question of further schooling seemed superfluous to Sandy. He felt that it would to her, especially after he had told her all that had occurred since morning. That she would approve he had no doubt. Molly was true blue as her eyes. Altogether, Sandy considered the petering out of the Molly Mine far from being a disaster. And, if Molly stayed west — for keeps — ?

Keith stayed in his car, smoking, ignoring the very existence of the ranch and its people. The afternoon wore on with the sun dropping gradually toward the last quarter of the day's march. At four o'clock one of the Three Star riders came in at a gallop, carrying double. Behind him, clinging tight, was Donald Keith, woebegone, almost exhausted, his trim riding clothes snagged and soiled, his shining puttees scuffed and scratched. He staggered as he slid out of the saddle and clung to the cantle, head sunk on arms until Sandy took him by the arm. Keith sprang from his car and came over. Sam and Mormon hurried up.

"What's this?" demanded Keith angrily, suspicion rife in his voice.

"I picked him up three mile' back, hoofin' it. He was headin' fo' Bitter Flats but he wanted the ranch," said the cowboy to Sandy, ignoring Keith. "We burned wind an' leather comin' in, seein' Jim Plimsoll an' some of his gang have made off with Miss Molly!"

"Where'd this happen?" demanded Sandy. "Sam, go git Pronto fo' me an' saddle up."

"That's the hell of it," said the rider. "The pore damn fool don't know. Plumb loco! Scared to death. Been wanderin' round sence afore noon."

Donald Keith sagged suddenly and Sandy picked the lad up in his arms. Weariness and fright, thirst, the changed altitude, had overtoiled his endurance. Sandy strode with him to the car and laid him on the cushions.

"Git some water," he ordered Keith. "We've got no licker on the ranch. Here's one of the times Prohibition an' me don't hitch."

Keith bent, opened a shallow drawer beneath the seat and produced a silver flask. He unscrewed the top and poured some liquor into it. It was Scotch whisky of a pre-war vintage. The aroma of the stuff dissolved in the rare air, vaguely scenting it. The nose of the wooden-faced chauffeur wrinkled. Sandy raised the boy's head and lifted the whisky to his pallid lips, gray as his face where the flesh matched the powdery alkali that covered it.

"Pinch his nose," he said to Keith. "He's breathin' regular. Stroke his throat soon as I git the stuff back of his teeth. So. Now then."

The cordial trickled down and Donald's eyes opened. Almost immediately color came back into his cheeks and lips and he tried to sit up. Sandy helped him.

"Now, sonny," he said. "Tell us about it. How'd this happen an' where? An' when, if you can place that?"

Donald nodded.

"Just a second," he whispered and closed his eyes. They were bright when he raised the lids again.

"Whisky got me going," he said. "I'd have given a whole lot for that flask two or three hours ago, Dad."

"Never mind the whisky, where did you leave Molly?" demanded Sandy.

"I don't know just where. I wasn't noticing just which way we rode. She did the leading. I don't know how I ever got back."

"Didn't she tell you where you were makin' fo'?"

"She didn't name it. It was a little lake in some cañon where Molly said there used to be beavers."

"Beaver Dam Cañon," said Sandy exultantly. "You left here 'bout seven. How fast did you trail?"

"We walked the horses most of the time. It was all up-hill. And I looked at my watch a little before it happened. It was a quarter of eleven. Molly said we'd be there by noon."

"Where were you then? What kind of a place? Near water?"

"We'd just crossed a stream."

"Willer Crick, runs out of Beaver Dam Lake. You c'udn't foller that up, 'count of the falls. Now, jest what happened?"

"We saw some men ahead of us. Molly wondered who they could be. Then they disappeared. We were riding in a pass and two of them showed again, coming out of the trees ahead of us. One of them, on a big black horse, held up his hand."

"Jim Plimsoll!"

"Yes. Molly recognized him and she spoke to him to get out of the trail. It was brush and cactus either side of us and we'd have had to crowd in. Grit was trailing us. Plimsoll wouldn't move. I heard more horses back of us and I turned to look. Two more men were coming up behind. They had rifles. So did the man with Plimsoll. He had a pistol under his vest. We couldn't go back very well and I could see from the way Plimsoll grinned that he was going to be nasty. Molly spurred Blaze on and cut at Plimsoll with her quirt. He grabbed her hand with his left. Grit sprang up at him and he got out his gun from the shoulder sling and shot him."

"Shot the dawg? Hit him?"

"Yes, in the leg. He fired at him again, but Grit got into the brush."

"Jest what were you doin' all the time?" Sandy knew the lad was a tenderfoot, knew he would have been small use on such an occasion, but the thought of Grit rising to the rescue, falling back shot, brought the taunt.

"The two men behind told me to throw up my hands," said young Keith, his face reddening. "What could I do?"

"Nothin', son. You c'udn't have done a thing. Go on."

"Plimsoll twisted Molly's wrist so that the quirt fell to the ground. The man who was with him tossed his rope over her and they twisted it round her arms. I had the muzzle of a rifle poked into my ribs. They made me get off my horse. And they made me walk back along the trail. They fired bullets each side of me and laughed at me when I dodged. They told me if I looked back they'd shoot my damned head off." Donald's eyes were filled with tears of self-pity and the remembrance of his helpless rage. "They kept firing at me until I'd passed the stream. I hid in the willows, but I couldn't see anything. I couldn't even see the men who had been firing at me.

"I didn't know what to do. I couldn't rescue Molly without a horse. I only had a revolver against their rifles and I'm not much of a shot. I tried to get back here but it was hard to find the way. I knew it was east but the sun was high and I wasn't sure which way the shadows lay. I was all in when your man found me."

"All right, my son. Keith, I'm goin' to borrow that flask of yores. Might need it."

He jumped from the car, flask in hand, and ran to the ranch-house. Kate Nicholson met him as he entered. "Has anything happened to Molly?" she gasped.

"That's what I'm goin' to find out," Sandy answered. "Mormon, git me my cartridge belt an' some extry shells fo' my rifle."

"I got to go git me my hawss," demurred Mormon who had followed him in. "Becos' I'm goin' on this trail."

"You can come erlong with Sam when the Brandon outfit shows. Or, if they don't show, you can bring erlong our own boys soon's they come in. But I'm hittin' this alone."

As he spoke he rummaged in a drawer and brought out the first-aid kit he always kept handy.

"You ain't takin' Sam?" asked Mormon, returning with the cartridge belt, Sandy's rifle and a box of shells. "I know you're goin' to ride hard an' fast, Sandy, but you got to go slow after you git tryin' to cut sign. Plimsoll's likely taken her over to the Waterline range country. They got a place over there somewhere they call the Hideout. It's where they hide their hawsses when they want 'em out of sight an' I reckon it's hard to find. I c'ud keep within' sight of you till you start cuttin' sign, Sandy, an' then catch up."

"Sam ain't comin'," said Sandy, filling his rifle magazine and breech, stowing away extra clips. "I'm goin' in alone. Mo'n one 'ud be likely to spoil sign, Mormon, mo'n one is likely to advertise we're comin'. They're liable to leave a lookout. Know we'll miss Molly some time. Figgered young Keith might git back some time. Plimsoll's clearin' out of the country an' I'm trailin' him clean through hell if I have to. Ef he's harmed Molly I'll stake him out with a green hide wrapped round him an' his eyelids sliced off. I'll sit in the shade an' watch him frizzle an' yell when the hide shrinks in the sun. This is my private play, Mormon. You an' Sam can back it up, but I'm handlin' the cards. I'll leave sign plain fo' you to foller from Willer Crick. They must have crossed at the ford below the big bend."

He left the room and they saw him covering the ground in a wolf trot to where Sam, astride his own favorite mount, held Pronto ready saddled. They saw Sam's protest, Sandy's vigorous overruling of it, and then Sandy was up-saddle and away at a brisk lope with Sam gazing after him disconsolately. Keith's car was turning for the trip to Hereford, spurning the dust of the Three Star Ranch forever — and not lamented.

"Ain't it jest plumb hell — beggin' yore pardon, marm — but that's what it is — plain hell!" cried Mormon. Tears of mortification were in his eyes, his voice was high-pitched and his chagrin was so much like that of an overgrown child that Kate Nicholson felt constrained to laugh despite the seriousness of the situation. "Me, I been punchin' cows, ridin' a hawss fo' a livin' fo' nigh thirty years," said Mormon. "I ain't what you'd call sooperannuated yit, if I am bald. I'm healthy as a woodchuck. But I'm so goldarned, hunky-chunky, hawg-fat I can't ride a hawss no mo' — not faster 'n a walk or further than two mile', fo' fear of breakin' his back. So I git left home to sit in a damn rockin' chair! Hell and damnation!"

"You're going to follow him, aren't you?"

"That was jest Sandy's way of lettin' me down easy. Sam'll go, but I'll stay to home. I'm goin' to give away my guns an' learn milkin'. Sandy's got about three hours of daylight. He'll go 'cross lots on the hawss, fur as he reckons the sign shows safe, an' no man can read sign better'n Sandy. Then he'll play snake an' he can beat an Indian at takin' cover. He'll drift over open country 'thout bein' spotted an', up there in the range, they'll never see, smell or hear him till he's on top of 'em an' his guns are doin' the talkin'. You ought to see him in action. I've done it. I've been in action with him, me an' Sam. Now all I'm good fo' is a close quarters ra'r an' tumble. He w'udn't take Sam erlong fo' fear of hurtin' my feelin's though even Sam 'ud be some handicap to Sandy on this trip of scoutin'.

"Sam can't take cover extra good, though he shoots middlin'. Sandy, he shoots like lightnin' fast an' straight."

"But there are four against him, at least."

"Fo' what?" asked Mormon with a look of scorn. "Plimsoll an' three of his cronies. Mebbe one or two mo' chucked in fo' good measure. What of it? Yeller, all of 'em, yeller as the belly of a Gila River pizen lizard. On'y way the odds 'ud be even w'ud be fo' them to git the drop on Sandy an' it can't be done. He's got his fightin' face on an' that means hands an' heart an' eyes an' brain an' every inch of him lined up to win. Sandy fights with his head an' he's got the heart to back it. Hell's bells, marm, beggin' yo' pardon ag'in, I ain't worryin' none erbout Sandy! I ain't seen him lose out yet. I'm cussin' about *me* — warmin' an armchair an' waddlin' round like a fall hawg."

Mormon slammed his hat on the floor and jumped on it and Miss Nicholson fled, a little reassured by Mormon's eulogy, anxious to talk it over with Sam.

Sandy, his eyes like the mica flakes that show in gray granite, his humorous mouth a stern line, little bunches of muscles at the junction of his jaws, held the pinto to a steady lope that ate up the ground, drifting straight and fast across country for the opening in the mesa that he had marked as the short-cut to the spot described by Donald Keith. Through gray sage and ferny mesquite Pronto moved, elastic of every sinew, springy of pastern, without fret or fuss though he had not been ridden for two days. Even as the man fitted the saddle, counterbalanced every supple movement of his steed, so Sandy's will dominated that of Pronto, making his mood his master's, telling him the occasion was one for best efforts with no place for wasted energy.

"We're goin' to cross a hard country, li'l' hawss," said Sandy. "But I figger we can make it. Got to make it, Pronto. An' we're sure goin' to. Doin' it fo' her."

Every now and then he talked his thoughts aloud, as the lonely rider will and, if the pinto could not understand, he listened with pricked ears.

"Grit must have been hurt pritty bad, I'm afraid. Still he might have trailed her 'stead of comin' back. Sun's gettin' to'ards the no'th."

He glanced at the luminary, slowly descending. "But the moon's up already an' she's full." He looked to where a wan plate of battered silver hung in the east. "We got some luck on our side, Pronto, after all.

"Wonder who the three were with Plimsoll? They've gone to the Hideout an' we got to find it, li'l' hawss. Some job, I reckon. But Plimsoll's goin' to be mighty sorry fo' himse'f befo' long."

As they neared the foot-hills of the range he lapsed to silence. He was taking chances, crossing country this fashion. He knew it fairly well, and he guessed at what lay behind the visible contours from the experience of years. Deep barrancas might crop up in their path, massed thickets of cactus that had to be ridden around for loss of time. The mesa, looking like a solid block of rock at a distance, was, he knew well, broken into tortuous ravines and cañons, eroded into wild thrusts of the mother rock, its central part eaten away by time and weather.

Part of the Three Star range, shared by two ranches, ran over the southern part of the mesa and it was close to its boundary fence that Sandy was heading. Then came the range of Plimsoll's Waterline, a rough country, unknown to Sandy, with scant food for many cattle, but sweet grass enough for a horse herd and containing pockets where the slicktails sometimes came.

Sandy struck the first rise. He was now a crucible filled with glowing white fury. Thoughts of what Plimsoll might achieve in insult and injury to Molly could not be kept out of his mind and they but added fuel. It was not Sandy Bourke of the Three Bar, riding his favorite pinto, but a desperate man on a horse infected with the same grim determination, a man with a face that, despite the fiery heat within, blazing from his eyes, would have chilled the blood of any meeting him.

He did not spare Pronto nor did Pronto attempt to spare himself, going at the task set before him with all the superb coordination of muscle and tendon and bone that he possessed. They slid down the sides of ravines that were almost as steep as a wall, the pinto squatting on its tail; they climbed the opposing banks with the surety of a mountain goat, a rush, a scramble of well-placed hooves, a play of fetlocks; then, with a heave of spreading ribs and hammer-strokes of a gallant heart under Sandy's lean thighs, they were over the top and away, with Sandy's eyes searching the land for the shortest, most practical way.

The place it had taken Molly and young Keith nearly three hours to reach in leisurely fashion, Sandy gained in one, splashing through the shallows of Willow Creek at the ford below the big bend and giving Pronto the chance to cool his fetlocks and rinse out his mouth in the cold water.

Ahead lay the chimney ravine that led around into Beaver Dam Lake, in which Molly and the boy had been attacked. Sandy viewed the chaparral, the trees that covered the lesser slopes, the stark cliffs above. Part of this lay in the Waterline territory. The chances that Plimsoll had left some one on guard were not to be slighted. But he rode on down the narrow trail. Once in a while he broke a branch and left it swinging as a guide to Sam when he should follow with the riders from the ranch. They would be coming in now and in a few minutes would start on remounts. Perhaps Brandon had come? Sandy wasted little time on surmise.

The tracks of Molly's Blaze and the horse Donald had been riding were plain as print to Sandy. He even noticed the slot of Grit's pads here and there in softer soil. He had picked them up at the coming-out place of the ford. Two more sets of hoofs came out of the chaparral and from there on the sign was badly broken. But Sandy knew the story and the interpretation was sufficient.

The shadows were getting longer, half the eastern side of the ravine was in shadow that steadily crept down as if to obliterate the telltale imprints. The moon was slowly brightening. Sandy's eyes, burning steadily, were untroubled by doubt.

The place of the struggle was plain. The brush was trampled. To one side of the trail there was a clot of blood, almost black, with flies buzzing attention to it. It must have come from Grit. He caught sight of another fleck of it on some leaves where Grit had raced into the brush out of the way of the crippling fire.

"I'll score one fo' you, Grit, while I'm about it," muttered Sandy as he dismounted and carefully surveyed the sign. He even picked up Donald's returning shoemarks. Six horses had gone on, one led.

Sandy swung up the heavy stirrups and tied them above the saddle seat. He stripped the reins from the bridle and pulled down Pronto's wise head.

"Hit the back-trail fo' home, li'l' hawss," he said. "If I need me a mount to git back I'll borrow one. I got to go belly-trailin' pritty soon."

He gave the pinto a cautious slap on the flank and Pronto started off down the trail. So far Sandy believed he had not been seen. If he had, a rifle-shot would have been the first warning. With the experience of a man who has seen shooting before, he had chanced a miss, knowing the odds on his side. It was twenty to one Plimsoll and his men had hurried off to the Hideout.

A buzzard hung in the early evening sky, circling high and then suddenly dropping in a swoop.

"Looks like Grit's cashed in," thought Sandy. "That bird was a late comer, at that."

But it was not Grit.

The ravine curved, forked. One way led to Beaver Dam Lake, the other rifted deep through rocky outcrop, leading to the Waterline Range. The boundary fence crossed it. Two posts had been broken out, the wire flattened. Through the gap led the sign that Sandy followed. He carried his rifle with him and he moved cautiously but swiftly through the half light, for the cleft was in shadow. The walls lowered, the incline ended, became a decline, leading down. The clouds were assembling for sunset overhead, the moon just topped the eastern cliffs, beginning to send out a measure of reflected light. A beam struck a little cylinder, the emptied shell of a thirty-thirty rifle. There was another close by. And scanty soil was marked with more hoofs. Sandy halted, wondering the key to the puzzle. Did it mean a quarrel between Plimsoll's men? Altogether he figured there had been a dozen horses over the ground. It was only a swift guess but he knew it close to the mark. Had Plimsoll been joined or attacked? And...?

His practised eyes, roving here and there, saw still more cartridge shells. Walking cat-footed, he made no sound but suddenly three buzzards rose on heavy wings and he went swiftly to where they had been squatting. A dead man lay up against the cliff, a saddle blanket thrown over his face. This had held off the carrion birds. The body was limp and still warm, it had been a corpse only a short time. Sandy took off the blanket.

It was Wyatt! Wyatt, whom he had seen not much more than four hours before, riding on the main street in Hereford, threatening vengeance on Plimsoll. A bullet had made a small hole in his skull by the right temple and crashed out through the back of his head in a bloody gap!

The row that had culminated at the Waterline Ranch, ending in the trouble between Plimsoll and Wyatt, had brewed steadily. It had been a reckless crowd at the horse ranch, practically outlaws by their actions though not yet so adjudged, yet knowing their tenure of immunity was growing short. There had collected, besides Plimsoll's riders, Butch Parsons, Hahn's and others of Plimsoll's following who had been forced from their livelihood as gamblers. They still hung together, waiting for Plimsoll to make a clean-up of his horses and move to places where they were less discredited.

Meantime they made their own crude liquors and drank them freely. They gambled and caroused late. There were some women at the ranch. There was little fellowship.

Plimsoll had lost caste as a leader. His moods were morose or bragging. His ascendancy was gone. The crowd clung to him like so many leeches, waiting for a split of the proceeds of the sale of horses that no one appeared eager to buy in quantity. Ready cash was short. There were frequent quarrels; through it all there worked the leaven of Wyatt's jealousy, fermenting steadily. There were men among them who had fought with gunplay and who had killed but, as they were cheats, so they were cravens, at heart.

When the split came, after an all-night session with cards and liquor, following the refusal of a dealer to buy the herd, it was not merely a matter between Wyatt and Plimsoll. Sides were taken and the weaker driven from the ranch. Preparations were made for departure. The frightened women fled back to Hereford.

"It's a rotten mess," declared Butch Parsons. "Wyatt or one of the others'll tell all they know. You ought to have shot straighter, Plimsoll. Just like cuttin' our own throats to let 'em get away."

"You did some missing on your own account," retorted Plimsoll.

"It was the rotten booze. You started it. If you'd plugged Wyatt right it would have ended it. Now we've got to clear out."

"There isn't two hundred dollars of real money in the crowd," said Plimsoll. "If Taylor had taken the herd...."

"He was afraid to touch it. We'll go south. That's my plan. You can find a buyer in Tucson. Put the horses in the Hideout. Leave one or two to look out for 'em an' turn 'em over later. We can arrange for a delivery if we make a sale."

"Who in hell's goin' to stay behind?" asked one of the men.

"We'll cut cards for it."

"Not me."

"What's the use of fighting among ourselves again?" suggested Hahn smoothly. "We can settle who's to stay later. There's grub in the Hideout and a safe place to lay low if anything goes wrong. They'll have a fine time proving up the horses are stolen. We've got to take a chance. Butch is right. We can't take them with us. There's a good chance of a sale in Tucson. Meantime we've got to figure on Wyatt. He'll likely try to get in touch with that Brandon outfit."

"Or that chap who said he was from Phoenix," put in Butch. "You made a misplay, there, Plimsoll. That chap was a ringer."

"You talk like a fool," retorted Plimsoll. "He sold us the bunch cheap enough. He never raised horses he'd let go at that price. He lifted 'em, like he said."

"Just the same, he didn't act like a rustler."

"It was his first trick. Young vouched for him."

"This ain't getting us anywhere," said Hahn. "Let's make for the Hideout and talk it out there. This place ain't safe."

Within an hour the herd, already corralled for the chance of a quick sale, was being driven to the glen known as the Hideout, a little mountain park with water and good feed where Plimsoll placed the horses that his men drove off from far-away ranches, or Plimsoll bought from other horse dealers of his own sort, keeping them there until their brands were doctored and possible pursuit died down. There were two entrances to the Hideout, one through a narrow gut almost blocked by a fallen boulder, with only a passage wide enough to let through horse and rider single file, a way that could be easily barricaded or masked so that none would suspect any opening in the cliff. The second led by a winding way through a desolate region, over rock that left no sign and wound by twists and turns that none but the initiated could follow. The place, accidentally discovered, was perfect for its purpose.

There were some horses now in the Hideout, the lot purchased from the man from Phoenix, whom Butch suspected. But Parsons was of a suspicious disposition and the rest had overruled him, though the purchase had taken most of the cash at their disposal, until they could make the sale that had fallen through at the last minute. There was feed enough for the entire herd for a month. There was a cabin in a side gully of the park, near the blocked entrance, the whole place was honeycombed with caves, in the towering sidewalls and underground.

Five of the nine left of the Waterline outfit drove the herd. Hahn and Parsons could both ride, but they were not experts at handling horses. They chose to go with Plimsoll and the outfit-cook, while the rest took the long way round to the other way in. The four lingered to give the rest a start. There was some liquor left and this they started to dispose of. At noon the cook got a farewell meal and they mounted.

"I hate leaving the country without evening up some way with the Bourke outfit," said Plimsoll. "Damn him and the rest of them, they broke the luck for us. As for the girl, if...?"

"Oh, quit throwing the bull con about that, Jim," said Parsons bluntly. "Sandy Bourke's a damn good man for you to leave alone an' you know it. Talk ain't goin' to hurt him."

"I'm coming back some time," said Plimsoll with a string of oaths. "Then you'll see something besides talk."

Parsons jeered at him. Plimsoll was no longer the leader and he knew it. But he hung on to the semblance of authority that an open quarrel with Butch might shatter. Butch was a bully, but Plimsoll respected his shooting. And Hahn sided with him. The cook did not count.

Plimsoll carried with him a fine pair of binoculars and, as they rode leisurely on and reached a vantage-point, he swept the tumbled horizon for signs of any strange riders. It was the caution of habit as much as actual fear of a raid. There were no Hereford County horses in his herd save those he had bred himself and he did not think Wyatt or the others who had left the outfit would be able to stir up sentiment against him in Hereford. It would take time to get in touch with Brandon. But they made it a point to be sure that no casual rider noticed them on the way to the Hideout, or coming from it.

At times Plimsoll rode aside from the trail to a ridge crest for wider vision. At last, coming up the pass of Willow Creek, he sighted Molly and Donald with Grit trotting beside them. It was the dog that confirmed his first surmise. He had heard that Molly had returned, but he had not dared a visit to the Three Star. Who the rider with her was he did not care. That it was a tenderfoot was plain by his clothes and by his seat. As he adjusted the powerful glasses to a better focus Plimsoll's face twisted to an ugly smile. He had a flask in his hip pocket and he swigged at it before he rode to catch up with Parsons and Hahn.

"I'll show you if I do nothing but talk," he said to Butch after he told them of his discovery. "We'll wait for them along the trail. We'll send the chap with her back afoot."

"And what'll you do with her?" asked Hahn. "We've had enough of skirts, Plimsoll. This is no time to be mixed up with them."

"Isn't it?" The drink had given Plimsoll some of his old swagger, and the prospect of hatching the revenge over which he had brooded so long took possession of him. "Then you're a bigger fool than I thought you, Hahn. That particular skirt, aside from my personal interest in her, represents about a quarter of a million dollars — maybe more. She's got a quarter interest and a little better in the Molly Mine. The Three Star owns another quarter. How much will they give up to have her back? Bourke's her guardian, remember. I think the chap with her may be young Keith. We won't monkey with him. He'll do to tell what happened. But we'll take the girl along and we'll send back word of how much we want to let her go. After I'm through with her. She may not go back the same as she came, but they won't know that and they'll pay enough to set us up and to hell with the herd."

Parsons and Hahn looked at each other, greed rising in their eyes. They had no love for the partners of the Three Star nor for Molly Casey. A big ransom was possible if it was handled right.

"You'll have the whole county searching the range," objected Parsons. "There's a lot know something about the Hideout and they'll use Wyatt to show 'em the way. Bourke'll guess where she is."

"Let him. Wyatt don't know about the caves, does he? We can take her some other place to-morrow. We won't say anything now to the kid about a ransom. We'll mail a letter after we fix details. But we'll take the girl into the Hideout now. That tenderfoot'll be lucky if he drifts back to the Three Star by nightfall afoot. We'll be out of the place long before that. And we'll put her where they can't find her till they come through. I'm running this."

The cook had ridden on ahead. Now he was waiting for them, looking back. Parsons shrugged his shoulders.

"How do we split?" asked Hahn.

"Three ways," said Plimsoll. "We'll take her to the cabin. The rest'll be at the other end. We'll keep Cookie with us — for the present. No need for the boys to know about it. We can manage that all right. Three ways, and I handle the girl."

Butch Parson grinned at him.

"I thought you'd lost all your nerve, Jim, but I guess I was wrong. All right, it goes as it lays. You handle the lady. You ought to know how. Now then, how'll we bring it off?"

Plimsoll talked glibly, convincingly. Butch Parsons had no extra share of brains, those he had had never been developed beyond the ordinary. Hahn was a good faro dealer. There his intelligence specialized and ended. Plimsoll was the master-mind of his crowd; they appreciated and acknowledged his capacity for details. That he had been unsuccessful of late they set down to his lack of nerve, dissipated in his encounter with Sandy. Their present lack of cash, the doubtfulness of being able to sell and deliver the horses, made ransom a glittering possibility. Hahn had some objections, but Plimsoll overruled them plausibly enough.

"I don't see the sense of letting the kid go," questioned Hahn. "He's good for a big split as well as the girl."

"You're a fool when it comes to looking ahead, Hahn. You always were," answered Plimsoll. What with the chance of revenge in sight over which he had brooded until it became a part of his consciousness, and the liquor still stirring potently within him, he felt that his ascendancy had become reestablished, "Keith — the old man — is too big a fish to monkey with. Got too many pulls and connections. He'd have the whole country out and the trick played up big in every dinky newspaper. That's part of his business — publicity. We've got one fish — or will have — no sense straining the net. We don't want the kid. Let him string along back best way he can. We'll get all the start we need. What else would you do with him?"

"Stow him away somewhere and send a tip where they can find him in a day or two."

Plimsoll shot a look of contempt at Butch, making the proposal.

"You and Hahn make a good team," he said. "No. One's enough. He may get lost — we'll take his horse — and that won't be our fault. He may make Three Star late this afternoon. I wish I could be with him when he tells what he knows. Time they locate the Hideout, we'll be miles away through the south end and they'll have one hell of a time trailing us over the rocks. The boys weren't over-keen about staying with the herd and they can vamose. We'll tell them it's best to scatter for a bit and name a meeting-place. The horses can stay in the park. If we put this deal over right we don't need to bother about horse-trading. We can get clean out of the country with a big stake, go down to South America and start up a place. There are live times and good plays down there, boys. All right, Cookie, we're coming. I'm going to take another look. It's ten to one they're making for Beaver Dam Lake — on a picnic."

He laughed and the two laughed with him as he went for his survey and returned, announcing that the girl and her escort were entering the ravine at the other end. They rode through the trees toward them. Molly and Donald came on so leisurely that Plimsoll feared they might have turned back and, with Butch, he risked a look down the trail, sighting them.

"They didn't recognize us," he said. "We've got to take Cookie into this. You and Butch ride on through the trees a ways, Hahn, till you get back of them. Then we'll get 'em between us. I'll wise Cookie up to what we are doing."

It was more than doubtful whether the three ever intended for a second to allow Cookie to share in the ransom money, but Plimsoll easily persuaded him that he would be a partner, adding that it would be foolish to let all the riders into the pot.

"She's Molly Casey of the Casey Mine," he told him. "Sandy Bourke's her guardian. We'll make him come through with twenty or thirty thousand, sabe? But there ain't enough to go all round and make a showing."

Cookie was a willing rascal and a natural adept at the double-cross. He raised no objections and the trap was set and sprung.

"You go ahead, Cookie, and open up the gate," said Plimsoll. Hahn and Butch were speeding Donald Keith on his way with close-flung bullets. "I'm going to have a little private talk with this lady. Go to the cabin and get some grub ready. There's plenty there. Spread yourself. We'll be along in a little while. That was a nice job of roping you did. I won't forget it."

"Allus c'ud lass' fair to middlin'," grinned the man through yellow, stumpy teeth. "That's why I tote a rope. An' I sure had a purty target."

Plimsoll scowled at him and he rode off. Molly, the lariat twisted about her upper body from shoulders to waist, constricting her arms, fastened where she could not reach it by a hitch, sat on Blaze, looking with steady contempt at Plimsoll, who held her bridle rein. He regarded her with sleek complacency and then his eyes slowly traveled over her rounded figure, accented by her riding toggery.

"Grown to be quite a beauty, quite a woman, Molly, my dear," he said. "Never should have suspected you'd turn out such a wonder. Clothes make the woman, but it takes a proper figure to set them off. And you've got all of that."

"What are you going to do with me?" she asked.

"I'm not going to tell you — yet. It depends upon circumstances, my dear. We'll all have a little chat after lunch. I'd take that rope off if I wasn't afraid I might lose you. You are quite precious."

She looked through him as if he had been a sheet of glass. From her first sight of him, back in childhood, she had known instinctively the man was evil. But she was not afraid. The blood that ran in her veins was pure and bore in its crimson flood the sturdy heritage of pioneers who had outfaced dangers of death and torture and shame. She was all westerner. The blood was fighting blood. She felt it urged in her pulses while her brain bade her bide her time. Rage mounted as she faced the possible issues of this capture, the flaunting dismissal of young Keith.

Plimsoll must be either very sure of his ground or desperate, she fancied. Both, perhaps. Molly had come into contact with life in the raw long before she went east. Education had not made a prude of her nor tainted her clean purity. She faced the fact and, for the time, she ignored the man. She had even time to think of young Donald turned tenderfooted into the mountains, to wonder whether he would be able to find his way back or get lost in the ranges. She heard the laughter that followed the rifle-shots and surmised that they were having their idea of a joke with the lad.

If he got back — then Sandy would come after her. She was very sure of Sandy and that he would find her. Until he did she must use her wits.

And Grit, gallant Grit, wounded and lying in the chaparral!

Though she still gazed through Plimsoll rather than at him, the scorn showed in her eyes and bit through his assumption of ease as acid bites through skin, eating its way on. He burned to wipe out his own trickeries, his cowardice, his failures, to wreak a vile satisfaction on this girl who sat so disdainfully, with her chin lifted, her lips firm, oblivious of him. She baffled him. A mind like Plimsoll's never had the clarity of prevision to see the strength of character that had been in the prospector's child, even as he had never suspected her unfolding to beauty. It roused the vandal in him — he longed to break her, mar her.

The return of Butch and Hahn brought him back to the fact that he was not playing this deal alone. While they might allow him some personal license, to them the girl represented so much money. Plimsoll's reprisals were only partly theirs, they would not permit him to balk them of their share. There is Berserker madness latent in every one that breaks out sometimes in the child that torments a kitten and ends by torturing it, maiming — killing. There had been nothing in what stood for Plimsoll's manhood to change such instinct, to restrain it where he held the will and power. But here he had to go carefully.

He cut short Butch's boast of the way they had scared young Keith. Both Hahn and Parsons felt a coil of embarrassment at the silence, almost the serenity, of their captive. They had expected her to act far differently, to rage, threaten, cry out. She almost abashed them.

"See if you can round up that damned dog, Butch," said Plimsoll. "I plugged him but we want to be sure he don't get away. He might help Keith's kid, for one thing. And he clamped my arm."

Parsons rode into the chaparral until he was barred by its thickness, trying to stir out the dog, without success.

"Dead, I reckon," he reported. "Crawled in somewheres. You hit him hard, Plim. Plenty blood on the leaves."

Molly bit her lips and paled a little, but turned away her head so that they could not see. She winked back the tears that came to her thought of Grit helpless, panting, bleeding.

They rode on up the rocky ravine that gradually closed in on either side with the rock walls set with cactus here and there, carved into great masses superimposed upon one another for a hundred feet. Presently they turned aside from the stony trail that left no record of hooves, and, Plimsoll in the lead, Molly next, walked their horses over a precarious ledge that zigzagged back and forth up to where a notch in the cliff had been nearly filled by a titanic boulder. To one side appeared a narrow opening, unseen from below by the curve of the great rock, just wide enough to admit horse and rider. A few feet in, they halted, and Plimsoll turned in his saddle while the other three men dismounted and carefully adjusted several rock fragments in the opening, piling them with a swift care that showed familiarity with their task, so placing them that they appeared as if a part of the wall. Butch clambered to the top of the great boulder and viewed the job from the outside.

"First-class," he announced. "That's sure a great scheme, Plim."

"Go on up to the tree and take a look," said Plimsoll. "Hahn, hand him my glasses."

Parson took them and climbed up to where a dead tree stood like a skeleton in a crotch of the rocks. It screened him from observation perfectly by outer approach.

"I can see Keith's kid," he said with a chuckle when he came down. "He's through the creek and he don't know which way to start. Looks as if he meant to follow down the creek."

"He'll not go far that way," commented Plimsoll. "Mount up. Cookie's getting grub and I'm getting hungry. He'll have to cook for the boys after we're through. They'll be showing up after a bit."

Below them, Molly saw the hidden park that lay so snugly back of the barrier walls. It was an irregular oval that appeared to curve at the far end. Gulches reached back, occasionally thick with timber that grew in clumps among the rocks and on the ledges, dotting the green grass of the floor. She caught the sparkle of a little cascade, the gleam of a streamlet. The cliffs were terraced and battlemented in red and white and gray. Their facades showed fantasies of weather sculpture that looked like ruined castles and cathedrals with cave mouths for entrances. Here and there a monolith of stone stood up out from the main cliff, spiring for a hundred feet or more. The grass was starred with flowers. Some horses were grazing a little distance away and stood at gaze, to break and wheel and gallop away with flying manes and tails. There was a good deal of underbush covering the talus.

The trail down was plainly marked. It forked after they reached the general level and the branch they took led into a side gulch where a log cabin stood, smoke coming from its chimney. Plimsoll took the rein of Blaze again and they broke into a canter. At the cabin Plimsoll took Molly from the saddle and carried her into the rude interior. There he set her on a chair. Cookie was busy at a stove frying ham and eggs, with coffee simmering.

"You'd better sit up and eat nicely, my dear," said Plimsoll as he unbound her. "You'll have to sooner or later, you know. No sense in being stubborn."

She said nothing but he saw a gleam in her eyes as she glanced toward the table where Hahn was setting out plates and cutlery.

"You'll eat with a fork, Molly," said Plimsoll. "Those steel knives are too handy for you. There's a nasty look in those blue eyes of yours that will have to be tamed — have to be tamed," he repeated as he took a demijohn from a corner and poured out a liquor that sent the reek of its raw strength sickeningly through the cabin. "Here's to your health, Molly — Molly Mine!"

The others laughed and drank their share before they ate the food that Cookie placed before them, talking louder, growing flushed with the crude whisky, while Molly sat facing the door, striving to catch something that might help, might give some clue. But the talk was all of the brawl at the Waterline with contemptuous mention of Wyatt and the rest. They seemed by common consent to ignore her once she had refused the food.

This attitude weakened her resistance though she strove against it. She had nerved herself to meet action. Now she seemed to count for little more than a bundle, of more or less value, that, having been secured, could wait its time for utility. Yet, before she had telescoped her vision to extend through and beyond Plimsoll, she had seen devils looking from his eyes, smug devils, but none the less menacing, risen from the man's own private hell pit.

Plimsoll looked at his watch.

"The horses should be showing up pretty soon," he said and rose, a little unsteadily. The effects of the liquor were patent on all of them. "Butch, you and Hahn go down with Cookie and keep 'em down at the south end. Get 'em to turn the horses loose. And get them out of the place as soon as you can after they've eaten. Better take what stuff you want, Cookie."

"I suppose you'd be jealous if we stuck around," said Butch, leering now at Molly. The whisky seemed to have been an acid test for his features, dissolving all that was not brutal. Hahn's cold sneering face was none the less evil.

"How long do you want us to give you, Plim?" asked the dealer. "No sense in our sticking round here that I can see."

"We've got to get the boys out of the way, haven't we? Keep your eyes peeled on Cookie," Plimsoll said in a lower voice as the ranch chef went out of the door with his arms piled with provisions. "He might take a notion to talk too much. We had to let him in, but he don't have to stay in. Soon as the boys are away you come back and we'll go out again this end, if all is clear."

"Where are you going to stow her?" asked Hahn "Leave her here in Split Rock Cave?"

The callous reference to her as if she was something inanimate chilled Molly. If only she had a gun! She had laughed at Donald's tenderfoot insistence upon carrying the one he had brought west as a part of his outfit and had never attempted to use. The cook's too well thrown rope would have probably thwarted any move of hers if she had had a weapon. Her fingers crept up toward her throat touching a slender chain upon which, ever since she had returned to the Three Star, hung a gold disk, the coin with which Sandy had gambled, the luck-piece. To Molly, even now, it was a talisman that held promise. If they left her behind them, somehow Sandy would unearth her. But that hope died.

"She'll stay in sight and touch," said Plimsoll. "Then we'll know she's safe. We'll make Windy Gulch to-night and stay there. It's as good a place as I know. One of us can ride over the mountain to Redding and mail the letter."

Butch nodded. "Come on, Hahn," he said. "Let's leave 'em together."

Molly cast an involuntary glance at the opening door, watched it close after the pair of blackguards and braced herself. The issue was at hand.

Plimsoll slid a bolt on the door, brought over one of the makeshift chairs and placed it in front of Molly, seating himself. His alcohol-laden breath reached her nauseatingly and she turned her head aside. As if a trigger had been released Plimsoll's face became inflamed with a passionate fury. The veins on face and neck swelled and writhed like little blue snakes, his eyes congested.

"Damn you!" he said. "Don't you turn your head away from me. I'll train you to better manners before I'm through with you. You'll be jumping to do what you think I want you to before long. You'll be begging me for favors. You may think you're too good for me now. You won't presently."

She saw that she had gone too far in her disdain; that she must try to leash the devils that had broken loose in his brain.

"Just what do you want?" she asked, and her voice seemed not to belong to her as she uttered the words that showed no tremor.

"You! Not for love, my beauty! Because you are good to look at — yes. But I'll take my time. I'll sip at the dish, my dear. I've got a big score to settle and I'll do it properly. We'll go over some of the items."

He got up and emptied a bottle that still held a generous measure. He staggered slightly and fumbled the chair as he sat down again. Molly watched him intently. If only he got sufficiently drunk. Before the rest came back. Perhaps she could get his own gun? Plimsoll laid a familiar finger on her knee and instantly loathing showed in her eyes. He laughed.

"Using that busy li'l' brain of yours, eh? Figurin' I'll get drunk. Want to play Delilah? Nothin' doin', m' dear. I made that booze and I know just how it treats me, sabe? Now then.

"Your guardian angel Sandy chiseled me out of my share in the Molly Mine belongin' to me 'count of grubstakin' your father."

"That's a lie."

"That's easy to say when it nets you a fortune. Easy to go back on a dead man's agreement. Four-flushing Sandy Bourke...."

Molly suddenly slipped back into the primitive. Something seemed to click and the refinement she had learned and used so far fell like a cloak that is dropped for freedom in battle. With the malignment of Sandy and her father she was Molly Casey, daughter of a Desert Rat, once more.

"That's another damned lie," she said.

"Haven't forgotten how to swear, have you?"

"I've heard how Sandy Bourke chased your rotten-hearted jumpers out off the claim and gave you until sun-up to sneak out of town. I've heard how you were afraid to look at him through the smoke but went galloping off while the whole camp laughed at you. Sandy a four-flusher! A coyote'll fight when it's cornered, but you...."

She had heard the whole story from Keith. It was a favorite tale of the promoter's. He used it as publicity across his dinner table. It gave the right touch of adventure to Casey Town. Plimsoll grew slowly livid.

"Heard all about it, did you?" he said slowly. "Then you know some of the score. And I can wipe off what I owe Sandy Bourke through you. And there are more items. There was the first time we met. I haven't forgotten that. There was the kiss you said you tried to bite out after you'd burned the doll I gave you. You told about that the next time I kissed you in the hammock at Three Star. You tried to rub out that kiss, too. Maybe the next ones will stay put."

"That was the time Mormon manhandled you." She saw the blue snakes crawl on his purpling skin, and she kept her eyes on them though her mental vision was on the holster beneath his vest. She deliberately taunted him to provoke him to an uncalculated move. Molly knew her own litheness, her strength. If she could get inside his arms, if even to endure a moment of his beastly embrace and could get a grip on the gun?

But there was something in Plimsoll that delighted in playing with a victim he felt sure of. It soothed his broken vanity.

"So," he said, "I'm going to get even with Sandy and with Mormon and that bow-legged fool Sam Manning who call you the Mascot of the Three Star, all at once; while I get even with you. And get what should have been mine at the same time. We'll have you tucked away while we mail the letter that will bring your ransom. Never mind the details of handling the money. I'll attend to that. But we'll bleed you dry. The price of all your stock and that of the three suckers at the Three Star at par — and all they can borrow on the ranch — that will be the price for you, my lady. With three days to deliver in."

"You talk like a crazy man, or a drunken one. They can't sell the stock in that time. And if you lay a finger on me they'll trail you to hell, Jim Plimsoll, and the devil himself won't stop them from skinning you alive."

Plimsoll shrugged his shoulders, but his eyes flickered and, for a second, his cowardly soul shrank.

"I'll look out for that," he said. "If you are delivered back to them as damaged goods they'll never know it till you tell them. Maybe you won't be over-anxious to do that." His eyes grew moody, his manner sullen. He was passing into another alcoholic phase. Molly sensed imminent danger.

"I'll take those kisses now," he cried and lunged for her, catching her about the waist as she rose from the chair. "And more to boot," he added thickly as he drew her to him, one hand at the back of her head, fingers twining in her hair, twisting her face forward, upward. She had both arms inside of his, her hands on his chest. With all her strength she strained and pushed away, her right hand slid up to the holster, groping.

The gun was not there. Plimsoll had reloaded it during the meal and left it on the table. His breath sickened her. She got her arm clear and struck him viciously on the mouth, breaking the lips against his teeth. Fighting like a cave-woman, she scored his cheek with nails that dug deep from the corner of his eyelid and brought the blood. As he shifted his hold she wrenched loose, leaving strands of brown hair in his fingers, and jumped for the door. In her spring she saw, too late, the pistol on the table. She drew the bolt, half opening the door before he caught her and dragged her back again.

"You wildcat," he panted. "I'll fix you."

Like a panther Molly fought, matching her young muscles against his, striking, clawing, biting. Her riding coat ripped, the neck of her waist was torn away. Maddened at her resistance he struck back. Once he got her about the throat, but her fingers were at his face, tearing at his eyes and he had to beat her off. The girl fought with all the sublimated despair of attacked womanhood, the man like a gorilla. The struggle was unequal, with more than forty pounds in favor of Plimsoll though, if Molly had possessed the puniest of weapons, she might have won. He held her at last, close to him, one arm wrapped about her, his right hand forcing the heel of the palm under her tucked-in chin, slowly, inexorably forcing it back while his bleeding, distorted face lowered. This time her arms were locked in, bent double, useless. Her kicks were futile, she had only her teeth left and she was going to try those. But she knew her strength sapped, knew in another moment or two she would be at the mercy of this brute who did not know the meaning of the word.

A shadow barred the half-open door, low down. A pointed head appeared with blazing eyes, with a neck-ruff flaring high. White teeth showed as red gums bared in hate and, forgetting the wounded leg that had held him back, Grit hurled himself in a staggering but magnificent leap. He could not reach Plimsoll's throat, he had lost much of his momentum through the damaged leg, he lacked power from loss of blood, but fury gave him strength for the spring that brought his teeth within reach of Plimsoll's right wrist, exposed; the cuff half-way up the forearm. Grit's teeth slashed like chisels, ripping through flesh, tendon and artery, sending jets of blood spurting before Plimsoll, with a yell of surprise and consternation, flung Molly into a corner, dazed and weak, and threw up his left forearm to guard against the dog's second leap.

It fell short. Plimsoll's right hand, scattering blood, groped blindly for the gun on the table behind him. He found the barrel and brought the heavy butt down with a crash on Grit's head, back of the ear. The dog dropped like a length of chain. Plimsoll kicked the body viciously, taking the bandanna from his neck and tying it tight about his wrist, fastening the knots with his teeth. With a look at Molly, crumpled unconscious in the corner, he sought for more liquor, found it and poured himself a big jorum, gulping it down while the blood dripped heavily from the bandage. He was soggy with shock and fatigue, the strong stuff half paralyzed his faculties and he dropped into a chair, gazing stupidly at his wrist.

His imagination was a curse to him. He had seen Grit's slavering jaws as they rose in the leap, the crimson glare in his eyes. To all intents the dog was mad. It had been lying wounded in the sun. Only madness could have given it strength to track so far. What if it meant lockjaw — hydrophobia? Through his dulled brain ran like a black thread the impression that he could feel the virus stealing through his veins, stiffening his body. How long did the damned thing take. And the horrible ending! He had seen a man die of it once, bitten by a mad collie, the same breed as the brute under the table. He had done for him, anyway.

Water — that was the test! There was water that Cookie had brought in for coffee, half a bucket, by the stove. He felt a sudden repugnance toward it. The slashed veins in his wrists burned and throbbed as if they were oozing molten lead instead of blood. And he was growing weak. If he didn't get a tourniquet fixed he might bleed to death. But what was the use?

Grit, who had opened a way out for Molly, lay still beneath the table. Molly, overtaxed, was in a swoon. Plimsoll sat in a stupor. The door swung wide. Cookie rushed in, his face muddy with alarm.

"The show's gone wrong," he cried to Plimsoll, who stared at him half-comprehending. "For Gawd's sake what's happened here? Gimme a drink." He snatched at the bottle and swallowed from the neck. "Here, you need a swig. We got to git out of here, pronto. Have you scragged the gel?" He thrust the bottle at Plimsoll who drank, senses rallying by the urge of danger that emanated from the cook like the sweaty stench of a frightened animal.

"Brandon's gang has come back," said Cookie. "It's the damndest streak of luck. They must have fell in with Wyatt or some of his pals. They must have been to the ranch. They cut off the boys and the horses over by Sand Crick! Reynolds got clear. He saw them comin' an' streaked it. They were shootin' like hell, he said. But he got a start an' he fooled 'em. Lost 'em, if they tried to foller him."

"And led 'em straight here," said Plimsoll with a curse, getting to his feet.

"Not him. He c'ud lose 'em twenty times between here an' Sand Crick. They were throwin' lead hard an' fast an' too busy to trail him if they saw him. He's gone out ag'in through the south end. Case they've got some one who does know the way in, he'll side-track by Spur Rock an' git through the pass at Nipple Peaks. It's hard goin', but we can make it unless we can git out this end. Hahn an' Butch has gone up to the lookout to.... Hear that?"

That was a single rifle-shot, followed by two others, the last almost as one.

"Hell!" cried Plimsoll, "they've got us this end. It's Wyatt. Just my damned luck for him to meet up with Brandon."

"Butch says it was the deal with that chap from Phoenix. He allus spotted him for a crooked one. They've planted hawsses on us to prove up. And Wyatt has been in touch with Brandon ever sense you took his gel away from him. Come on, I'm goin'."

He ran outside and Plimsoll followed to the door, lethargy leaving him in the face of disaster though he could not think fast or clearly. Hahn came clattering over the rocks on his horse, his face chalky white. He was reeling in his saddle, the horse spraddling, wild-eyed, almost out of control. Cookie jumped for its bridle as Hahn slumped sidewise in the saddle, clutched for the horn, missed it and was falling when Plimsoll caught him and helped him to the wall of the cabin where he leaned weakly. A blotch of blood showed on his left shoulder.

"Go get him a slug of whisky," Plimsoll ordered Cookie.

But Cookie, his face twitching with fright, jumped for his own mount and went galloping down the valley to the south.

Plimsoll sent curses after him, reaching for his own pistol before he remembered it was inside, dragging Hahn's half out of its holster and then quitting as the fleeing cook tangented and disappeared behind some timber.

The handkerchief about Plimsoll's wounded wrist was now a sodden rag, but the loss of blood had cleared his brain. He set his left arm about Hahn and helped him into the cabin. Molly was stirring and Plimsoll scowled blackly at her. He gave Hahn a drink.

"Brace up," he said, "what happened? I know about Reynolds. I mean at the lookout."

Hahn finished his glass, pushed it out for another, gulped that.

"Got to make our getaway," he said. "Butch is done for. They got me here under the collar-bone. I reckon they touched the lung. I never saw such shooting. But Butch got Wyatt."

"Tell it straight," demanded Plimsoll. "How many of 'em? What did they do?"

"We no more than made the lookout," said Hahn, "before six men came riding along, heeled for trouble. One of them was the black-bearded guy from California who was here with that Brandon, first time they came nosing around. And another was Wyatt, God blast his rotten soul in hell for a twisting hound! Wyatt was just starting to point 'em out the entrance when Butch lets him have it. Hits him smack in the forehead. Before he could show 'em the way in. He may have told 'em about it on the way up. But Blackbeard must have caught the shine of Butch's barrel. He fires back — they all had their rifles handy cross the pommel — the bullet goes plumb through the tree and knocks Butch down. Went through both hips. He falls against me and I show in the open, sliding on that damned slippery boulder, sliding inside and out of range, but they got me.

"They'll be through any minute, Plim. They'll go careful until they find there's no one firing back at them, then it won't take 'em long to figure out the way in. You can't tell how much Wyatt told 'em on the way up. They've got me. I can't ride. My lungs are filling up. Butch is paralyzed — if he ain't dead. A hell of a wind-up! You can make it out the way Reynolds did. None of the gang that left with Wyatt knows about the side-trail by Spur Rock. But you'd better beat it. Me, I've turned my last card. The case is empty!"

His head fell forward on to his arms. A trickle of scarlet came from the corner of his mouth. Plimsoll looked at him calculatingly. Hahn could not ride. But he wouldn't die for a while. To leave him here where the raiders would find him might mean a confession wrung from him that would tell of the getaway trail by Spur Rock and Nipple Peaks. He shook Hahn by the sound shoulder.

"Brace up," he said. "You can hide in Split Rock Cave. I'm going to put the girl in there. Take another drink. Pick up some grub. There's water in the cave. You can come out soon's the coast is clear."

"I'll not be coming out," said Hahn huskily. "But it's a good move." He weakly collected the bottle, some scraps of food.

Plimsoll stooped over Molly, coming out of her faint, and gagged her with her own scarf as her eyes opened and looked at him. He took off her belt and strapped her arms behind her back. Then, despite his wounded wrist, he lifted her easily enough and strode with her out of the door, Hahn following.

Hahn's horse was standing there obediently with pendent reins anchoring it! Blaze and Plimsoll's black were nipping grass in the little corral where they had been placed. Blaze whinnied at the sight, or the scent, of his mistress. Plimsoll passed the corral and went through a grove of quaking asps close to the wall of the side-gulch, keeping to the rock as much as possible. He turned into a cleft, stopping at a rock whose almost flat surface was level with his feet, a great mass of granite that some freak of weathering or convulsion of earthquake had split almost in half. Into the crevice a wild grape-vine had twined, and died.

"Can you make it, Hahn?" he asked.

The dealer nodded and knelt, using his sound arm to aid himself by the tough fibers, bracing with his knees. Down some ten feet in the crack he looked up, his ghastly face pallid in the shadow, with an attempt at a grin.

"Good-by, Plim," he said. "Good luck! What do I do with the girl?"

"Keep her from calling out. She's gagged but she might try it. Make her nurse you. Do anything you damn please with her!"

Hahn dropped out of sight. Plimsoll did not wait but picked Molly up from where he had deposited her, a helpless bundle, on the rock.

"The bottom's soft down there," he said. "Sand. It ain't more than fifteen feet. Down you go, you hellcat! They'll have a fine time locating you. And you've got a dying man for company. He'll be a dead one before morning."

He lowered her, feet down, released her and watched her disappear. He swung about and ran back to the corral, his hurt arm throbbing with his exertion. He had entertained a brief thought of hiding in the cave himself, but the fear of madness from the bite had not left him, the suggestion of it coming on in an underground cavern sickened him with horror. He craved the open. He flung himself into the saddle of the black horse, once leader of a slick-ear herd of wild mustangs, magnificent for speed and symmetry, worthy a better master, and galloped out of the corral, out of the side-ravine, into the open park. The rough towel about his arm was becoming soaked. Every jump of the black horse seemed to increase the bleeding. The spurt of fictitious energy that had carried him through since the arrival of Cookie was dying away. But he was on a mount that none could match, he was going on a trail that was hard to follow, practically unknown. Unless he was headed off, he could break through. At Nipple Peaks he could rest, attend to his wound.

A shout, a bullet whistling past that nicked the stallion's ear and sent him plunging and bucking, warned him that his enemies had found the way in and were after him. He did not look back, but bent forward in his saddle and sunk the spurs into the black's flanks. The half-tamed mustang's indignant bounds spoiled the aim of the marksmen, and, though the steel-nosed missiles hummed like bees about them, they gained the shelter of the same trees that had covered Cookie. Belly almost to ground, the black swept over the cropped turf at racing speed, the drum of his hooves like distant thunder, crest high, crimson-satin nostrils flaring, mad at the sting of the red notch in his ear.

Round the elbow of the Hideout, with Brandon's men distanced, into the gorge at the south end. A wild scramble up a steep slope and the way to Spur Rock was clear. Plimsoll smiled grimly. "Damn them, I'll beat them yet!" For a second he was silhouetted against a skyline, then he plunged down. Fresh droppings told him that Reynolds had won clear. He was safe from pursuit. If the wound — he should have cauterized it. But....

He reined in for a moment. The sound of a shout rang in his ears. It was an echo, he fancied, it must be an echo, flung back from the mountain walls ahead. But it could mean nothing else than a view-halloo. Some one had glimpsed him disappearing beyond the ridge.

CHAPTER XX
MOLLY MINE

Sandy, replacing the blanket on Wyatt's face, examined his guns and started climbing up to the big boulder. He could not see the rocks displaced by Brandon's men from below, but he picked up the bloody imprint of Grit's pad, with other smears of blood less distinctly marked. Soon he discovered the narrow opening and proceeded cautiously. The moon was quite bright now and the daylight almost vanished. Only the afterglow still flamed in the eastern sky back of the violet cliffs. The touch of night chill was already threatening, great stars were assembling court about the moon.

To Sandy's right was perpendicular rock, to his left the curve of the blocking boulder with the skeleton tree topping it, withered in the cleft that had first nourished, then denied it nourishment. It gleamed silver gray, attracting his attention. As he gazed his sharp ears caught the tiny crack of a brittle branch. Instantly he dropped to all fours as a spurt of flame showed from the tree and a bullet whined over him, to smack against the rock and fall flattened.

Sandy did not move. He knew that, to the man firing, his fall might have seemed a hit, that he had beaten the missile by the space of a wink. He heard more broken boughs, as if his assailant were clumsily, assuredly, clambering out of ambush, and he shifted silently into position, rifle set down, both guns ready. There came a strange thrashing sound, a groan of mortal anguish, silence. If this was a trick it was a crude one. Sandy waited. That groan, half sigh, half rattle, could not be mistaken. He half circled the boulder, gliding up a flattened traverse, and saw, lying outspread over a low bough of the withered tree, face to the moon, gun away from the curling hand, Butch Parsons.

With ready gun Sandy reached him, bent, turned him on his side. A bullet had ranged through both hips, shattering them. The spine must have been injured. There were puddles of blood that told the injury was some hours old. Butch had lain there paralyzed, passed by Brandon's men as dead, lingering like the traditional snake until sunset to see and recognize Sandy coming through the gap, to use his last remnant of life to pull trigger and so to die, the injured vertebrae giving away to the effort, the spark of life pinched out.

Sandy left him and returned to the gap. He could still read sign, plain as it was on every side. He found the side-gulch, saw the cabin, saw Hahn's saddled horse grazing free, Blaze in the corral, the cabin door open with the moon streaming in. He had pieced out the puzzle to his own satisfaction. Brandon and his men had arrived and, in Hereford, they had run across Wyatt, procuring horses there and saving themselves the trip to the Three Star. Butch's body was evidence that they had not been unsuccessful, Wyatt's that the fight had not been all one-sided, the surprise not perfect. And, if Plimsoll had been warned, what had become of Molly?

He got an answer that made his heart stand still, then pound in a rush of action. On the floor, in the beam of the moon, lay the luck-piece, a few links of gold chain attached to the coin. Stooping for it, he brushed a strand of brown hair. Then he saw Grit's body beneath the table. Fury boiled in him, chilled to icy wrath and determination. He put away the coin and hauled out the dog's body into the moonlight. It was limber and still warm. Sandy rose from his squat and swiftly examined the cabin. He discovered a lantern with oil in it, which he lit. The condition of the fire, corroborating other signs, told him that the fighting was long over with, the issue passed on. He had no fear of interruption. Before very long Sam and the Three Star riders would be along. The sight of Blaze suggested that Molly was not far away. If she had gone, by force, or her own free will, the probability was that her own mount and saddle would have been requisitioned.

Sandy's capacity for reading sign was almost without limit. He was better at it than an Indian because he had equally good observation and better judgment. But, to find Molly, with the ground about the cabin cut by arriving and departing feet and hooves, with Blaze in the corral, was a miracle that called for more than eyesight and deduction. If he could revive Grit...?

He found water warm in a kettle; he had the first-aid kit with its bandages, iodine, lint. And, above all, he had Keith's silver flask, half full. He did not fail to note the empty bottles on the table, the blood marks where Plimsoll's veins had sprinkled and Grit had stained the floor. He found, too, a button of horn with a fragment of black and white check, torn from Molly's riding coat in the struggle. Sandy's anger crystallized into one ambition beyond the finding of Molly, and that was to kill Plimsoll, if possible with his hands. He pictured the struggle between the gambler and the girl, desperate on one side, brutal on the other and, whether the stake had been won or lost, he resolved that Plimsoll should die for that attack.

Now his hope hung on Grit. He squatted on the floor by the lantern, a gun handy in case of need. He took the collie's head on his lap and examined the blow made by the butt of Plimsoll's gun. It had laid bare the bone but he did not think it either splintered or fractured. Grit's tongue lolled out from between his teeth and his muzzle was dry, yet Sandy fancied breath still passed the nostrils and that there was a faint beat of heart beneath the heavy draggled coat, matted with the blood that had drained life from him. Sandy knew that dog or wolf or coyote will lie in a torpor after being badly wounded and often recover slowly, waking from the recuperating sleep revitalized. But, if he could bring Grit back, he must make fresh demands on him.

He washed the wound on the head and poured iodine into it. He did the same with the hole in the leg, cleansing it from the dried blood and hair. It had stopped bleeding. He disinfected it, stitched it, closed it, bound it with adhesive tape and strengthened it with a bandage adjusted as expertly as any surgeon could have done. He pried open the jaws with but little resistance and let the tongue slip back before he poured in a measure of Scotch and water between the canine and incisor teeth. He tilted Grit's limp head, shut off his muzzle, stroked his throat and let the restorative trickle into the gullet. For a moment there was no response, then Grit coughed, choked, swallowed. Sandy repeated the dose with less water. It went down naturally. Almost immediately he felt the heart stroke strengthen. Grit sneezed, opened his eyes and feebly thumped his tail as he licked Sandy's hand.

"Grit, ol' pardner," said Sandy seriously, the dog's head between his hands, "yo're sure mussed up a heap an' I hate to do it, but I got to call on you, son. Mebbe it won't be such a long trick, but I can't git by without yore nose, Grit. It's worth more'n all I've got. An' I know yo're game. I'm goin' to give you some mo' of Keith's special Scotch, which I sure had a hunch w'ud come in handy, an' then we'll try it."

Grit wagged his tail more vigorously and tried to get on his feet, but Sandy prevented him until the third dose was administered. Then he carried the dog outside to save him every foot of unnecessary progress, and set him down. The collie stood up, wabbly on one foot but able to stand, looking eagerly at Sandy, commencing to snuff the air. Sandy let him smell the coin, the strand of hair, the piece of cloth and, with his keenest sense stimulated with the perfume that stood to Grit for love, the dog wrinkled his nose and cast around. But he led direct to Blaze and stood by the horse uncertain while Blaze nosed down at him.

"Carried out of the cabin, son," said Sandy. "We'll guess at Plimsoll. He's got clear of the locality. Blaze knows but he can't tell. We've got to cast about." He picked up the dog again, puzzled, and looked about him in the gulch, suffused with moonlight. "There sh'ud be soft dirt under those asps, let's give a look-see there."

They had not gone five feet into the trees before man and dog made a simultaneous discovery. For Sandy it was a heel-mark left by Plimsoll, treading heavily under his burden, a slight depression enough, but plain to Sandy. Grit began to struggle in his arms. Molly's hair or body must have brushed against lower boughs at the same height that Sandy carried the wounded Grit and the scent still clung.

"They c'udn't go fur in this direction by the looks of the place, Grit," said Sandy. "See what you can make of it." He put him down by the heel-print. Grit uttered a low growl deep back in his throat, his ruff lifted. Hatred replaced love, but the two odors and emotions were inextricably linked for Grit that day. He started off, hobbling along, leading truly over rock or sand, into the cove where the split rock lay, its crevice black, the vine curving down into it like a serpent. Where Plimsoll had laid her down Grit halted and raised his head, his tongue playing in and out of his jaws in his triumphant excitement, his eyes luminous, his tail waving like the plume of a knight. Sandy gently patted him, pressed him down to a crouch.

"Down charge, Grit," he whispered in his ear. "You've got it. You stay here." Sandy had left his rifle at the cabin when he carried Grit out, now he spun the two cylinders of his Colts, lowered himself into the split, holding on to the vine, looking straight into Grit's lambent eyes.

"Stay here, son," he said softly, and Grit licked the face now on a level with his own. "I'll be back."

Sandy doubted whether he would find Plimsoll in this rock hollow, or any one but Molly. There had been the one horse saddled and grazing free, but that might have belonged to the dead man by the withered tree. It made little difference. There was, to him, the certainty that Molly was there and there was no other way of finding out or getting to her. He had adventured more dangerous chances than this.

He felt his legs dangle into space and his hands found a curving loop in the vine trunk that sagged slightly under his weight. Extended at full length, his toes touched bottom. Letting go, he dropped lightly and stood in blackness, the crevice above him showing a strip of azure light. Sandy listened, wishing for Grit. He might be able to get him down, now that he knew the depth of the descent.

There was only the sound of dripping water. He had a vague sense of empty spaces all about him. He ventured a match, holding it at arm's length in his left hand, flicking friction with his nail, an old trick. The match caught and began to blaze instantly in the still air. Low down, and to the right, there showed a stab of flame, the roar of an exploding cartridge, the reek of high-powered gas seemed to fill the cavern. The bullet passed through Sandy's coat sleeve. If he had held the match in front of him he would have been shot through heart or lungs. His right-hand gun barked from his hip, straight for where the flame had showed, then to right of it, to left, above, his left-hand gun joining in the merciless probe. No second shot came in answer.

Sandy lit another match. Its flare showed him a sandy floor, slightly sloping, moist in one place, a charred stick almost at his feet. It was a pine knot, half burned, and he lighted it easily, advancing toward the spot where he had flung the shots he knew had silenced whoever had fired at the first match. He found Hahn, crumpled up, shot through the right arm and a thigh, besides the other wound in his shoulder. There was not much life in him, he had suffered a hemorrhage twice before Sandy came; the shock of the two bullets had brought on another.

Sandy turned him over, brought Keith's flask into play. Hahn looked up at him and essayed a grin.

"Yo're game all right, Hahn," said Sandy. "You ain't the man I was lookin' fo', but you fired first. I see I wasn't the first to plug you. Mebbe I can fix you up a bit?"

Hahn shook his head.

"'Twouldn't be a mite of use," he said huskily. "I'm empty of blood as a prohibition flask. I reckon it will be prohibition for me from now on. They say it's sure dry where I'm going. No grudge against you, Sandy. I thought you one of Brandon's gang. They got Butch and me an' they're chasin' Jim Plimsoll to hell and gone — over Nipple Peaks — if he beats 'em to Spur Rock he'll fool 'em on the black — I couldn't ride — he left me here — with the girl — but the case is empty and the bank's bu'sted — cashing — in — time and no chips."

He was wandering in his mind, speaking without control, but Sandy's mouth tightened at the mention of Nipple Peaks, relaxed again on the word "girl." He gave Hahn the last few drops of whisky.

"Where in hell'd you get that?" asked the dealer weakly, coughed violently, collapsed, shuddered, writhed a little and was still before he could answer Sandy's eager question about Molly.

He found her without much searching, rolled down a little slope beyond the crevice. Under the light of the torch her eyes looked up at him. Her hair was in disorder, her raiment torn, her slender body wound about by the lariat rope, her mouth and chin hidden by the tightly drawn bandanna, but her gaze, reflecting the flare of the pine knot, held so much of welcome, of faith, of pride and courage, all sourced in something deeper, far more wonderful, moving beneath the surface like a well spring, that Sandy's heart swelled with glad emotion, knowing she was unharmed, knowing that his coming was no surprise, however welcome.

He found himself trembling as he untied her bonds and took away the gag from the mouth that lifted to his. She snuggled into his arms and, as the torch sputtered out, leaving them in the darkness, save for the luminous beams that stole down from where Grit whimpered in joyous impatience, her hair showered down over both of them.

"Sandy. I knew you'd come in time!" she whispered.

He held her close and hard for a tense moment that gave all his world to his embrace.

"Molly — girl," he said brokenly, his voice broken with passion.

Her hand crept up and a soft palm cupped about his chin. He kissed the edge of it. He rose easily, still holding her and lifted her high to where she could reach the vine, swinging up after her, Grit dancing a three-legged reel of joy as they came up into the free air and the moonlight.

Blaze greeted them in the corral. Molly mounted, and Sandy set Grit on the saddle in front of her.

"Where's Pronto?" she asked.

He told her.

"I figger Sam an' the boys'll be erlong soon," he said. "They may meet up with Pronto. Anyway, they'll likely bring Goldie fo' me. She's up. An' Pronto'll be too tired fo' what I want him to do ter-night."

She sensed the change in his voice, intuitively guessed but, womanlike, asked:

"What do you mean, Sandy? Aren't you coming home with me to Three Star. If it wasn't so far I'd love to go back just like this, without meeting anybody." She had taken off Sandy's Stetson and she ran fingers through his hair, thrilling him to the intimacy of the caress. But, if there was any plan in her actions, it did not deter him from his.

"Plimsoll's makin' fo' Nipple Peaks an' he's likely to git clear. Me, I aim to head him off an' settle the account."

"Sandy." There was a plea in her voice that plucked at his heart strings. "Don't spoil to-night. Please!"

"That ain't Molly Casey talkin'," said Sandy. "That's somethin' you must have picked up back to Keith's."

"He didn't harm me, Sandy."

"He tried to."

Her hand slipped to his shoulder, touched his cheek. She reined in Blaze. Sandy stood beside her, straight and stern, his eyes implacable.

"He ain't fit to live," he went on. "I w'udn't be fit to go back to Three Star where yore daddy lies an' know he was there in his grave while I let that coyote go loose. I found the luck-piece on the floor of the cabin, Molly, with a lock of yore hair he must have tore out, a button an' a bit of yore dress he nigh tore off you. I was in hell when I thought of you fightin' him off an' if I have to wade through it knee-deep in flamin' sulphur I'm goin' to find that snake an' make sure he quits trailin'. Why, it's my job, Molly. What w'ud you think of me if I let him slide?"

"I know," she answered.

A horse whinnied from down the ravine. Blaze answered.

"That'll be Sam an' the boys, Molly." He cupped hands and sounded a "Yahoo!"

The answer came back clear through the evening, multiplied by the rocks about them.

"I'm afraid," she said.

"Afraid?"

"I know. I never was before. But...." She broke off, leaned swiftly down from the saddle and kissed him.

"Come back to me soon, Sandy," she said.

CHAPTER XXI
THE END OF THE ROPE

Pronto had chosen his own trail and gait back to the Three Star. It was Goldie that Sandy rode under the stars toward Nipple Peaks. He was alone, refusing any company of Sam or the riders. Molly's last kiss had been the key that turned in the lock of his heart and opened up to reality the garden of his dreams where the two of them would walk together, work together all their days. It could have meant nothing else. And she had been afraid — for him. Plimsoll living was a blot upon the fair page of happiness. Though Molly, thank God, had come through unharmed, to Sandy the touch of Plimsoll was a defilement that could only be wiped out by his death.

Nipple Peaks he knew by sight, two high mounds of bare granite above the timber-line, barring the way to a jumbled country of peaks and ravines and cross cañons among which lay Plimsoll's Hideout. Spur Rock he knew only by rumor. That there was a pass between the peaks he did not doubt. And he rode to meet Plimsoll coming down out of it. To have returned to the Hideout and attempted to follow a rock trail by moonlight, despite its brilliance, would have been sheer folly. Plimsoll had from three to four hours' start, he figured. And he calculated that, with luck, with common luck and justice, he would pick him up before he reached the base of the mountain, before he got into the timber. If not, sooner or later he would cut Plimsoll's sign and follow it to the end.

As he rode over the finny ridge of Elk Mountain and saw the Nipple Peaks gleaming above the black pines across the valley, with Elk River gleaming in the middle, he realized that he had said nothing to Molly of Keith, of the shutting down of the mine and his own action in her name. While she had asked nothing of young Donald. For the time it had been as if the rest of the world had been fenced off from them and their own intimate affairs.

He compressed his knees and the mare answered in a lope that stretched into a gallop, fast and faster as she reached the levels and sped toward Elk River. Sandy was not going to waste time looking for a ford. The mare could swim. The moon, sloping down toward the west, still above the range, helped by the big white stars, made the valley bright almost as day. He scanned the mountain toward the peaks, passed over the dark impenetrable pines, surveyed the stretch of gently rising ground between the Elk and the trees and shifted his guns in their scabbards. His rifle he had left with Sam. Either Plimsoll had not passed the peaks, was in the woods, or he had come and gone. Something told Sandy this last had not occurred. Travel beyond the peaks must have been hard and slow and roundabout for Plimsoll while he had tangented fast for the cut-off.

The mare took the cold river water about her fetlocks with a little shiver, wading in to the girths, sliding to a deep pool where she had to swim a few strokes before she found gravel under her hoofs and scrambled out. Suddenly, while Sandy hesitated how best to arrange his patrol, a horse came floundering out of the pines less than a quarter of a mile away, a black horse, shining with sweat, tired to its limit, staggering in its stride, the rider hunched in the saddle more like a sack of meal than a man.

Before Sandy could turn the mare toward them three riders burst from the trees like bolts from a crossbow, spurring their mounts, the two in the lead swinging lariats. They divided, one to either side of the foundering black stallion, one at the rear, gaining, angling in. The ropes slithered out, the loops seemed to hang like suspended rings of wire for a second before they settled down, fair and true, about the neck and shoulders of the black's rider. They tightened, the lariats snubbed to the saddle horns, the horses sliding with flattened pasterns. The black lunging on, pitched forward as it was relieved of a sudden weight and its rider jerked hideously from the saddle, hands clawing at the ropes that choked his gullet, wrenching, sinking deep, shutting off air and light with a horrid taste of blood and the noise of thundering waters.

The ropers wheeled their mounts and galloped back toward the woods, the limp body of their victim dragging, bouncing over the ground. The third rode to meet Sandy. It was Brandon. He hailed Sandy with surprise.

"How'd you happen here this time of night, Bourke? Not looking for me?"

"No. I was looking for the man you've just caught. I was about a minute too late."

Brandon glanced curiously at Sandy, caught by the grim note in his voice. But he made no comment.

"Sorry if I spoiled your private vendetta, Bourke. You can have him, what's left of him, if you want. We were going to swing him from a tree with a card on his chest presenting him to Hereford County, with our compliments. As it is, Bourke, I'd be relieved if you'd keep out of this entirely. Even forgetting you'd met us. We're within our rights, but we've done some cleaning up to-night that we might have to explain if we stayed too long in the state. We got the goods on Plimsoll; one of his men whose girl Plimsoll had stolen helped us to pin them on him. We met him at Hereford. I'm going to send the facts and proofs to your authorities. They may not approve of lynch law these days, but they wouldn't act — and we did. I don't fancy they'll bother us any. He wasn't worth the ropes he spoiled. Just as well you kept out of the mix-up."

Sandy said nothing. There was no need to mention Molly's adventure.

"Want to be sure it's him?" asked Brandon. "Let's look at the black first. He gave us a hard chase, but we were too many for him and rounded him up."

They found the black stallion stretched out on the turf with its neck curiously twisted. Tired out, it had fallen clumsily and broken the vertebrae. It was quite dead. Both men looked at it silently, with a mental tribute to a good horse.

The body of Plimsoll lay at the foot of a big pine. The loops were still tight about his neck. One of the ropes had been tossed over a bough. The two men had dismounted. They nodded to Sandy as he came up with Brandon. He had seen them before on their first unsuccessful trip to the Waterline. They were horse-owners, responsible men, who considered they had administered justice, who felt no more qualms concerning the dead man than if his body had been the carcass of a slaughtered steer.

"Waiting for the rest of the boys to come up," said Brandon. "We'll hit the trail home to-night. Bourke wants to identify the body, boys."

Sandy looked down at the contorted, blackened face, and his disappointment at having been forestalled, sedimented down. The gambler's features had not been made placid by death; they still held much of the horror of the last moments of that relentless chase, his horse failing under him, foreknowledge of sudden death and then the whistling ropes, the jerk into eternity...! It was a thing to be forgotten, a nightmare that had nothing to do with the new day ahead.

"It's Plimsoll," said Sandy shortly. "I'm ridin' back to Three Star. I found him hangin' to a tree. Good night, hombres." He left them standing about their quarry and turned the willing mare toward home. Peace settled down on him under the stars that were fading, the moon below the hills when he rode into the home corral.

A figure was perched upon the fence, waiting. It was Molly, and she leaped down almost into his arms as he sprang from the mare. In the gray dawn her face seemed drawn and weary. There were the blue shadows under the eyes that he remembered seeing there the time they had ridden over the Pass of the Goats. She came close to him, her hands up against his chest.

"You're safe, Sandy. Safe!"

"I was too late," he said. "Brandon's men had been ahead of me."

"I'm so glad, Sandy. Your hands are clean of his blood. They are my hands, now, Sandy."

He swept her up to him, kissing her mouth and eyes, the eager pressure of her lips returning all with full measure. A streak of rose glowed in the east behind the amethyst peaks. Her face reflected it like a mirror. The tired lines were gone as he set her down.

"How long have you been waiting, Molly?"

"Ever since I got back. I slipped out of the house when the rest had gone to bed. If you hadn't come back, Sandy, I should have died."

"I don't have to go back east," she said presently. They had left the corral and were under the big cottonwoods by Patrick Casey's grave. "Do I?"

"I don't reckon you can, even if you wanted to," answered Sandy. "I forgot to tell you, Molly, that you're bu'sted, so far's the mine is concerned. Listen."

She laughed when he finished speaking.

"Is that all?" She patted the turf on the green mound. "I'm sorry, Daddy, for you, it didn't pan out bigger. But I guess what you wanted most was my happiness — and I've got that." She turned to Sandy. The big bell of the ranch boomed brassily. Molly put her hand in Sandy's. "It may be most unromantic, Sandy dear," she said, "but I'm hungry. Let's go in to breakfast."

CHAPTER XXII
THE VERY END

There was a council held later that day, that was almost a council of war. Sandy was in the chair, Mormon and Sam present, Molly the indignant speaker-in-chief.

"I'm very much ashamed of all of you," she said. "An agreement is an agreement, and we were to share as we arranged. We shook hands upon it. I've had three times as much as any one of you, as it is. I haven't spent all of it, Sandy tells me.

"I've got to accept Sandy's share of it, I suppose, because it goes with Sandy. As for you, Sam Manning, you'll need your third when you marry Kate Nicholson."

Soda-Water Sam gasped.

"Marry Miss Nicholson?"

"Certainly. She expects you to."

"She — Molly, it ain't no jokin' matter with me. She wouldn't look at a rough-hided cuss like me."

"You ask her, Sammy. Mormon, I suppose you'll have to hang fire until you find out about that third wife. I hope the fourth time will be the charm. It will if you marry Miranda Bailey."

"You're sure talkin' like a matrimonial boorow, Molly," said Mormon. "I sure think a sight of Mirandy. She's different from my first three. They all married me, fo' me to look out fo' them. If Mirandy can be persuaded to take me it's becos she is willin' to look after me. She 'lows I need it," he added sheepishly. Then he chuckled.

"I've knowed the whereabouts of my third fo' some time back," he said. "She got a divorce six years ago. I've kept the matter secret as a so't of insurance policy. I've allus been sort of unbalanced in my leanin's to'ards the sex, you see. An' it sure acted as a prop an' a defense so fur."

"Then the meeting is closed," said Molly. "I accept your apologies and you keep your money."

Mormon and Sam rose. With a glance at each other that ended in a wink, they left the room. Molly turned to Sandy.

"You didn't give me back my luck-piece, Sandy."

"What does a mascot want with a luck-piece?"

"She would like it made into an engagement ring, Sandy."

"Why not a weddin' ring, Molly, Molly mine?"

THE END

9 788027 275854